Desmond McFarlane:

My Cuban Odyssey

Billroy Powell

Dedication

I dedicate this book to my friend, Carole Foster, who incessantly encourages me to put words on paper. She convinces me that I am in the best position to weave the story into a fictional novel. This one is for you, from me, with love.

Contents

A cursory look

This historical romance novel is a work of fiction inspired by a true story describing the experiences of a Jamaican student who spent four years, along with other Jamaican students, in Cuba undergoing training in Physical and Health Education mid-way through the latter half of the twentieth century. The story is bifurcated into a main plot, the student's academic pursuit, and a subplot, the student's romantic involvement with a Cuban girl. The main plot is written using regular Arial font, and the subplot is written in Arial Italic font to differentiate the two experiences as they occurred independently but simultaneously.

About the Author

Billroy was born and raised in Jamaica and spent several years studying in Cuba before immigrating to Canada. The cultural experiences from these three countries inform his work. His book, settling in Canada: Jamaicans have a Story to Tell is a classic account of the Jamaican experience settling in Canada over more than five decades. He has published several policy papers pertaining to higher education. He began his career as an educator and is passionate about sharing knowledge and creating work that advances learning. He is fluent in English, Patois, and Spanish. He speaks and writes conversational French.

Foreword

I was a little apprehensive when Billroy asked me to write the foreword for his book Desmond McFarlane: My Cuban Odyssey. After all, I haven't used my literary skills, other than reading since I graduated from university decades ago. However, having read an early draft of the novel, I was charmed and happily agreed to do it.

I have known Billroy Powell for over 25 years as a close relation of my beloved spouse and have always known him to be educated, open, and always ready to lend a helping hand. I was impressed with his first book: Settling in Canada: Jamaicans have a Story to Tell, a "classic" account of the Jamaican experience settling in Canada for five decades, starting from the 1950s and lasting until the 2000s.

I have long respected Billroy as a detailed and straightforward non-fiction author. What I didn't know was that he had a talent for historical fiction and romance!

Desmond McFarlane: My Cuban Odyssey is set in a fascinating place, which places the world of sports in the context of a Pan-Caribbean cold-war pilgrimage. Our protagonist, Desmond, is a youthful and optimistic Jamaican Physical Education teacher/trainee who finds himself accepted into a rigorous program in the revolutionary island of Cuba in the 1970s. We are treated to a fascinating description of the trials and ordeals the students, Desmond, and others are subjected to in a Cuba that is struggling with scarcity in the context of the United States embargo, which includes regular bouts of agricultural labour.

Desmond readily adapts to the rigour of the program, quickly masters communicating in Spanish, and takes a leading role in his cohort of Jamaican trainees. This is where the book takes a sudden romantic turn, as Desmond meets the girl of his dreams, Belkis. From here, the book becomes a captivating, sometimes steamy, description of young love and longing.

As a Jamaican-born immigrant who moved to Toronto, Billroy Powell spent several years in Cuba, training and becoming familiar with the people and culture of the island. This makes him an ideal guide to the non-tourist life that is so richly described in Desmond McFarlane: My Cuban Odyssey. I highly recommend this book to anyone who is interested in understanding cross-cultural relationships and to those who are fascinated by the relentless power of young love in exotic places.

Steven Stunell

Chapter 1

It was early one Friday evening in 1979, and my friend Alvin and I were busy collecting stones, cutting trees, uprooting shrubs, and clearing logwood brambles under the hot evening sun in Santa Cruz, St. Elizabeth, quite possibly the hottest place in Jamaica, when a familiar voice rang out, "Desmond and Alvin, a word please."

I looked, but I did not have to because I was quite aware of his distinctive voice. It was Errol, our youth leader, the architect behind our youth club formation, and who was working with the Ministry of Youth, Sports, and Community Development in Kingston.

"In a moment, brother Errol," Alvin and I replied simultaneously, and I gazed over in the direction from where the voice came.

Alvin and I ceased working and moved across the small, cleared area just big enough for a soccer scrimmage game.

We had just formed the youth club and had no playground in the community. So, before we played in the evening, we would undertake to remove whatever obstacles we could to create and increase the play area systematically. We were building a playground with officially approved dimensions for men to play cricket and soccer and for the ladies to play netball.

The atmosphere was still, with no wind to cool down our bodies. For that purpose, we had to rely on our profuse perspiration, which needed a steady water intake. As we approached Errol, a woody smell permeated the environment. He was standing relaxed on one of his bowed legs with one hand akimbo and carrying a broad smile on his slightly large triangular face.

"I have good news for you, I hope," he said.

"What would that be?" I asked, and Alvin nodded with approval of my question.

"I have arranged for you two to be interviewed to go to Cuba on a four-year sports program, if you're interested."

The news surprised me, but I was elated just the same. A life-changing opportunity, I thought, despite the awful news I kept hearing about Cuba and Communism from individuals and media outlets in Jamaica.

Both Alvin and I thanked him for thinking of us and for offering up our names for the program; we took turns hugging him.

"I consider it fulfilling my civic duty," he told us.

"Civic duty or not, I appreciate you going out on a limb for us," I assured him.

"You'll receive a teaching certificate after you successfully completed the program."

This could be an excellent opportunity, I thought to myself, but how would I support myself while I was studying or who would assume that responsibility?

"If you're successful in the interview," Errol began listing off his fingers, "the Jamaican government will provide a stipend while you're learning Spanish in Jamaica, pay your airfare to and from Cuba each year of your study, and deposit a modest sum to your Jamaican bank account, while you maintain enrollment in the program. While you're in Cuba, the Cuban government will assume responsibility for your keep there: food, shelter, education supplies and uniform."

"When and where does all this begin?" I inquired.

"To get the ball rolling, you'll have to go to the National Arena in Kingston for a screening interview this Monday at 10 a.m. That should give you sufficient travel time to get to the Arena if you gonna go to Kingston on Monday morning. You could travel with me on my return to work on Monday. That way, you'd only have to worry about coming back home."

Alvin and I regarded each other, and I confirmed with Errol on our behalf. "We'd love to travel with you on Monday."

"I'll at least attend the interview and take it from there," Alvin assented, and I muttered in agreement.

"Then it's settled," Errol declared.

However, I asked Errol, "Can you keep a lid on this information until after the interview, at least?"

"Of course," he responded with a smile.

At this time, the sun was just a few meters away from docking on the western edge of Santa Cruz Mountain, and our scrimmage game time was drawing nigh, so I halted work for everyone. I was vice-president of the youth club and chair of the disciplinary committee, and the one leading the work-before-play initiative.

"Hey guys, we're having an early game this evening," I announced, which invited shouts of "Yahoo!" Yes!" and Cool!" from all around us, and in the passing of a few minutes, everyone gathered around to be selected for either of the two teams that usually play the game. After the game, I approached Alvin, he's a lanky black guy with low-cut black hair, the president of the youth club.

"Where'll we meet up on Monday? "I asked him.

"At Errol's home, at about 8 a.m.," he replied.

With this bit of information, I dashed over to where Errol was having a conversation with a few individuals. I quickly interrupted to tell him the plan.

"That's fine," he said and nodded in agreement.

The younger of my two brothers and I were still living at our parents' house. They had migrated to England in the nineteen sixties and left us and two other siblings in the care of our maternal grandmother who had recently moved away since we were by then able to care for ourselves. Hence, it was fitting that I communicated with him in some form or the other about the new opportunity presented to me. When I got home that evening. I told him, "I'm going to Kingston on Monday, so when you wake up, I may be off already or getting ready for my departure."

He looked at me in astonishment, but before he could speak, I said, "I'll fill you in on the details when I get back," and he nodded in agreement.

Both Alvin and I lived within walking distance from Errol's home, and at 7:50 a.m. I was in Errol's driveway waiting. Within a few minutes, I spotted Alvin approaching. He was elegantly dressed, sporting a sky-blue shirt tucked into his dark pants, grey blazer, and dark suede shoes. Not long after, at about 8:07

a.m. Errol was in his dark midnight-blue Mini Cooper. He started it and invited us aboard.

On our way to Kingston, we talked mostly about the youth club and its development. We also discussed the loss of Alvin and me leaving the youth club at the same time while being president and vice-president.

"We didn't discuss any handover or replacement if we're successful in the interview," Alvin remarked.

"Don't worry about that now," Errol dismissed.

We arrived at the National Arena at exactly 9:30 a.m. and noticed that there were several youth around, other potential scholarship awardees, just hanging about. The Arena was a huge white rectangular building with a flat roof that hung over at the front and sides.

Our interview appointment was pushed back half an hour to 10:30 a.m., and at that time both Alvin and I were called and guided into a small interview room, possibly eight feet by eight feet, where the smell of the fresh off-white paint still lingered. In the room, sitting behind a large red oak desk with paper piles and folders covering almost the entire surface area, was the interviewer, he was hazel-eyed, with straight black hair, and appeared to be of East Indian descent.

The interviewer stood to greet us. He was small in stature, maybe five feet two inches and plump. He stretched out one of his hands, "My name is Christopher Maragh, but just call me Christopher. I will be conducting the interview."

"Alvin Daley, it is a pleasure to be here."

"Desmond McFarlane, it is a pleasure to be here," Alvin and I spoke alternately while shaking Christopher's hand, following which Christopher plopped back down into his seat.

"I assume Mr. Jones filled you in on some details of this meeting. You are sent by Mr. Errol Jones, are you not?" Christopher asked.

"Yes, we received a snapshot of what the program entails," Alvin responded.

The meeting turned out to be more of an orientation than an interview.

"Before going to Cuba, you will have to learn Spanish in order to perform competently in the Cuban education settings. You may begin classes tomorrow at the language training centre or any day between now and next week Friday, just report to the receptionist who will confirm your enrollment and give you the relevant instructions and information."

"We did not come prepared to start classes this week. We would prefer if we could start next Monday, which would give us sufficient time to make needed adjustments back home since we are from the country," I explained on behalf of both Alvin and me.

"Okay, just as long as you start before next Friday. The language centre is located in Premier Plaza, at 8 Constant Spring Road, building number one. The Spanish course will last approximately six months. During this time, you must learn Spanish and attain a minimum proficiency level of three out of five, to manage the program courses comfortably in Spanish. This may seem like a formidable challenge, but others have surmounted this task, and so I am confident that you will be able to as well. One last thing, should you qualify to go to Cuba, you must travel with your passport and high school certificate." The meeting lasted approximately 10 minutes.

In parting, Alvin inquired, "Can you give us directions from here to Premier Plaza? and expounded, "We want to get a feel for the lay of the land before coming back for our first day next week, given that classes are in session right now."

"Take the number 27 bus across the road from here, the final stop is at Half Way Tree Park. Half Way Tree Road is straight in front of you when you get off the bus, just walk north on Half Way Tree Road, which turns into Constant Spring Road. Walk on Constant Spring Road to Premier Plaza, which is on your right."

Kingston is located more than seventy miles from where I lived in St. Elizabeth, and my knowledge of Kingston was not extensive, to say the least. Therefore, I needed a bit of handholding. I phoned Errol, using the public telephone, at his sister's home, where he was living while working in Kingston, the same night after I got back home following the interview with Christopher.

"I'm instructed to start classes at the Ministry of the Public Service language training centre any time before next week Friday. I have no place to stay in Kingston, and I don't know of anyone in Kingston besides you to assist me. As you are aware, one of my younger brothers lives in Kingston and is an apprentice in the appliance trade, but he is in no position to offer any assistance. Do you know how I could go about getting accommodation apart from foraging through the newspapers?"

"My batchmate, Delroy, who attended Munro College with me, has an aunt living in Kingston, and from time to time, she takes in boarders," Errol said pensively.

"Any assistance would be much appreciated."

"I'll inquire from him the possibility of you boarding at her place. I should've news on this for you before the week is over."

I did not have a telephone at home, so waited anxiously until Friday evening for Errol to come to the country from Kingston.

"I spoke with Delroy, and his aunt has accommodation available."

"Did you find out from him how much it's gonna cost me?"

"The cost to you is $300 per month, two meals provided, per day: breakfast and dinner, Monday to Friday. The bathroom facility you will have to share with other male boarders. The house is off Molynes Road in a community somewhere between Red Hills and Hughenden communities."

"When will you be going back to Kingston? I'm wondering, could I get a ride with you?"

"I'm going back to Kingston on Sunday evening. You can ride with me, and I'll take you to the address," he stated.

It was a little after 8 p.m., Sunday night when we arrived at 25 Cherry Crescent. I exited Errol's Mini Cooper and strolled behind him as we approached the main door of the enormous flat-roofed house, made visible by the lighted streetlamp located at an angle a few meters to the left of the property's gate. The grill was open, and Errol pulled one of the wings to one side and knocked on the large dark-brown pine-wood door. A young man appeared in the doorway and greeted us: "Good evening, my name is Winston."

Errol and I introduced ourselves.

"My aunt isn't at home, but she asked me to receive Mr. McFarlane."

"Please call me Desmond," I told him.

"Come inside, please," he said to us.

"Since I have delivered you safely, I'd best be on my way," Errol told me. We shook hands, then he bade us goodbye and disappeared into the night.

Chapter 2

To attend classes in Premier Plaza in Kingston, I had to travel on Molynes Road to Half Way Tree by autobus during rush-hour traffic. Often times the bus was overcrowded, and passengers had to stand crouched, fitted against one another like sardines in a tin can. In the morning, when I boarded the bus, it was already filled with passengers; I was barely able to squeeze in. In the evening, when I got to the bus stop, the lines were already several metres long. I was never able to get a seat because of the locations and times of day I boarded the bus.

Furthermore, I had to endure multiple kinds of smells: cigarette and marijuana smoke, perfumes, and strong and weak body odours. Then there were on any given day the shouts of profanities over the least bit of annoyance— "bomboclaat," "pussyclaat," "bloodclaat," "rassclaat"—and the threat of physical violence by some passengers towards one another. There was an almost intolerable volume of reggae music blaring from loudspeakers installed on the minibus. This way of travelling was new to me, and I had to learn and adapt quickly in order to endure my stay in Kingston. I also had to be mindful and aware of my surroundings because pickpockets were everywhere, ready to pounce on unsuspecting passengers and relieve them of any items of value. One evening Rachel, a tall, dark, slim lady who constantly wore a beautiful smile, and one of the boarders living at the same house where I was living, had her handbag snatched from off her shoulder.

"A motorcycle rode alongside me, and the pillion rider grabbed my handbag, and they disappeared into the evening dark shadows. It happened just after I dismounted from the minibus and began walking home. I did not even bother to call the police and report the incident."

"Did you get a chance to see who the culprits were?" I asked her.

"No, because it all happened so fast; I didn't think of getting a description of any kind."

The idea of learning a new language made me excited and anxious to begin classes; therefore, I was not overly concerned with all the commotions and distractions around me.

On the first day of classes, we were administered an auditory test to determine our aptitude and proficiency level in order to place us in the appropriate learning group. I could have done better on the test. However, I could not understand or discern any of the words that were dictated to us. I had to listen and write what I heard, and nothing made sense to me. So, I was placed in a beginners' group, and there were three beginners' groups. I was not happy with the decision, but I had no choice but to accept the result. However, as the classes began and time passed, I realized that I had nothing to be ashamed of, given that even those who were selected for the more advanced classes were not better than me at learning Spanish.

Incidentally, I have no idea of how well Alvin did on the test, I did not get a chance to inquire from him because after the test he disappeared, and I never saw him again until several years after I completed my studies in Cuba—He never pursued any studies in Cuba.

Classes were held at two separate locations: in Premier Plaza, on Constant Spring Road, on the second floor in a three-storey building managed by the Ministry of the Public Service, and at Half Way Tree Road in an old collectorate or tax office building. The group that I was a part of was selected to attend classes in both locations. We had to alternate between both locations at least once per day.

"I'm somewhat overwhelmed by this Spanish thing, any advice?" a female voice came from behind me while I was standing in the corridor of the old collectorate building. I was not sure if I were the one being addressed, so I remained pensive about how events have turned out for me. Suddenly, I was face to face with an attractive, petite young lady. She had dark brown eyes, snow-white teeth and sported an afro, all to go with a shapely body.

"Hi, my name is Heather," she proclaimed, "and yours is?" she asked.

"My name is Desmond, and before you ask, I'm from the country: St. Elizabeth."

"You seem to be very perceptive; how did you know I was gonna inquire of your where about?"

"Everybody seems to be looking for some connection if not family, then parishioners," I told her.

"How are you liking what we've been learning so far? I don't know about you, but I'm struggling with the assignments and comprehending the teachers: they're speaking too fast for me."

"We have six months to learn the language. I believe if we're patient and methodical in our approach, we'll overcome any barriers that the language poses."

"To tell you the truth, I'm a little scared I won't make it."

"Nonsense, we must do our best to repel fears and anxieties, try and learn at a moderate pace, and remember, it takes a lifetime to learn a language, and even then, there's never enough time."

"You're one of confidence," Heather told me.

I explained to Heather, "Let's look at this exercise from the vantage point that we get the opportunity to travel between our two learning locations every day, which is a short distance, and we can easily go and come without contravening the course schedule."

"So, what'll I do about this situation?" Heather asked.

"Take this opportunity to scan the environment and pull commonly used English vocabulary and translate it to Spanish at your own pace in a practical sense. If you make this a practice every day and connect this vocabulary to your class instructions, the barriers will slowly disappear." I reassured her.

"You make it seems so easy, some of our colleagues could benefit from talking with you," she told me.

"I observed that some of the students, mostly the males, are finding the language difficult to learn and, therefore, aren't motivated to attend classes," I told her.

"Often, they extended their lunch break by sitting around conversing in the park and aimlessly strolling the shopping centres," she added.

"Our success in life is inextricably linked to the choices we make," were my parting words to her that day.

Despite the low attendance at the beginning of the classes, the teachers stuck to their schedules and tasks. They delivered class content and assignments to those of us who were present and interested in learning the language. The teachers were very resourceful. Classes were offered orally with learning aids such as charts, symbols, and an overhead projector. We started with basic everyday needs and things in Spanish. We learned to greet one another, ask, and respond to simple questions, like what is your name, and the words to describe the human body and how to take care of it, for example, shaving one's beard. We were also treated to television lessons sometimes. The instructors were Cubans, Peruvian, Venezuelan and Cuban-Jamaican.

I found Spanish easy to learn. I quickly began leading discussions and debating issues of the day, like the border conflict between China and Vietnam. The debates in Spanish were lively and hilarious—it was amusing to listen to my colleagues fighting with themselves to recall words. The frustration among most of us was noted because we were anxious to speak the language, which was important for us to go to Cuba and study.

The teachers advised us, "Please be patient, follow the in-class work and exercises; no one cares about the clowns you are making of yourselves and in front of one another."

Those of us who were serious about succeeding saw learning the language as a challenge to overcome. It did not matter the field we were in because we were all going to pursue a career, and that was significant for many, if not all, of us. For several of us, this would be difficult, if not impossible, in Jamaica. There were no formal sports training program encompassing multiple disciplines in Jamaica at the time, not to mention the financial burden one would have had to endure in order to attend postsecondary studies.

One of my colleagues, Gregory, and I discussed the limitation the lack of funds placed on us. Gregory was short, light brown in complexion, and he walked with a slight limp and with one of his hands arched inward at the elbow.

"The Ministry gives all the language trainees a stipend to assist us with living expenses. I receive one hundred and fifty dollars per week; I was made to understand that where one comes from makes a difference in how much they receive," Gregory told me.

"I'm from the country, so I suppose I will get the same amount as you," I remarked.

"The people from the rural areas receive one-hundred-and-fifty dollars per week. However, I don't know how much the people from the metropolitan area receive, but it could be anywhere from fifty to a hundred dollars per week," Gregory rejoined.

In those days, the Jamaican dollar was much stronger against foreign currencies than it is today. The exchange rate at the time was approximately five Jamaican dollars to one American dollar.

"Even though it's a far cry from what I need, the one hundred and fifty dollars would be my lifeline in Kingston, as I have no other source of funding. It'll pay for my room and board and provide me with Lunch and transportation," I told Gregory.

"I'm in the same boat as you, but lunch is a low-priority item for me since it's the only expense that gives me a bit of flexibility."

"What do you do for food now?"

"I often seek out cheap eateries because most of the time, all I can afford are two patties and a soft drink. Entertainment isn't in the cards for me."

Transportation to the language centre was two dollars round trip. Nevertheless, I made the most of the precarious situation. On weekends, Errol provided the means for me to travel to the country on those occasions when I had to go down to check on my parents' property, and while I was at it, I got my laundry taken care of–I washed my clothes myself by hand. I would travel down with Errol on Friday afternoon and return on Sunday evening or on Monday morning and head straight to class instead of going to my boarding home.

"How're things working out with you, your host, living conditions, money and the training," Errol inquired.

"The living accommodation isn't great, but it's not bad for the rate I'm paying. I would give it a rating of three points out of five. I adapt and make myself comfortable with the situation for the most part. The food is a challenge sometimes, but I don't let it bother me. The house owner, Miss Adams, and her daughter Pat are courteous to me, but we don't see one another much because they both work—Miss Adams is a nurse, but I'm not sure what is her daughter's occupation."

"What about the other boarders? Do you get to interact much with them?"

"Yes, there're two other men and a lady, as well as the owner's two nephews and the housekeeper, all under the same roof—it's a bit crowded sometimes."

"It seems like a challenge for you; too bad my sister doesn't have the space to accommodate you. She's has only one guest room, and I'm occupying it."

"Don't worry about it, I'm managing okay. Besides, my self-imposed austerity measures provide the kind of self-discipline that'll come in handy," I told Errol. "However, I miss the country and its slow-paced lifestyle, fresh morning air, newly harvested produce, the comradery of the youth club members and the activities we do."

"Change is always difficult, especially away from home." Errol reminded me.

"This seems like a precursor to what's in store for me in Cuba."

"All I'm sure of is that things won't be the same in Cuba as in Jamaica," Errol advised me.

Chapter 3

A deep voice grabbed my attention, "Let's go for a stroll around the block; you seem spaced out. John and I are going to browse through the plazas," and a tall, slender black figure plopped down beside me on the park bench.

"My name is Tom, and we're in the same class; and I already know your name—Desmond, right?"

"I'm not comfortable walking around in the plazas, if I am not purchasing anything."

"We look around to check out what is available and the price ranges, and if things are reasonably priced, we'd return to acquire them when we've the funds," John said.

"Isn't there a law against loitering? I can't afford to be detained, not now especially," I replied.

"You'll be detained if you take items out of the store without paying for them. No one'll detain you if you're walking around and looking business-like."

"You've no plans on stealing anything?" Tom asked, jokingly.

"Not in a million years," I responded.

"Our female colleagues often go window shopping in the stores in Premier Plaza and the other adjoining plazas: Kings, Queens, and Manor Park Plazas. Why can't we?" John enlightened me and asked.

"You may be right, but we don't have to do what the ladies do, do we?" I inquired.

"Besides, if you care to join us, the men hangout in the park at Half Way Tree from Monday to Thursday, in the afternoon, where we discuss politics, hit on women passing by, and reminisce about high school times, events, remarkable teachers, and those that were perceived as wacky. On Friday evening, the meeting moved down to Cross-Roads near to downtown Kingston," Tom told me.

"You're both from Kingston, I presume?"

"Yes, our homes are within walking distance from the training centre, though, we take the bus to avoid the long walk," Tom said.

"How do you pass the time? What're the popular attractions that you guys patronize and would recommend?" I asked.

"Often, we would opt to go see movies in the Odeon or Carib cinemas at Half Way Tree Road and Crossroads; attend sport events at the National Stadium and visit the beaches," Tom said.

"There's also the Tom Redcam Library which is frequented by high school students, and it's always buzzing with them and their activities. You might find it interesting as you seem to be studious," John observed.

Visiting the Tom Redcam Library on Tom Redcam Road became my favorite pastime. I borrowed books and chatted up older high school female students. I often borrowed books just to pass the time reading at home, which was for the most part lonely since I spent most of my free time in my room. Even though there were other people living in the house, they were not always there and when they were, they also locked themselves in their room. On weekends, they all left to spend time at their permanent residence, which was in rural Jamaica.

The owner of the house had another property in one of the upper-class neighbourhoods in Kingston— Forest Hills. The times when I spent the weekend in Kingston, she and her daughter would slip away for the weekend, and I would not see them again until Monday evening.

"How've you been spending your leisure time in Kingston, Desmond?" John asked.

"During the week, after class, my friend Erroll treats me to a couple soccer games at the National Stadium. I also have a younger brother who is living, and learning a trade, in Kingston going on three years now. Whenever I stayed over in Kingston on weekends, he occasionally arranges for us to meet up and go to dinner or a bar to have a few drinks," I said.

"I understand you're not from Kingston," Tom said with an inquisitive look on his face.

"No, I'm not," I answered.

"So, have you found a girl in the city yet, Desmond?" John inquired, and continued, "There is an abundance of them around, you should try and hook up to help you pass the time."

"No one firm, but I'm ferreting," I told John, "My brother who is quite a ladies' man arranged a couple of double dates for him and me. We went out with a couple of women and have an enjoyable time socializing."

"Where do you go?"

"We go to clubs, movies, and to the beaches—Hellshire and Port Royal."

"Where do you connect with the ladies?"

"My brother is popular with female students from Short Wood Teachers College, and they're our main targets to visit the various attractions in Kingston," I explained.

One of several unforgettable experiences that I had in Kingston and connected to the language centre was with two of my classmates, Yasmin, and Andrea, who subtly showed interest in me romantically, and even displayed streaks of jealousy. One morning, during breaktime, I was standing near the entrance to the old collectorate building talking to Yasmin; and Andrea walked by and accidentally brushed against Yasmin's shoulder. For that, they got into a heated discussion about who was in the way, and who should have moved out of the way, and so on. I stood by and witnessed the verbal altercation without making any attempt to intervene. However, a couple of other ladies came by and insisted that the quarrelers put an end to their bickering and reminded them that they needed to get along because they were going to spend four years living together in Cuba.

I felt more drawn to Yasmin and was attracted to her, so I asked her for a date.

"Yasmin, would you like to attend Boys' Champs with me?"

Without any protest or hesitation, she said in a moderate to low, soft ladylike, voice, "Let's meet-up in the Half Way Tree Park on Saturday at 9 a.m., even though the events usually scheduled to start at 10 a.m. We should give ourselves enough time to make sure there're no surprises."

We both entered the park at the same time from opposite ends. From afar, I could see why I was attracted to Yasmin: she was beautiful. She was about five feet seven inches tall, dark bronze skin colour, dark brown permed hair pulled to the back of her head in a bun, heart shaped face, and was outfitted in dark pants and a pale pink blouse. She walked across the park smartly towards me. We greeted each other, and I said to her, "Gosh, you're so beautiful, I could steal you."

"Where'd you hide me?"

"I could make you invisible."

"Go weh wid yu ugly self."

"Really," I said.

"Yes, really."

"Why're you going out with an ugly guy?"

"Because those are the kinds I like," she rejoined.

However, as luck would have it, as we stepped down from the park on to the sidewalk, a middle-aged man bumped up against her side and she shouted, "Ouch!" In that moment, I seized the opportunity to tell her, "You see, my powers are working."

"Go weh fraahn mi boy, you tink mi come fraahn country?" she said jokingly. This is a remark that implies people from rural areas believe in witchcraft and voodoo or obeah as we call it in Jamaica.

Boys Champs is an athletic event that is held annually at the National Stadium in Kingston. We arrived at approximately 9:30 am, and I bought our tickets for the bleachers, and entered the Stadium to find seats that gave us a bird's eye view of the track and field. Unsure of myself, I tried making "small talk" with Yasmin in between events. I have never dated a city girl before.

Back then, Kingston and Montego Bay were the only two big cities we had in Jamaica, and I lived far away from them. There was a rumour that city people are crafty and very alert. Therefore, I waited for her to take the initiative, but it did not occur while we were in the Stadium. At about 3:30 p.m., Yasmin asked me, "Can you take me home?" Which was really to accompany her to the park and from there she would find her way home.

"Yes, I'll take you home," I said with a smile.

When we reached the park, we had a brief conversation. I asked her, "Did you enjoy Boys Champs?"

"Athletics is not really my "cup of tea," further there is too much of a time gap between events, and the Stadium was very hot, and there was a foul smell blowing across our area."

"I'm sorry you did not have a good time," I said.

"Would you go out with me again?"

"Sure," she said, "but it got to be a more animated event and maybe even romantic."

"This'll be a date assignment for me to complete over the weekend, which I'll invest some time in to make sure I get it right, so you'll be pleased," I told her. I held her hand for a moment and told her, "Goodbye and be careful."

She came close to me and kissed me on the cheek and smiled. She emitted an alluring minty smell and the warmness of her cheek against mine sent subtle inviting messages through my body. I reacted voraciously and leaned into her body and face and kissed her on her lips right in the park in public view, and she did not protest. I would say that she welcomed my advance; and therefore, I went home happy and pleased with myself.

The following week at the language centre, Yasmin and I spent a lot of time together, talking, eating lunch, and strolling around the plazas. In addition, we decided to meet up with several of the other guys the following

Sunday and explore the streets of Kingston, as a way of making acquaintances and getting to know one another better. We met in the Half way Tree Park as was customary, and chatted, joked around, and listened to passersby making weird remarks, as well as the music belting out of the nearby record shop, across from the park, at the corner of Hagley Park Road and Half Way Tree Road.

"It would be nice to go for a walk, I have had enough of the park. I would like a change of scenery and location," Yasmin spoke.

"Yes, let's walk around, it's a Sunday morning, even though the sun is making its presence felt, the streets are practically empty," James intervened, smiling.

Gregory reminded us that, "On our walk, we could stop at the convenience store down the road at the gas station to pick up snacks."

While a few of the guys went into the store, several of us remained outside under the shelter of the gas station. I was happy to escape the blistering morning sun and heat. I stood on the platform that hosted the gas dispensers, and Yasmin came and leaned against me, with her back against the front of my body. I put my arms around her neck, forming a V shape from her neck down across her chest. We were both in a relaxed position.

Suddenly a car pulled up across the aisle from us and a man came out and rushed towards us, yanked off a tuque Yasmin was wearing, and muttered, "A dis yu dah a road a do, tannup wid mon han ron yu neck?"

I immediately discerned that it was personal, lovers' discontent, so I backed away and gave them space to sort out their issues. There was a heated exchange of words between them, and the man, angrily, went back into the car and drove away.

I was dumbfounded, scared, weak in the legs, nervous and confused. I decided to stay aloof from everyone, however, one of the guys, Joshua, who never made it to Cuba for personal reasons, came over and explained to me that, "The person who was reprimanding Yasmin is her baby father, and they're living together in a common law relationship."

"That's news to me. I didn't even know she has a child. I could have been in mortal danger and not the least bit aware."

I went back into the group but away from Yasmin and I avoided spending too much time around her for the rest of my stay in Kingston, and the four years in Cuba.

From then on, anytime I asked a girl for a date, I insisted on knowing if she was in an existing relationship, and depending on the answer, I managed my approach accordingly. Incidentally, I never asked any of the other girls at the language centre for a date, not then or since.

The cost of living in Kingston began to move beyond my purchasing ability. During the final few weeks at the language centre, after the rent was about to increase for the second time in six months, I started looking for alternate living accommodation.

"I must find somewhere reasonably priced to live for the next three weeks, or else I'm going to starve," I told one of my classmates, Howard Johnson.

"I'm staying at Garfield Higgins' place; I'll talk to him tonight to find out if it's possible for you to stay with us. He's an okay fella, and he might just be opened to the idea of you staying with us for the next three weeks."

The next morning, I anxiously awaited Howard and the outcome of his conversation with Garfield.

About 10 minutes before classes began on Friday morning, I heard Howard softly said behind me, "Desmond, I've good news for you, Garfield is happy to have you stay with us."

"Howard, you're a life saver," I told him, as I turned around to face the person who uttered those relieving words.

"How much is the cost?"

He looked at me furrowing between his eyebrows and responded, "It'll cost you nothing."

"Are you sure? I don't want to be a freeloader."

"Please bring your belongings with you on Monday morning, your stay is expected to start Monday night," Howard said with a smile.

I knew that Howard walked to and from the training centre every day. I heard him telling Andrea, so I figured, with the cost for transportation erased, I would have a few dollars freed up that could go towards paying my boarding cost. But Garfield Higgins, a once famous Jamaican soccer player, insisted he would not accept any money from me—hence I got an unexpected break.

I did not go home to the country that weekend. Hence, Sunday evening, I packed my luggage. I did not have a lot of clothes in Kingston. I asked the housekeeper to tell Miss Adams, who was away for the weekend with her daughter, that I will not be back on Monday evening.

Monday morning, I saw Howard standing in the passageway at the collectorate building and I told him, "I'm ready to go to your place this evening."

"I'll hail you when I'm leaving this evening," he responded.

That evening when Howard and I arrived at Garfield's home, 32 Rose Lane Crescent, it was a large grey stone single family bungalow with two nearby accessory dwellings painted in canary yellow. The three structures were situated on about a half-acre of land. Howard led the way into the open concept living and dining room. Garfield and his pregnant wife were sitting at the dinner table, having just started to eat.

"This is Desmond McFarlane," Howard presented me.

"Sit down please, or rather wash your hands, and come back to the table. Howard, show your friend where the washroom is," Garfield directed.

When I returned from the washroom, Garfield stood up and said, "I'm Garfield and this is my wife, Masie."

Garfield was tall and slender, dark brown skin, low cut afro, rectangular shaped face. He sported sideburns but was otherwise clean shaven. Masie was short, with brown skin, shoulder length permed hair, and she radiated beauty.

"Please join us for dinner, there is lots of food for everyone, I hope you have a big appetite, Desmond," Garfield said as he sank back into his chair.

The smell of the food was tantalizing, and it was quite a spread. On the table, there were: roast beef, curried goat, mashed potato, rich beef gravy with a touch of cinnamon, coleslaw, fresh garden salad, and sweetened carrot juice. Dessert included potato pudding, and ice-cream, which was still to come from the kitchen.

"Don't be shy; dig in, Desmond," Masie encouraged me.

"I heard you are quiet and intelligent, but I can see you have more going for you, you are quite handsome too, straight nose, thin lips, light brown skin colour and a symmetrical face" Masie partially described me.

"Thank you for the compliment."

"Where are you from Desmond?"

"I'm from St. Elizabeth,"

"You seem to speak English quite well contrary to what I have heard about the people from St. Elizabeth's speaking ability."

"What exactly have you heard?"

"Mostly, I have heard that people from St. Elizabeth don't speak proper English, they even speak Patois badly."

"I would say the people of St. Elizabeth are being stereotyped. St. Elizabeth is the third largest parish in Jamaica and is also heavily populated. Besides, if schools are a good indicator of peoples' intelligence, St. Elizabeth has three grammar schools, one technical school, four secondary schools, one teacher's college and several training centres."

Hastily changing the topic, she blurted out, "You must have a lot of girls chasing you, Mr. Handsome?"

"I'm not taking notice; besides I'm shy and intimidated by the ladies."

"Then it is time you do and move beyond the trepidations" she countered. Have some dinner and payless attention to me, I was just making conversation to get you to relax and feel at home."

"Well, you have succeeded because I feel like I'm a part of the family already," I assured her.

For some reason, I had no appetite, I barely touched anything on the plate. My grandmother's Monday evening gungo peas soup with pieces of renta yam, sweet potato, and sun-dried cassava bread on the side arrested my thoughts—though it has been a while since I had any of my grandmother's cooking.

After dinner, Howard showed me to one of the accessory dwellings, and told me, "This is where you'll be staying for the next three weeks. In the morning you must be up by 5 a.m., we're going over to Rockfort Mineral Bath, it is part of Masie's pregnancy routine."

"I'm game for that," I told him.

He smiled and disappeared into the bungalow.

It turned out, I got more than just free boarding, I also got free breakfast and dinner and routinely taken to the Rockfort Mineral Bath. When I became aware of this development, I approached Howard in protest, "This is too much."

"Think nothing of it. Garfield sympathizes with our circumstances and is only too happy to help out."

After living and learning Spanish for six months in Kingston, it was time for us to receive feedback on how well we had performed. The teachers and officials at the language training centre organized a graduation ceremony on Friday, July 27, 1979, to present us with our certificates and provide us with refreshments to celebrate the culmination of our language learning experience.

At approximately 3 p.m., the event began. One by one, we were called and given our certificates and comforting remarks were made on how satisfied the teachers and officials were with our accomplishments. Everyone was given a passing grade, and I received a 3+ grade, which was among the highest awarded to the beginners' groups. I was ecstatic about my achievement considering that when I started, my Spanish competence was zero. The results put everyone in a joyous mood, which was an appropriate segue into the breaking-up events.

Each class was encouraged to plan its own event on any topic they wanted. Students volunteered or were selected to perform skits and recite speeches in Spanish. Some were brave enough to take on these roles, while others shied away. In the end, all the events were successful, and students were happy and proud of their performances. After the events, people hung around and chatted for a while and then bade one another farewell as some would never see one another again. Depending on their academic pursuit, they would be sent to various locations in Cuba.

"Congratulations Desmond, your achievement made us all proud. I inquired from one of the teachers for the reason you weren't given a grade of four and she told me, it is because you aren't a native speaker. Apparently, it is unlikely that anyone would get a four if Spanish it isn't their first language," Andrea told me.

"I didn't know, and that shouldn't be, one should be graded based on their performance and not on whether they're native speakers, but I'm not discouraged. Thank you for letting me know this bit of information,"

Tom inquired from me, "Why didn't you participate in the on-stage activities, Desmond?"

"Others needed to participate and assume leading roles so that we can all develop our innate and acquired abilities," I responded.

"But it'd have been so much more fun with you playing a role," Andrea countered.

"Thank you for the vote of confidence, but I believe I'd been taking on too much of the speaking roles, debates, speeches, and dialogues in class and as such leaving little room for others to participate."

"Desmond, you chickened-out of the closing events!" Heather teased with accompanying chicken clucks.

"I don't see you volunteering for any activities, you've to be told or asked to participate in all of our activities."

"I don't speak Spanish as well as you do, and I don't want to embarrass myself."

"That's the best way to go about learning as you challenge yourself to avoid mistakes. In other words, you learn best from your shortcomings," I explained.

"Well, I'm happy this leg of the journey is over. I'm so looking forward to going to Cuba now that I know and can articulate a few sentences in Spanish. I wonder what is in store for us and if we'll be able to adjust to the Cuban system and way of life," Tom said in the presence of John, Andrea, Heather, and myself.

"I'm going with an open mind, ready for whatever comes my way, I'm a survivor," announced John.

"I'm hoping that I'll be able to manage the assignments and get good grades because I wonna go on to higher studies when I return to Jamaica. It might seem too far ahead but that's my plan because I wonna build a solid career," Heather said.

"I'm taking one step at a time and hoping that I'll enjoy the experience. I believe I'm well prepared linguistically and mentally for the imminent journey. According to our teachers and the officials of the language training centre, we're now ready to fly into Cuba and begin our studies," I reminded everyone.

Chapter 4

Between 1972 and 1980, the People's National Party governed Jamaica by principles akin to democratic socialism. These principles provided the basis for developing close relationships with Cuba, which resulted in important collaboration between the two islands. The relationships produced opportunities for Jamaicans to pursue postsecondary studies in a variety of fields in Cuba.

Therefore, in 1979, as well as the previous year, approximately two hundred individuals were selected to go to Cuba to pursue studies in a variety of disciplines, like sports, medicine, fisheries, agronomy, dentistry and so on. I was selected to study physical and health education with the expectation that I would return to Jamaica to share the knowledge and expertise that I would acquire in Cuba and promote sports, physical and health education in schools, colleges, and communities across the island.

On Friday, August 31, 1979, at approximately 7:30 p.m., 34 of us, physical and health education trainees: nine ladies and 25 men, as well as other students both in sports and in other disciplines, departed the Norman Manley International Airport, on board an Air Jamaica flight, the national airline then, bound for Havana, Cuba, José Martí International Airport. That same evening, we landed at approximately 9 p.m. after being one hour and 30 minutes airborne, with the mental preparation of continuing to Santiago de Cuba via ground transportation to begin classes on Tuesday, September 4, 1979. We cleared customs expeditiously.

However, upon exiting the airport, we were told by an official, Juán Peres, of the Instituto Nacional de Deportes, Educación Física y Recreación, INDER, or the National Institute of Sports, Physical Education and Recreation, who received us at the airport: "Your college, the Escuela Provincial de Educación Fisica, EPEF, or the Provincial college of Physical Education, is not prepared for your arrival due to the summer break and a slower than usual start to the academic year." He also informed us that we would be staying in Havana for at least a week before going to Santiago de Cuba.

"Where will we be staying? I inquired. I hope at a hotel," I said after.

"You will be staying at the La Finca compound until it is time for you to continue your journey to Santiago de Cuba."

With no choice in the matter, we resigned ourselves to the newly received information. We soon discovered that there was another group of sports students who were one year our senior, and they also would be sharing the location with our group for the same reason.

The news that we would not travel immediately to Santiago de Cuba took us by surprise and disappointed us, since we were hyped about our destination.

Furthermore, we were made to linger far away, relatively speaking, from the Havana city centre and its activities. We were hosted in crudely constructed dormitories furnished with bunk beds. We were assigned two to each bunk bed which were individually covered with mosquito nets. We learned later that mosquitoes were rampant and a nuisance to everyone living in Cuba. In the general population, it was customary for every home to be fitted with mosquito nets as a means of controlling any possible outbreak of diseases carried and transmitted by mosquitoes.

Cuba's landscape is predominantly flat; therefore, when it rains the water does not run off quickly—it tends to settle in puddles indiscriminately across the island, thus creating the perfect breeding ground for mosquitoes. During our stay in Cuba, the mosquitoes came out almost exclusively at night so that was when we humans had to take measures to protect ourselves from them.

Given that we had no protection outdoors from the mosquitoes, we became quickly aware of our vulnerability in the La Finca. Hence, the threat of mosquitoes was often a topic of conversation amongst members of our group.

"There are a lot of mosquitoes in a dis yah place sah, and mi no bring any mosquito repellants. And from the look of things, the nets are the only repellants available to us. You would think someone would have alerted us to the situation so we could at least come prepared to deal with the mosquitoes," Andrea said.

Andrea was always thinking of things we could do ourselves to make life more bearable. She was a talkative type, attractive, a little anxious but pleasant, short, sported a short-coiled hairdo which she sometimes straightened, and walked with short and quick steps.

Heather informed us, "I inquired about mosquito repellants, and I was told that there's no solution or lotion available comparable to those in Jamaica or other countries in the Caribbean, to guard against these insects."

"I hope no one's allergic to mosquito bites, because it seems there's a good chance that we're gonna be bitten by these insects. This isn't a good way to begin our stay in Cuba," Gregory declared.

"While we're staying in this compound, in the evenings and nights, we'll have to keep moving around, go to bed early or go out to the streets, which we're unfamiliar with, to avoid contact with these mosquitoes," Tom said.

"Going out to the streets requires money to at least be able to travel around, I don't know about you, but I don't have even a cent of any kind in my pocket," I announced.

"I've a few dollars," John said, "but I understand, I'll have to convert them to Cuban pesos because foreign currencies aren't accepted on the streets."

Except for a television in the comedor or canteen, the compound was desolate and without any form of entertainment such as music or even a radio. Fortunately, a few of us brought cassettes and cassette players, so we were able to listen to a variety of songs according to the taste of the owners. The television in the canteen provided additional entertainment despite having to compete with the noise of the patrons. Occasionally, we were treated to a variety of local and international songs. Whenever Michael Jackson was featured, every Cuban on the compound, chefs and all would glue themselves in front of the television for the Michael Jackson TV airing.

"This isn't what I was looking forward to, I feel like a fish out of water, I'm bored," James said with a solemn look on his face.

Although several of us had no money, those who had foreign currency quickly converted them to the Cuban currency and offered to share. Therefore, to help pass the time, most of us elected to go out to the streets and traveled by bus to explore Havana's day as well as night life.

The transportation system was not very developed compared to what we were accustomed to in Jamaica. The buses passed infrequently and by the time they arrived the lines to board them were very long. Thankfully, for the most part the Cubans would not attempt to cut in front of us. There were, however, the odd occasions when younger individuals engaged in pushing. The bus ride was cheap; the cost was no more than 10-cents for a one-way trip within the parameters of the city.

"It helps that the cost of travel in the city isn't prohibitive and allows us to travel the city leisurely," John said on our first outing.

"I like the slow pace; Havana isn't like Kingston with everyone in a rush to get where they're going. You can take time to breathe the air and scan the environment. Though the buildings are antiquated, I like the architecture and foremost the way they are rowed along the streets—not much room for trash," Andrea remarked.

"The streets are bare, hardly anyone around," Tom said.

"Maybe people are at work, I read in books and papers that unemployment in Cuba is very low. If you're not working, it's because you don't want to." I asserted.

Very early in our street exploration, we discovered the Havana Club Tropicana, which was a buzz to us, and kept us out late at night—a welcome diversion. We went there four out of the eight nights we spent in Havana, but we were only able to gain entrance twice. On those occasions the entertainment was fabulous. We enjoyed the performances that were done mostly by Cubans dressed in colourful costumes and dancing to Cuban and Latin music. We had a few drinks: beers, and the famous Havana Club rum. The two nights we were unable to access the club, we hung around outside trying to make conversation with Cubans or just simply walked around the blocks to get a feel for the locale. The lack of entertainment was not our only complaint during the nine days we spent at the La Finca, the food was far less appealing than we anticipated.

The Cubans through INDER provided us with three meals everyday plus snacks, even though some of us had difficulty eating the food because we were not accustomed to the Cuban dietary habits. Cubans were big fans of pork, while some Jamaicans detested eating pork; therefore, we frowned upon the meals that were provided.

"If we don't get the pork in its natural form, we are sure to get it in the oil that is used to prepare the meals. It's in the rice, fried eggs, fried jurel or jack mackerel and other meat," James said.

"I don't know if I can survive this constant barrage of pork," Gregory added.

"Don't they get tired of eating this?" John asked.

"The US embargo limits their food choices, and pork is home grown providing an escape from the restrictions of the embargo," Heather reminded everyone.

"One thing I'm certain of, I'm not gonna eat any. Bread, though it was suspected pork oil was included in it, and water are gonna be my staple diet whenever pork or its by-products are on the menu," I told them.

The canteen was always a noisy place; one could hear the murmuring and often the shouts of discontent among us when food choices did not allow for options without pork. About one third of us did not eat pork in any form and another third would prefer not to eat it and the final third did not mind eating it.

To get our meals, we had to line up one behind the other, pick up a tray from a nearby counter. Then we would move across a serving hatch to select our food, and finally on to one of the four-seater tables.

El desayuno, breakfast, provided the best options to avoid eating pork. Breakfast offered choices of bread, dairy cheese, guava cheese, fried eggs or omelets, boiled eggs, porridge, and coffee and milk. Those of us who did not eat pork avoided fried eggs or omelets, because lard was used to prepare them. The other items were much appreciated and welcomed. Often, we left the canteen with stacks of bread and cheese just in case lunch or dinner was not to our liking.

El almuerzo, lunch, was always challenging, as it was difficult to find anything to eat that was devoid of pork. Lunch was made typically of white rice, chickpea, kidney beans potage, fried jack mackerel, shredded beef, and hard-boiled eggs in tomato sauce. Everything, except for the boiled eggs was to some degree made with the support of pork. At lunch time it was certain to hear a litany of Jamaican profanity as several of us expressed our displeasure at the menu that was prepared for us, despite the Cubans' awareness of our aversion to pork and its by-products on a whole. Almost everyone pleaded with the cooks and servers to make more bread available.

La cena, dinner, was also difficult for us non-pork eaters. Dinner was made typically of white rice—white rice is another staple of the Cubans diet—chicken, pork, shredded beef, bologna sausage, chorizo, chickpea and kidney beans potage and hard-boiled eggs in tomato sauce. Here again, the chattering and frustration could be heard and seen as some of us inquired and learned about what went into preparing the meal. Most of us requested and received milk and bread as a substitute for the prepared pork-laced meal. Some, who could afford to, went out to the streets, and purchased expensive food in locations predominantly reserved for or frequented by international tourists.

Not all the above items were prepared and served daily but any amount of them could be seen in the canteen depending on the day of the week. It was likely that only one kind of meat would be available on any given day. Portions served to us were also small. Therefore, after meals, there was always a desire to have something more to eat. Hence, the pastry counters and ice cream parlours in the streets were handy fallbacks to supplement the offerings of the Cuban cuisine.

"The chefs show great understanding to our needs especially with respect to food. They tried their best to accommodate us with what they've on site," said Andrea.

"We only have to ask, and they do whatever they can to ensure our comfort. However, at times I can see the frustration in their faces as we hail profanities in English and Spanish, and they seem to think that we're directing our anger at them," Tom said.

"No doubt about it, we've caught-on quickly to the Cuban profanities: "maricon, hija de puta, chingao, pendejo." I wish we wouldn't use them so much. It's obvious that the Cubans in the compound are annoyed when they hear them from us. It is amazing how much more easily we learn the street lingo than we do the formal language which is more important for our training," Andrea said.

"I wish I was already in Santiago, the suspense is getting to me, besides, I wonna settle and not having to think about another move," I remarked.

"I say amen to that, Desmond," Heather agreed.

"Do you think we'll be able to make telephone calls to Jamaica?" John inquired.

"I think we may have to beat the drums for distance communication," responded Tom.

"Don't you see that most things that we're accustomed to are either unavailable or nonexistent here?" Andrea questioned.

"It seems Cuba is cut off from the rest of the world, there seems to be no obvious path to shaking the past," James said.

To cope with the isolation and boredom, members of our group started to develop intimate relationships, mainly between guys from the previous year's group, and girls from the new group. Most of those relationships did not last long after our arrival in Santiago de Cuba since they were formed based on the need for social interaction more than anything else. However, two of the relationships lasted about three years but ended when the partners in the previous year group graduated and did not have to come back to Cuba.

The isolation and boredom in Havana, for nine long days, was about to end, finally with a time set for our departure to Santiago de Cuba.

Prior to leaving Havana on Friday, September 7, 1979, at 4 p.m., an impromptu meeting was held to elect a group leader. I learned of the meeting to choose the group leader approximately 30 minutes before it happened.

The chair of the meeting, Keith Davis, welcomed and thanked members for attending the meeting and quickly announced the purpose of the meeting and asked the group to vote on a motion to proceed with the agenda—no other issues were proposed or discussed at the meeting.

"The floor is now open to nominate a group leader, can someone put forward a name or can I get a volunteer," Keith announced.

"I nominate Desmond McFarlane to lead our group in Cuba," Andrea shouted.

"I second that," Heather sanctioned, immediately following the nomination.

The decision to elect me to be group leader was made amongst the rest of the group, it seemed, in discussions unbeknownst to me. I certainly did not express any desire to lead the group nor canvas anyone to vote for me.

No other nomination came forward. Then there was a brief silence.

"If there isn't any other nomination, the floor is closed and Desmond McFarlane will lead our group," Keith declared.

This was met with thunderous applause and laughter. But I was flabbergasted. My surprise was such that, I neglected to thank the group for "selecting" me group leader in my acceptance speech, and one of the ladies called me out. I proceeded to thank the group for the honour they bestowed on me and let them know that I would try to provide the best leadership possible in Cuba.

After the meeting, I approached Andrea and John who were walking by the canteen, "What just happened?" I inquired.

"We chose you as group leader," Andrea said.

"Why wasn't I consulted? When was this decision to nominate and select me made? What if I'd declined the nomination?" I asked.

"A group of us planned it so it'd be hard for you to decline. We figured it'd be hard for you to back out of the situation if all or almost all the group members showed their support. By the way did you notice that there was no objection?" Andrea spoke.

"Why did you select me to be leader?" I asked.

"You're articulate, speak Spanish well, and besides, most of us admire you," according to Andrea.

"You're the best choice among us, and you're going to do a fine job, I'm sure," John said.

"I never anticipated this; I told John and Andrea. Although, I never expected this vote of confidence, I do believe it's a good decision to select a leader, so we can hit the ground running, once we arrived in Santiago de Cuba."

They both smiled and Andrea asked, "So, you aren't mad at us?"

"Absolutely not," I assured her.

Up until that moment, I was never caught off guard like that before. It was the biggest surprise and compliment I had ever experienced.

Chapter 5

We left Havana in the evening on Saturday, September 8, 1979, destined for Santiago de Cuba. At about 3 p.m. in the afternoon, we loaded our suitcases onto a coach bound for José Martí International Airport where we would embark on a plane to travel to the Antonio Maceo Airport, located in Cuba's second largest city—Santiago.

Our journey began at about 4 p.m. with the coach carrying the two groups of physical and health education students, from the compound where we had been staying for the past eight days, to the José Martí International Airport.

On the way, we talked and laughed about the experience of the past eight days, and how it was an eye opener. We marveled and commented on the picturesque landscape of the city which we had not previously beheld, because when we first traveled from the airport to the compound it was after darkness had fallen. The trees were lush green, and the shrubbery was skillfully organized and groomed in a fashion that delighted the eyes with splendour.

As we traveled along Avenida Guzman or Guzman Avenue, we encountered some of the most well-kept antiquated buildings that seemed over 200 years old, and cars bordering on 40-50 years old. The houses were tall and dull as though they were longing for a "new dress."

Most of the cars were classic American cars that were made or assembled in the 30s and 40s. These cars were to us a stark contrast to what we were accustomed to seeing on the streets of Kingston, which had the latest in American, Japanese, German, and British-made vehicles.

"A weh dem get demyah ole car from?" James inquired.

"These are similar to those we see in American movies from the 1930s and 40s," Gregory asserted.

"With an enforced American trade embargo, Cuba is unable to do a lot of import and least of all American merchandise. Most of the goods we'll see in Cuba are gonna be Soviet made. So, you better start conditioning your way of thinking to that reality," I told them.

In addition to sightseeing, we chatted and wondered about the welcome awaiting us in Santiago. The most salient points discussed were the gastronomy and eating habits of the Cubans.

"We'll have to be careful about the menu and options," Heather reminded us.

"We may end up having to choose between eating pork and scaled-back portions," Tom said.

"Can we change the subject of eating pork," I asked, "I'm not too keen on hearing about it because just thinking about it makes my stomach turn."

"I agree with Desmond," John said, "we'll deal with whatever the situation is when we get to Santiago and learn of the available options."

Within 35 minutes we found ourselves in front of the airport near the customs and immigration area of the airport. We alighted from the bus, unloaded our belongings, and took a curt view around us. The airport was a long two-storey rectangular building with a slight hotdog curve at the front and an appearance of being well kept, which made it difficult to judge its age even though it was obvious that it had not received a coat of paint in many years. The corridors were clean and the grounds in front of the airport were green and well-groomed with several small palm trees, and flower beds artistically situated in front and along the laneway leading to the main building.

Once we thanked the bus driver and bade him farewell, we moved cautiously into the building to check in at customs. We formed three lines in front of our assigned immigration officers who reviewed our travel documents and directed us towards customs. The custom officers separated us from our luggage and waved us through to the awaiting Cubana Airline. We did not have to wait for our luggage to be checked as had been the case in Jamaica just over a week ago.

In less than an hour, we went through immigration and customs and were ready to board the aircraft to continue the pen-ultimate leg of our journey. We moved casually out of the airport and approached the aircraft with a mobile staircase attached to it and ready for our boarding. The aircraft was stationed about 25 feet from one of several rear exits of the airport with the staircase inclined towards the aircraft door and away from our assigned exit door.

On exiting the airport, we slowly mounted the stairs one by one. Looking back, I saw a group of Cuban workers, some of whom it seemed were air-traffic controllers, moving around briskly to get the aircraft going. We entered the aircraft and took possession of our seats, which were arranged in pairs of two on both sides of the aisle. The aircraft was not large but was big enough to accommodate the approximately 75 of us that were on board—first and second-year students, pilot, co-pilot, and flight attendants.

The flight time from Havana to Santiago de Cuba was approximately one hour and 25 minutes and we spent most of that time in silence. However, occasionally, those of us who believed we had a fair command of the Spanish language tried to strike up conversations with the airhostesses. That did not go over too well for our ego, as we struggled to find words in our limited vocabulary to have a sustained conversation. The airhostesses understood our dilemma but nonetheless had a few laughs at our expense.

The airhostesses tried their best to assist us with the needed words and sentences in our attempt to convey what we wanted to tell them. They spoke English which was helpful in the cases where Spanish was a barrier in communicating our ideas. The main topics of our conversation was about what life was like for them in Cuba, and what they knew about life in Santiago de Cuba. We were interested to learn about Santiago de Cuba as it was going to be our host province for the next four years. It turned out they knew little about Santiago de Cuba, since they were from Havana and Villa Clara.

We arrived at the Antonio Maceo Airport in Santiago de Cuba while the sun was still up and shining in a cloudless sky. The pilot, co-pilot, and flight attendants located themselves on both sides of the aircraft doorway to greet and wish us well as we moved to descend the staircase pinned to the aircraft in front of the entrance. We alighted from the aircraft with our carry-on luggage in hand, and once we were on the ground, we moved quickly towards the interior of the building, and were directed by ushers to the locations where we needed to line up to process our travel documents.

There were several immigration officers, with quiet and serious demeanour, waiting, each beside a wicket that leads to the luggage collection area. The officers were seated and neatly dressed in immaculately clean white shirts, and dark pants and purple bowties. They summoned us one by one, requested our passports and inquired as to the purpose of our visit—routine I supposed. We told them we were students coming in to attend the sports college, and without further questions, they stamped and returned our passports to us and directed us to move through the passageway next to the wickets.

We walked over to the area where our luggage was left for us to collect; there were no carousels installed back then, everything within the airport building had to be done manually. We collected our suitcases, put them on trolleys, and exited the building without any further checking or inspection.

The airport was small, much smaller than the José Martí Airport in Havana but exhibited many of the features and characteristics of the José Martí airport.

"Welcome to Santiago de Cuba compañeros, we are happy you are finally here," said José Ramos, the assistant director of the college, as we exited the airport, "How was your flight?"

"Fine," we all said in unison.

"We wish we could have been here sooner" remarked, one of the second-year students.

"You are here now, and that is what counts," José replied.

"How far is it from here to the college?" Gregory asked.

"The distance from the airport to the college is about 30 minutes' drive," one of the bus drivers responded.

"Señores, all on board, we must get to the college in a hurry to allow the kitchen staff to complete their day," another driver told us.

As we set off on the final leg of our journey, the driver and the college's officials began explaining some of the landmarks to us. Moving through the city, José pointed out, "There is the General Hospital—the largest in Santiago. Also here are the Moncada Barracks, the place from where the Cuban revolution was launched."

The barracks were kind of straw yellow and sat close to the Central Road, about 10 minutes' drive away from our destination—the college.

A few minutes later, the bus driver called for our attention. "This is the central bus terminal that serves local, national, and international travelers. We are almost at the college. There is the baseball stadium, baseball is Cuba's favourite pastime."

The baseball stadium was a large enclosed oval building about 500 feet away from the sports college.

Santiago reminded me in many ways of Havana: the landscape and architecture bordering the road from the airport to the college were like what I had seen along Guzman Avenue in Havana. The buildings were tall and dull with a lot of patch work to the walls indicating that they were undergoing or recently experienced a bit of face lifting or simply to prevent other areas of the granite from eroding.

We arrived at the main entrance of the college just at the beginning of nightfall, there was hardly anyone there to meet and greet us. Then we sat in the bus and murmured amongst ourselves for a while about the strangeness of the locale and buildings that were going to be our home for the next four years. Next, we sluggishly rose from our seats, grabbed hold of our hand luggage, and eased ourselves off the buses. Once we were out, we collected the remainder of our luggage from the baggage compartments, and I began visually surveying the environment in complete awe and amazement. The college's surroundings were filled with lush green vegetation of trees and shrubs that were exquisitely manicured. The college grounds were clean: no waste or garbage anywhere in sight.

The college was a three-storey building designed in a rectangular shape, displaying an opening of about thirty-five metres wide, which formed the entrance to the college yard, each section of the building was connected to the other with easy access for movement from the dormitory to the classrooms without having to exit the building. The building walls were painted in an off-white colour and displayed matching salmon pink jalousie windows and pine-wood doors.

The building columns and beams as well as the retaining walls and the perimeter of the benches were painted in royal blue. As we proceeded from the parking area towards the college yard, which was framed by the college building, we could see kitchen staff congregated in front of the canteen door staring at us with some apparent anxiety. They must have been weary, and wanting to go home, because at that moment, José announced to us, "Hurry up and get ready for supper, because the kitchen staff are having a long day."

They probably knew it would be a while before their day would be completed, since we had not even gone up to our dormitory to put down our luggage yet. They were going to work another two hours at least before they would be able to go home that Saturday evening.

As we were told, we hurried up to our designated dormitories: men on the third floor of the north wing and women on the third floor of the east wing of the building. In pairs, we claimed our bunkbeds and rested our luggage on the beds, top and bottom, according to our choosing. We then scurried to the washroom to wash our hands, and without examining the quarters which would house us for the ensuing four years, we dashed downstairs to the canteen to collect our grub.

The canteen was a large square room, painted in the same off-white colour with salmon pink trimmings as were the doors and windows. The area was rowed with long, rectangular tables covered with laminated, yellow Formica tops. Each table was outfitted with six very light chairs made with dark brown metal tube frames and plywood seat bases.

Dinner included paella, chickpea soup with pork rinds, guava cheese and cold dairy milk. For those who preferred to drink water, there was a large fountain with ice-cold running water. We were welcome to request a drinking glass from the kitchen staff and help ourselves.

To receive our food, we formed a line, one behind the other from inside the canteen doorway up to the serving hatch.

The kitchen staff were dressed in blue uniform with a white apron and hat and were all wearing face masks. One at a time, they pulled a tray from the pile and served the repast which we individually picked up and moved along to the seating area. Some members from the second-year group had their own eating vessels in which they collected their meals and went back up to the dormitory to eat while the rest of us remained in the canteen to eat. We fumbled our way through the meal, picking what we wanted to eat. Once we were finished eating, we returned our food trays and utensils to the counter at the side of the serving hatch where a member of the kitchen staff gestured, we should leave them.

That evening we spent about an hour in the canteen eating and talking about the meal and what little we had seen of Santiago thus far. Then, we hung about for a bit, in the corridor, making conversation primarily with members of the second-year group about what could be expected from the college in the coming days. We also questioned them about life in Santiago and where we could go for entertainment and social interaction. They provided us with names of centres, clubs, and streets, and recommended that the best way to learn about the city was to let them show us around, since we were not yet familiar with the city.

The following day, we asked the college's maintenance crew about the college's features and learned that it was equipped with a basketball court, two swimming pools—an Olympic size and a small training pool—a soccer field, a baseball field, and a gymnasium designated for indoor sports: volleyball, fencing and various disciplines of gymnastics. Furthermore, the college was in a sports village, near to the baseball stadium, and a soccer stadium. The sports village also served as a training camp for national athletes in training and pre-game preparation. In addition, there was a construction yard, which was incidentally, home to a group of Jamaican brigades acquiring skills in construction; and a military camp which was completely cordoned off from on-lookers.

It was approximately 8 p.m. when I was approached by a couple of guys from the second-year group of students with a request, "We'd like your permission to take out a few of the first-year ladies," Alton said.

"I've to deny the request until I speak with the college's director and have a better understanding of the rules governing our stay in Cuba and the college," I told Alton.

And I instructed the ladies, "Please turn in for the night and we'll talk about leisure outings when I know what the rules and protocols are surrounding outings. Furthermore, Señor Juán Peres had warned us about travelling without a travel pass or authorized Cuban identification." The look on the faces of the aspirants was one of displeasure as they walked away without further supplication.

This request placed me in an awkward position because I did not want to start off my relationship with students from the second-year group and those from my own on a sour note. However, my responsibility as group leader outweighed any thoughts of being perceived as a mean and authoritarian leader. However, the following day, I learned from other ladies in the group, who did not go out, that moments after I was out of sight, those females who wanted to go out came back down and sneaked away with their male counterparts. I was uncomfortable that my directive was not observed, but I did not let it bother me since as the person responsible for representing the group with the college's administration, I had advised against the students leaving the campus. After all, we were all adults between the ages of 18 and 26 years old; and therefore, bore personal responsibility for any consequences our actions may have produced.

That night, my stay in the corridor was interrupted by an attack from mosquitoes, and I headed back up to the dormitory for refuge. In the dormitory, I rummaged through my luggage for my hygiene kit and headed to the washroom to prepare for bed. The area where we brushed our teeth and washed our hands and faces was a tall trough fitted with six water taps. Facing the trough were four stalls each containing a lid-less flush toilet. Behind the toilets, separated by a concrete prefab panel wall, were four shower stalls, facing the opposite direction. In each stall there was a pipe protruding out of the wall without any fixtures. We were obligated to take turns showering given the limited number of shower stalls.

It did not take long for me to freshen up and hustle onto my bunk bed, which was covered with a mosquito net. Someone turned off the lights, and the groups chatted a bit in the dark until there was complete silence. On Sunday morning, I was awakened by an audio system hollering music in English and Spanish alternately.

Then at precisely 7 a.m., I heard the announcement that the canteen was open, and that breakfast was going to be served between 7 and 9 a.m. We, immediately got out of bed, hurried to the bathroom, freshened up, changed into some casual clothing, and descended the stairs to the canteen. We were the only students on campus, and the only other people were a few members of the grounds and teaching staff. Almost all of us converged on the canteen at the same time. Therefore, once again, we were told to form a line one behind the other to receive our breakfast.

We collected our breakfast and moved slowly across the serving hatch to the seating area and made ourselves comfortable. For breakfast they served egg sandwiches, and we had a choice of warm or cold milk and sweetened cocoa with milk in a small glass. Like the evening before, we conversed with one another for the duration of the meal. Except for a few of us, who did not have any eggs, we ate the meal that was served to us.

Once we were through eating, we exited the canteen and hung about in the corridor in front of the canteen. Some of us sat on some concrete benches, while others remained standing to continue the conversation that was started in the canteen.

"I can't wait to see the Cuban students. I'm brimming with curiosity. I wonder how they'll react to us being in their spaces," James uttered.

"This afternoon is almost here, we'll know then," Gregory responded.

"I'm sure they are going to have a lot of questions for us. Are you guys ready to answer in Spanish? Better yet, have you been practising mock dialogue? Call me crazy if you will, but I'm already having make-believe dialogue in my mind," I told everyone.

"Desmond, you don't have any need to do that, you are already speaking like a Cuban," Heather said.

"I'm leaving nothing to chance. On my part, it won't be for a lack of trying."

"Okay Mr. Wise Guy," Andrea remarked.

Not long after, we began dispersing in all directions: some went back up to the dormitories and others went about getting an intimate view of the campus. Within the space of about 20 minutes, the guys were engaged in some form of sport activities in the college yard. We were all over playing soccer, basketball, and cricket. The ladies did not participate but remained in their dormitory.

A few Cubans took the time to observe us in action and we could sometimes see them laughing at our aggressive behaviour during the contact sport exhibitions. We shouted and lunged into one another forcefully to win possession of the ball.

Our little entertainment lasted for about an hour. That morning the sun was extremely hot, and we were perspiring profusely, drenching our bodies and garments. After the exhibition, we sat around for a while to cool down and regain our normal body temperature and composure. Once we were satisfied that we had regained some normalcy, we slowly ascended the stairs. Upon our arrival in the common area facing the dormitory some of us decided to play chess and dominoes while the rest either stood around to watch or went off to catch a shower.

At 12 p.m. the college's public address system announced that lunch was ready, and the canteen would be open until 2 p.m. Before long we were once again lining up to receive our lunch, so we moved calmly up to the serving hatch, and each of us picked-up an aluminum tray and drinking glass, then lazily headed to our preferred seating location. We placed our trays on the table and went over to the water fountain, which was brimming with ice-cold water, helped ourselves to some water and returned to our table. Our platter boasted white rice, black bean potage, baked chicken, and orange marmalade.

"I'm happy that we can eat a meal without having to worry, except for the potage, about the ingredients," I said.

"Amen to that, and I'm going to pray that we continue receiving similar servings in the future," Heather commented.

"I don't believe prayer is gonna do it for us. Remember, members of the Cuban authority aren't religious, and the Gods may not be willing to intercede with them on our behalf, it might be better to consult with the devil," Tom concluded jokingly.

"For the first time since our arrival in Cuba, no one has complained audibly about the food, and this is good. We know this treatment isn't going to last for long, though. Furthermore, it is common knowledge that Cuba is a developing country that is experiencing a hostile and cruel trade embargo imposed and maintained by the United States which contributed to a dearth of food products in the island. The Cuban diet consists mostly of home grown produce and made goods or, alternatively, Soviet imports such as shredded beef, some pork products, and chickpeas," John reminded us.

"We just have to accept the food situation for what it is and navigate the meals as best we can with the knowledge that we should never raise expectations too high or else we'd be at risk of disappointment," I told the little gathering at the table.

Our time in the canteen lasted a little longer than usual that Sunday afternoon, given the conversation we were having about the food and expectations of what were to come in the evening with the return of the Cuban students to the college campus for their first semester of classes in 1979. Once we had finished eating, we returned the dirty eating and drinking vessels to their designated location. Having done that, we exited the canteen and proceeded to climb the stairs towards our respective dormitory. On the way, the guys discussed the different options we had for the afternoon. Some decided to just chill out in the dormitory, others decided to head for the streets and attraction park close to the college, and still there were others who decided to remain in the common area of the dormitory to play chess and domino games. In the meantime, we were treated to some ballad songs from Cuba, Brazil, and Spain.

Chapter 6

We knew the Cuban students were arriving when we began hearing chatter in Spanish. It was after 2 p.m., and the Cuban students were coming in buses, and the entire campus came alive with strange voices and live bodies that were sparse in the previous eighteen hours. Most of us hung around the windows and began peering outside to see what was happening. To our delight, we saw students, most of whom were dressed in college uniforms: guys dressed in pink tops and red pants and girls dressed in pink tops and red skirts cut above their knees.

The students' racial diversity was limited to white and black and a large pool of brown in between. It was not long before several of us ventured out to get near the Cuban students who were just as curious as we were to learn about one another. Those of us who understood and or could string a few words and sentences together had to take on the role of information brokers and translators.

We were bombarded with personal questions, a common one being, "How long are you going to be in Cuba?" This was natural since, previously, Jamaican sports students spent short stints at the college: anywhere from one to three months. Besides, the Cuban students apparently were not given any information about how long we were going to be in Cuba, and even if they were, they demonstrated little knowledge about the duration of our stay in Cuba. Furthermore, several of the Jamaican students who were now in the four-year program had previously participated in those short stints. While we chatted with the Cuban students, one of the first things we noticed and shared among ourselves was that the Cuban students spoke with a nasal tone which was quite strange to us since we were not accustomed to hearing this kind of speaking. In Jamaica, we speak with a more guttural tone. Overall, the Cuban students were friendly and eager to speak with us and wanted to follow up with our conversation the next day.

One of our most fascinating experiences was observing their social behaviour amongst one another. It was quite enlightening for us to watch how the Cuban students greeted one another without reservation. They approached one another, screaming and shouting with lots of hugs and kisses on both cheeks. Then again, this might have been since they had not seen one another over the summer because they were from different parts of the island. Even though Santiago de Cuba's population was large enough to support the college with students, at least two other provinces were feeding into the college—Guantanámo and Granma.

Many Cuban students third-and-fourth year did not return for in-class participation because they had to fulfill their practicum obligations with the college. Students were required to complete two stints of practicum, each of a six-month duration, to be eligible for graduation. Those who were returning arrived steadily in buses and on foot. We figured out that the students that came late in the evening were mainly from the city of Santiago because they were walking in and not brought in by buses. The greeting and conversation among students went on all afternoon and well into the evening until dinner time.

For the first time since our arrival in Cuba, we would have a meal in the company of Cuban students. Once dinner was ready to be served, we were called up to the canteen to collect our meal, as was done before the arrival of the Cuban students on campus. We collected our meals and proceeded to sit at the tables. Apart from a few second-year Jamaican students, the Jamaican and Cuban students sat separately. The process went smoothly, and within an hour and a half, the canteen was empty, and we were back in the college's hallways conversing with our Cuban counterparts.

A second-year Cuban student with a typical profile: brown skin, approximately five feet eight inches tall, straight black hair almost shoulder length, muscular and slightly top heavy, approached me and we began a conversation.

"How many new 'Jamaiquinos' came this time? By the way, my name is Amaury Lopez, and I'm from Guantanámo," he introduced himself.

"My name is Desmond McFarlane; I'm the jefe for the Jamaican group. 34 of us came," I told him.

"When did you arrive in Cuba?" He asked.

"We arrived in Cuba the week before last Friday, August 31, spent a week in Havana, and came to Santiago yesterday," I said.

"Did you come to Cuba by boat or airplane? I never traveled outside of Cuba. I want to go to Méjico; mi padre lives there. He is an estomatólogo. The Cuban government sent him there to work as an internationalist. Let us continue our conversation another day; here comes my girlfriend," he proclaimed.

Within a few seconds a young lady approached us, and Amaury threw an arm around her, leaned into her, and kissed her on the neck.

"You need to find a Cuban girl to help you pass the time; las Cubanas are very sabrosas," he declared, looking back at me, and giggling with one of his hands floating over the girl's backside. I returned the smile without any further remarks.

As night began to fall, we could see and hear signs of intimacy all around us as several student couples got closer to one another and started making out. They kissed and fondled each other and then wandered off into dark areas around the college campus.

They would be out of sight for brief spells, and when next you see them, their hair was ruffled, and their clothing without the neatness of which they arrived on campus earlier, and some of the girls even had blouse buttons undone. One could easily get the impression that they were making up for the time they lost over the summer. The men were not shy to tell us that they had just had sex with easily identifiable girls by indicating with their fingers and motioning with their heads.

It was surprising and entertaining for most of us who had never had the experience of living in a coed learning environment. On the one hand, it was surprising because of the raunchy behaviour of some of the students, who were not shy to demonstrate their sexual desires and even acted them out in almost plain sight. On the other hand, it was entertaining because we could easily imagine what was happening in the dark corners.

A sexual act is always appealing, even if you only get to think about it happening in proximity. Never mind having to listen to the girls saying, "Hay papi meta me la, give me all of it; it feels so good," and the guys saying, take it all, mami, it's yours, open it; I'm going to make you tremble and wet."

This behaviour went on until about 9 p.m. when we heard the public address system informing us that it was time to head on up to our respective dormitories. In less than 15 minutes, the corridors were empty, and the college guards patrolled the grounds and the corridors. The lights were on in the dormitories, and we could hear laughter and chatter emanating from within the Cuban student's quarters. It sounded like bees in their hive; in other words, there was no clear word articulation. Our inability to hear and understand Spanish clearly, especially from afar, was not helpful in deciphering what was being said. But it was not hard to imagine that they must have been sharing their summer experiences.

At approximately 10 p.m., the PA system announced that all lights should be turned off in the dormitories. This instruction was followed almost instantaneously; suddenly, there was silence and darkness throughout all the dormitories. We, Jamaicans, chatted amongst ourselves in the dark about our recent experiences down below. Two of the guys from the second-year Jamaican group, Jason, and Patrick, related their welcoming experience as well.

They confirmed to us what we heard from the Cuban students earlier downstairs. They connected with their girlfriends from the previous year and wasted little time rekindling their relationship in the most salacious fashion against the walls of the college building in dark corners. They even went as far as to explain in detail the responses from their Cuban girls in their moment of gratification: "Oh yes, daddy, give me more, do not stop, fuck me please," Patrick told us.

Jason told us, my girl said, "I missed you so much that it aches, I'm burning up with yearning, this is paradise, devour me, honey, I'm yours any time you want me."

Through these vivid accounts, one by one, we fell off to sleep, while our colleagues bragged and narrated their experiences, from exciting to boring, depending on how one feels or appreciates certain descriptions.

Chapter 7

Monday morning, at about 6 a.m., we woke up to the PA system's announcement that it was time to rise, and the canteen would be open from 6:30 a.m. to 8 a.m. We got out of bed and took turns going to the bathroom to shower and freshen up before heading downstairs.

That morning, after breakfast, I learned José was on campus and in his office. I approached the office and found the door ajar, and peeked in. We made eye contact, and he beckoned to me with his hand and a nod of his head to come inside. I entered the office, and he stood and extended his hand for a shake. He was approximately six feet seven inches tall, dark-brown skin colour with black curly hair. We introduced ourselves, "I'm José Ramos."

"Desmond McFarlane, I'm the leader of the first-year Jamaican group."

"How has your experience been thus far?" he inquired.

I explained to him as best as I could in Spanish, "Things are going fine. We are trying our best to adjust in order to have a pleasant stay in Santiago. However, several of us do not eat pork, including myself. As such, at times, we do not have enough to eat, which was causing anxiety among some of us."

He was sympathetic when he learned of our eating habits, but he told me, "I'm powerless to do anything about the situation since the decision is not under the college's control. The dietary decision is made at the provincial level in accordance with prescribed direction from the Ministry of Sports through the Instituto Nacional de Deportes, Educación Fisica y Recreación—the INDER. However, I will investigate the possibility of getting you some of what you are accustomed to eating, at least on weekends when the Cuban students are usually not on campus."

I assume that the investigation did not go anywhere because no meaningful change was noticed on the meal front in the ensuing months or years, for that matter.

Further, I told him, "My real reason for coming to your office is to find out when it would be possible for you and me to have a conversation about college protocol, like comings and goings. I could meet with you this afternoon once I'm through with a bit of housekeeping regarding our integration into the college's norms. Would 3 p.m. work for you?" I inquired.

"My preference would be 4 p.m. if you don't mind,"

"Then 4 p.m., it will be," I told him.

We then bade goodbye, and I said, "Hasta luego."

As I exited his office and walked towards the lobby of the college, several of my colleagues were sitting on concrete benches in the yard, and I headed towards where they were, and before I fully arrived, they revealed their curiosity. They wanted to know and asked, "Who were you talking with?" Andrea spoke.

"The assistant director," I replied.

"What's he like? Did you find out when the college administration is gonna meet with us?" James inquired.

"I'll have the answers to your questions later this afternoon."

However, after lunch, I was summoned to the director's office and met the director, Luis Pacheco, a short man with light brown skin, low-cut salt and pepper hair, round face, and a serious demeanor, José, the college's principal secretary, Juanita Suarez, a tall white lady with a rectangular face and long blonde hair; and our would be group godmother, Linda Euclides, a short, chubby black lady with a triangular face and short black permed hair were there waiting to confer with me.

The director welcomed me and informed me, "I would like to speak with your group at 3 p.m. tomorrow afternoon to provide you with important information regarding the college's routines, expectations, and your comportment as members of the college community."

"My colleagues and I are anxious to meet with you; therefore, tomorrow afternoon would be perfect," I responded.

Luis then requested that José and Linda explain to me the order of business over the next few days.

"You won't be attending classes tomorrow but rather you will get through some housekeeping activities such as receiving your college uniforms. Your Madrina, Linda, will provide you with a bit more detail," Luis said.

"Don't hesitate to bring your issues and concerns, if any, to my attention, and I will endeavour to address them within our realm of possibilities," José added.

"Thank you. That is encouraging to hear and know," I replied.

First, Linda provided me with a sheet of paper containing the course schedule and explained: "During the first semester, your group will be attending practical activities in the morning and classroom instructions in the afternoon. The schedule contains the courses you are to attend, the name of the instructors, and the location of each class. Next, she explained, "Your sportswear is your responsibility, but the college will provide uniforms for classroom instructions."

"We were informed before leaving Jamaica that our sportswear was our responsibility," I acknowledged.

Linda instructed me, "Please convey to your group that at 10 a.m., everyone should go to the college warehouse to collect their uniforms."

"Where is the college's warehouse?" I inquired.

"Al lado del comendor, por la derecha, she responded in Spanish. It's very important that you all adhere to the canteen schedule because if you miss any of your meals, there is no way for you to make up for them. You will have to wait for the next meal on the schedule. Breakfast is served between 6:30 a.m. and 8 a.m., lunch between 11:45 a.m. and 12:45 p.m., and dinner between 5 p.m. and 7 p.m."

The instructions were all communicated to me in Spanish as though I was a native of Cuba. After hearing the instructions, I thanked the college administration for the orientation.

Luis inquired, "Do you have any questions?"

"Not for now. I already explained our primary concern to José," I replied.

"Then we're finished here," Luis declared.

I excused myself from their company and went back to the dormitory to inform my male colleagues. I also sent a message to the females that I needed a meeting with everyone to bring them up to date on the information I received from the college's administration.

Not long after returning to the dormitory, I called an impromptu group meeting in the male dormitory's common area since I forgot to inquire from the administration about available meeting space. I shared with them the information I received from the college's administration. The information was received civilly by everyone present. I inquired if anyone had any questions, and no one expressed any desire to delve into the situation.

"Remember now, everyone, let's be on time to receive our uniforms because each person needs to be there to confirm his or her sizes. I suggest that we meet at the college warehouse entrance at 10 a.m. to collect our uniforms."

"I hope we can find the right sizes and that they are new, and we won't have to settle for any old hand-me-downs that the Cuban students have rejected," John said.

"That I can't speak to since I'm in the same "boat" as all of you. Besides, my understanding is that once you receive your uniforms, they are yours, and you are not required to return them, even if you decide to quit the college," I responded. At that point, I dismissed the group, and everyone returned to their respective lodging area.

The next morning, while we were waiting for our appointment at the warehouse to collect our uniforms, we got a chance to see a myriad of physical activities.

In the yard below and in front of the canteen, we saw students lifting weights, and further down another level, we saw an instructor supporting students to practice pivoting and shooting basketball hoops in an area displaying markings of a basketball court.

Further away from the yard were the two swimming pools. Both were buzzing with activities as instructors shouted out instructions in Spanish, and students dressed in swimwear plunged into and exited the water and shouted to one another in Spanish. Observing the activities and students' participation in them helped us to pass the time, and we quickly approached 10 a.m. without realizing it.

At 10 a.m. sharp, we were all present at the college's warehouse entrance, which separates the interior from the exterior by a door cut in two halves: the upper half formed an open window, and the lower half offered a counter to place articles. In the warehouse, there were four attendants ready to look for and find our appropriate-sized uniforms. I stood at the threshold to assist with translation since not every member of our group spoke Spanish well enough. One by one, our students came to the wicket and described their clothing sizes, I would translate if needed, and the attendants rummaged through several boxes to find the appropriate sizes as per the individuals description.

Each student received two sets of uniforms: two red pants and two pink shirts for guys and two red skirts with built-in shorts, and two pink blouses for the girls. We also received footwear: guys received above-ankle boots, and the girls received below-ankle shoes. It took about 40 minutes for the process to complete.

When we returned to the men's dormitory, John remarked, "These uniforms are ugly, and they don't fit properly, but I guess this is it; we must make the best of the situation since classes begin tomorrow."

"The uniforms aren't for formal occasions, and besides, both Cuban and Jamaican students would be outfitted in the same fashion, and no one is going to notice, even if there're minor differences. If there're any significant concerns, we have an opportunity at 3 p.m. to air them with the college's administration," I declared.

"Stop complaining, John; remember, this is Cuba, everything is behind the times, but they are still useful," James intervened.

My most pressing desire at that point was to get started in both physical and theoretical activities. It seemed tomorrow was a lifetime away. However, time sped by, and before long, the public address system announced that it was lunchtime. Students rushed to get in line to receive their lunch. All the Cuban students were attired in their uniform, and a few wore necktie indicative of their senior role among the student population in the college.

The students who had physical activities in the morning were released 30 minutes before lunchtime to change and get ready for lunch. Hence, initially, they were not all present to receive their meal, but they slowly joined in the lines as time passed. Those who had theoretical instructions in the afternoon were all lined up together to receive their lunch.

Even though I was not delayed by having to change, by the time I got to the canteen, it was still hard to find a place to sit and eat comfortably. Besides, the chatter and noise from the Cuban students were deafening, and I just wanted to get out of there as quickly as possible. Cuban students were trying to strike up a conversation with me—they wanted to know when the Jamaicans were going to begin classes—but I was in no mood. I had never attended a boarding school in Jamaica; and was not accustomed to the rush to collect the meal, eat, and get out of the canteen.

Finally, lunchtime was over, and the Cuban students who attended the morning theoretical instructions and were in uniform headed off to their dormitories to get changed and ready for the physical activity portion of the day's activities, and those who had physical activities in the morning went back to their dormitories to collect their classroom equipment and streamed across the overpass to their respective classrooms.

As we did in the morning, we gathered to watch the Cuban students practice their physical activities. Except for swimming, the afternoon activities were all different.

Weightlifting was replaced by gymnastics and basketball with volleyball. There were other activities taking place in locations not visible from where we were gathered, such as baseball, soccer, and rhythmic gymnastics, among others.

A few of the Jamaican students wandered off to observe the other activities that were occurring around the campus. However, I remained seated on one of the benches in the college yard close to the lobby of the college administration building in anticipation of our 3 p.m. meeting.

While I was there, one of the maintenance employees of the college came over to make conversation with me without any form of introduction.

"I noticed that most of your colleagues are black, and you are one of four exceptions and the one that stands out the most. Are there a lot more people like you in Jamaica? I like las mulattas. They are delicious," he told me.

"You don't like black women?" I asked.

"Yes, but I prefer the mulattas," he said.

"I don't discriminate; I like everyone?" I told him.

"Have I offended you," he asked.

"No, but you disappoint me."

That line of questioning made me uncomfortable, given that I considered myself a black person regardless of my pale skin colour. I listened to his prejudicial remarks, but I was not in the mood to be confrontational, and neither did I want to be impolite.

Furthermore, I was aware from reading certain literature that many Latinos, including Cubans, despite their cultural revolution, were colour prejudiced—racist. Cuban officials refer to those individuals as analphabetos or illiterates. Time was on my side, and I told him, "I must go. I'm meeting with the college's administration." And I bade my goodbye and never spoke with that person again.

It was minutes to 3 p.m., so I gestured for the other members of our group to come closer to where I was sitting. "I'm going up to the administration office and will signal to you once I have confirmed that the meeting is ready to start."

By the time I got in front of the exterior door of the meeting room, I noticed a door inside the room was open to allow Luis, along with other senior members of his team, to enter. I immediately signaled to my colleagues to approach me, and I heard Luis simultaneously say, "Entra por favor."

"Can you give us a minute, please? My colleagues are not far away." Almost momentarily, my colleagues crowded around the doorway, and I told Luis, "We are now ready to enter the room."

"Come on in and have a seat," he told us.

The room was small for the thirty-four of us, along with the director, two assistant directors, godmother, and the college secretary—the college's administrative corps. Still, there were seats to accommodate all of us despite the small room size. The ceiling was very high, and the supporting exterior wall had a set of open awning windows approximately six feet above floor level, which allowed for fresh air to enter the room. The walls of the room were painted light grey, and the smell of paper and typewriter ink filled the atmosphere.

Once we were seated, Luis stood up and welcomed us all to the college and meeting. For formality purposes, we took turns naming ourselves. After we were through, Luis expressed: "I hope you are settling into the college comfortably, and for your information, the college's administration is disposed to ensure that your stay at the college and in Cuba will be pleasant. Have you collected your uniforms? Are you satisfied with the fittings?"

"Yes, we all collected our uniforms even though we discovered some of the sizes were a bit off, but we will be able to make do," I responded.

Luis continued, "I recognize that you are older and more mature than our Cuban students, and we expect you to always exhibit good behaviour and maintain discipline, especially when you are around them. We are hoping that you will be role models for our Cuban students, failing which could lead to difficulties for the college's administration."

A major concern was our comings and goings during the week.

Luis impressed upon us, "Do not leave the campus on weekdays or on weekends without your identification card. You should not travel individually, and you should keep away from deserted areas. Also, try to avoid relationships with Cubans on the streets. There are elements in our society that could bring harm to you because of their ignorance and lack of support for some of our government's initiatives."

Luis then asked José to address us on some of the college protocols.

José then proceeded to explain procedures to us, "First and foremost, no brawls or fights will be tolerated on campus, the likes of which will be met with expulsion from the college, and that applies to all students. Expletives are acts of disrespect and should be avoided, especially in the common areas and even more so in class. Proper attire is essential for particular activities. Furthermore, gentlemen must wear low-cut hair and be clean-shaven—the hair salon is in the college's basement, and it is open Monday to Friday from 7:30 a.m. to 4 p.m. During the evening, certain classrooms are off-limits because of other ongoing activities. The college provides dedicated time for mature students to study for their bachelor's degree between 5 p.m. and 8 p.m. However, there are class reserved for students, Cubans included, to engage in curricular and extra-curricular activities. Any concerns should be taken up with Linda, who will help you to adjust to life at the college. Hence, now is a good time for her to speak to you. If you have no pressing questions, I will turn things over to Linda to finish the orientation," José concluded.

Linda announced. "Each member of the group must always carry a photo identification card and especially on the streets. The photographer will be in on Thursday to take your pictures, and in approximately 10 days, you will receive your photo identification card. You will receive a stipend of 30 pesos (P) per month to expend in a fashion you see fit anywhere in Cuba. You must collect the funds from the administration's office on the second floor on the first Friday of each month. Also, when you return to your dormitories, you will find the college's caretaker has placed soap to bathe and wash your clothes as well as toothpaste on your bed. The caretakers shall change the bed linen once a week during class time, and bathroom tissue will be provided daily. Your personal laundry is your responsibility; you are responsible for washing and pressing your own clothes, including your uniforms, even though the uniforms do not need pressing. Students in the college are required to do autoservicio. This includes washing food trays and cutlery in the canteen and helping with the orderly conduct of students while meals are being served and consumed. The schedule will be done according to the nine student groups, but it is up to each group to select the students who will participate in autoservicio when it is their turn to go on duty. Students will take turns doing dormitory duty Monday to Friday. This involves cleaning all areas of the dormitory, including the common area, and performing guard duty to prevent larceny and ensure the security of your content. One student, el Cuatelero or la Cuatelera, shall remain in each dormitory daily for duty. In addition, you are required to assist with yard duty. You must fall in with the Cuban students to help maintain the aesthetical appearance of the college's grounds. This is done through regular collection of trash, removal of shrubs, and cutting of grass where the lawn mower has difficulties getting the job done adequately. I have for you several copies of the class schedule; there is enough for each of you to have one."

Before adjourning the meeting, Luis asked once more, "Do you have any concerns or questions?"

"For the time being, two questions: first question, will there be entertainment and extracurricular activities for us, given that we will be confined mostly to the campus" I inquired.

"What do you have in mind?" Luis asked.

"Parties, stage performances and movies," I responded.

"Usually, we don't facilitate those kinds of events on campus, but I'll see what can be arranged," Luis said.

"Second, we would like to know if there was anything that could be done about the food. Several of us do not eat pork, and even those who eat it are hoping that it would appear less frequently on the menu," I said, and inquired from my colleagues, "Do any of you have anything to add or ask?"

"Give us a bit more time to settle in," Yasmin remarked.

Luis then adjourned the meeting, and all five Cubans went to stand by the doorway to shake our hands and wish us well for the next day and beyond as we exited the meeting room.

After the meeting, we gathered for an informal chat about what we had heard in the meeting and went over the class schedule. The schedule showed that we would have physical activities in the morning and theoretical classes in the afternoon.

For the first semester, the morning classes were: basic gymnastics, athletics, weightlifting, recreation, and school games. The afternoon classes were mathematics, physiological anatomy, physics, chemistry, and Spanish. Our first class the following day was basic gymnastics. Most of us had never practised this sport before because it was never widely included in the Jamaican public schools' curriculum at any level. Therefore, we could only conjecture as to what we were in for, but no one made a big issue out of anything that was anticipated over the ensuing weeks and months.

Chapter 8

The next morning at 9 a.m. sharp, all thirty-four of us were in attendance to begin our basic gymnastic class on time without any absences; however, the instructor was already waiting for us. He asked us to form dos filas or two lines and verified that we were all present by taking attendance. He took the attendance slowly, and after calling each name, he lifted his head to observe who was answering the name he had called. After completing this exercise, he introduced himself: "My name is Vincent Muñoz, your instructor for the semester," and explained to us the activities for the morning class. Vincent was short, with light brown skin and low-cut hair. He had bowed legs and walked with a limp and elbows semi-flexed away from his body.

Vincent started off the class with warm-up exercises, and prior to each core activity, he explained, in a high-pitched voice, what it was and demonstrated what was to be done. First, we did some stretches and jogging on the spot, followed by military-style drills of a left-right-left-right-turn-around pattern. It took some time for us to get the hang of the coordination. For the first five minutes, there was confusion everywhere. We kept making the wrong turns and bumping into one another. Hence, we had to repeat the moves several times until we found our groove. It was obvious to all of us that Vincent and the other Cuban onlookers: the students, and workers and staff, were having a healthy laugh at our failure to plunge perfectly into a rhythm. As a result, the warm-up lasted almost 30 minutes, 15 minutes beyond the allotted time.

Once we completed the warm-up exercises, we were directed to an area where two mechanical gymnastic horses were set up for us to perform some core exercises. Parallel to each other were the pommel and vaulting horses surrounded by canvas-covered sponge to minimize hard landing on the concrete ground. Vincent demonstrated how we should jump over the vaulting horse and land without falling to the ground. Our inexperience was noticeable to all; several of us were not able to execute the jump on the first day, and it took several days and sessions before most of us got the hang of it. Several of us, me included, never mastered the technique of jumping over the vaulting horse.

Our approach to the pommel horse was hardly any better as, one by one, we tried and failed to maintain our balance on the equipment. We struggled until it was time to do the cool-down exercises. Vincent made fun of us by imitating some of our moves but promised that we would get better as time went by, and we got to practise more of the routines. The cool-down exercises were simple breathing exercises, and we had no challenges in executing them. For class dismissal, we were required to reform the two lines as we did at the beginning of the class, and then we were dismissed.

Next on our agenda was the weightlifting class, and the location was just a few metres away from where we received the basic gymnastic class. The class began with all of us standing in four lines horizontally facing the instructor. The instructor introduced himself as Isaac Gonzalez. Isaac took our attendance, similar to how it was executed by Vincent. Afterwards, we were invited to sit and take some notes about the mechanics of the discipline we were going to be learning over the ensuing weeks and months. Approximately 20 minutes of notes were dictated to us in Spanish, and then we were asked to stand again for the start of the physical activity portion of the class.

Unlike the class in basic gymnastics, we were not required to do general warm-up exercises, but instead, we started by practising the mechanics of the moves with light bars and plates, according to Isaac's demonstration. We took turns at the moves and learned from one another's mistakes. The techniques of this discipline were not difficult to manage with the light irons and plates, but as Isaac instructed us to add more plates to the bars, those of us who were out of shape physically found it a bit challenging to complete the lifts in a single motion from ground to overhead.

"The bar is too heavy for me, professor, and my arms are paining me," Heather squealed.

"Put only as many plates on the bar as you can manage. Next month you will have strong muscles, and soon you will be able to lift and hoist anyone of your classmates over your head," Isaac responded, smiling.

Isaac was patient with us, and we learned the techniques slowly, step by step. However, not before Guys and girls alike struggled to get a handle on the moves and techniques as it became apparent that most, if not all, of us, were new to the discipline. Soon an hour and 15 minutes went by, and it was time for dismissal. Once again, we were asked to stand uniformly and listen to Isaac's parting words. He expressed his pleasure to have met us, worked with us, and was looking forward to our next class—la proxima semana.

It was now 11:30 a.m., and our physical activity classes were over for the day. Several of us hung around talking to the instructor and amongst ourselves while others ascended the stairs to shower and get ready for the afternoon classes, which were to follow lunch. Before long, we were all ready, and we waited for the public address system to announce the group whose turn it was to move into the canteen for lunch. At 12:10 p.m., our group, 11A, was summoned to the canteen, and we all hurriedly converged into the canteen at the same time. We quickly ate and vacated the lunchroom to prepare for the afternoon classes as well as to free up space for the Cuban students to be called in for their lunch.

Lunchtime concluded at 12:45 p.m., and classes were to begin at 1:05 p.m. At 12:50 p.m., the public address system announced that students should descend the dormitories and assemble in the college yard in front of the corridor adjoining the canteen and snack shop. As instructed, we went down to the assembly and received instructions about comportment. Here is an example of what the second assistant director, Alfonso Soriano, told us: "Students should not aimlessly hang about the college yard. After the assembly, you are to proceed to your respective classes and be silent in the corridors," Like so many other Cubans, Alfonso was short and bulky, had a figure which leaned to his right, and he walked with a bounced and spoke with a carrying voice.

Our first class of the afternoon was Spanish. Upon reaching the doorway of the classroom, an older lady greeted us. She was about five feet four inches tall, had silver-greyish hair and had a light brown complexion. She spoke with a deep voice and wore a serious countenance. The second-year Jamaican group debriefed us about her beforehand and told us they called her Granny.

"Buenas tardes alumnos," Granny greeted us.

"Buenas tardes profesora," we all responded in unison.

She had us lined up outside the classroom door along the corridor, looked us over and advised: "Button up your shirt, those of you who have two or three buttons undone. Tie your shoelaces. Tuck your shirt into your pants all the way around your waist. The men must get your hair cut and ensure that you are all clean-shaven for class next Wednesday."

"This lady must be from the old school, she doesn't joke around, and Desmond, you are gonna look strange without your beard, but I look forward to seeing you without it," Heather remarked.

"I guess this is the trade-off for getting a professional education and career," I responded.

The lady then invited us into the classroom and told us to be seated. She introduced herself, "I'm Clarissa Santana, and I will be your Spanish instructor while you are here at the college." She slowly took attendance, pretty much like the physical and health education teachers in the morning.

Clarissa pronounced our names like someone who speaks English fluently, even though, except for our names, she never once uttered a word in English in our presence.

I informed her, "Each of us received a pseudonym from the Spanish teachers at the language training centre in Jamaica."

"That is silly; you should use your real names. Please never use those pseudonyms in my class and desist from using them outright. I want to learn your real names so that I can properly identify you," she stated. No one contradicted her, and she proceeded to deliver her class material.

Clarissa started off the class with a history lesson, specifically, the Moors' invasion and conquering of parts of the Iberian Peninsula. For most of the semester, we read and discussed the character El Cid Campeador a.k.a. Rodrigo Dias de Vivar, who fought bravely to rid Spain of the Moors' rule. Despite the historical account of 11th-century Spain, Clarissa was very focused on Spanish grammar and pronunciation. She asked us to repeat words several times over until she was convinced that we got the right pronunciation. She emphasized the difference between prose and poem as a way of explaining the different writing styles. Notwithstanding, the frustration was noticeable, as revealed by the facial expression of many of us, as we struggled to understand the language and Clarissa's insistence that we pronounce the words correctly.

Clarissa's countenance was one of unflinching seriousness. She never sat during class and never moved beyond the front row of seats. As a matter of fact, for the four years, I spent at the college, I never witnessed a smile from Clarissa, neither in nor out of class.

At 10 minutes to 2 p.m., Clarissa dictated the assignment to be completed for the next class, and at five minutes to 2 p.m., she dismissed the class at the indication of her watch. There was no clock in the classroom, and neither was there any announcement from the PA system or any other type of signal to inform us that the class was over. However, we hurriedly left the classroom to get to the next class, which was physiological anatomy. As we exited the classroom, we were thrust into the path of Cuban students moving back and forth in the corridor, trying as well to get to their next class. Some of them greeted us in passing, and others just skedaddled on their way without acknowledging our presence.

We spent the next two hours learning about physiological anatomy and physics. Like all the teachers before, these too knew their material, but Spanish was a barrier for several of us. The most difficult part to handle was taking notes, especially having to spell and write new and scientific terminology.

To their credit, the teachers were patient, and they understood our predicament: it would have been next to impossible to acquire sufficient vocabulary, auditory prowess, and fluency in speech in only six months at a language training centre and be able to master the requirements of the several subject areas in a matter of days. Furthermore, the training had not been conducted in a Spanish-speaking environment. If it had, that would have helped us with our listening skills and thought processes.

Our physiological anatomy teacher was the second-year group's godmother, and she understood our situation better than any of the other teachers, because she had experience working closely with the Jamaican group from the previous year. She deliberately spoke clearly and loudly in order to enable us to take notes. She repeated her dictations as often as she was asked by us to the point of falling behind in giving us the entire prepared lecture.

Our physics teacher also made a gallant effort to assist us as much as possible to take copious notes so that we could review the material prior to his next class. He administered a quiz at the beginning of each class to keep us engaged with the material before the formal tests. Even with the slow pace of dictation, many of us, understandably, struggled to keep up. We lacked oratory fluency, vocabulary, and familiarity with the professional language, which would take months to develop sufficiently despite continuous daily practice.

During the delivery of the physics class, one of the girls, Winsome, fell ill with stomach problems, and I accompanied her to the college's health centre. This was to become a regular occurrence for me personally since I was the leader of the group and, at that point, the one who spoke Spanish relatively well. This individual fell ill weekly, approximately three times per week. On one occasion, the resident doctor told me, "There is no need for you to accompany students to the clinic because I understand English very well."

"I wasn't aware of your linguistic ability," I responded.

"What is that word you used, linguistic?" She asked.

"I thought you understood English very well," I responded.

"I know enough to discuss with my patient their needs," she said with a smug smile.

Henceforth, I never again accompanied anyone to the clinic.

After about six weeks in Cuba, that student declared that she was not going to continue her studies in Cuba and wanted to go back to Jamaica. She expressed her desire to the college administration and explained that she was not keeping good health. The matter was reported to the Jamaican Embassy in Havana, and arrangements were made for her to leave Cuba almost immediately. The rest of the group never found out what was the cause of her illness and often wondered if it were real or just made up because she wanted a way out of having to undergo the rigours of studying in a Spanish-speaking environment.

In quick succession, two more members of our group were sent back to Jamaica: one at his own request and the other for disciplinary reasons.

A former table tennis player, Trevor, elected to return home because table tennis was not one of the disciplines offered at the college, and that was where his interest lies. I knew that Spanish was not a huge barrier for him, because he understood the language even though he did not speak it well.

The other student, Orville, was an excellent swimmer who spent most of his free time in the swimming pool with Cuban students, but he was a mischievous fella who was also short-tempered. He regularly got into bruhaha with the Cuban students, and when these bouts became physical, the college's administration recommended that he discontinued his studies at the college. The Jamaican embassy in Havana was consulted, and he was returned to Jamaica within a couple of months after his arrival in Cuba.

Chapter 9

It was not long after we arrived in Cuba that several of my colleagues started picking up bad habits as strategies for survival. They made friends on the streets, in the neighbouring communities around the college and even in some rural enclaves. Several members of our group began selling their belongings to Cubans on the streets in order to raise funds to eat at the local hotel and street restaurants.

The little group of students with which I often confer—Tom, John, James, Andrea, Heather, and Gregory—and I chatted often about the problems we were up against in Cuba, mostly about the gastronomy and the responsibility it seemed we had to one another on a terrain that was not always amenable to disparate dispositions. We often had our little stock-taking discussions. In one of those discussions, Heather raised a few interesting points. "Yes, we are all Jamaicans and share certain commonalities such as music and food, but we are different from each other as night is from day. To one another, we are strangers who never met before, and if we did, it was only in passing. First, we are not from the same village in Jamaica, and second, we are certainly not friends. Hence, we are in Cuba equally to develop a relationship among ourselves as much as we are here to be trained as physical and health education instructors."

Heather was short and always wore a smile. She was petite and walked with a rocking waist style.

"This is what makes our journey interesting and our experience valuable. We just need to reinforce our commitment to our purpose of coming here and stay clean and away from prohibited activities," I added.

"I think it's up to each of us to make our own survival choices," John remarked.

John was a bulky guy of medium height with a dark complexion and laughed a lot in a deep booming whoop.

"Whatever you guys do should be within the confines of the law because to do otherwise may result in expulsion from the college and deportation from Cuba. If the situation is unbearable, it is better to ask for a release from the program and return home," I encouraged.

"Jefe, you can always take the high ground; it seems that the conditions don't bother you," Gregory said.

"Don't forget that you elected me to lead the group, and unlike the rest of you, I'm expected to set examples. Besides, this, for me, is a test of will; how much can I endure? I would rather hold my nose and eat the pork than resort to illegal conduct."

"Jefe, I support that, and I'd join you in that," Andrea concurred.

"Without reservation, we're overwhelmed by the rapid changes we're experiencing away from home, friends, and families. Some of us are away for the first time ever," James said.

"I wish someone had told us what we should have expected once we arrived in Cuba. Instead, we're thrown into this situation without any inkling of how to deal with the challenges," Gregory added.

"The culture shock and shift are pronounced, yet we're expected to adapt to the new society and culture as though we're devoid of human feelings and needs," Tom added.

"Yes, our diet and eating habits are completely rearranged, and we've little or no choice in the matter; we either eat what's provided to us or resort to dealing in illegal transactions with Cubans on the streets, for me the latter is a non-starter," I said.

"The Cubans are enamoured with jeans, banlon shirts and sneakers. Sales of these items can fetch us a lot of cash. A pair of jeans can fetch an average of 150 pesos, and good quality jeans are likely to fetch even more; a shirt, depending on the quality, can easily fetch 80 pesos; a pair of sneakers can fetch anywhere between 150 pesos to 200 pesos," John told us.

"My position is reduced to advise only; your choice is your responsibility, and given the cost of living in Cuba, you'll be wallowing in cash before long. You may certainly be in an advantageous position, but I can't support you in this behaviour," I emphasized.

"That's fine. I don't expect you to support me," John said.

"So, we're clear on that matter," I retorted.

There were times when some of my colleagues exchanged the above-noted articles for American dollars directly, and this allowed them to replenish their merchandise by shopping in the local hotels or special stores. These locations were created specifically for foreign tourists. Particularly Cuban Americans, to purchase gifts for their Cuban families and friends, and for themselves, if they wished.

Cubans were not allowed to make purchases in the designated tiendas de tourismo or tourist shops. Hence, the Cuban racketeers would solicit the help of foreign students to make the purchases for them in these shops for a fee, usually in foreign currency, primarily American dollars. Foreign students could make purchases in these shops because we retained our passports, and our Cuban identity cards bore the word extranjero or foreigner.

The Cubans peddlers would purchase foreign currency from tourists who were inclined to exchange their money for Cuban pesos—one American dollar was worth 25 Cuban pesos—and made deals with our students which led to frequent exchange of goods and cash. These illegal practices went unchecked for almost the entire four years we spent in Cuba.

This was a lucrative way for some of my colleagues to raise funds to support their eating habits that were not being met by the college's canteen.

Fortunately, no member of our group was ever caught dealing directly in the aforementioned activities. If they were caught, it would have resulted in immediate expulsion from the college and Cuba.

Notwithstanding, there were several of our students, me included, who resisted the temptation and never succumbed to extravagance.

"While you guys are busy trying to take advantage of the Cuban foreign-exchange system, I'm going to find myself, una jeva, a girl to help me through this challenging time of my life; I noticed a few of them giving me the eye. One even took up one of my books and kissed it," I declared.

"I think you have the right attitude, Desmond; we need positive distractions, not negative diversions," Andrea declared.

Chapter 10

*T*o cope with life in Cuba, we developed intimate relationships with Cubans and other foreigners. We were young, so not many of us had left committed relationships back in Jamaica, and even the few who did, they did not hesitate to go astray. Furthermore, the Cuban students and women in the community alike showed interest in having relationships with Jamaican men, and we were only too happy to oblige them.

One evening after dinner, I decided to go over to one of the classrooms to have some quiet time and do my class assignments for the next day. As I was walking on the connecting overpass from my dormitory to the classroom, I noticed several male and female students sitting on some concrete benches that were laid out close to the enclosing wall near the edge of the overpass, and so my eyes started roaming, and I spotted the most attractive girl I had ever laid my eyes *on: she was petite; had long wavy black and golden hair. She had a light brown complexion without a single blemish. She had perfectly proportioned lips, and her eyes were big and bright. She was completely devoid of any facial makeup. Although she was sitting, I could tell that she was not tall. She was still dressed in her college uniform and wearing clean black shoes and lily-white socks. I approached her and stood close enough for her to hear me whisper, "Can I sit beside you?"*

"No," she replied with a beautiful smile "because I'm waiting for my friends to join me."

I took no for an answer and did not linger, but as I walked away, I gazed back at her and noticed that her eyes were following me. I pretended not to see her staring at me and went my way.

For the next three evenings, I made it a point of duty to walk along the overpass at approximately the same time as the first evening I saw that beautiful girl, but I was never lucky enough to see her again.

Weeks later, I learned of a swimming competition that was to take place in the college and decided to attend as a form of distraction and relaxation. Several sports centres were participating, but it was being hosted at our college. Then, suddenly, at one of the 100-metre events, I heard our Cuban college students yelling the name "Belkis" repeatedly. It seemed then that Belkis was a crowd favourite, so I asked a female student, "Who is Belkis?" and she indicated that she is the competitor in the second lane. I watched the competitor in the second lane arrive at the finish line in a blistering second place.

After the competitors exited the pool and removed their swimming cap, I discovered that Belkis was the girl I had been yearning to see for weeks. We glanced at each other for a moment, and then she disappeared with a group of students, seemingly her friends. They were fussing about her performance: screaming, shouting, hugging, and congratulating her.

A few evenings later, as I was again walking across the overpass to my usual classroom to review my homework and other material the teachers had assigned our class, I noticed Belkis sitting on the same bench in almost the identical spot where I first saw her. I pretended not to see her, but as I was walking by her, she called out to me with a "Hi;" when I gazed in her direction, she asked me over both verbally and with her outstretched right-hand motioning with the palm of her hand facing the ground and her fingers flexing. My heart skipped a beat, but I did find the courage to walk over to her unhesitatingly. She smiled at me and asked me to sit, and I obliged her. She inquired, "Why do you go across the overpass every evening?"

"I go mostly to get some extra work and homework done for my teachers the next day," I replied. "How do you know I go by every evening?"

"I'm spying on you from my dormitory," she said.

That night, we spent over an hour trying to learn about each other; I learned that she was nineteen years old and in her second year at the college and was interested in synchronized swimming. Her parents were separated, and she lived at her father's home in the city centre. Her mother was living not far away from the college and close to the general hospital, Belkis' father worked at a construction yard where they made prefabricated building panels, and her mother worked as a maintenance personnel in a local historical museum.

I took the opportunity to tell her that she was beautiful, and I would like us to be friends if it were okay with her.

She said: "We will see!"

At about 8:30 p.m., the point when most students were heading to their dormitory, she announced that it was time for her to head up to her dormitory.

"Could I see you again at this same location?" I asked.

"Maybe!" she said:

The next day when I was crossing the overpass on the way to my classroom, she was there as if she was waiting for me. I looked at her and approached her; as I drew closer to her, she greeted me: "Good evening."

She stood and embraced me and kissed me on both cheeks. She looked radiant, beaming with elation, as the smell of sweet magnolia emanated from her shapely harmonized physique. Naturally, I responded, "Thank you and good evening to you too," and I reciprocated the warmth she shared with me.

We both sat down and rekindled our conversation from the day before. "Do you have homework or get assignments?" I asked her.

"Yes, but I usually complete my assignments and homework immediately after class," She responded.

The following week on Tuesday evening, there was to be a baseball game at the stadium between the Santiago de Cuba team and a team from another province. Usually, when there is a national game at the stadium, we were allowed to stay out until the game was over. I let her know that I like baseball, and asked her, "Would you like to attend the game with me?"

"I'm not a fan of baseball, but we could go for a walk in La Feria near the stadium," she replied.

This meant that I would not see her again until five days later. Nonetheless, we agreed to meet at 6:30 p.m. in front of the college's auditorium, which was located next to the staircase leading up to my dormitory.

The weekend took forever to end, but Tuesday evening did eventually arrive, and we were both on time. She was smiling as beautifully as she had ever had for me, and I noticed that she was again not wearing any makeup. This was particularly unusual for a Cuban lady, but I was not bothered in the least, because I like ladies in their natural appearance.

We greeted each other, and I asked her, "Are we ready to go?"

"Yes," she responded.

There were some other Jamaican students sitting along the ramp of the auditorium, and they began whistling and making comments. She inquired about the reason for their behaviour, and I told her that they approved of her. We exited at the back of the college, which faces the road that runs alongside the baseball stadium and provides access to La Feria. When we crossed over the road, which constituted the main entrance to the college, and was out of sight of the college students, I tried to hold her hand, but she resisted, and I asked her, "Are you afraid of being seen with me? Do you have a boyfriend that I should be aware of?" I inquired further.

She replied, "No, I never had a steady boyfriend, and neither have I ever been with a man."

"So, you are a virgin?" I blurted out.

"Yes," she answered.

At that moment, I realized that the task ahead of me was arduous and required patience, tenderness and understanding. I did not try to hug her or hold her hand again for the rest of the evening, and she made no attempt to initiate any physical contact until the end of our date. We entered La Feria proper and headed for one of the benches to sit down. I began to question her celibacy, given that she was nineteen years old and was in a co-ed college with lots of muscular men walking around, showing off their physique, and constantly trying to impress the ladies.

"I kept my distance because I learned early that Cuban men are mostly interested in scoring, and I don't want to be on anyone's conquest list. I'm not in any rush to have sexual intercourse with any man. Furthermore, I'm looking for Mr. Right: someone who is mature and cultured," She made it clear.

She asked me about my rendezvous with girls, and I told her: "There have been a few, but I had no real serious relationship because I want to first put in place what I need to survive in this world."

"What if that never occurs?" She asked.

"Then, I'm going to live a lonely shut-away life," I told her.

She refused to believe that I was serious. "Anyway, your expectations are too high," she told me,

"You're not that different from me in terms of expectations, since we are both holding out for the unknown as nothing in life is certain," I told her.

Around us, the temperature started to fall, and she wanted to return to the college and dormitory. And so, we headed back. At the bottom of the staircase to her dormitory, we lingered a bit, chatting about when and how we would meet again; when suddenly she kissed me on the cheek, said goodnight and ran off up the stairs towards her dormitory.

For the next week and a half, I saw Belkis twice per day. At lunchtime, she would present herself below my dormitory and yell for me all the way up to the third floor, and when I peered through the window and recognized her, she would demand, "Bajate" or "Come down." In the evenings, we would meet on the overpass before I went to do my assignments and before she returned to her dormitory after dinner. We talked about almost everything—but she made me promise to not discuss politics—from the flora and fauna to extraterrestrial and outer space events. Belkis was fond of the world we inhabit and had plenty of ideas about how it should be protected. She abhorred destruction of the environment and the waging of wars.

The Cuban students received a pass once per month when they could stay out until 10 p.m. on a Wednesday evening. They could use this time to visit home, and friends and go wherever they wished. On one such Wednesday evening, we decided that we would use Belkis' time to go and see a movie in the city centre. We agreed to meet at the back entrance of the college at 6 p.m. We were both on time and exited the college compound and headed for the bus stop; in order to make it in time for the first run of the movie for the evening, we had to get on the earliest bus possible. We made it to the movie theatre just in time. Belkis purchased the tickets, and we entered the theatre and sat in the middle of the hall.

The movie was an American suspense, Jaws, which suited me fine because I did not have to read the subtitles. After the movie, we stopped at an ice cream parlour, purchased ice cream, and then walked to the city centre park, sat on one of the benches and ate our ice cream. Once we were finished eating, we headed to the bus stop and caught a bus almost immediately. When we reached our final stop in front of the inter-provincial bus terminal, we dismounted and decided that we would walk through La Feria and not on the street back to the college.

When I checked, the time was approximately a quarter after 9 p.m., so we decided to kill some time in La Feria before returning to the college. We sat on a bench in an area where the light was partially blocked by a couple of tall trees and exchanged a few thoughts about the movie and discovered that we both liked it. And then there was silence, neither of us spoke and suddenly Belkis drew herself close to me and leaned her head on my shoulder and whispered, "Te quiero papi," and I raised her head from my shoulder and looked piercingly into her eyes and reciprocated the sentiments. I ran the back of my hand down the side of her smooth face and around the back of her neck. She smiled at me and leaned into me and put her soft lips against mine, and we kissed passionately and emitted sounds of pleasure.

Suddenly, I felt a kind of tingling all over my body, it was not just the arousal I acquired from her voluptuous lips and succulent and tender kiss but also a sense of helplessness, which made me feel as though I was losing control of my being and in that moment, I concluded that I was caught and shackled with nowhere to run or hide even if I wanted to. The kiss lasted for about three minutes, and when she pulled back, I was relieved and dejected at the same time: Relieved because I could regain my composure and dejected because she was no longer vulnerable and would return to her aloof behaviour.

For a moment, I believed that I was in a confused state of mind. However, I stood up and pulled her up and in close to me and lifted her off the ground and sat back down with her on my lap and planted another kiss on her. Suddenly, we both acknowledged simultaneously that time was against us, and we needed to get back to the college before 10 p.m., so we uncoupled, stood up and headed back to the college. We did not say much on our way back, but whatever was happening to us was understood because we stopped several times along the way and kissed with tenderness and passion.

For the next several days, I lost my appetite; I could not eat or drink—food was tasteless, and I had trouble sleeping at night; all I could think about was Belkis Sanchez. My heart was feeling as though it wanted to explode, and my head was heavier than any other time I could remember. I was in agony all the time, worrying about tomorrow and how long the relationship would last. Will Belkis dump me like all the other guys she flirted with throughout her teenage years? I believe this kind of feeling only comes along once in a man's lifetime because I never felt that way before and never again. I wondered, could it be love? And if it were, why did it have to consume me in such a strange manner, to the point where it hurts?

As time passed, I became anxious to see Belkis. I wanted to see and be with her all the time. I made myself conspicuous in places where I knew she was likely to trod—in the corridors, hallways, by the swimming pool, in the gymnasium, and the most obvious of places—in the college yard. When I did see her, my first instinct always was to embrace and kiss her, even when the location was not conducive to making out. I had to exercise immense control over my feelings and urges, and I believed she had to do the same from the way she held me and looked at me; it seemed she was experiencing a bittersweet metamorphosis.

Belkis and I did not get together too often for a few days because we both had to prepare for upcoming examinations—even though I found it difficult to study or even to go to the scheduled revisions. However, we agreed to meet in La Feria one Sunday evening on her way back from visiting with her father for the weekend. She was going to stop by her mother's, and after spending some time with her mother, I was to meet her at the bus terminal opposite La Feria. I arrived about

10 minutes before Belkis and waited until she came; we hugged each other and kissed, and walked through La Feria to the bench, where we shared our first moment of passion.

It was about 8 p.m., give or take 15 minutes, and we sat down to talk about the weekend and what we did. Our conversation veered into our feelings for each other, and then spontaneously, we started kissing, and I tried to fondle her breast, but she would have none of it, and I did not insist. Moments later, we stopped kissing, and she suddenly said, "I'm feeling chilly."

I gave her arms a quick rub to try to warm her before I continued talking again about the upcoming examinations. Then, abruptly interrupting me, she asked: "Can we go back to the college?" She immediately stood up, and I followed automatically. I put my arms around her shoulder, and we walked back to the college. We did not say much to each other along the way, but when we reached the foot of the staircase to her dormitory, she pulled away from me and asked: "Why didn't you offer to lend me your windbreaker when I said that I was feeling chilly?" At that moment, I was speechless, and I looked down at my person to see the windbreaker. I did not remember that I was wearing a windbreaker, so I failed to offer it to her, and that was not good on my part because it demonstrated insensitivity at a time when I should have been showing her how much I loved and cared for her.

"I wasn't thinking clearly, and I'm sorry," I told her. She took off up the stairs without even saying good night.

Chapter 11

The end of our first semester in Cuba was fast approaching, and soon it would be time to test our knowledge acquisition. Just before the examinations began, Linda informed me, "Your group is scheduled, as part of the first-year group of students, to spend a month in the country where you will perform agricultural work on a sugar cane plantation."

"Really? Don't you think you should have given us a heads-up earlier on so we could at least condition our minds for this kind of activity?"

"I received this information yesterday; I'm just as surprised as you are."

"I had heard of the idea floating around previously that every year first-year students go to work in the country on either a coffee or sugar plantation, but since I wasn't officially informed of the event, I didn't let it concern me or the group for that matter. This information may not go over well with the group," I cautioned Linda.

"The group may like this kind of activity, let the rest of the group know, and we will go from there," Linda encouraged.

"Some of these students have never done manual labour in their lives, never mind working and living in the country for a whole month," I said.

"They might surprise you," Linda said.

I called an impromptu meeting with our group and informed them of the new development. I must say, not everyone was excited about the prospect of going to farm country as they described it, especially the ladies—there were even some profanities hurled.

I tried to explain the situation as best as I could and asked that they view it as an opportunity to give back to Cuba for all that it was doing for us and Jamaica. But I also told them we did not have any choice in the matter since it was an exercise that the entire college's first-year students must undertake.

After two weeks of examinations, we boarded a college bus to a sugar cane plantation on a Sunday evening in late December 1979. On the bus, we had the company of Linda and other teachers who were going to work with and supervise us.

After several hours of driving, the bus made a stop at what turned out to be the men's encampment at about 9 p.m. Once the guys vacated the bus completely, it continued to the girl's encampment. We were shown by the teachers and site keepers into a barracks-looking shed, about 50 feet long and 35 feet wide, lined with four rows of hammocks. Inside the barracks, humidity and musty smell overpowered me. I got the impression the barracks were uninhabited for some time.

Shortly after, the Cuban students arrived. We were shown specifically where the Jamaicans and Cubans students would be separately bunking. After we were settled into our designated corner, we were invited to partake of sandwiches and Guava juice. For the sandwiches, we had three choices: guava cheese, dairy cheese or ham and cheese sandwiches. If anyone did not care for any of the three choices, they could have plain bread.

While we were eating our snack, the Cuban students were teasing us and laughing at the idea of us coming to the sugar cane plantation. They painted a dismal picture for us about life on the plantation. They dwelled, especially, on insects like mosquitoes and wild boars that we would encounter both at night in the barracks and in the cane field during the day. We did our best to ignore them, even though a couple of us hit back at them. Tom told them, "We would yell for your help if we had the misfortune of any perilous encounters, and you would get the opportunity to save us and display your courage."

"We're good for any situations coming our way. We're survivors," Gregory added.

At about 10 p.m., we were told that the lanterns were going out and we should get some rest because we would start working in the morning.

At approximately 6 a.m. the next morning, we woke up to a gong-like sound and the smell of whole-wheat porridge and hot bread. It was still dark outside, so the lanterns were lit for us to see around in the barracks. Before breakfast, we were given work clothes and boots and hoes and machetes to work in the cane field.

When the day began breaking, we streamed outside to survey our new environment and were greeted by lush green vegetation everywhere: sugar cane plants and shrubs of all kinds. The air was fresh, and a sweet fragrance from several plants and trees swirled around us, much different from our barracks experience the night before. However, there were no houses or buildings in sight and no humans around except for us in the encampment.

We did see a pile of old and new Soviet-made machinery, mostly tractors and cane harvesters. There was a long stretch of dirt road running in front of the barracks, which went beyond the girl's barracks in the west, and I had no idea how far it went in the east. It was not long before we were called to receive breakfast. The whole-wheat porridge was delicious, and I thought that both Jamaicans and Cubans relished it because I heard no complaints, only slurping from the diners.

Once we were finished eating, we returned the containers to the makeshift kitchen and thanked the cooks. Already dressed, we were led into the field to begin working. We were randomly selected and put in groups. Then we were assigned several rows of canes and told to remove the unwanted plants and weeds. However, soon it became obvious that the unwanted invaders were far and few between the rows of sugar cane plants.

James and others were in rows beside me; James was of medium height, slim built, and walked lackadaisically as if he had not a care in the world.

"There isn't much to do; why did they bring us Jamaicans here?" James asked.

"I don't get the point of this exercise," Gregory said.

"I believe it's an attempt to introduce us to rural living and give us a taste of what the rural inhabitants' daily life is like," John said.

"The evidence of that isn't far away from us. Look, the campesinos are working hard at clearing unwanted weeds and plants, and their task is much more arduous than ours," I drew my colleagues' attention.

We "laboured" until 1 p.m. when we were told that it was the end of the workday, and we should return to the camp. When we arrived at the camp, lunch was ready, and the cooks were waiting for us with serving utensils in hand. We collected and ate our meals and shortly thereafter began chatting about the morning experience. Several of us decided we were going to walk down to the girls' encampment to see them and hear about their day while others stretched out in their hammocks for an afternoon snooze.

About half of a mile down to the girls' encampment, I spotted a running stream with clear water, and I told the other guys, "I'm not going any further."
They all laughed, and I heard James uttered, "The country boy finds his heart desire."

I knew he was spot on, so I did not respond to the comment.

I went close enough to the stream and observed that the water was flowing by fast enough to wash away any impurities that might have been thrown in from farther upstream. I sat on the bank of the stream with my feet hanging to reach below the surface of the running water. I noticed that the water was gushing over some large rocks and pebbles, and I was satisfied that the stream was naturally furrowed and not artificially cut. I dipped my hands in the water and scooped up some of it and brought it up to my nose, and smelled it in search of any foul odour, and there was none that was noticeable.

I stayed by the stream for nearly two hours, contemplating the beauty of the area, absorbing the solitude, and observing the wildlife in general. It was a delight to see the several species of birds flying around me, perching on nearby branches, and chirping their delightful melodies, which brought peace and serenity to my being. I was able to observe other wildlife, such as butterflies. These insects, with their dazzling array of colours, were plentiful along the water's edge where there was an abundance of plants flowering that provided them with needed nectar and pollen to replenish the plants over time through pollination and which would result in the birth of new seedlings.

I believe that people who are natives of rural settings tend to appreciate the natural habitat much more than the folks from urban and suburban settings.

I fell in love with the area by the stream and the stream itself, so much so that for the rest of the week, I went down there every day to bathe in the refreshing cool water and meditate on life. None of my colleagues showed any interest in joining me, and I could not have been happier because it gave me time to enjoy that tiny part of nature, my own company and reflect upon my situation and the circumstances that were conditioning my life for the foreseeable future.

Furthermore, I thought about the generosity of the Cuban government and its people who have given their lives so we could find opportunities to improve ours and those of our countrymen and women back in Jamaica. I also contemplated that Jamaicans should not have to leave their homeland in search of opportunities elsewhere. My thinking might have been wishful, but I could not help the way I felt. Although my homeland was small, and the people impoverished because of a lack of resources and mismanagement of its economy by successive governments, I knew that pride, ambition, and determination are like "fires" burning deep, deep down in all of us; if not, how else could we have survived?

The stream and its surroundings helped me gather some perspectives on life which may not have occurred under other circumstances. I resolved to complete my studies in Cuba, and while I was at it, I was going to comport myself in a manner that was exemplary to all those who may need a role model to inspire their work and efforts.

Almost every evening after my trip to the stream and my return to the encampment, I received a visitor from the female camp. Young Cuban girls wanted to talk and hang out with me, and I perceived perhaps more. This reminded me of times when several of the girls back in the college came up to me and embraced and kissed on both my cheeks and, on occasions, left the shape of their lips in my books through the colour of their lipsticks. I also remembered several of them asking me if I noticed that they existed and why I was so aloof.

I must say though, that I was flattered by the fact that they would walk a mile to be with me, knowing that I was not even a Cuban. However, I was an average of seven years their senior and could not in good conscience take advantage of their youth and mental immaturity. Each evening, a different one would show up, and I dutifully walked her back to her camp without so much as flirted with her. We discussed every and anything except sex and relationship because I was not prepared to frolic around with 14, 15, and 16-year-old girls.

One evening while accompanying one of the girls back to her encampment, we met three of my Jamaican colleagues, John among them, who themselves were returning from a visit to the girl's encampment. John asked me, "Can we run a battery?" Meaning all four of us taking turns sexually with the girl. I did not respond to the request, except I looked him sternly in the face, and he withdrew his remarks with the excuse that he was only joking. However, I did not believe he was joking, but I assumed that when he caught up with himself and that he was addressing the leader of our group, he must have felt ashamed.

Unbelievably, when the guys were at some distance behind us, the girl said to me, "I wouldn't have minded."

"Do you understand what was being asked?"

"Yes," she said.

I know she did not speak a word of English, so I surmised that the expression on John's face revealed his intention.

Nevertheless, I told her, "If you want to take the guys up on that kind of offer, you are welcome, but it certainly wouldn't include me."

She became embarrassed, and we did not speak again for the rest of the journey or for the rest of my stay at the college.

No sooner than we arrived at the encampment, and that girl had disappeared, than I was beckoned over by another girl who wanted to speak with me. Several of my Jamaican colleagues, both guys and girls who were around took notice. The girl asked me to join her in a room without windows or doors near the roadway. I agreed and went into the room, and my fellow Jamaicans were apparently unaware of where we went.

In the room, there were some concrete benches pinned around some wooden tables, and no other students were inside the room. The girl invited me to sit, and I obliged her; she started a discussion by questioning me, "So what life is like in Jamaica? Why did you come to Cuba to study?"

"Jamaica is in many ways like Cuba, except for two significant differences: we speak different languages, and our skin colours are different: Cubans are mostly white, and Jamaicans are mostly black," I told her.

The questioning was relentless.

We spent close to an hour talking about ourselves, our interests, and our college life until it began to dusk. At that point, I told her, "I must go because the night is falling, and I don't want it to fall completely on me. Besides, I don't want to be ravaged by the mosquitoes on my way back to the camp."

"I understand," She smiled and told me.

I left her with a hug and kiss on her cheek. The following day several of my colleagues, when they saw me, started laughing and whispering to one another that I had broken my duck. However, I did not confirm or deny their assertion then or at any other time.

One may inquire, Why the intense interest in me by Cuban girls? I have been told by Jamaicans and Cubans alike that my looks were remarkably close to that of a Cuban. I'm multiracial: predominantly Indian, White, and black, in that order. Hence, it seemed, I was especially attractive to the Cuban women.

Several of my colleagues often criticized me for not being more aggressive in trying to have sex with the many Cuban girls who apparently wanted to go romping with me. However, I took my responsibility seriously and wanted to lead by example to encourage discipline without reproach.

On the Saturday of the weekend of our very first week in the country, I learned that the Jamaican female students had returned to the college and would not return to the encampment. I asked when the next bus was leaving for Santiago, and I was told the next day, Sunday, so I told the rest of the guys, "I understand that the girls went back to the college for good, and I was going to Santiago to bring them back." I was furious at the decision to return the girls to Santiago without even informing me.

Therefore, on Sunday at midday, I boarded the bus and travelled to Santiago, and when I got to the college, no one from the administration was available to speak with me about the decision. Early the next morning, I asked Juanita, "Can I get an appointment with Luis? I need to speak with him about the Jamaican female students who had abandoned their assignment in the country."

"Desmond, he is very busy, but let me check to see if he has any openings."

In short order Juanita confirmed, "Luis has agreed to meet with you at 10 a.m. in the boardroom and said that he is going to bring with him additional members of the administration."

"That is fine with me, and can you arrange for José and Linda to be there?" I requested.

"I will let Luis in on your request," she said.

At 10 a.m., I was already seated and waiting for the arrival of the other meeting participants, at about one minute after 10 a.m., we were all convened and ready to start the meeting. Included in the meeting were Luis, José, Linda, and Juanita.

"Why were the Jamaican female students brought back from the country?" I Inquired.

Luis asked Linda to respond. "The girls are not accustomed to working in the field and they complained about insects in the cane field and blisters and calluses forming on their hands."

"Who authorized their return?" I asked.

"I did," Linda said.

I asked her, "Are you aware that I'm the leader of the group; and therefore, for a decision like that, I should have been consulted?" I continued, "I think that it is important for these girls to experience country living. They need to overcome and move beyond the things you said they were complaining about. Besides,

I don't believe it is fair that the first-year Cuban girls had to persevere the conditions that the Jamaicans are fussing about. If the Jamaican girls were going to be released from the country, then the Cuban girls should have been released too. I want the Jamaican girls back in the country as soon as possible," I remarked.

Luis agreed and sent for the girls, and they came. There were eight of them.

"Please be seated," Luis said. "You have to go back to the country because every student must fulfill their responsibilities, and no exception can be made," he told them.

"I'm 100 per cent behind the decision for you to return to the country. Furthermore, it was disrespectful for you to leave the encampment without informing me," I let them know.

"Would the following day be okay for them to make the trip back to the country," Luis inquired.

"Yes," I answered.

The Jamaican female students were not happy with my intervention, and they had no qualms about registering their displeasure with and about me. They criticized me with the second-year Jamaican group. Later in the evening, I was confronted by the guys of the second-year group who wanted to convince me to let the girls stay in Santiago. To me that was understandable coming from them because I knew several of them were intimately involved with several of the first-year girls. I argued with them forcefully and extensively about my responsibility, and I was not going to be a party to favouritism, "If the Cuban students are required to do agricultural work, then so must the Jamaicans. I'm convinced that my position is fair and principled, and I can't relent," I told them.

I was determined that the girls were going back to the country, irrespective of how they or their lovers felt about my decision.

The next morning at 10 a.m., Linda, all eight girls and I were on a college bus heading back to the country. For the entire journey, I was my own company, no one exchanged a word with me, and I did not try to speak with anyone. We arrived at the girls' encampment at about 2 p.m. and dropped them off the bus, and I returned on the bus to the guy's encampment. I explained to the rest of the guys that the girls were back, and that Linda had fallen for their whining, and she took upon herself the decision to take them back to the college. There were mixed reactions to the information, but to me, what was done could not be undone, and we needed to move on.

Unfortunately, that was not the end of the matter, and before the end of the week, I was informed by a male teacher from among us that all of us Jamaicans were going back to Santiago. Linda had asked him to relay the message to me. When I spoke with Linda later that day, she told me that "the college's administration had requested that all the Jamaican students return to the college." Again, I was furious, but I did not make any attempt to challenge the decision this time around, and I did not ask for a reason, and none was provided.

I was disappointed that I had to return to Santiago without completing the month in the country as was previously suggested, and even more so because the Cuban students had to remain in the country while we Jamaicans were back in Santiago not doing anything productive. Suddenly, I had a lot of time on my hands because classes were not scheduled to begin until nearly another three weeks and boredom and loneliness became my companions, and I needed to cut them loose.

Chapter 12

Several weeks went by, and I did not set my eyes on Belkis or hear from her, and I was missing her terribly. For weeks and days, I was restless, tormented and felt abandoned. I was also beginning to understand that love is not only beautiful, but it is also ugly and painful, and there is not much I, by myself, could do to make the latter less intolerable. It was as though a part of me had been amputated, numbed, robbed, and I was in no position to recover my loss, and there was no one anywhere I could go to for help. It was all up to me to pick myself up, dust off and take charge of myself thereafter.

I finally decided that I had to find a way to release the energy that was pent up inside me and bound up emotions that were beginning to play tricks on my mind. In order to release energy and control my emotions, I began to do daily runs, mostly during the week, on the college's athletics track; hoping to run myself to exhaustion so that I could at least sleep well at night. Before the run, I would walk out to the newspaper stand and buy myself two newspapers: *La Granma* and *La Juventud Rebelde*, the two most popular newspapers in Cuba at the time—official organs of Cuba's communist party.

After I ran myself to exhaustion, I would go up to the dormitory, shower, and crawl under my mosquito net into bed, and read in Spanish until my eyes and seeing sense gave way to sleep.

After a few days on this routine, I noticed a female student began appearing in the corridor at the back of the college and sat herself down on one of the concrete benches that were lined along the corridor. I could see that she was observing me even though it was some distance away. Then one evening, she got bold and came down to the track when I was almost complete for the evening.

She introduced herself, "I'm Amparo."

"My name is Desmond."

Soon a conversation ensued, which began with her asking me, "Are you training for an event or for some special reason?"

"No, I just want to stay in shape and keep my thoughts clear in order to concentrate better on my studies."

Amparo was incredibly beautiful and perfectly proportioned. She had big eyes, beautiful white teeth, and extremely long black hair, and, like Belkis, her colour was light brown. She was 21 years old, specializing in rhythmic gymnastics and was in her final year at the college.

Despite Amparo's beauty and captivating smile, I was not enticed. I was still thinking of the girl I fell in love with a few months ago. Besides, it crossed my mind that Belkis may have been behind Amparo's *advance towards me, and I was not prepared to be outwitted. As the days went by, I found it difficult to indulge that thought because I knew Belkis' best friends who were in her cohort, and Amparo was not her friend as far as I knew. I had never seen them together. I concluded that only a dear friend would engage in that kind of behaviour. Notwithstanding, I decided to inquire from the second-year Jamaican male students about Amparo, not because I was interested in her but instead to get a better understanding of the person I was chatting with for a fair amount of time in the evenings—I was more curious than anything else. I learned from the Jamaican male students that Amparo was popular with them and other foreigners from the medical school across the street.*

Amparo and I became talking buddies and she revealed to me that she was not happy with her life in Cuba. She hated the government and the revolution and wanted to escape to a non-communist country: anywhere as long as she did not have to live under the rules of communism. Amparo was the first Cuban that admitted to me that she did not like the political system that governed Cuba. Amparo made every effort to avoid talking about politics and the Cuban revolution with me.

Once I discovered that such discourses made her uncomfortable, I avoided dwelling on them, but I was also uneasy about being seen with her just in case she was under observation from the Cuban authority. I believed she understood that I was trying to disengage from our relationship, because she became estranged from me and the back corridor of the college. However, I continued my routine and extended my running time every evening as I became more accustomed to the drudgery of keeping my body in tip-top shape. In addition to extending my running time at the college, I looked for outlets away from the college.

I spent my weekends going down to the city centre and hanging out at the several parks: garden parks, monumental parks, and commercial parks. They provided me with the opportunity to talk to Cubans and foreigners alike who were roaming about, just relaxing or sightseeing. I also, by myself, went to the movie theatre every Saturday afternoon to see movies. Sometimes I saw other students I recognized, Jamaicans, and Cubans, and we would link up.

My favorite location to hangout was the Parque Céspedes, monumental, in the centre of the city which wore the design of a round-a-bout. The park was surrounded by streets and on those streets were many historical buildings and others such as hotels, arts and crafts stores, boutiques, and a couple of municipal buildings. Traffic constantly flowed around the park; there were buses traveling to and from the north, west, south, and east, dropping off and picking up passengers, many of whom were tourists.

There were several five-feet-long concrete benches placed around the park, to the inside of the enclosing wall, and I usually randomly sat on one of them depending on their availability. Often, someone would join me on the bench that I was sitting on, sometimes more than one person, and I would try to make conversation. Many of them could barely speak Spanish, and I realized immediately that they were tourists: I met Portuguese, French, Germans, Canadians, British, other Latin Americans like Nicaraguans, Chileans, Mexicans, Brazilians, and several others.

A lot of the times, my conversation had not gone on long before we started running into language barriers. Unless they spoke English or Spanish, our conversation was reduced to, "What is your name, and where are you from?" Whenever I was lucky to speak with someone who was fluent in Spanish and or English, the conversation would go on for several minutes with mostly questions about what I was doing in Cuba and how long was my stay and if I liked it in Cuba.

Every Saturday night at 8 p.m., it was customary for a band to play music in the middle of the street beside Hotel Venus, which was quite popular with tourists. I would usually wait around to listen to the band and watch the people dance. I enjoyed the dances, and it always amazed me to see how fast the dancers rhythmically coordinated their several moves to the beat of the music. I tried it a few times, but I never was able to get it right, so I gave up and resigned myself to watching.

During this musical, no alcohol was served or sold, and I never learned the reason for the restrictions. I surmised that because the gig was close to the hotel, the authorities may have been trying to control the public's behaviour as much as was possible. However, I did notice couples frequently veering off between buildings, and sometimes I catch sight of them making out. Interestingly, I never saw anyone from the college at these musicals and maybe that was a good thing because that way I did not have to rebuff any advances from female students.

Chapter 13

*A*mong the several unwanted advances I had from female students in the college, the one that I am not likely to forget has connection to Marbelis, the girlfriend of a student from my neighbouring parish in Jamaica. One evening Marbelis interrupted my running to tell me about the ancient army Sea Fort, El Morro, on the southwest of the city of Santiago that she and her boyfriend were planning to visit. Marbelis had planned a hooked up for me with Maritsa, another student at the college, of which I was unaware and would never have consented to in the first place. "El Morro is a landmark that is frequented by international and local tourists alike, and Ian and I are wondering if you would like to join us on a trip up there," she asked me.

"Yes, I would be thrilled to join you guys on the trip; that way, I would get a chance to decompress and unwind, I told Marbelis."

We agreed on a meeting location from which to begin our journey to El Morro. We arrived at the meeting location in tandem; they were ahead of me. As I approached the bus stop, I noticed they were having a conversation with a young lady, and I was unaware that she was going on the trip with us. When I got up close enough so we could touch one another, I was introduced to Maritsa; I gave each of the ladies a friendly hug, and I shook hands with my colleague.

"This is a friend of ours who will be journeying with us to El Morro," Marbelis told me.

There was a designated bus to El Morro, which made the trip to and from every 2hrs, and we were not to wait long before the bus arrived. We ascended the bus, paid the 10-cent fare, and chose our seats. My compatriot and I sat together, and the two ladies sat together until we reached our destination.

Once we were at the final stop, we dismounted the bus and walked up a peak while chatting about the beauty of the environment and the picturesque landscape that surrounded the nearby hotel—Balcon del Caribe. Spaniards built the Fort during the period of their colonization of Cuba, to protect the city from potential invaders. It was situated on a peak overlooking the sea and provided an unobstructed view for several miles out into the ocean.

On top of the peak, we went through several passages to get to the edge of the Fort, which was hanging over the sea. There were a few plaques placed on top, and on the sides of the enclosing passage walls with names and messages imprinted on them. There were still several well-maintained old cannons on display, and which were pointing out to the sea. While I was browsing around the Fort, Marbelis and Maritsa came over to where I was, and Marbelis revealed to me that she invited Maritsa for her and me to get acquainted, and that I needed to forget about Belkis because she was crazy. I looked at her and asked, "Is that so?"

"Yes," Marbelis said.

Strange as it was, I did not bother to ask what she meant by crazy.

She then walked away and left Maritsa standing near me. Maritsa was about four feet seven inches tall and of light complexion and buck teeth. I looked her over and concluded right away that she was not my type.

Even though I was not the slightest bit interested in her, I started questioning her, "Where do you live? What is your family like? What sport are you specializing in at the college? How old are you? How long have you been at the college?"

"I live in Vista Alegre with my parents, an older and younger brother; I'm specializing in gymnastics, I'm 18 years old, and I'm in my second year at the college," she answered with enthusiasm.

For a moment, the message on one of the plaques caught my attention, and I began to focus on the words which were preceded by dates in the 16th century.

I stooped a bit to read a few of the plaques, and while I was reading one in the stooped position, to my amazement, Maritsa bent around me and kissed me on the lips. I was dumbfounded and speechless. Nothing like that had ever happened to me before, and it was not expected and certainly not from someone I barely knew. I looked at her and began to move away in disgust and anger; she recognized my discomfort and started to apologize.

Talk about Belkis being crazy! That little drama marked the end of the relationship between Ian and me, not because it was his fault but rather because I did not want to be around his girlfriend anymore.

From that moment until the visit was over, I tried not to initiate any conversation and spoke only when I was drawn into a conversation, specifically by my name. Ian asked me several times, "What is the matter with you?"

"I'm fine don't worry about me," I repeatedly told him and refused to give any explanation.

That was the way it continued until we were back in the city. I bade them goodbye and headed to the college and my dormitory and went to bed under my mosquito net without eating anything that evening. Besides, after that little escapade, I had no appetite for food and could only think about Belkis and if we were ever going to be together again.

One evening after I finished running, I sat down on the grass inside the circle of the track to ponder how I was going to cope with more than three years of Cuban life to come; I noticed a girl coming towards me, and when she was close enough, I recognized her, Magdalena, an attractive brunette. She walked briskly with an appealing style. She was one of Belkis' two best friends. She came and stood over me, and looking at me, she blurted out, "Why are you treating Belkis so mean?"

"Magdalena, worry about your own affairs," I told her.

"There is no need to be impolite. I'm only trying to help you."

"Help me with what?" I asked.

"Belkis talked about you a lot in the dormitory, hallways and in the meal lines—she is crazy about you," she said.

"If that is the case, then Belkis should not have been avoiding me. I know she has reason to be mad with me, but I did apologize for what happened, and

she never accepted my apology. Instead, she distanced herself from me and kept out of sight."

Magdalena confided, "Belkis misses you and wants you and her to be on speaking terms again; you should send for her during your off times."

"I'll not be the initiator of any rekindling," I replied.

"Chico tú eres bobo; you need to let go of your pride," she said and walked away.

I then rose to my feet, slowly ambled to the college building, and walked along a path where I knew it would be unlikely to encounter anyone, and since dusk had begun to fall, I felt very safe from that possibility.

I climbed the staircase to my dormitory on the third floor, and when I reached the top of the staircase, several of the guys were there playing chess and dominoes. I snuck by without them consciously noticing me and headed to my bunk bed. I occupied the top bed, so I pulled out the mosquito net that was tucked under the mattress and pushed my head under the net, and I stood there with my forehead against the bedframe and thought about Belkis and the idea of me approaching her to make up.

During those moments, I felt the energy draining from my body and the emotions dissipating from all over my being. Unexpectedly, I felt very tired and wanted to lie down; my legs were unable to bear me up. Feeling that way, I decided to climb into bed without taking a shower or reading my newspapers as was customary for me. When I woke up the next morning, it was time to go down for breakfast. I rushed into the bathroom and secured an available shower stall and quickly showered, dried myself off, got dressed and scurried downstairs to the canteen.

I picked up my breakfast, moved hurriedly to a table and sat down to eat. Then I began thinking about the discussion I had with Magdalena and the scenario of the energy escaping my body. At that moment, I began to feel as though I had been relieved of an enormous burden. The information that Belkis was still in love with me led me to infer that my newfound joy and peace were my subconscious responses that were helping me to overcome sadness and alienation. I ate my breakfast heartily and rushed back upstairs to fetch my notebook, pen and pencil and descended the first flight of stairs to the overpass that took me across from the dormitory side of the building to my classroom. Though I was elated that Belkis wanted to be with me, I was convinced that she should make the first move, and I was too stubborn to cave.

Later that morning, after classes but just before lunch, I decided to change my route from the overpass to the ground floor corridor, and as I was passing by the tuck shop, which was located on that level, I saw Belkis and her friends making purchases. Our eyes made contact, but I did not greet her. Her face appeared a bit leaner; I noticed the sadness in her eyes as she stared at me. It was the kind of sadness that softened my heart; for a moment, I wanted to go back and speak with her, but soon after, I was back to my old stubborn ways. I walked on and ascended the stairs to my dormitory and thought to myself, "How much longer can I keep this up?"

After lunch, I climbed into my bunk bed and started to read the newspapers that I had purchased the evening before and which I was unable to read because of my meltdown. Not long after, I started reading the papers, I heard the sweet-sounding nasal voice of my Belkis yelling, "Desmond, Desmond, Desmond, from three floors below." My whole body began to shiver with delight and eagerness.

I put the papers away and got out of bed immediately and went over to the window and opened the louvers wider so we could see each other. She gesticulated with one hand for me to come down. I quickly tucked my shirt into my pants so that I appeared neat and rushed downstairs to be with Belkis. Once I reached the bottom of the stairs, I slowed my strides, because I was uncertain of what to expect. Furthermore, I did not want to appear anxious just in case my assumption about the purpose of her call was misplaced.

We made eye contact and moved in closer to each other, my emotions were welled up, I also discerned that she was exhausted from the effects of our separation.

"Can we sit?" she asked.

"Of course," I said.

So, we sat on the edge of the ramp to the auditorium about a foot away from each other and began talking about our misgivings over the last several weeks.

"I was miserable because I was not able to talk to you even though I saw you every day. I always observed you running around the track through the windows from my dormitory," she told me.

"I missed you a lot and thought about you all the time we were separated," I said.

She pulled herself in closer to me, "Abraza mi por favor," she requested.

I put my arms around her shoulders as she leaned on me.

We were sitting side by side, so we angled ourselves to face each other, and I looked into her big eyes and noticed that they were partially red, and tears were trickling down her cheeks. Simultaneously, we both blurted out: "I love you a lot."

We kept talking about the experience of being apart for the last while and how foolish we both were to be holding out on each other.

"I don't know why I was obstinate because my heart was aching for you day and night," I confessed.

"I was miserable and in agony and longed and waited for you to seek me out, but you never did. Sometimes the hurt was almost unbearable. I missed several meals because, I had no desire for food," she said.

"Well, here we are together again, let's not dwell on the past anymore," I told her. When it was almost time to go to class, I told her, "Your face is a mess with tears' streaks all over, so go up to your dormitory and freshen up before you go to class."

"I need to change out of my sportswear and into my uniform anyway. I have theoretical classes in the afternoon," she added.

We left each other with a hug and agreed to meet again on the overpass after dinner. I was impatient for classes to be over, so I may quickly swallow the dinner and get another chance to hold my girl, squeeze her small body against mine and kiss her alluring and voluptuous lips.

Once dinner was over, I did not have to wait long for Belkis to appear on the overpass. As we saw each other, we rushed into an embrace and shivering; we pulled apart and sat down to chat. We avoided trying to make out because we did not want to put on a show for other students who were nearby or passing by.

"I want you to meet my mother, brothers and sister," she told me.

"I would love to meet them, but are you sure about this," I asked her.

"Yes, that is why I suggested it," she told me.

"When will this rendezvous take place?" I inquired.

"This Saturday at 11 a.m., the address is 112 Calle Bueno across from the general hospital," she told me. We did not try to see each other again before then.

Chapter 14

Saturday could not have come soon enough, not only to meet Belkis' family but to see her and be near her again. I arrived at her mother's at exactly 10 minutes to 11 a.m., and the door was open, and Belkis was already there sitting in a rocking chair. Once she saw me, she shouted out to her mother, "Mummy, Desmond is here," and she rushed into my arms and kissed me on the cheek, and her mother, Lorena, came from around the back of the house where she was preparing a meal. Lorena, like Belkis, was a slim light brown lady with long black hair and was about five feet six inches tall; she had on a pair of slippers and dragged them and herself around.

Belkis' two brothers, Felipe, Lionel, and her sister Gladys were also at home. Felipe, the brother that followed Belkis was dark with coarse, curly black hair and about five feet 10 inches tall, of medium built; and Lionel, the younger brother, was of a much lighter complexion with soft curly black hair and about five feet eight inches tall; and Gladys, her skin colour was lighter than everyone else's. She had long straight brown hair and was about five feet three inches tall. We greeted one another, and they invited me to sit down.

"So, you are Belkis' boyfriend?" Lorena remarked, and before I could answer, she continued, "I heard so much about you and wanted to meet you for a long time, but Belkis was timid to bring you home for an introduction."

"Thank you, all in good time, and it is a pleasure to meet you all," I said.

"Make yourself at home because I'm in the process of preparing something for us to eat," Lorena told me.

"Thank you," I replied.

Belkis excused herself to go outside; later, she came back with a couple of young ladies to show me off.

We greeted one another, and one of them uttered: "So, I heard you are Jamaican."

"Yes," I responded.

"Be careful of Cuban women; they are heartbreakers," she said.

"I'm very much aware of that already," I told her.

We chatted for about 15 minutes about my stay in Cuba thus far and what were some of the differences between the two islands.

"Do you miss your home? Is there a girlfriend waiting for you back in Jamaica?" One of the ladies inquired.

"I have already explained that to Belkis, so you should inquire from her," I told her.

They both smiled and soon after, they bade me farewell and disappeared onto the sidewalk, which was just a step down from the house.

After the young ladies left, I took the time to survey the environment. I noticed that the house was an elongated structure and semi-detached. The living room was in front of a bedroom to the right and a passageway on the left from the entrance; behind bedroom number one, there was bedroom number two and the space behind bedroom number two and the end of the passageway was shared between the bathroom on the right and the kitchen on the left.

The kitchen was small and arranged so that the family could eat in it. The house could only be entered and exited from one door at the front. There was a window in each of the bedrooms as well as the bathroom. The door was painted in brown, and the rest of the house in Persian green. The aroma from the cooking in the back of the house seized the surrounding space. The house was extremely hot because the roof was the only barrier above, between the inside and outside: there was no ceiling to cushion the direct sun heat from outside. However, there was a small floor fan in the living room, and Belkis turned it on and focused it on me, and as a result, the heat was not so unbearable.

Felipe, Lionel, and Gladys remained in the living room with me, chatting; they asked me about Jamaica, my family, and personal questions about myself and my motivation to study in Cuba.

I inquired from them about their vocation and learned that Felipe was completing secondary school and would be going to Havana in the fall of 1980 to study general chemistry. Lionel was in the second year of his secondary education, and Gladys was in elementary school.

As the conversation continued, I could recognize my Spanish improving by the minute, and I was excited about the fluency with which I was speaking. I described, in the best possible way I could with limited Spanish vocabulary, the beauty of Jamaica: our music which was popular in Cuba because of Bob Marley, the beautiful beaches surrounding the island, the United States' influence on our daily living and much more.

Lionel, the most talkative of the three, wanted to know, "Do you like Cuban food, music, women and generally communism?"

I answered his questions as diplomatically as I could: "I have just begun the Cuban experience. I still have a lot to see and learn, but up to this point, I would prefer not to have to choose whether to eat pork."

"Los Cubanos love el macho," Felipe said with a laugh.

At about 12 noon, I was rescued when Lorena announced that the meal was ready, and we should come to the table. I was amazed at the quantity and types of food that were on the table: frijoles negros or black bean stew, arroz blanco or white rice, filetes de carne de res frito or fried beef steak, ensalada de avocado or avocado salad and limonada fria or ice-cold lemonade.

"Everything looks delicious," I remarked.

"Que aprovechen," Lorena said.

There were smiles from everyone including me. I was partially served, and I helped myself with what else I needed to eat; not long after I started eating, Lorena told me, "No tengas pena there is more food." However, I only ate from what was originally placed before me on the table. Though the meal was scrumptious, I avoided asking for more because I did not want to overfill my stomach.

Lionel was the only one who asked for more. Belkis and Lorena both asked if I wanted more, and I replied in the negative.

After we finished the entrée, pastry was offered, but I refused to eat anything more and asked only for a glass of water at room temperature with an added squeeze of lime. Everyone was mocking me, and Gladys remarked, "Desmond is shy and ashamed of eating in front of us."

"I'm not putting on a show. I'm just not a big eater, and it will be proven to you in the months and years ahead," I told them.

They all claimed that they were going to hold me to that statement. We all remained at the table until everyone was finished eating, and then Belkis began clearing the table; I handed her my dishes, and so did everyone else, and Lorena took charge of removing the assorted-coloured placemats and folding the nylon table covering.

Felipe suggested that the guys head for the living room and leave the ladies to tidy up the kitchen. Belkis waved with her hand that I followed them, and I did.

"Thank you for the sumptuous meal and welcome," I told Lorena.

"Think nothing of it," she said.

I followed the guys into the living room. Lorena, Gladys, and Belkis remained in the kitchen and from what I overheard, they were doing the dishes and chatting about me in positive terms.

Felipe and Lionel did not hang around for the ladies to exit the kitchen. They told me, "Vamos a dar un paseo. We will catch up later."

"Don't get lost," I joked.

"We are Santiagueros," they responded.

When the ladies were finished in the kitchen, Belkis and Lorena came and joined me in the living room, but Gladys went into her bedroom. Lorena sat down and told me, "You need to eat a lot more than you are now eating, especially since you are always engaged in physical activities—*you need your strength. Los Cubanos comen mucho. Belkis hardly eats, and you shouldn't let her influence you.*"

"*Thank you for the advice, but I'm not accustomed to eating a lot,*" I told Lorena.

Suddenly, a lady who was casually dressed, looked a bit haggard, appeared in the doorway and wanted a word with Lorena, it turns out she was the next-door neighbour.

Lorena introduced me as Belkis' boyfriend and asked Belkis, "*Will you guys be going soon?*"

"*No Mummy,*" Belkis responded.

Lorena immediately asked to be excused and went through the door with the lady and pulled it up behind her.

Belkis and I were sitting opposite each other; I was sitting in an armchair, and Belkis was sitting in a rocking chair.

"*What do you think of my mother and siblings?*" Belkis asked.

"*They are fine people, but I need more time to give an informed answer.*"

She smiled and said, "*You are being diplomatic.*"

"*Don't you think I need more time to know them better?*" I inquired.

She smiled again and said, "*You have a point.*"

"*My mother tends to overdo things sometimes.*"

"*That doesn't bother me,*" I said.

"*What are the plans for the rest of the day?*" I asked.

"*We are spending it here with Mummy, but later, we could go for a walk in La Feria, but right now I want to be with you.*"

Belkis got out of her chair and came over to me and sat on my lap, put her arms around my shoulder, *and said, "I think my mother likes you, and I'm happy you came to meet her."*

Her nasal voice and warm and tender embrace were drowning me with desire. I looked into her eyes and then on her lips repeatedly, and I told her, "I'm glad that I did too," and then she put her sweet lips to mine and laid a juicy kiss on me.

The longing for her and the excitement running through my body was mesmerizing.

As she latched on to my body and heat penetrated and overwhelmed me, I found my right hand wandering up her skirt, but she was a girl with amazing control, and she gently pushed my hand away. Next, I moved towards opening her blouse in order to caress her breast, and she "dished" out a similar treatment as before. However, she kept on kissing me; I was on fire. I fondled her breast from outside her blouse, and she allowed me to do that without interference.

We remained in each other's embrace, and we kissed until we heard Lorena's voice close enough that it suggested she was almost at the door. We hastily pulled apart, and Belkis returned to her seat looking all ruffled and vulnerable. Her mother passed us by, without taking any intense notice and inquired of us, "Are you guys okay"? And went towards the back of the house.

"We are fine, Mummy," responded Belkis.

There was an old television set in the living room, which was not working properly, and I fiddled with it until I got it going. Belkis and I spent more than an hour watching television, and for a while, I was alone watching a documentary on the Escambray rebellion that followed the triumph of the Cuban revolution.

During the documentary, Belkis spent most of the time in the back talking with Lorena. Once the documentary was finished, Belkis invited me to go for ice cream in La Feria, and we excused ourselves from the house and went out. The sun was extremely hot, so the ice cream was a welcome treat, and the occasion gave us the opportunity to enjoy the breeze and shade La Feria had to offer.

When we arrived at the ice cream kiosk, Belkis ordered two cones with vanilla-flavored ice cream and paid for them—they cost ten cents each. We sat on a bench in La Feria and relished our ice cream and talked about her family and mine. I discovered she had extended family members on her mother's side living in another province—Holguín.

On her father's side, they were living in the city of Santiago, and in the region of Palma in the province of Santiago de Cuba.

"Mummy has two sisters and two brothers, and my father has two sisters and one brother."

"My parents are living in England, and I have two brothers and two sisters. Our grandmother cares for us in the absence of our parents."

We spent a total of two and a half hours in La Feria talking about our feelings for each other and any and everything that popped into our heads. However, we never discussed our future, we were just content to let time decide our destiny. We ended up eating three cones of ice cream before we went back to her mothers' place. Upon our return, Lorena was again in the kitchen preparing another meal—dinner.

Belkis and I were alone in the living room, and we were all over each other; we kissed and hugged, while the television was on, and we were unable to hear anyone coming. Lorena entered the living room without us having any warning of her approach.

"Do you eat fried eggs?" She asked me.

"Yes, I do."

She caught us, Belkis, and me, in an embrace and kissing. She did not remark on what she had seen. Lorena left the living room without saying anything else and went back into the kitchen. At that moment, I was feeling a little embarrassed and a bit shivery, but Belkis put my mind at ease when she said, "Don't worry, my mother understands." She reminded me of when her mother went out earlier to talk to the neighbour and pulled up the door behind her— "She was giving us some privacy."

We did not have to wait long for the light dinner: fried eggs and "pan caliente" and salad made from lettuce, tomatoes and cucumbers and small bottles of refrescos. Even though Felipe and Lionel had not returned from their walk-about, the rest of us were called to the table to eat. We ate and chatted a bit about Cuban eating habits, which were a light breakfast, moderate to heavy lunch and light dinner, depending on what was prepared and served at lunchtime.

Monday to Friday, lunch is normally heavy, and dinner is light and on weekends, lunch is light, and dinner is heavy, but exceptions are made for special occasions. I surmised that lunch was heavy that day, because I was invited, and they wanted it to be special for me.

After the entrée, a small pumpkin pie was brought to the table, already cut into several pieces, for dessert.

"Desmond, help yourself to a piece," Lorena said.

"No thank you, but can I have one of the ripe bananas instead?" I inquired.

"You don't have to ask," Belkis said, and reached for one of the fruits sitting in a transparent glass dish on the kitchen counter.

Just as we were about to leave the table, Felipe and Lionel arrived and headed straight for the kitchen. They remarked simultaneously, "So you guys have already eaten. Disculpenos for being late, but we got caught up in conversation on the street," Lionel declared. They sat at the table.

However, Lorena told them, "Guys you will have to help yourselves because I'm not going around the stove again for the rest of the evening."

"Okay Mummy, we will," Felipe muttered.

In that moment, the remaining four of us exited the kitchen and went into the living room and after about 15 minutes of chatting and laughing, Belkis and I agreed that it was time for us to leave. She had to go back to her father's home, and I had to return to the college. Belkis announced our departure, and we got a signal of approval from everyone.

"Don't be a stranger, Desmond; you are welcome back anytime," Lorena told me.

I embraced and shook hands with the hosts, and Belkis kissed her family members on their cheeks one by one.

We exited Lorena's house and put our arms around each other's waist and strolled along to the bus stop. Belkis commented, "My mother likes you."

"It certainly seems that way," I responded.

We stopped several times along the way and kissed and embraced tightly. When we reached the bus stop, Belkis hugged and kissed me and bade me goodbye— "Until Sunday afternoon," she said.

"I'm going to accompany you to the city centre," I told her.

"I don't want you to do that because it is already too late," she replied.

I insisted, and she relented and said, "Only to the bus stop."

I agreed to her suggestion.

We sat beside each other on the bus and joked about Felipe and Lionel having to prepare their own supper— I wondered aloud, "Do they know what they are doing in the kitchen?"

"They are used to fixing their light meals because Mummy is a member of the Communist Party and the Committee for the Defence of the Revolution. As a result, she frequently attends meetings of these organs; and therefore, my brothers are accustomed to doing things for themselves."

"What about Gladys?" I asked.

"Mummy always takes care of her before she leaves the house," she responded.

It was not long before we reached the bus stop, which was a block away from her home in the city centre, and she kissed me on the cheek. "Until tomorrow my love."

"I wish we didn't have to spend the night apart from each other."

"Too bad," she said.

She descended the bus and walked across the street behind the bus and glanced back and waved a couple of times. Suddenly the bus pulled away from the stop, and she was out of sight. I stayed on the bus until it reached its final stop in the Frank País district because I was going to take the same bus back to my stop across from the inter-provincial bus terminal for my return to the college.

The driver of the bus spotted me on the bus after everyone had dismounted and asked me, "Where are you going?"

"I'm staying on the bus to go back to the inter-provincial bus terminal," I told him.

"We are at the end of the trip, and if you want to go back, you will have to pay again," he told me.

The driver apparently recognized that I had an accent that was not local and asked me where I was from and what I was doing in Santiago.

"I'm not a Cuban, I'm a Jamaican, but I'm in Cuba at the invitation of the Cuban Government to study physical and health education."

"We are very generous in this country," he remarked, and he began to tell me about all the different nationalities that were in Cuba studying multiple disciplines.

We chatted a bit about Jamaica and Cuba, and he asked me, "Have you found a Cuban girlfriend yet?"

"Yes, and she is the reason that I'm on the bus at this time of the night."

"Be careful now, Cuban women are caliente," he warned.

"I have already found that out."

He then asked, "How long now have you been in Cuba?"

"I'm in Cuba for approximately six months," I replied.

"Good for you," he said.

After about 10 minutes, the bus was off and making stops for passengers along the way. The driver and I did not speak again until I was getting off the bus—and he bade me farewell.

"Be careful, there are some bad characters roaming about," he told me.

"Thank you for the advice, and have a good night," I replied.

I proceeded to cross La Feria at a brisk pace. I may have passed about 10 people on my way, the majority of whom were couples making out in the dark. In a short space of time, I was at the college. Most of the lights were off, and the silence was deafening. I silently climbed the stairs, went by my bedside to get my toothbrush, and paste from my closet and tiptoed into the washroom in order not to wake or disturb anyone. Once I was through freshening up, I stealthily traversed the dormitory to my bunk and climbed into it quietly to sleep for what remained of the night.

Chapter 15

After our return from the country and non-productive work, we got to idle for two weeks because our new class schedule was not due to begin right away. I developed my own routine, and the other students also made their own plans. There was quite a contrast between us. I spent most of my time developing my Spanish skills by reading extensively, practicing verb conjugation, and putting what I learned into practice by conversing with Cubans willing to talk with me.

Furthermore, I joined in with other Cuban students to keep the campus clean. While so doing, I took advantage of the opportunity to develop my listening skills while learning bits and pieces of the vernacular language of multiple and different regions in Guantanámo, Granma, and Santiago de Cuba. As for the other Jamaican students: except for a few who were learning French and had to attend French classes, the girls were mostly in their dormitory. However, the guys were mostly out on the streets except for the periods before meals when they could be seen and heard playing chess and or dominoes in the dormitory's common area. They made friends in the surrounding communities and were learning the street lingo of those environs.

The new lingo was brought to our dormitory daily to show off or to practise on those of us who were not making the streets our centre of learning. Most of us knew that when classes resumed, these forms of expression would not be tolerated. Notwithstanding, there were benefits to learning the street lingo because one gets to develop listening skills, new vocabulary, and the ability to speak with a fair degree of fluency. Conversing with regular Cubans, pertaining to their customs and culture, contributed to a greater understanding and use of the official language over time. Even though I was not in favour of the relationships that my colleagues were building in the communities around the college, I agreed that acquiring the street lingo was essential to making friends, unwinding, and developing new perspectives. These would go a long way in reducing the susceptibility to isolation and language barriers and pave the way progressively for unhindered conversation between members of our student group and members of the city's communities.

Jamaicans' ability to make friends wherever they go is one of the attributes they rely on to navigate new environs. Therefore, our students went about exploring the surrounding communities and their inhabitants and made several connections in the process: some good and some not so good, depending on one's perspectives. Once connections were made, we began to see outside visitors, in the college at hours before lights out in the night, men and women. These visitors frequented the campus in the evenings and on weekends: they usually hang around at the bottom of the staircase and inquired about individual Jamaican male students, and occasionally, some of them ended up in the common area of the men's dormitory. In one instant, to my amazement, I encountered a man and two women visitors, relaxed, conversing with a few of my colleagues in our dormitory.

"Non-college visitors are not allowed in this area," I told them.

"Why not?" The man inquired. "We aren't creating any disturbances or problems, are we?" he asked.

"No, but it is against the college's regulations, and I take my cue from the college's administration. I would rather not have to inform the administration of this scenario," I replied.

"I think we better leave," said one of the women.

They did leave but with some hesitation, crass stares, evocative body language, and unpleasant utterances. There were also grumblings from the entertainers but nothing that I could decipher.

From their own sources, potentially the college's caretakers, the college's administration became aware of these visits to the college and asked me to discuss their concerns with the group: security, safety, violation of college protocols, attracting unauthorized, depraved, and inappropriate behaviour towards the general student population. I did as I was requested to do, but my efforts were futile, and I was unsure of how to manage the situation save from reporting the matter to the Jamaican Embassy in Havana. Therefore, I pretended as if all were under control—which was a sham. I was relieved when it was time for our classes to resume and activities to occupy students' time, thus reducing contact between students and the surrounding communities, and I hoped that the visits would have tapered off.

The new semester began with an increase in physical activity class time, 90 minutes, and shorter theoretical activity class time, 50 minutes. In the mornings, we had aerobic gymnastics and athletics, and, in the afternoon, we had mathematics, physiological anatomy, psychology, physics, chemistry and Spanish.

Several of our students were competent, given their high school background, preparedness for college or university, and discipline in study habits, which afforded them the ability to progress despite not being able to speak Spanish fluently—especially the girls. However, like the first semester, a few students struggled due to inadequate high school preparation, not being fully committed to the program, questioning the value of certain subjects, and a lack of confidence.

In the area of physical activities and specifically in the discipline of gymnastics, students with inadequate physical preparation had a tough time manoeuvring certain activities like working the parallel bar, doing somersaults, walking the balance beam, and maintaining equilibrium—and therefore, easily lost concentration. Those who were unprepared academically had difficulty keeping up with the teachers, dictation, explanation, and material while managing their assignments. The fact that they were not acquiring the necessary classroom skills in Spanish greatly impeded their ability to grasp the fundamentals of the courses, which led to frustration on both the part of the students and teachers.

Those of us who were better prepared did our best to assist our less prepared colleagues and encouraged them to work with us in their free time, evenings, lunch breaks and weekends to get needed support. We also pleaded with the teachers, with success, to speak slowly, elevate their voices, and frequently repeat key themes in the lessons.

While a few students were experiencing difficulties managing aspects of the physical and health education program, a few others, particularly the guys, were excelling in two areas of sports: soccer and athletics. Those participating in soccer wore the city's uniform and made stellar contributions to the city's team. They had the opportunity to travel the province on a regular basis and see what the rest of us were unable to see, according to their report back—historical sites, the beautiful landscape that adorned the provincial countryside, war museums, parks, different customs, and different segments of the population that were not as diverse as those in Santiago.

Home competitions were always well attended by students from neighbouring secondary schools, colleges, universities, polytechnics, sports centres, and the public in general. Overwhelmingly, there was no lack of support for our Jamaican competitors. When inter-college athletics competitions were in progress, the athletes were treated with thunderous roars and applause, and special cheers for specific competitors. After each event, the competitors circled the track, waved their hands, and threw kisses at the cheering crowd. Most of the times, the Jamaican athletes placed in the top three and quite frequently in first place. Once the competition was over, several of the attendees gathered around the athletes for the opportunity to shake their hands, embrace them and hoist them into the air repeatedly in joy and jubilation.

Even though several of the athletes were strong candidates for inter-provincial competitions, they were not allowed to compete there because they were not Cubans. The rationale provided was that national sports competitions were designed to prepare Cuban athletes for international competitions, and Jamaicans were not eligible to represent Cuba in the International arena. The local coaches advocated for their inclusion in the inter-provincial lineup, but Cuban officials, INDER, refused to authorize their inclusion.

Midway through the semester, the college's administration attempted to mitigate the monotony of college life by staging a cultural event at the college one Friday evening. Hence, one evening on my way out of the canteen, Linda approached me and informed me of the plan.

"The college's administration would love the Jamaican students to participate in a cultural event it is planning for students' entertainment. It would give you all a chance to unwind and relax."

"I will discuss the administration's suggestion with my colleagues and get back to you," I assured Linda.

I discussed the administration's request with my colleagues, and the response was positive.

"My colleagues would be happy to participate in the cultural event. A couple from the second-year student group would like to perform dances, and a few first-year students agreed to perform a short play," I conveyed to Linda the next day.

"We need an emcee for the event, and we believe you should do it. It would be a great opportunity for you to practise your Spanish," Linda encouraged me.

"I'm not sure I'm brave enough for the task, but I will give it a shot," I told Linda.

"You'll do fine," Linda assured me and told me also: "The administration will provide the band, dancers, singers, and instrumentalists to help stage the show."

Even though I accepted the offer, I was terrified. I was not sure how well my Spanish would hold up in front of a live audience, some of whom were not from the college's population and might criticize and mock my performance. However, my desire to practise the little skills I had in Spanish outweighed any reservations that were gnawing at my confidence.

When I broke the news to my colleagues about confirming to emcee the event, most of them congratulated me and expressed some sentiments of elation. However, there were a few skeptics who reminded me that I was not a native Cuban. One of them was my buddy, Tom.

"Are you sure you can manage this assignment without embarrassing yourself doing it? In the end, it's your decision," Tom said.

"Any opportunity to practise my Spanish, I welcome wholeheartedly. Furthermore, I have already given my word, and I can't back out now," I told Tom.

"If you're up to the challenge, go for it," Gregory encouraged me.

"I wish I had your confidence," Heather added.

"I will never know whether I can do it if I don't try. Besides, what's the worst that could happen? I may occasionally draw blank in search of words, but that's no-good reason not to take the stage."

The reaction from my colleagues made me more determined to emcee the event, and the mere fact that no one outright discouraged me from doing it helped to calm my nerves, which usually get wacky, even under normal conditions.

On the night of the event, at about 7:30 p.m., the students and outside audience gathered in the college yard in front of the stage; the band had arrived and began setting up, and the performers were prepared and anxious to get the show moving, college administrators seated themselves on one side of the stage, and the ground keepers and other staff were seated on the opposite side. I walked onto the stage with a sheet of paper in one of my hands; it had a list containing names and positions of the performers' appearances during the night.

The microphone was on its stand, positioned about three feet from the edge of the stage in front of the band. I gently removed the microphone from the stand, noticed that I was not nervous, all the usual stomach butterflies were gone, and I tested the microphone to make sure the audio was on and functioning properly. I introduced myself, the band, and its accompanying members, welcomed the college performers, and thanked the audience for their presence. One after the other, I called on the performers to perform their acts which they did flawlessly. After each performance, the crowd applauded to demonstrate their approval and appreciation of the performance. In return, the performers waved to the crowd and bowed their heads in appreciation.

The second-year Jamaican students dance duo brought everyone into sharp focus; by dancing the Rumba to the music of "Los Muñequitos de Matanzas." In about the middle of their routine, their moves were so enthralling, exhilarating, and perfectly coordinated that the crowd went wild. When the dancers reached the end of their routine, almost everyone wanted them to continue; they did provide a short encore before leaving the stage amid screams and shouts of gratitude.

With the microphone in my hand, I got comfortable and was rocking my upper body to the sound of the music. Suddenly, shouts burst out from the audience.

"Dance for us, maestro!"

"I can't dance," I told them.

"Why not?" they asked in unison.

"I have two left feet," I said.

That little gimmick brought a resounding laughter from the audience. Shortly afterwards, another request came for me, "Sing us a song!" someone said.

I hesitated for a moment and said to myself, "why the hell not?"

I told the audience that, "even though I had no prior experience and had never done any public performance in my life, if the band plays it, I will sing a Roberto Carlos song." They quieted down, drew themselves closer to the stage and waited attentively, smiles beamed across their faces as they stared at me in amazement. The song was popular in Cuba at the time. I told the band the name of the song: Qué Será De Ti, and they agreed to play it.

I found the courage, and suddenly, I began to sing in Spanish. You could hear a pin drop if it were not for the playing of the band and the sound of my voice. When I was through singing the song, I heard lukewarm applause, and at that moment, I began to question the wisdom of having decided to indulge the audience. Fortunately, I did not hear any booing or mocking, which was somewhat comforting and went a long way in my recovery for the night. For the rest of the gig, I received no other request, and I did not volunteer to do another performance.

Even though I was shaken a bit, I continued in my role until the end of the show and tried my utmost to stay calm and positive, making jokes and sneaky comments about the show and the performers, to which the audience often roared in ecstatic pleasure. After the acts, I brought the concert to a close by thanking the entertainers for their contribution, the audience for their patience and tolerance, and the college's administration for making the show possible.

Before I left the stage, the band leader approached me and said, "You have a good voice, but your singing was offbeat with the music. Nonetheless, good job. I will give you full marks for your effort. I know it must have taken a lot of courage to stand in front of an audience and sing, especially in a language that you are still learning."

"Thank you, and I'm glad you didn't abandon me midway through the song."

When I left the stage, some of my colleagues and several Cuban students pretty much restated what I had heard from the band leader.

I was even more reassured when two of my colleagues, Tom, and Jordan, approached me a few days later and asked me to join them in forming a singing group. I was excited about the confidence they had in my ability to sing. The opportunity to practise and coordinate my singing with the beat of instruments playing was alluring, and so I accepted. We started to rehearse almost immediately on the second floor of the college's academic wing of the building and were slowly building an audience—several members of which were providing advice to us after each practice session.

As soon as we began to feel good about our effort, one evening during rehearsal, the potential lead vocalist, Jordan, began to cough intensely, and when he spat, we noticed blood was mixed in with the saliva coming out of his mouth. With that adversity, we put our practice on hold for about three weeks, hoping that when he recovered, we would resume where we had left off. Unfortunately, when he returned and we restarted rehearsing, the hemorrhaging re-emerged, and we gave up on the idea for good.

Another spinoff from the concert was our dancing duo, Earl, and Joan, were invited to participate in a dance competition scheduled for the city centre one week after the night of the concert. The couple spent the evenings of the entire week practising, dancing to Cuban, Caribbean, and rock-n-roll songs in order to prepare themselves for the dance contest. They put their heart, mind, soul, and body into their routine with grace, poise, determination, and devotion. The college's administration was pleased that Earl and Joan decided to participate in the contest because it accomplished two things—it provided representation for the college, which would have been nonexistent without the Jamaican duo, and the opportunity for the other Jamaican students to attend the event and alleviate boredom.

The college's administration provided transportation to take us—Jamaican students, Cuban students, and several teachers—to the theatre. After we arrived at the building, we descended the bus and were directed by the teachers to the area where the contest was going to occur. The seating was arranged in auditorium fashion, and since we arrived at about 9 a.m., and at that time, there were more than enough seats to accommodate all of us. However, minutes later, several more people entered the theatre after the college's spectators had been seated, and the number of available seats was reduced significantly.

We were yearning in expectation when, at about 10 a.m., the competition got underway. Most of us were there to support and cheer on our colleagues, Earl, and Joan, who were listed fourth in line to dance. The duo that danced before them was energic, strong, flexible, synchronized with their movements, and they put on quite a spectacle. Several of us began to wonder about the ability of Earl and Joan to compete with such displayed talent. Nevertheless, we were hopeful that they could pull it off, make us proud, which would go a long way in lifting our spirits at a time when positive emotions were declining, and homesickness was beginning to dominate our consciousness.

Finally, the moment we had been waiting for arrived, and Earl and Joan glided unto the dance floor, dressed in mismatched colours, Earl in dark pants and a blue shirt, Joan in a white blouse and yellow skirt, and began their routine, in earnest, to the applause of all the Jamaican students as well as several Cubans in the theatre. Their routine was exquisite, and flawless and left the audience in awe—we were pleasantly surprised.

The number of contestants were six pairs: one Jamaican and five Cubans. The contest went on for more than an hour; each duet danced to three different songs in Spanish, after which there was a delay in getting the results and when it was announced, everyone was in disbelief. To the chagrin of the audience, Earl and Joan's routines were awarded third place. Spontaneously, there were shouts of wrong and fraud coming from all corners of the theatre, but no one took any time to explain the decision to us. However, we Jamaicans concluded that it was a fix because it would have been embarrassing to admit that Jamaicans defeated Cubans at their own game.

Chapter 16

Sunday evening at about 6 p.m., we had already eaten dinner, and I was in bed under my mosquito net reading a book, "History Will Absolve Me," by Fidel Castro Ruz, and unexpectedly, I heard Belkis shouting my name at the top of her nasal voice. Like so many times before, I peered through the window's louvres, and she spotted me and motioned with one hand for me to come down from my dormitory to the first floor to meet her. I wasted little time in getting into the appropriate attire and hurried down to the first floor. As I reached the bottom of the stairs, at the last flight of the staircase, she was there with her captivating smile and glowing face. She sprung into my arms with her feet off the ground and was within a hair's breadth of toppling me over. Luckily, I was in a walking position with my feet in tandem, and I was able to keep them firm, after a bit of wobbling, on the ground. Almost *instantaneously, she lodged a succulent smacker on my lips and rubbed her warm face against mine.*

She whispered softly in my ears, "I brought you something, mi amor," and motioned to a purple bag resting on the edge of the ramp leading into the theatre. Without letting go of me, she said, "Go on and open it."

I reached for the bag with one hand and the other keeping her from weighing down too much on my shoulder. I picked up the bag, and she let go of me, then took the bag away and began removing its contents. One by one, she pulled out the items: guava pie, dairy cheese, soda, and cigarettes.

She looked me in the face and asked, "Do you like them?"

I nodded as well as answered in words by saying, "You made my day, but I had no idea you were going to bring me stuff." I went on to say, "You shouldn't have gone through the trouble and expense."

She looked at me with an air of disappointment and said, "So you don't like them; well, I must tell Mummy that you don't like the gifts she bought for you."

I said, "Oh no, I like them very much, but I didn't want you or your Mummy to incur unnecessary expenses."

She countered by saying: "You told me you weren't eating properly because you don't eat pork, and it is always on the menu."

At that moment, I said to her: "Okay, you win; you can bring me things whenever you are so inclined. I appreciate it a lot. You are a darling."

Once we were settled on the gifts, we decided to sit and talk for a while before heading off to our respective dormitory for the evening, and so we sat on the edge of the ramp to the theatre and talked about how we spent the weekend while we were apart from each other.

Neither of us had engaged in any activity away from our domicile; our descriptions were similar: we read books and newspapers, watched television, and in my case, I played soccer and chess with my colleagues.

"I slept and assisted my madrastra with the household chores. While conversing with her, I let slip that I have a boyfriend who is from Jamaica and is studying at my college."

My stepmother was surprised and asked me, 'Estás loca? When are you going tell your father?'

"When I find an opportune time, I told her."

She said her stepmother laughed and said, 'I hope you know what you are doing.'

"In matters of the heart, one never really knows what the right thing is to do; besides, I have already introduced him to my mother, brothers and sister, and they have raised no concerns, at least not with me," she said she told her stepmother.

I was aware that my situation with Belkis was a delicate one because of the differences between us in culture, language, and customs. Perhaps the most distressing was the fact that my time in Cuba was limited and task-oriented, and sooner rather than later, I would have to say goodbye and return to Jamaica. However, if she was bothered by it, Belkis never showed it, never wanted to discuss it, and it seemed she was contented to live each day as if it were her last—She was a very carefree girl and did not dwell on what ifs of the future or negative thoughts. Our conversations varied from astronomy to life sciences, nature, culture, family, and movies, arts, and relationships—certainly not our situation.

Even though I was concerned about our tomorrow, I kept my feelings buttoned up because I was in love and wanted to be. My feelings for Belkis were extraordinarily strong, deep inside me. I had no control. My emotions were immensely elevated, and I often wondered, when I was alone, in deep meditation, shut off from others and things, trying to reach a place of calm and serenity, how did I get where I was? Was there anything I could do about the situation? Did I even want to?

As the days rolled on, Belkis and I continued our rendezvous, and we did our best to see each other as often as we could: afternoon and evening. We were inseparable.

One morning after physical education classes, we were talking on the level section of the ramp to the auditorium, and suddenly, we got the urge to kiss, and hence, we entered the auditorium hugging and kissing, unaware of, and not checking, whether anyone was inside the auditorium. Unexpectedly, a voice rang through; it was the second assistant director, "Students, you are on college property; please cut out your brazen behaviour."

There were also several students taking dictation from him; when we cast our attention in their direction, all eyes were on us, waiting for our reaction. However, we stopped kissing, let go of each other, looked each other in the eyes, then hung our heads and quickly disappeared from the view of the onlookers.

Once we were out of the auditorium, we began laughing, "We must never again be caught in such a compromising position on campus," I told Belkis.

Belkis responded, "We should make ourselves scarce for a couple of days; I'm embarrassed."

"We need to cool off a bit until we are comfortable knowing whether or not the matter is going to be taken up at the college's administration level," I said.

On Friday, late afternoon, before Belkis left for her home, she sought me out and requested, "Let me take your uniform home for washing and ironing. I want to do things for you, and I noticed that you are wearing your uniform with wrinkles, and that must stop."

I asked rhetorically. "Are you sure you want to take on this responsibility?"

"Of course, I'm sure; otherwise, what would be the point of asking?" She replied.

"Wait a moment, let me get my uniform as well as some other dirty casual clothes that also need laundering, if you don't mind?" I asked.

She agreed and said, "One of my aunts who lives in the same complex as me and my father has a washing machine, and so the washing will not be done by hand, only the ironing. Please walk me to the bus stop."

I didn't hesitate, "Gladly. I like being with you, and it gives me the opportunity, which I'm always longing for, to hug and kiss you, far away from the nosey eyes on campus," I told her.

Just before we reached the bus stop, she asked me, "What are you going to do this weekend?"

"I'm going to hang out with the other guys, play soccer, dominoes, and read, and review my assignments," I told her.

"If ever you feel bored over the weekend, give me a call," she said.

During that weekend, I was not feeling bored, but I called her anyway just to hear her sweet, charming nasal voice and chat with her, even if it were only for a short period of time. At about 3 p.m. on Saturday afternoon, I went over to a restaurant near the college campus and called Belkis.

"I'm happy to hear from you. I'm just about finishing up the laundry and hanging the clothes out to dry. What are you up to?" She asked.

"Nothing important that I couldn't leave or interrupt. If you have no big plans for the evening, could we go to the movies? We could go to the movie theatre, which isn't far from the college campus," I impressed upon her.

"We would meet at the bus stop at 6 p.m., just outside the theatre, across the street," she said.

I got to the bus stop a little early, which gave me enough time to get into the line to purchase the movie tickets before Belkis arrived.

The bus carrying Belkis arrived at about 6:15 p.m., which gave us about 15 minutes before the start of the movie and time to go to the Coppelia and buy ice cream. No food or drinks were allowed in the theatre, so we ate the ice cream in less than 10 minutes and were soon seated, away from the screen, in the back row, where it was dark. We could barely see the individuals on either side of us in the theatre. We held hands, Belkis, and I, in the movie, "The Heiress," starring Olivia de Havilland and Montgomery Cliff, began exactly at 6:30 p.m. About 20 minutes into the movie, with our arms around each other, suddenly I felt an arousal and leaned around in front of Belkis face and kissed her on the lips, and she whispered, "Control yourself, papi, there are people all around us."

"I don't care; besides, it is dark, and no one is paying attention to us."

"But I do; I can never be sure if anyone is looking," she said.

Though I was burning inside with desire, I heeded her request; out of respect for her feelings, I did not want to offend her in the least bit.

For the rest of the movie, I repressed my sexual urges and was content to just lean against the upper portion of her chest that was next to my neck and head—In my mind, I wondered. "If she is so careful, will

I ever get the opportunity to make love to her?" I wanted so badly to ravish her; I was beginning to get desperate. I told her, "When I'm with you, time pauses just for you and me. After meeting you, I want to live forever; if it is your wish, I want to be your slave in every way imaginable. But we aren't "bearing the fruits" I'm itching to devour."

The movie was over just before 8:30 p.m., and we both decided to chill out for a while in the nearby park before going back to our place of lodging. The evening had already faded, and night was upon us when we crossed the street and spotted an empty bench under a tree where the night's shadow was much more noticeable than anywhere else in the park. We hurried over to take possession of the bench before anyone else could deprive us of such an enviable location. We sat on the bench and began talking about the calmness of the night, shadowless sky, moonlight splendour, stars disappearing and re-emerging, and the academic year that was coming close to its end.

We were beginning to realize, without saying it out loud, that soon, I would be going back to Jamaica for at least two months over the summer for vacation, and we were going to be separated—by distance in airspace and waterway—not knowing with certainty if we would ever see each other again. We pretended as if reality was imaginary, just a surreal bliss that was devoid of purpose, meaning and importance.

Neither of us needed to express in words our feelings, the heightened emotions, transposition of warmth from my body to hers and vice versa because our embraces and kisses spoke volumes—I loved her so much it was excruciatingly painful.

As the evening wore on, I observed buses making stops close to the park where we were sitting and a lot of people dismounting them wearing shorts and thin jersey tops. "What is going on?" I asked Belkis.

"It's nothing serious, just beachgoers returning from Siboney Beach; it is like this every weekend along this street," she replied.

"What is the distance from the city to the beach?" I asked her.

"Approximately an hour and 15 minutes," she replied.

"I haven't been to the beach since my arrival in Cuba, and I would like to go to one," I told her, then asked, "Would you be interested in going to the beach with me?"

She said, "Let us talk about it during the week after I speak with my mother about it and make arrangements with her for meals and a sleepover."

I agreed. "It is time for us to return to our residences," I suggested, "Because it is getting late, can I accompany you?" I asked her.

She refused and reminded me, "The bus stops only a block away from my home. "But you be careful." We squeezed each other's hands and bade each other goodbye,

On my way, walking slowly back to the college, I stopped by the only restaurant on the street and went inside. These types of restaurants typically only serve liquor with meals to their patrons, but I inquired from one of the waiters, a white man dressed in a black and white uniform, "Can an exception be made in my case? I don't want to eat; I just want to drink one beer."

"Wait a moment," he said. Shortly after, he came back and told me, "Have a seat over there," and motioned to an empty chair in the corner close to the back of the room. "You must drink the beer inside the restaurant—drinking alcohol on the street isn't permitted in Cuba."

I believe he figured out that I was a foreigner. "I wouldn't have it any other way," I replied.

He brought me the beer, which I opened by twisting off the top and put the bottle to my mouth and in one gulp, I almost half the bottle. Having noticed me, the waiter returned to ask me, "Would you like another?"

"No, I'm not big on drinking alcohol," I replied.

He smiled and walked away.

The remainder of the beer in the bottle took me almost 20 minutes to complete, my thoughts about Belkis were running wild: 'This luck of mine was no good; why did I have to fall in love? And even more ill-fated, why did I have to fall in love with a virgin? There were so many girls around, in the college, in the city, on the streets, who were showing interest in me, but I ignored them and stuck with this one girl with whom I was not hitting the bonanza.

I finished the beer, paid the waiter, and gave him a 10 cents coin for tip. He thanked me, and I slowly got up from my seat, shook his hand and exited the restaurant. As I journeyed back to the college, the feeling of melancholy began taking hold of my being, and I again started thinking about how tender, kind, loving and warm Belkis had been to me. Somewhat selfish in my thinking, I just wanted to see her again; Sunday could not come soon enough; I was impatient for her to return to the college, to hear her nasal carrying voice below my dormitory, calling me, and beckoning to me with her hand to come down.

Chapter 17

Sunday did arrive, and this time, I did not wait for Belkis to come and shout me down from my dormitory, I went and sat on the steps at the back of the college where I knew normally, she entered from the street.

At about 6 p.m., I saw her coming from afar, and as our eyes made contact, we smiled; I got to my feet, and she began walking briskly. She had her bag over her shoulder, my uniform on a wire rack in one of her hands, and we dashed into each other's arms. We did not kiss, but we looked each other in the eyes, greeted each other gently, courteously, and affectionately. To smother the temptation, we quickly pulled ourselves apart. We began talking about how much we missed each other between Saturday night and the present time. While we were talking, Belkis handed me my uniform and asked me to hold it while she took *something from her bag. She took from the bag a sandwich wrapped in paper and handed it to me.*

"I made it for you, and I hope you like it," She beamed.

"Thank you, can I start eating it?"

"Certainly, it is yours, and I hope you will before it gets stale."

I bit into the sandwich and began chewing. "Would you like a bite?" I asked her. She hesitated for a moment, said nothing, but took my hand and brought it up to her mouth and dug into the sandwich for a small piece. I protested, "Certainly, you can do better than that!"

"I have just eaten, and I'm full—this is yours," she responded.

We hung around for a while, sitting on the side of the steps beside each other without blocking the passersby. I told her about my stopping at the restaurant for a beer on Saturday night.

"Did you have something to eat? How many beers did you drink? How late did you stay out? Did you see anyone I know? What time did you get to the college?" she questioned me.

I told her as it happened blow by blow, "One beer, no food, I stayed at the restaurant for about 25 minutes, I didn't see anyone you and I know, and I arrived at the college at 9:30 p.m."

I did not inquire about her Saturday evening because I was not about to engage in tit-for-tat. Besides, I had complete confidence that if she had anything to tell, she would not hold out on me. At about 7 p.m., we agreed that it was time to call it a night, I thanked her for cleaning my uniform, embraced her, pinched her arm, ran the fingers of my free hand down her cheek and said goodbye, and she smiled at me, and I at her.

"Until tomorrow," we both uttered simultaneously.

The following day, Monday after her theory classes, Belkis saw me in the corridor between dormitories and stopped me to talk about her math class, "I'm having difficulty understanding the material; I'm going to fail the subject if I don't get help, and what can I do to improve my knowledge in mathematics?" she asked me.

"Bring your assignments with you this evening to the overpass; let us see if we can figure out a way forward. You must remain at the college, acquiring knowledge and a credential, and of course, I want to continue seeing you."

We met on the overpass and agreed to go into one of the classrooms. It was empty, and quiet, but occasionally teachers and maintenance staff did their rounds to check in and see what students were up to— if there were any present.

Belkis brought the pieces I had asked her to bring, and I leafed through her books, assignments and noted the teacher's concerns and where she was making errors or failing to perform the assigned tasks. She was having difficulties conceptualizing the subject matter, Algebra particularly, methods to help her use factors, completing squares and using the quadratic formula to solve equations. I supported and tutored Belkis almost every evening from then until the semester ended, and the final exam was held. In spite of her challenges in mathematics, needing support, and tutoring, Belkis was successful on her math examination—she scored 85% on her final examination and 73% on the course overall. Thanks to my insisting that she practises the sample problems every day, and at every available opportunity.

Chapter 18

We agreed to go to the beach on Saturday. Belkis suggested the meeting time; she wanted to wash and dry our clothes before leaving for the beach because it was likely we would not be returning early that afternoon—and if so—on Sunday, she would only have to do the ironing. We met at 11:30 a.m. at the bus stop across the street from the one where we saw the beachgoers dismounting from the bus the previous Saturday night.

The bus arrived almost on time—two minutes behind —and Belkis was on it, sitting at a window seat, smiling—she got my attention and beckoned for me to get on board the bus. I mounted the bus to find that she unofficially reserved the seat next to her for me by placing her bag on it to ensure it was not taken by any of the other passengers. I sat down, greeted her, put my arms around her, and kissed her on the cheek.

"Have you gotten your chores done according to your plan?" I asked her.

"Yes, my cousin was kind enough to help; the washing machine was a time saver," She answered.

I noticed several more people mounted the bus dressed in shorts, uncovered bikini tops, wearing sandals, running shoes and casual clothing; it was obvious that they were also going to the beach. Once all the passengers were on board, the driver requested, "Move to the back of the bus as much as possible, please, señores."

Once passengers cleared themselves away from the front door, the bus pulled away from the stop, and we were on our way. The bus made several stops to let off and pick up passengers until we reached the last stop to the beach. We arrived at approximately 1 p.m. and decided that we were going to have lunch before we headed into the water. There was a line-up outside the restaurant, we joined the line, but the restaurant was at capacity. We were hungry, and if we did not eat then, we would have to wait until dinner time or when we got back to Santiago, late in the evening.

We remained in the line until it was after 2:30 p.m. before we were seated. "What would you like to order?" the waiter asked.

"White rice, chicken fricassee and fresh garden salad for both of us, please," Belkis ordered.

We waited for another 40 minutes before we were served the meal. After we were served, we ate leisurely and gave our stomachs time to digest the meal. At that time, the restaurant was close to empty, and no one was hurrying us off since lunchtime had passed.

At about 3:45 p.m., we exited the restaurant, "Let us head over to the beachfront," I told Belkis; "the water looks calm, clean, and suitable for bathing," We just needed to remove our outer layers and hop into the water. We already had our bathing suits on under our clothes.

I looked at Belkis and was amazed to see her, "Your beauty, perfectly sculpted body, well-proportioned figure, looking like a supermodel, if there is a goddess, I'm now in her presence," I remarked.

"Aren't you the romantic type?" She asked.

"Around you, I'm always romantic," I responded.

I had seen her in a swimsuit before, the night when she competed in the competition that was held at the college's swimming pool, but not this close and certainly not in the sunlight. I moved slowly towards her with the intention of cuddling her in my arms, but she ran and jumped into the water in a manner that I had only read about, like a mermaid, in a fairy tale. For several minutes, I was unable to tell where she was, I glanced around, peeking between bathers, and unexpectedly I felt pressure weighing down on my shoulders and back—I felt cold water on my body and warmness from her body against my back. I ducked under the water to lose her, but to no avail, she was too good of a swimmer. A wanna be synchronized diver who was not afraid of the water, I told myself. I did not try a second duck because I realized it was not worth the effort and so I played along with her.

Not long after, she was in front of me, with her arms around my neck and her thighs and legs tied tightly around my waist—I was shackled. She looked me in the eyes and said, "I love you, papi," and kissed me on the lips.

"Are you sure about that?" I asked her.

She pulled loose from me.

"Why do you ask if I'm sure?" she asked.

"Because you refuse to go all the way with me!"

And she returned to hug me and told me, "Don't be impetuous, we are going to make love, you and I; you *will be the first man that I have been with in my life, but it must be when I'm ready—I promise you."*

I lifted her chest high, dejected, embarrassed, bashful, dominated and somewhat exasperated; I threw her in the water away from me. I swam around her a little. We began frolicking, ducking each other, splashing the water, making short sprints, racing against each other, and competing for who could hold their breath the longest underwater. We played around until we were both exhausted.

We exited the water to lie in the sand and let our bodies absorb the sun's heat. Belkis had left a bag with some trappings against the trunk of a tree close to the beachfront, which she quickly retrieved and among its contents were a large towel and a tube of sunscreen. We coated each other's body with sunscreen and spread the towel on the ground.

"Come lie beside me," she invited me.

I hesitated a bit, but she grabbed hold of my hand and pulled me onto the towel and her body.

"Are you still mad?" she asked me.

"No, but I have needs. However, I don't wish to coerce you into doing something that you aren't yet prepared for or comfortable doing," I replied.

Though I wanted to caress her exquisite body, I restrained myself, suppressed my yearning, erased all promiscuous thoughts from my mind, and made myself content to lay my head on her chest. I contemplated the light blue sky, watched the sun slowly descending into the sea far, far, far away, and observed the yellow rays of the sunshine touching and lifting as they danced with the top of the ocean; my self-imposed discipline allowed me to control my otherwise wayward behaviour, while Belkis examined and leisurely ran her fingers through my hair and against my neck and ear.

Once the sun disappeared below the ocean, we discussed and agreed to go into the water for one last dip, wash the salt water off our bodies, got dressed, and prepared to head back to Santiago.

We went into the men's and ladies' stalls, respectively; I washed myself with fresh water, removed the wet clothing, dried myself off, put on my dry clothes and hurried out to meet Belkis once she exited the ladies' stall.

"Let us go over to the bus stop," I told her.

"We should try to catch the earliest bus possible," she said.

Within 10 minutes, we were on a bus heading home. On the bus, we sat beside each other and talked about the two hours spent at the beach and that we should do it more often because the massaging effect of the water was good for our bodies, especially since we performed a lot of physical activities at the college.

During our conversation, Belkis said to me, "I want you to come with me to Mummy because you may not make it for mealtime at the college, and I don't want you going through the night with an empty stomach."

"Is Lorena expecting me for dinner?" I asked.

"No, but she is expecting me, and whatever is left for me, I will share with you."

On that note, I remained on the bus with her until our final stop.

We descended the bus and walked with our arms around each other's waist to her mother's, and the moment we stepped onto the patio, Belkis' mother greeted us at the open door and told us, "Pasa, pasa y siéntense. I hope you guys are hungry because hay bastante comida aqui," she remarked.

I looked at Belkis inquiringly.

"Don't worry, Mummy always prepares more food than is needed," Belkis said.

"Whatever you say, my darling," I replied.

Felipe and Lionel were not home, but Gladys was, and she and Lorena prepared the table and meal for us to eat. We washed our hands in a large palangana and dried them in the clean toalla provided by Lorena and sat down around the table. The meal was placed on the table, and the menu included: chickpeas and white rice, chicken fricassee, salted avocado in some sort of cooking oil—I did not inquire what kind—and ice-cold water.

I served myself a modest amount of food; Belkis and I set about eating, and Lorena reminded us: "There is a lot more food, so don't be shy."

I ate and told them that it was delicious—it was the truth.

"I wish I could eat more, but I have already had enough," I told them.

Belkis had herself a large serving, but she did not go for a second helping. Once we were done eating, Belkis told me, "Sit and wait for me in the living room while I clear the table of the dishes."

Lorena told her, "Leave them; I'm going to do them."

Belkis would not relent, and she washed the dishes and was soon sitting in my lap. She inquired, "Are you full and satisfied?"

"Very much so," I responded.

"Good, because I want you to be pleased," she said.

Neither Lorena nor Gladys came to sit with us in the living room; Belkis turned on the old black and white television, and we watched a Cuban soap opera for about 20 minutes and then began making out. Soon the fatigue from the long day, swimming at the beach, and the desire to lie down and sleep was purged from my corps, and I was extremely excited. We kissed, hugged, and caressed each other's body, Belkis, and I. I looked into her eyes, and they were drowsy; her lips were larger than usual, her face glowed, and the tan she acquired at the beach was pronounced on her skin. Suddenly, one of my hands was in her bosom and easing out her breasts from her bra, and she did not protest, so I began kissing them, put her nipples in my mouth, sucked them and rubbed my face against her warm upper body.

I heard her breathing heavily, panting, throbbing, and moaning softly, and I noticed her body shifting around, expanding, and contracting, and the heat leaving both of our bodies was mesmerizing. She groped my crotch and sucked and squeezed hard on my tongue, and my hand travelled slowly between her legs up to and touched her mound; she pulled back from my hand and then settled back down, I repeated the action, only this time, my hand lifted her panties, and I ran my finger over her aroused bud, pressed, rubbed against it. She whispered in my ear, "Papito, don't penetrate me, please."

I obeyed her and reminded myself that Lorena and Gladys were inside the house, and we needed to be respectful. However, I knew that she was enjoying my antics, so I continued running my fingers over her aroused love bud. She rocked her hips rhythmically to my kneading fingers on her bud; I occasionally flicked her petals teasingly; suddenly, her body contracted forcefully, she climaxed and shuddered like seismic waves. She sighed heavily as if a huge weight had been lifted off her being. In delight, she kissed my face all over and with a beautiful smile, whispered in my ear,

"Thank you, mi amor."

"You are welcome."

"Do you want me to hacerte la paja?" she asked in a whisper.

"No, I want to make love with you."

"Be patient."

But I knew then something had changed, and I told myself, It would not be too long before I sail her pleasure island—little did I know, I was in uncharted waters, and I would have to hone my navigating skills a lot more before I could sail into her harbour.

The academic year was ending, and soon I would be going to Jamaica for a two-month vacation; no Belkis, no cuddling, no rush of blood to my vital organs, no elevated body temperature, no trembling fingers exploring forbidden places, no necking in the park or at her mother's house and at the bus stops.

Just hours before I left Cuba for Jamaica that summer, I learned from a friend that Belkis desperately wanted to consummate our relationship, but she was scared that once I slept with her, I would lose interest in her and move on to another girl. I was told that she and a few of her girlfriends rented a beach cabin with the intention of giving me a goodbye present, but she got cold feet and abandoned the idea.

Chapter 19

We had two visits from Jamaican officials during the final leg of the semester, none before and only once after—except for a brief, surprise stopover by the Jamaican Prime Minister just before the 1980 plebiscites—during our four years in Cuba, they were members of the People National Party Youth Organization (PNPYO), the youth wing of the governing party of the country at the time. The first visit was marked by two events: a meet and greet Saturday with all the students in Santiago, followed by a meeting with a select group of students who were members of the PNPYO from back in Jamaica. The meeting was convened at the Medical School in Santiago; sports and medical students were the only two groups of Jamaican postsecondary education students in the province at the time. The meeting was conducted over two days, Saturday, and Sunday, with intervals for meals only.

A couple of months later, another visit with two of the officials from the first visit requested to meet with us. This time the meeting was held in another province, Villa Clara, at the medical school in that province. Therefore, we, eight participants, travelled by train and bus to the medical school in Santa Clara, the capital of the province. The distance by train from Santiago to Santa Clara took about 11 hours plus about 20 minutes of bus travel in the city of Santa Clara to the medical school. Most of the journey was covered in daylight, and we had the opportunity to observe the contours of the scenic countryside that decorated the land along the wayside—sometimes as far as the eye could see and other times as near as the closest hillside or clumps of shrubs and trees. The only stops that were made were for bathroom breaks, picking up and dropping off passengers, and if rushed—and the lines were not too long—to purchase sandwiches, pork and cheese or cheese only. I had a cheese-only sandwich on one occasion for the entire journey. Like the meeting in Santiago, the meeting lasted two days with intervals for meals.

The two meetings were similar in nature: the discussion was centred around the political climate in Jamaica and a document of principles that the PNPYO was hoping to get input from us on and adopt to its mandate before the next general elections in Jamaica were held. The meetings were not student-focused; no one investigated our situation in Cuba, what our concerns were, whether we had adjusted to the Cuban social and political culture, whether we were breaking the language barrier, or any interest in knowing how we were progressing in acquiring the education that brought us to Cuba in the first place. This was disappointing, given that we were hoping that our efforts would have been recognized and encouraged, if only because we were preparing ourselves to return to Jamaica with tools ready to contribute, we physical and health education trainees, a repertoire of sporting and physical and health education programs and disciplines in the island schools and colleges, and medical students to the network of health care providers in the island.

The information we received about the political climate on the island, through the media, was chilling, heart-wrenching, sad, uninspiring, and cold-blooded. Our discussion at the meeting only made the distressing situation even worse and concerning, given that our families, relatives, and loved ones were the subjects of violence and cruelty to both their persons and property.

We learned that because of direct political violence, over five hundred people lost their lives in two months, as well as hundreds of injuries to people. There were attacks on the governing party offices in several parishes and its headquarters in Kingston, destruction and burning of persons' home–a senior citizens' residence was burned to the ground, and several of its occupants lost their lives due to the fire. Roadblocks were set up, and fires set up and burned on most of the veins and arteries leading in and out of the city of Kingston daily to prevent travel. These were all activities to bring down the government or to convey the message that the country was in chaos, and disarray and the governing party was incapable of maintaining peace, stability, order, and control.

As a result of these developments, the PNPYO wanted to revise its mandate document to include measures that would strengthen the organization regardless of the outcomes of the upcoming elections. We spent several hours discussing the language in the document and weighing the pros and cons until we were all comfortable with the implication of the amendments. In the final analysis, we agreed that it would have been important for the organization to continue supporting the governing party. And given the political climate in the island the government should be encouraged to use the security forces to protect persons, and properties and prevent the escalation of violent behaviours and activities. No militia group should be tolerated, or sanctioning of any retaliatory measures, outside the purview of the legitimate security forces of the island.

The meeting ended Sunday late afternoon, and the officials disappeared without a formal goodbye, and we returned to our respective residences. Those who were from the sports college in Santiago, up on our return, were met with the ire of our colleagues. In my case, I was asked to explain why the entire student body was not included in the discussions. Further, a debrief was demanded of what had been discussed in private over the course of both meetings. I was told that "We are all Jamaicans and had the right to know what the content of the meetings were." I explained that the meetings were confidential and were germane only to members of the PNPYO. That explanation seemed satisfactory to the challengers, and the anger dissipated.

Chapter 20

The pressures of the final examinations did not dampen some of my colleague's propensity to roam the streets and the community, frequenting restaurants and bars as well as visiting the homes of acquaintances, maintaining relationships and friends they had assembled over the course of the year. They took the opportunity to sell what clothes they had remaining. In the meantime, my little discussion group took some time to reiterate the importance of finishing the year on a high note.

"We need to leave Cuba satisfied that we've completed the academic year successfully," Heather remarked.

"Let's work hard to be prepared, be confident, to succeed honestly, and be proud, because it is critical that no one attempts any cheating," Andrea pointed out.

"We all know that it is important to avoid cheating because if were caught, that would mean the end of our scholarship. We vowed at the outset that no one would support anyone in any dishonest conduct so as not to tarnish our name in Cuba, and that still stands as far as I'm concerned." I chipped in.

"The work isn't hard; I did some of these things in high school, they may not be exactly the same, but they are close enough to give me a flashback. The Spanish is my biggest problem," Heather said.

"My biggest fear is the gymnastic equipment. In Jamaica, my sports experience was limited to soccer and running, and I don't know if I will ever get the hang of these things," James said.

"No one is expecting us to perform like professional athletes; I believe the expectation is that we execute the technique correctly; just do the best we can. Effort sometimes goes a long way in bettering the impossible," Andrea assured him.

In the area of physical activities, we had only two subjects to prepare for, aerobics, gymnastics and athletics. On the one hand, in athletics, we had to prepare for long jump, high jump, throwing javelin and shot-put, which were not difficult for most of us except for a few of the ladies. On the other hand, gymnastics was much more challenging for several of us, given our inexperience, ignorance, and lack of familiarity with the sport.

"Even if we don't completely dominate the movements and techniques, we must demonstrate our commitment to overcome the obstacles," Heather declared.

"I know there's a certain amount of nervousness because of the unknown, but if we pull together and support one another, we can overcome," Tom continued.

"You're quiet, John," Andrea remarked.

"I've nothing to add. I agree with what you're all saying," John responded.

"How about you, Gregory," Andrea Asked.

"I'm cool; I'll be okay because I'm getting help from two of my teachers who always encourage me to approach them whenever I've difficulty or need something explained or clarified," Gregory responded and added that his concern is everyone's: "the availability of the gym equipment."

"We've to move quickly to take possession of them once they're not in use by the Cuban students. There's a shortage of sports equipment in Cuba," John finally intervened.

"We need to stake out the gymnasium and sports ground, wait for opportunities, and take possession of equipment and space once the Cuban students are disengaged from them. We'll have to put in a lot of time and effort," I told the group.

There was no overt selfishness on display; we encouraged and assisted one another as if our lives depended on succeeding.

"I'm not prepared to carry any subjects over to the coming year," Gregory said.

"I couldn't endure the humiliation of having to join a first-year Cuban group to achieve the required credits," Tom joined in.

"I'm prepared to hit the books at every available opportunity," I told the group.

To prepare for the theoretical exams, night after night, most of us remained in the dormitories, lights on, under our mosquito nets, in complete silence, reviewing the material from the beginning to the end of the semester. During the day, we got together in small groups discussing possible scenarios, practising mock questions, picking one another's brains, and ensuring we were all comfortable with the material that was presented to us in Spanish over the course of the semester. We even solicited the help of teachers whenever it was possible after revision classes to ensure we grasped the material they imparted to us. Every teacher held revision classes to review their material because it was as important to them as it was to us that everyone succeeded in finishing the year successfully. We made the necessary effort, worked together, studied hard, asked for help, prepared ourselves for the final exams and were successful in achieving the required grade point average. Our grades were averaging 75 to close out the year.

Chapter 21

In 1979-80, there was a reasonable amount of pastime activities once we became immersed in the Cuban society. The most salient of them all was the carnival celebration, we able to experience the pre-carnival celebration, which commemorated the attack on the Moncada Army Barracks on July 26, 1953, in Santiago, which started the Cuban revolution and ended with Fidel Castro Ruz as the president of the Cuban people. In addition, there was the Cubans' favourite pastime—baseball. The regular season ran from November to April, and playoff games began in May and ended in July. Home games usually attract thousands of people from all over the province.

Aside from the in-person attendance, games were usually broadcast on national and local television and radio stations; Cubans could and usually tuned in to see or hear the play-by-play description of the games. Even those watching the games in-person brought their radios with them into the stadium to listen to the commentators describe play in real time. The description by the commentators of spectacular actions on the part of the players was quite riveting at times—their words were spellbinding.

The stadium was always clean, with no sign of trash, mud, bottles, or waste. Even though smoking was permitted inside the stadium, neither carousers nor alcohol was allowed inside the stadium. Notwithstanding, in the stadium, fans often got rowdy and excited when they approved or disapproved of any actions on the field from the players of both teams.

During the games, the streets were scanty, save for children, people going to and coming from work, buses running irregular schedules, and a few non-baseball fans loitering on the street corners—especially couples taking advantage of the empty and lonely streets to make out. Making out on lonely dark street corners—behind lush, treed areas—was another favourite Cuban pastime.

I missed a few games, and sometimes, on those nights, I walked the parks and side streets. I heard the lovers' rumblings as they got consumed in heightened pleasure. Cubans, at the time, mostly lived in single-family homes, generally pre-revolutionary dwellings, in need of significant repairs, and their income did not permit them to enjoy the luxuries of hotels very often—once per month would be a modest statement. Therefore, especially the young, sometimes lovers would do their hanky-panky on street corners without concern for passersby. These romantic encounters were noticeably more frequent after the end of the academic year and as carnival time approached. As I had learned the following year, alcohol, food, and sex were staples from about July 12 to 26.

Precipitously, after the end of classes, we were advised that we would be leaving for Jamaica in a week: Thursday, July 3, 1980. Our departure was set for 5 p.m., and we were told to prepare for the bus trip to the wharf at approximately 3 p.m. We were all excited at the prospect of going home after a full year away.

Those of us in the first year of the four-year physical and health education program were hopeful that we would return to Cuba in September 1980, after the two-month vacation and separation from the relationships that we had kindled in the local Cuban communities.

We were sad to leave Cuba, the friendship we developed within the local communities, and the teachers at the college. We became part of an extended family because several of them invited us into their homes to enjoy their hospitality and friendship and share what little they had, sometimes at great inconvenience to themselves. The teachers, especially, expressed regret that we were leaving; the sadness in their voices was noticeable, along with the melancholic expression on their faces, even though we were due to return in two months' time.

My colleagues wasted little time in announcing to their friends the date of our departure, and before long, the college was being overran by individuals from the streets. On the one hand, though many came to express their discontent that we were going home, others were on campus to make requests for things: clothes, shoes, and electronics, to be brought back for them upon our return. I learned of these entreaties by overhearing conversations between Cuban and Jamaican students, Jamaican students among themselves, and even from our teachers, some of whom were themselves making requests for specific items, including music cassettes and tapes and movie videos. On the other hand, several of my colleagues went on shopping sprees, acquiring household items such as pressure cookers, tabletop stoves, books, magazines, tapes with political speeches of Fidel and Che Guevara, and paintings. They decided to take advantage of low-cost items, especially since goods were priced according to the purchasing power of the Cuban people.

On July 3, 1980, at about 3 p.m., we gathered around the designated college bus that was to take us to the wharf. A few teachers and a couple of individuals from the college's administration were present to see us off. Otherwise, the campus was empty. We boarded the bus and departed, with most of us wearing a sombre and solemn expression on our faces as we began our journey away from the place, we had called home for the past year and proceeded towards the point where the ship was to set sail from to Jamaica.

The bus was slowly driven along busy streets, allowing us to view the streets and nearby buildings, wave to pedestrians, and savour the beauty of what was perhaps the most charming colonial city in all of Cuba. Minutes before the bus pulled into the parking lot, several members of our group began rendering verses from one of Bob Marley's songs, "One Love," which before long moved everyone to join and chant verses which were very popular in Jamaica at the time.

On arrival at the wharf, we noticed Cubans from the local communities and the arrival of the students from the medical school. The ship was already in the harbour and appeared to have many travellers on board. I later found out that all Jamaicans studying in Cuba—Havana, Villa Clara, and Santiago de Cuba—would travel together on the same ship to go home. We unloaded our luggage, suitcases, bags, and boxes from the bus and tarried to chat with our Cuban friends who had come to see us off and bid us safe travel. Cubans and Jamaicans alike huddled, embraced, and kissed amid tears, smiles, and a fair amount of laughter.

Then came the announcement that we should approach the luggage compartment with our belongings for them to be stored, and we also should proceed to the cabin area and get settled for departure.

We quickly made final gestures to our Cuban well-wishers and ascended the ramp into the ship, and in a matter of seconds the outside world was invisible.

In the ship, old friends and acquaintances began to chatter about experiences in Cuba, including food, entertainment, friends, hospitality, transportation, roads, architecture, lovers, relationships, off-springs, prejudices, racism, and beaches, and what it was like to be going home after a year away from Jamaica.

Soon it was approximately 5 p.m., and the captain ordered the ship anchors to be pulled. In an instant, I felt the ship drifting away from Cuban shores. We were advised that the journey would last approximately 12 hours. Furthermore, we were shown the staircase to the deck area and told that we could go back and forth if we were so inclined. The vast majority of us remained seated and continued our chatter. In addition to getting reacquainted and exchanging our opinions on the political climate in Jamaica, we discussed current affairs, which according to several media reports, were not encouraging.

Our concerns were compounded by the fact that within a few months, Jamaicans were going to the polls to elect a new government—the ruling political party was in danger of being voted out of office, putting at risk the relationship between Cuba and Jamaica that had been established and fostered over the previous eight years and made possible the opportunity for us to study in Cuba.

had been established and fostered over the previous eight years and made possible the opportunity for us to study in Cuba.

Chapter 22

About a week prior to our return to Cuba, the Jamaican Ministry of the Public Service sent us each a telegram reminding us of the departure date. It appeared as if, within the twinkling of an eye, two months had vanished. The summer vacation was over; it was that time again to leave behind family, loved ones and friends, and the jewel of the Caribbean. On the day of our departure, those of us who were returning to Cuba arrived at the Norman Manley International Airport on time and ready for another year in Cuba. However, we were anxious about the political climate in Jamaica and the dreaded prospect of the governing party of the day losing the general elections and putting our fate in jeopardy.

The opposition party made no secret of its intention to sever diplomatic relations with Cuba in favour of aligning itself more closely with the United States. Friday, August 29, 1980, a chartered Air Jamaica flight returned the medical students and us to Cuba to begin the second year of our study program, but not the other group of sports students who, according to their curriculum, remained in Jamaica to undertake their practice teaching. They were slated to complete two six-month stints of practice teaching in Jamaica: the first in the third year and the second in the fourth year of their program.

Before going through customs, I could not determine if everyone were present to make the trip back to Cuba. However, once we were in the departure lounge, I did a quick headcount and saw that all 31 of us were checked in, and almost everyone was engaged in conversation. Listening intently, one could overhear about different events, encounters, and experiences that saturated our summer vacation. Students talked about working and earning money so that they could purchase items that were scarce or unavailable in Cuba, and travelling to the United States, the Cayman Islands, and Canada, going to the various beaches, visiting the Blue Mountains, and many other tourist attractions in Jamaica. After about thirty minutes in the departure lounge, we were advised by a female voice over the public address system to proceed to Gate 3 for check-in on the Air Jamaica flight to Havana, Cuba, and receive our boarding passes. We checked in our hand luggage, showed our passports for verification, exited the terminal, ascended the airstairs, entered the aircraft, showed our boarding pass, and were told which seat number each of us was assigned.

After one hour and thirty minutes airborne, the plane began to descend the sky. The plane touched down at approximately 7 p.m. at the José Martí International Airport in Havana. Without exiting the airport, we were hustled onto a Cubana Airline at the call of our names from a list containing all the names of those bound for Santiago de Cuba. We boarded the airline, and at approximately 8:15 p.m., we were again in the sky, this time in Cuban airspace. Then came a voice from the public address system informing us that the sky was clear, the temperature was 95 degrees Fahrenheit, the flight would be free of any turbulences, and the flight time would be one-and-one-half hours. We were served snacks while airborne: natural orange juice and sandwiches made of buns with ham and cheese and buns with just cheese alone.

At 9:50 p.m., we landed at the Antonio Maceo Airport in Santiago. Once we descended from the plane, we were led through the airport by a Cuban official, with our luggage, without having to go through customs or even show our travel documents for inspection. Outside the airport, there were two buses waiting: one for sports students and the other for medical students. We hurriedly said goodbye to the medical students and boarded our bus for the final leg of our journey.

On the bus, there were a couple of college employees, teachers, and administration workers, who made the trip because there was nothing else to do at the college. These individuals were from remote areas of the province and were provided residence at the college for them to avoid having to travel to work every day and lengthy delays because of unreliable transportation. Several of my colleagues talked with them about their vacation in Jamaica, and the Cubans described their summer break, which they said was heavily weighted on partying, carnival, beach-going, and generally having a good time.

We arrived at the college after 40 minutes and found it to be sparsely lit, desolate, empty, and showing hardly any signs of life, except for the groundskeeper and caretaker. This was expected and quite natural given that it was approximately 11 p.m. at night, and most, if not all, dwellers had already turned in for the night. Furthermore, most of the Cuban students were expected back on Sunday or Monday, just in time to restart classes on Tuesday. We quickly unloaded our suitcases, bags, and boxes off the bus, and several of us began to move our belongings from the bus to the dormitories while others kept watch to ensure that none of our items went missing mysteriously.

During the transfer of luggage, we noticed that the ladies were struggling with moving their bags, and several of us men pitched in to assist them in ascending the stairs to their dormitory on the third floor. When we finally settled in, it was almost midnight. Everyone wanted to sleep. We turned out the lights, and it was not long before we heard the PA system instructing us to come down to the canteen for breakfast. Not having gotten enough sleep, several of us were annoyed that on a Saturday morning, we were awoken early as though it was a regular day of classes.

Regardless of the sentiments, discomfort, and annoyance, it was 7 a.m., and the kitchen staff needed to get breakfast underway, so they could finish in time to begin preparing lunch and dinner. After all, it was the weekend, and they may have wanted to get home early to their families, spend time with their significant others, visit friends, bask in entertainment such as attending parties, go to the movies, or just relax. Furthermore, this was unofficially the last weekend of the summer and the time of year when those who worked in the education milieu: teachers, administrators, and support staff, began conditioning themselves for the academic year ahead of them.

We had a one-hour window in which to breakfast. Hence, we freshened up, got dressed and headed down to the canteen as quickly as possible. When we entered the canteen, the kitchen staff expressed delight in seeing us; several of them came from around the serving hatch, embraced us, kissed us on the cheeks, shook our hands, and greeted us warmly as though we were long lost family members who suddenly turned up. Once we collected our breakfast and were all seated, several of the kitchen staff came over to our tables to chat with us. One of the more courteous staff questioned me. She provided me with bread in the previous year when nothing on the menu appealed to me.

"How were Jamaica and the family?" I was asked.

"They were all fine," I replied.

"Was the family happy to see you, and did they miss you?"

"Yes, everyone was delighted to see me and wondered if I missed my home."

"What did you do in Jamaica for your vacation?" I was asked.

"I worked so I could earn money to purchase items I need," I responded.

"Were you anxious to come back to Cuba?"

"Yes, I wanted to come back so I may proceed with my studies."

"Did you miss Cuba?"

"Yes, I did; Cuba is a beautiful country."

Overall, they seemed happy to have us back—though prior to our going to Jamaica, most of them were aloof, coy, and pretended as if we were never in the college. But now they were extremely friendly and even invited us to their homes to meet their families.

After breakfast, while several of us played indoor and outdoor games, others wasted little time hanging around but instead headed for the various communities to rekindle their relationships and sought out acquaintances with whom they had arrangements and promises. Amazingly, at that time, no outsiders were to be found on campus; apparently, our arrival was a well-kept secret, thanks to the limited means of communication tools in Cuba. Electronic devices: telephones, mobile phones, and emails were not yet common household items. Letters and telegrams were the widespread available means with which to communicate, and they could not be relied on to deliver information fast and on time in Cuba. Even so, the existing relationships were entrenched, so much so that several of my colleagues did not bother to return to the campus for the rest of the day. They had lunch and dinner wherever they had been, I assumed.

As the day wore on, it was noticeable that outside visitors and a few Cuban students began trickling onto the campus. The visitors and several students inquired for several of my colleagues by name, most of whom were not on campus, while a few were around and were summoned to the ground floor corridor to report to their friends, allies, partners, and associates in clandestine activities. The remainder of the weekend was marked by these activities until Sunday evening when most of the Cuban students and several teachers rolled back onto the campus.

The air was filled with excitement, jubilation, exhilaration, and celebration as the news broke that the Jamaican students had come back. Friends, significant others, and admirers came calling and looking for those with whom they had developed close ties and agreed on promises. Furthermore, in almost every corner of the college campus, the myriads of lovers' activities were underway: conversing, kissing, caressing, hugging, and as night approached, eroticism and lovemaking were right there in the middle of things. People were catching up after a two-month hiatus. The atmosphere was like rain making an appearance and quenching the "thirst" of the earth, plants, and animals after a long and arduous drought. Not surprisingly, while the wild behaviours were underway, at about 8:30 p.m., the public address system announced it was time for all to report to their dormitories and lights must be turned off by 9 p.m.

The following day, Tuesday, we began the new academic year and semester with a full course load, nine subjects, each of which was offered at least twice per week: they were mathematics, psychology, physiological anatomy, physics, chemistry, Spanish, Marxism, pedagogy in the morning, and rhythmic gymnastics, athletics and soccer in the afternoon.

In many respects, like the past year, several of my colleagues could not see the value in doing some of the courses. They protested Marxism, chemistry, and physics vociferously in the hallways, in the dormitories, in between sessions, on courts and fields, and frequently after classes in the evening. In my view, they were oblivious to the worth of a well-rounded education, which illuminates and expands the mind, builds vocabulary, increases knowledge, provides information, and liberates the thought process.

The majority were mainly interested in physical activities without stopping to think that their future was going to be dominated by the task of facilitating children's learning which was going to require a fountain of information in order to stimulate and guide their thought processes.

Rhythmic gymnastics was particularly not well received by several of my male colleagues. They held the view that the program elements were better suited for girls and guys who were perceived as "sissies." They detested working with the hoops, ribbon, rope, and clubs and were even hesitant to practice the movements that were required to demonstrate good balance, flexibility, coordination, and strength. They participated in the classes reluctantly, lacklustre at best. They were always conscious of the possibility that their colleagues could mock them for moves that were out of sync or discordant. Suffice it to say, laughter was a common feature during most of the classes, as male students were mocked because they executed certain movements awkwardly, uncoordinatedly, unharmoniously, and clumsily.

The teacher was practically supplicating my colleagues to participate actively in the class, and she went as far as to threaten to fail them if class participation did not improve, if the exercises were not executed with evidence of sincere effort, if she were not taken seriously, and if she were not shown the respect that demonstrated appreciation.

The ladies, for their part, were not enthusiastic about participating in activities that required frequent body contact, constant running around, competitive force, rough plays, stamina, and endurance. Except for the execution of the technical elements of these activities, which were coached by the teacher in a non-competitive manner, the girl's participation was inconsistent. The girls' participation in soccer was passive. Occasionally, a couple of them joined the guys in playing scrimmage, but they avoided the rough and tumble altogether; waited for the guys on their team to deliver the ball to them, which they occasionally received but quickly lost to the opposing team. As a result, they seldom received the ball to carry to the opponent's goal. Besides, tackling the opponent for the ball was not likely for them. They constantly complained about how rough the guys were playing and whined about not regularly receiving the ball from the guys. They never perspire or get dirty during the games, which is very unusual to occur if one is actively participating in a game like soccer.

The Cuban teachers tolerated our reluctance to participate in all the required physical activities fully. They overwhelmingly graded our participation on how well we performed the technical elements of the exercises or games. For example, in soccer, it would involve heading the ball, kicking the ball with the different parts of the foot, controlling the ball with the chest, thighs, and feet, and keeping the ball up without it hitting the ground for several seconds or minutes. The teacher emphasized and encouraged us to practise the techniques while the ball was in play, but they did not put much grading weight on our execution of them during the games.

Had they graded every single aspect of our performance, several of us would have been in trouble regarding successfully completing the subject or even the physical and health education program. I assumed it was understood that there was no jack of all trades, and no one was going to impart all the various sports after graduation.

Chapter 23

Added to the vicissitudes of the new semester, I was treated to a couple of unexpected surprises. First, I was surprised by a visit from the Jamaican Prime Minister, Michael Manley, accompanied by the Cuban leader, Fidel Castro, and the Jamaican Ambassador in Havana, Cuba. And second, I was treated to a trip to Pinar Del Rio. I had no prior warning of these events, but they made me feel special and appreciated.

Early in the semester, one evening just before dinner, we were informed by Luis that the Jamaican Prime Minister was due for a visit to Santiago later in the evening, and he had asked to meet with us, the sports, and medical students. We were also told to be on the alert because as soon as it was clear that his party was approaching, we would be informed of the meeting location. This news was certainly a surprise, but it was delightful, and we were impatient for the moment to arrive. At about 8:30 p.m., in the dormitories, we received news that we should go down to the soccer field immediately. Unbeknownst to us, the helicopter carrying the Prime Minister had already touched down. We rushed down to the soccer field, still in our uniforms. It was dark, and we did not immediately recognize that anyone was present, but as soon as we got onto the field proper, I heard talking and noticed a chopper on the ground. As we drew closer, the occupants began descending. The first to hit the ground was the Jamaican Ambassador to Cuba in Havana, then the Jamaican Prime Minister, followed by Fidel Castro—talk about surprise! We had no idea that Castro was included in the visiting party.

We encircled the visitors and exchanged greetings and handshakes with them. Soon, we were having informal conversations in little groups, and my group was chatting with the Prime Minister. His focus was mainly on the economic turmoil Jamaica's economy was experiencing because of economic sabotage by specific elements within the Jamaican population. However, not long after he began to lay bare his case to us, the Jamaican Ambassador came and whisked him away, and we were left wanting to hear more.

However, Castro was still talking to students, and we joined in to listen to him. He was inquiring from individuals about their studies, which discipline they were pursuing, how long they were in Cuba, and the remainder of the time they had before completion. Suddenly, he asked: "How many Jamaicans students are in Cuba?" And at that moment, everyone went soft. No one expected such a question; therefore, none of us knew the answer, especially since we were unaware that Castro was going to pay us a visit, given that, we were not concerned about tracking that sort of information. Realizing that we did not know the answer,

Castro volunteered the answer, "There are 280 Jamaican students in Cuba undertaking professional studies." We all looked around at one another in amazement.

"How do you know that information Comandante?" a student inquired.

"I'm aware of the number of all non-Cubans in our country."

After several questions and answers, the chopper engine began roaring, the propeller turning slowly; we received well wishes and bade goodbye. The visitors ascended the chopper and waved to us, though hardly visible, because of the darkness, and soon the chopper was airborne and disappeared into the night sky. The visit lasted approximately 30 minutes—in hindsight, I concluded that it was a farewell visit from the Jamaican Prime Minister since his governing party was not looking strong for the upcoming elections.

After the visitors disappeared into the night's sky, we slowly headed back to our dormitories, talking, thinking, conjecturing, and wondering what the Prime Minister was officially doing in Cuba. It was after 9 p.m. when we arrived at the dormitories. The lights were out. The guys left the chattering outdoors and headed to our bunks in almost complete silence except for a bit of rustling from individuals looking for their nightwear. As the date for the Jamaican elections approached, the recently concluded Prime Minister's visit was not the only surprise that we were in for, or I should say, I was in for.

One week after the Prime Minister's visit, I was informed by José that I was required to attend a meeting in Pinar Del Rio, which was organized by attachés with the Jamaican Embassy in Havana. The instruction was that I was going to travel, leaving Friday evening at 7 p.m. sharp by minibus, making several stops along the way, and picking up students from Santa Clara, Matanzas, and Havana to Pinar Del Rio. Yes, the drive was long: 644 miles in a non-air-conditioned vehicle. The drive was also not smooth sailing, the vehicle having had several mechanical failures along the way—radiator overheating and gear problems. This was a pre-revolutionary vehicle that was not suited for the lengthy journey. However, both the driver and the other students and I persevered, taking things in stride, telling jokes and stories in Spanish, swearing whenever anything went wrong, and blaming the problem on the United States trade embargo. We ended up spending more than twenty hours on the road between stops, and when the minibus was not prepared to cooperate with the driver.

Along the way, we had very little to eat; no provision was made for us either to take with us on the trip or for us to stop and eat. I believe the expectation was that the drive was going to be without glitches and that we would arrive on time for a late breakfast. Even though we had money to purchase food, there was none available overnight, and the following day when the eateries were operating, everywhere was stocked with pork sandwiches only, and I had to endure hunger until we reached our destination. By the time we arrived, it was after 2 p.m. Saturday, five hours later than anticipated.

Upon our arrival, hungry, exhausted, perturbed, and anxious, we were instructed to head to the meeting room for a briefing. The meeting was convened for two days, Saturday and Sunday, on behalf of the People's National Party Youth Organization (PNPYO). Only members were invited to attend, and there were two attendees who came up from Jamaica to participate in the meeting. After the briefing, we were advised to break immediately for something to eat and reconvene in 30 minutes. We complied and had a sumptuous late lunch, with meat choices like brown stew lamb and chicken fricassee served with white rice, lettuce and tomato, and ice cream for dessert. We reconvened for approximately four hours.

The meeting was primarily focused on the pending general elections in Jamaica and the violence associated with it. We had not heard anything different from what we had discussed months before in Villa Clara, except that there was a chance that we would be able to continue our studies in Cuba regardless of the outcome of the elections. If the opposition, the Jamaica Labour Party (JLP), were to win the elections, there were no assurances that we would enjoy their support. However, the People's National Party would continue to support us as the official opposition if the Cuban government held up their part of the agreement.

We appreciated the information that was shared with us. However, we were concerned because if the new government chose to recall us as Jamaican citizens studying in Cuba, there was nothing anyone could do about it save for us to seek and obtain asylum in Cuba. Nonetheless, the meeting and the discussion provided us with an update on what was ahead of us for the next two and a half years should we choose to complete our studies in Cuba.

The two-day meeting was adjourned at approximately 3 p.m. on Sunday following a speech from one of the attendees from Jamaica. He spoke about Jamaica's last eight years under the leadership of the PNP: the achievements relating to women's and workers' rights, access to fertile farmlands, the bauxite levy in the interest of all Jamaicans, the campaign against illiteracy, rural electrification, greater access to purified running water, and more accessible roads and so on. He also talked about what our role should be in the country when we return to Jamaica: education of the masses, especially in rural communities. We got the impression that it was a foregone conclusion: the PNP was going to lose the elections.

After the speech, we were advised to go to the canteen to have a meal, and picked up some sandwiches before leaving—cheese, ham and cheese, guava cheese and roast beef. We hung around for a few minutes after the meal to say goodbye to the kitchen staff and to those who were not travelling with us back on the trip. We started out at about 4:30 p.m. making the required stops along the way to drop off the students who were not going the full distance with us. The drive back was much better, as it was hindrance free: breakdowns and mechanical problems were absent.

We slept intermittently, made small talk, and debated, lively in English, the political situation in Jamaica. Apart from washroom breaks, our only other stops were for fuel and coolant or water top ups: the engine was overheating and, by the "same token," was using up the coolant much faster than normal. However, these issues did not prevent the driver from making it to Santiago well within the normal estimated time.

The return trip took about 14 hours. By 7 a.m., we were dropping off the medical students at their residence, and at 7:15 a.m., I was descending the minibus at the sports college. I did not linger for breakfast since I was not hungry, having filled up on the sandwiches during the night that I had brought from the meeting eatery.

I dashed up the stairs to the dormitory to get a shower before class time. Physiological anatomy was the first class of the morning. Upon entering the dormitory, I noticed several of my colleagues in the common area; I greeted them and received no response; their faces were not welcoming; I went by them to my bunk, unloaded my bag, grabbed my shower towel, soap, and toothbrush, headed to the bathroom and located a vacant shower stall. After I had freshened up and finished with the bathroom, I headed back to my bunk, and no one spoke to me, and I reciprocated the silence.

Upon reaching the bunk, I lifted the mosquito net, inserted my head to hang over the bed, organized my paraphernalia, and sorted my books, pens, and pencils, which I normally kept on my bed next to my head and pillow. In those days, unlike the present, I never tossed and turned, so there was little chance of my stuff falling off the bed. When it was announced that it was class time, I strolled over to my class in silence and alone. After the class, I approached Tom. He was generally a quiet person, tall in stature, and walked with a lean posture. He was one of my sounding board buddies, but he too was behaving strangely towards me. However, he was willing to respond to my inquiries.

"What is going on? Why the silent treatment, sulking, cross appearance?" I asked him.

"Most persons were upset because, as the leader of the group, you left without informing them of your absence, destination, and nature of business. They wanted to know if there were some clandestine activities planning and connected to the elections in Jamaica. They believe that events surrounding the elections in Jamaica would impact them, and they'd a right to know," he explained.

I told him, "I was instructed by the college's administration not to communicate with anyone regarding my trip and meeting, and besides, the meeting was organized by members of the PNPYO for its members in Cuba, and it didn't in any way affect, compromise, or undermine the general Jamaican student population here." Furthermore, though I was not giving him a message to anyone, I told him, "I'm not at liberty to share details of my trip with the members of our group because the content of the meeting is organizational matters which are restricted to members only." Seemingly, he acknowledged the need for secrecy and understood my position in the matter.

Later that afternoon, when classes were over for the day, there was open hostility towards me, and several guys from the group confronted me in the common area of the dormitory. Rambunctiously, they demanded to know where I went and the purpose of my trip. One of the members even threatened me with physical violence. Somewhat shaken, I stood my ground and refused to divulge any information, only that the activity I attended was organized by the PNPYO and only members were invited. Moreover, I advised them, "If you are interested in the affairs of the PNPYO, you should become members; otherwise, buzz off the lot of you." This last remark seemed to have made an impact, and the boisterousness died down, and individuals went their separate ways with mumblings, which I was unable to decipher.

I withdrew from the common area into the dormitory and climbed into my bunk. I calmed myself down by looking through and reading an old newspaper. I did not speak to anyone for the rest of the day, and neither did I go down to the canteen for dinner. The following day the situation normalized, and everything was back to normal as though nothing had occurred. I totally understood the anxiety of the group; the elections in Jamaica were near at hand, we faced an uncertain future, and everyone was on edge as the anticipation was an imminent loss for the ruling PNP.

The elections were finally held on October 30, 1980, and the results were expected but nonetheless devastating; the governing PNP lost the elections 9 to 51 seats to the victorious JLP. This was disappointing. Melancholy rocked the group; the defeat was felt by all, and several members cried and sobbed for most of the day. Notwithstanding the demoralizing outcome of the elections, we had to and did go to classes that day, despite the uncertainty we then faced. The college's administration offered no comment even though other members of the college staff, teachers, maintenance workers, canteen, and kitchen staff as well as some students expressed their sympathies to us. Jamaica and Cuba had a very close relationship, and so the elections were monitored and discussed widely throughout Santiago.

No one came to discuss or talk to us, Cubans, or Jamaicans, about our fate in the immediate aftermath of the elections, though it was not far-fetched on the part of Jamaica. Particularly because Jamaica had no consular representative in Santiago, only in Havana, and the newly elected administration was hawkish about Cuba's role in Jamaica and made it clear that diplomatic relations between the two islands would be severed. Besides, members of the victorious JLP were, before the elections, spreading misinformation about what we were doing in Cuba. That is, Jamaican students in Cuba were being trained in guerilla combat activities.

The frustration of not knowing increased among us, and rumours spread like wildfire about what was in store for us: recalled to Jamaica, put in jail, investigated individually, and denied the opportunity to resume normal life on the island. Moreover, all of us would be blacklisted and prohibited from employment in Jamaica's public sector.

Despite the aforementioned, there were no changes in treatment and attitude of the college's administration towards us:

- We stayed out late at night as before without reprimand.
- Parties were convened for us to socialize.
- Food on weekends was mildly improved.

We were treated to the occasional out-of-province and municipal excursions. These distractions were welcomed, and most of us took advantage and participated in them. However, nothing was able to soothe the anxiety from the lack of knowledge that we experienced for the remaining two-and-three-quarter years we stayed in Cuba after the defeat of the PNP in Jamaica's general elections.

Chapter 24

Soon after our second year had started, I saw Belkis in the corridor between the administrative department and the canteen with several of her friends. I passed by them without greeting her or them, no running into each other's arms, no kissing or embracing, she did not extend greetings to me either. I purposely ignored her because I wanted to get a reaction as an uneasy jealousness consumed my mind. Had anything shady occurred in my absence? Did she miss me? Had she found a new guy? Were we going to continue our relationship? Several days went by, and we did not try to see each other, but all along, I knew it was up to me to make the first move because I was the one who went away. However, pride and distrust took hold of me. My lack of action left much to be desired, and undoubtedly, jealousy was unbounded.

The uncertainty was mesmerizing, and for a while, my judgment was impaired. Before too long, I got a grip on myself and reality and sent her a message to come and see me one afternoon at lunchtime because I had a gift for her from Jamaica. Not that she had ever asked me to bring back anything for her—she was not like that. She had never asked me for anything or made any demands of me. Even though, it was commonly discussed in the male dormitory by many of my colleagues how the Cuban girls were always asking for foreign items—clothing mainly.

Not long after I sent the message, Belkis was at the bottom of the stairs shouting for me to come down. I was in my bunk reading, so I jumped out of bed, got out of my shorts and pyjama top, put on some casual clothing, combed my afro, patted it down so that it was smooth all around, exited the dormitory and descended the stairs forgetting to take with me the gift for her.

Belkis was there with her eyes red and swollen as though she was crying, and before I could say a word, she said: "I know what you are thinking, but I'm not that kind of a girl; if I were going to discontinue our relationship, I would be sure to let you know before I hooked up with another guy. Goes to show that we don't know each other as well as we thought we did," she told me.

"You are right, I should have trusted you much more than I did, and it'll not happen again," I told her.

"I understand; the same thoughts went through my mind all summer long. The separation was unbearable. I was always lonely. I longed for your embrace. I missed your kisses. I pined for your hands and fingers, probing my body in the most intimate places. Oh, I didn't know how much you meant to me until you were out of my reach and sight. All my friends invited me to the beach and to go out at night to revel in the carnival,

but I declined all the invitations I received because I figured I wouldn't enjoy any outings without you by my side," she whispered.

"I felt the same way over the summer. I missed you. I dreamt about you over and over, and I wrote you several letters. I know you received my telegram because I received yours. The letters you may not have received because the mail is very slow between Cuba and Jamaica, but over the next few weeks, you will receive them," I told her.

At that moment, I took her into my arms and squeezed her tightly against my shivering body, and she did not protest; I recognized she was shivering too; I pushed her around in a full circle to examine if there were any physical changes; I lifted her off the ground to determine if she had gained or lost any weight, she did not, she remained the way I had left her, I ran my fingers through her hair; caressed her cheek and neck and pulled her in against my body and kissed her with all the tenderness that I possessed then, and she reciprocated with warmness and excitement which I was happy to receive.

We took no notice of the audience that we were entertaining, even though they made every effort to let us know that we were being observed. We reminded ourselves that we were still on college campus, and we pulled apart; also, because lunchtime was over, we had to go to class. We agreed to meet again after dinner, about 7 p.m.

"I will bring your gift down at that time," I told her.

She smiled and said, "Anytime you are ready, I will be waiting."

After dinner and a quick freshen up, I ambled over to our meeting place with the little bag containing the gifts for Belkis. She was not there yet, and I sat on our usual concrete bench and waited for her while other students passed by and greeted me.

"Waiting for Belkis? Don't be impatient, she will be here soon, she is talking to a couple of girls in the corridor downstairs," one of them told me.

"Thank you," I told her.

They laughed amongst themselves and continued on.

Not long after, Belkis came running up the stairs and onto the overpass and out of breath, "I'm sorry, papi. I would have gotten here earlier, even before you, but I was detained by two of my classmates who wanted to know if we were still together and what you had brought me from Jamaica—inquisitive the lot of them."

Without hesitation, no small talk, no canoodling, no wisecrack, I just handed her the bag containing her gifts.

She thanked me and said, "I'm not going to open the bag now; I will, when I get back to the dormitory."

But I insisted because I wanted to know then what would be her reaction. She relented and opened the bag and took out the items; shoes, blouses, skirts, underwear—my sister purchased them for me—and a make-up kit. She leaned over against me and kissed me on the cheek.

"They are beautiful, papi," she said,

And I asked, "Do you like them?"

"Yes, but I don't believe the shoes will fit; they are too small," she responded.

She kissed me again and said: "Don't look so disappointed; I can get rid of them easily; my cousins will find buyers for them unless you want to take them back."

"No, you do whatever you wish with them; they are yours," I told her.

She returned the items to the bag and leaned against my shoulder, pulled my face around to hers, leaned in, and kissed me long and tenderly on the lips.

"So, how did you spend your vacation? What did you do for fun? Had you any romantic encounters?" she asked.

"I was too busy working and thinking about you," I told her.

"What kind of work have you done?" she inquired.

"I was delivering baked products to shops and supermarkets. I was on the road every day and, for most days, 12 hours or more. I practised speaking Spanish in front of my mirror. I visited family and friends. I played some soccer over at the youth club that I was involved with before I came to Cuba in 1979. I occasionally spoke to my mother on the phone," I told her, then asked: "What did you do over the holidays."

"Mostly, I relaxed. I read five books. On the last night of the carnival, my cousins, their boyfriends, and I went out, near our home, to listen to music bands play. We danced and observed the party revellers dancing and shouting in the streets," she explained.

We remained on the overpass until it was time for us to turn in for the night, according to the public address system. I walked with her to the bottom of the staircase to her dormitory, embraced and kissed her good night, and I told her to dream about me; I waited for her to disappear up the stairs and then headed over to my dormitory. That night my mind was awash in thoughts about how long I would have to wait to make love to her. I asked myself, "What are the right things to say and the best time to bring the subject up with her?" All because I was aware that she was ready to make the leap, though I did not hear it directly from her.

Further on the subject, I schemed in my mind, tossed, and turned in the bunk, but the ideas were not flowing for me, and I eventually went into deep breathing and meditation; without realizing it, I fell asleep, and then I was awoken by the public address system instructing us to go to the dining room because breakfast was ready and serving. I went to the bathroom, freshened up and put on my uniform, and slowly walked downstairs; when I hit the landing at the bottom of the stairs, I recognized Belkis; she was sitting on one of the concrete benches across from the entrance to the canteen, making eye contact with me, she stood up and walked briskly towards me, with a bounce in her stride as if she was stepping on a hot surface barefooted. She stopped immediately in front of me, took my hand, and led me into the canteen; we were among the second set of students that morning; no need for a lineup.

"We are going to sit together for breakfast today, for the first time on campus since we have been dating," she said.

"Whatever you say, my love, you are in control."

As we walked hand in hand up to the serving hatch, I could "feel" the piercing eyes all around; everyone was staring at us, including the kitchen staff. Unlike Belkis, I glanced around at the onlookers.

Belkis protested, "Don't let them know you are aware of their gawking."

Upon reaching the serving hatch, and while I was in the process of collecting my breakfast, one of the kitchen staff blurted out: "Are you guys an item?" I didn't respond,

"Is there anything wrong with that, inquisitive gossipmonger?" Belkis asked.

The lady did not respond; we took our breakfast and ambled over to a table and sat down to eat. I did not realize it then, but afterward, days later, I started thinking about that little exhibition, Belkis was showing off, letting everyone know that we were together, no more secret meetings on campus, from now on, all in the open, this is her man, and she was proud to be with him.

After breakfast, I accompanied her to the bottom of the staircase to her dormitory; we kissed on the cheeks. Just before leaving, Belkis reminded me that we were included among a group of students who were scheduled for a visit to a historical site—the Moncada Barracks. I said to her, "I remember." She smiled and ran up the stairs, and I went to my dormitory to get ready for class.

Late that afternoon, an announcement came over the public address system asking the students who were going on the tour to come down to the parking lot. Two buses were in the lot with their engine running, and we were called by names to each bus, Belkis and I were on different buses, and we were disappointed. Nonetheless, we boarded, and off we went. At Moncada, we walked in groups and looked around at photos of fallen revolutionaries, Belkis and I separated, of course, from one another. About 30 minutes after our arrival, we were asked to gather in a semi-circle facing a podium with a lectern and microphone installed. Not long after we had gathered, an official from the Municipal government approached the microphone, greeted, and welcomed us, and began speaking about the significance of the day in the development of the Cuban Revolution. His message focused on the achievements of the revolution and the responsibilities of the current generation as educators.

After the speech, we were told to board the buses to head back to the college. The boarding was not as orderly as when we departed the college. We could board either of the two buses if we could find seats.

Belkis and I were on the same bus; we made sure of that; something weird happened: Belkis was standing, and I invited her to sit on my thighs: big mistake; after about 30 seconds, she stood up and was crying.

I asked, "What is the matter?" but she continued crying. I asked her again and tried to put my arms around her, and she pulled away from me; at that point, I let her be and I sat back down, perplexed, angry, and sulky. I refused to go near her or even talk to her again for the rest of the journey.

When we arrived at the college, I was sitting almost in front of the bus's rear doors, double doors, and as soon as the bus stopped, I scampered out and away from the bus, and I heard my name shouted repeatedly; I looked back without stopping, Belkis was running and calling after me. I stopped and asked, "What is it you want?" Her face was red, her eyes swollen, and white tear marks streaked down her cheeks.

"I was upset with myself, I was embarrassed, I shouldn't have sat on your thighs, we were still engaged in college activities, it was as if we were on campus, it didn't look proper, there are rules against such behaviour, and I'm now only hoping that I'll not get reprimand by the college's administration," she explained.

I really felt bad about the whole thing at that moment because I knew I was equally responsible; I was the one who encouraged her without thinking of the appropriateness. We both did not think about the perception that could be engendered by our action. "Let's not worry about it now because it was now out of our control. We must wait and see if there are any reactions," I told her.

It was nearing the weekend anyway, and the Cuban students were getting ready to leave the campus to go back home and visit their family. However, time went by, and no one ever mentioned our presumed indiscretion to us; maybe no one in authority was taking notice.

Chapter 25

Not long after, one Friday afternoon, Belkis sent me a message with one of my colleagues for me to come downstairs, and I should hurry; I did as I was told and went down to see her. She informed me, "I'm going home to the city centre, my father's home, and I'll not be visiting with my mother this weekend."

I said, "That is fine; you do what you have to do, but I'm going to miss you."

"I will be thinking of you though. Get your uniform, please. I'm going to do laundry, and I will include yours," she told me.

I went and got my dirty clothes and brought them to her, "They are all here; thank you very much for being so considerate."

She smiled and said, "Please, walk me to the bus stop."

We walked down to the bus stop, and when the bus arrived, it was packed to capacity. She forced her way onto the bus without any opportunity to glance back at me.

Once the bus was off and out of sight, I walked slowly back to the campus and towards my dormitory.

On the way towards the stairs up to my dormitory, I looked across the college yard and noticed a pretty girl sitting by herself on one of the many concrete benches, and she beckoned for me to come over to where she was, and I complied, she invited me to sit, but I chose to remain on my feet.

"Why did you call me over?" I asked her.

"You don't even know that I exist, do you? You seem to have eyes only for Belkis; what is so special about her?" she asked.

"I'm in love with her," I replied.

"Are you going to marry her?"

"We haven't discussed such matters, and why do you ask?"

"If you aren't going to marry and take her with you to Jamaica, why don't you make friends with other girls, like me, for instance? You only have four years in Cuba, and you are now into your second year; you need to loosen up and explore," she followed up.

Suddenly, I began thinking it may be a trap to find out if I really care about Belkis, as I have been demonstrating for more than a year now. Could it be that Belkis had put her up to this shenanigan? Could it be that Belkis' friends were behind it? Or just maybe she was jealous, envious, that Belkis was in a devoted relationship. At the same time, I was very aware that Cuban girls are not shy to make the first move with a guy they like, and this could be one of those times.

Nonetheless, as the evening dragged on, a couple more girls came over and joined in the conversation.

They were all saying the same thing, "You need to loosen up, explore possibilities, enjoy life, and date other girls, you're un muchacho guapo; lots of girls will fall for you, your stay in Cuba is short, and your young days are for experimenting and experiencing life as much as possible because you will never get a second chance at it."

At that point, I decided to test the sincerity of these girls' intention.

"I'm free this weekend, and I would like to take you up on your offer of exploring life's possibilities. So, which one of you girls wants to go to a movie with me tomorrow night?"

"I would!" They responded in unison.

The first girl who invited me into the conundrum, Marisol, was selected to go to the movie on Saturday night with me. This was an opportunity for me to verify, Was this real? Was someone setting me up? Was I that appealing, in demand, attractive and irresistible?

Hence, I called Marisol aside and told her: "You are my date for tomorrow night."

"Really! You want to go out with me?" she asked.

"Yes, didn't I ask you?" I inquired.

She seemed pleased that she was chosen; the others looked at her and around at one another and said, "Disfrutate."

I told Marisol, "I will confirm with you the time and place we will meet tomorrow; look out for me at lunchtime tomorrow. Goodbye, see you soon." And I went up to my dormitory.

I had an acquaintance, Brea, who lived close to Lorena's house whose parents had a telephone at their home, so I went down to Lorena's about 10 a.m. the next day and asked her to call Brea for me, she did, and Brea did not hesitate, in a matter of minutes, he was entering Lorena's living room, and I greeted him, and asked him, "could I use your telephone to call Belkis.?"

"Yes, of course, anytime," he responded.

I called Belkis and told her what was happening, the conversation I had with the girls, without naming anyone, "a few girls are interested in going out with me, I let one of them know that I would go out with her, and we made a tentative date to go to the movie later-on this evening, "But I'm calling for your approval before confirming the date and to let you know that nothing unscrupulous was going on between the girl and myself."

"I can't believe you have accepted to go out with someone while I'm at home," Belkis responded in alarm. Immediately, I knew she was not behind the scheme.

I explained to her, "There is nothing going on between the girl and myself. I wouldn't do anything to hurt you, embarrass you, or disrespect and dishonour you. I just want to find out what this girl is up to and how far she is prepared to go with her charade." Belkis acquiesced to my attempt at manipulation to get to the bottom of things.

"Who is it? Which year of study is she in? What does she look like? Is she pretty?"

"I will provide all the details you need after the date – just trust me," I told her.

I met with Marisol after lunch and confirmed our date, time, and place to meet; she seemed enthusiastic about the whole affair. I got nervous as the time drew closer to starting our date; I began thinking, why did I agree to this escapade? What was going through Belkis' mind? It must have been agonizing and tormenting for her to know that I was going out with another girl—I was remorseful, to say the least. One thing I was certain of, I trusted myself and would not ruin things with Belkis. She had never gone beyond kissing and fondling; she was a virgin, she wanted me to be her first, and I desperately wanted to give Belkis her first taste of paradise.

Despite my awkward feelings, I met up with Marisol at about 6 p.m. on the street that ran alongside the sports village, where Cuba's young and promising athletes frequently stayed for specialized training and very often competition. I suggested this location because even though Belkis is aware of my date, I did not want anyone on campus to get wind of the fact that I went out with Marisol while I was courting Belkis. I wanted Belkis to be free of gossip, hallway talks, lunchroom tattles, and dormitory whispers.

Marisol was on time; she walked towards me with short steps at moderate speed; we greeted each other with words only; she looked stunning. She was donning a purple dress that cut above her knees, hobble style, which kept riding up her hips, and she kept pulling it back down, revealing her petite body in a respectful manner. Her arms were covered to her elbow; her cleavage was not exposed; in other words, she was looking proper, decent, and attractive—very beautiful. The sweet-smelling fragrance and smile she wore were captivating—the temptation was smothering me.

After we undressed each other with our eyes, "You look fabulous, Marisol," I remarked.

"So do you, Desmond."

She smiled and winked at me in a saucy kind of way; our chosen movie theatre was within walking distance from the college. "Shall we go?"

She came close to me and walked by my side; she was alluring; though we did not make body contact, my blood was overheating, the desire was taking control of my being, my mouth was salivating, my heart was pounding, and for a moment I felt like pulling her into *me and kissed her, but I did not give in to the temptation.*

I sensed that she, too, was burning with desire. She constantly looked over her shoulder at me and shared her captivating smile; the pressure was building; it was almost unbearable; I wondered how much more I could take before relenting to beauty and its tantalizing intrigue. Now more than before, I was questioning my judgment, wisdom, confidence, and will—one can never be too self-assured when it comes to the power of sex and attraction. Luckily, the movie theatre was suddenly visible, and lights were everywhere as if they were focusing on us to reveal our indiscretion should there be any.

We joined the line in front of the ticket wicket, and when it was our turn, I purchased the two tickets for us to get into the movie theatre. We immediately went inside the theatre, no hanging about outside the theatre. No ice cream, no sandwich, or soda for either of us, as we both had eaten at the college not long before leaving the campus for the movie theatre. The lights were on in the theatre, everything was conspicuous, and patrons were everywhere around us and staring at us as if we were aliens because, in my opinion, Marisol was strikingly beautiful, a delight to behold and be with.

While we were waiting for the theatre lights to go out, a preview of upcoming movies, and the running of the movie credits, I thought I would strike up a conversation with Marisol.

"Where in the province are you from?" I asked her.

"I'm from Guama. It is the most beautiful region of Santiago de Cuba, with excellent beaches, running streams, manicured landscape, and detached houses made mostly of wooden walls and zinc and thatched

roofs. You should come to visit before you finish your studies in Cuba and return to Jamaica," she told me.

"I might just oblige you because you never know what tomorrow will bring your way," I replied, "What year are you in at the college? I inquired.

"Fourth year, and I will be graduating next semester," she responded."

"How old are you?" I asked.

"I will be twenty just before I graduate college next semester," she replied.

Unexpectedly, the lights went out before I could ask any more questions. Previews began running, then the credits for the movie, and in about 20 minutes, we were watching the movie "Dial M for Murder," an Alfred Hitchcock thriller; I held Marisol's hand next to me on the right so as not to appear aloof with our fingers in an interlocking position.

We watched the movie without any hanky-panky; besides, the movie was suspenseful and intriguing. After the movie, the evening was still early, so we went to get ice cream, sat in the nearby park for a while and continued our conversation. I learned that her parents were divorced, and she had two siblings, both younger than her, a brother who was living with their father and her younger sister who lived with her and their mother.

Once we were done eating, we decided to head back to the college, and on our way, Marisol proposed that I spend the night with her.

"Most of the students went home for the weekend, and those that remained usually stay indoors, so no one would ever find out our little secret."

I declined the offer, but Marisol was persistent.

"I wouldn't tell anyone; it would be our secret. What are you afraid of?" she asked.

"Belkis is my girlfriend, and I couldn't cheat on her; we trust each other; I could never betray that trust; she doesn't deserve my indiscretion," I said.

Marisol went silent for a while, but she held on to my hand and occasionally leaned against me as though she wanted me to cuddle her, but I resisted the enticement.

When we reached the sports village, the lights were dimmed and faded in certain sections.

Marisol stopped me and stood in front of me and said: "I really need to spend tonight with you."

She looked into my eyes; hers were dreamy and suggestive. Then she said, "I'm burning with desire. Please don't let me spend the night alone; I want to give myself to you so badly."

I was almost persuaded, weakness was invading my body and mind, and for a moment, I was dazed; I was aroused and burning with desire, too; I pulled her close to me, so she was aware of my physical state of being, she wedged against me like a tick on to cow. Suddenly, I remembered Cubans are not known to keep secrets; information passed with ease and spread like wildfire. I firmly believe that what more than one Cuban knows is no secret. I kissed her on the forehead and told her, "Maybe some other place and time; I may take all that you have to offer, but not now."

So as not to forget my primary mission, I asked Marisol the all-important question: "Did you and the other girls plan beforehand to seduce me yesterday afternoon?"

She looked at me in dismay and replied, "I don't know about the others; I was acting on my own; I do things my way without company. Remember, I was alone talking with you for about 10 minutes before the others joined the conversation?"

Cheekily, I said to her, "I thought you needed help to persuade me."

"Not at all. No way. I'm not like that," she said.

I wanted answers for when I had to update Belkis. Feeling more reassured about Marisol and her intentions, I walked her to the staircase of her dormitory, waited for her to say goodbye, and ascended the staircase, she embraced me, kissed me on the cheek, began walking up the stairs, and she asked one last time. "Are you sure you don't want to spend the night with me?"

"I'm sure," I said to her.

She smiled and disappeared up the stairs, seemingly disappointed.

I then went up to my dormitory. The lights were off; my colleagues were talking over and around the bunks; I undressed, put on my pyjamas, and climbed into bed. I thought to myself that was a narrow miss, but I had no regrets; Cubans are known for their gossiping; furthermore, I did not want to mess things up with Belkis. After all, I was going to see her the next day and wanted to be able to look her in the face without a glimmer of guilt. Therefore, I did some deep breathing, meditated for a bit, lay on my side, tried to forget the earlier part of the night, relaxed my body and mind, and fell asleep.

On Sunday evening, at about 6 p.m., Belkis arrived on campus. I was in my bed thinking about her when I heard her shouting my name. I looked through the window, and she saw me and gestured with her hands for me to come down. I went down, and she kissed me on the cheek as was customary with Cubans and took my hand and led me towards the gymnasium and signalled that we sit on the steps but to the side so we would not block the entrance. The first thing she said to me was that "I brought you some goodies, pastries, sandwiches, and sodas for you to snack on as long as they will keep, and maybe you can gain a little weight." I was slim and was always teased about it by both Cuban and Jamaican students.

Belkis usually brings me things whenever she returned from her home on the weekends, but never so much before, I looked at her in an inquiring fashion, and she said, "Don't look so skeptical; my cousins were able to sell the shoes, they were too small for me and them as well; there was no point in hanging on to them,"

She offered to give me 10 pesos, the equivalent of 10 American dollars, in the official bank, at the time, but I refused to accept it, "They were my gift to you, and you shouldn't even buy me things from the proceeds. Not that I don't appreciate your kindness and consideration, but I'm not comfortable benefiting from my own gifts," A grim look befell her face, and tears began streaming down her cheeks; she was offended by my refusal to accept the money, my scolding words; though I did not mean for it to sound like a rebuke, it did. So, I had to console her and reassure her that her action did not hurt me. I dried the tears from her eyes and cheeks, put one of my arms around her shoulder, kissed her on the lips, and tickled her side until I got a smile from her.

"I love you very much, cosita linda, I don't like to see you upset, and I'm sorry if I offended you," I said.

"Let us forget the whole thing, pretend it never happened," she said.

This was just one of many misunderstandings we had as we went forward.

Strangely, she did not ask me about my date or what I had done for the weekend; she showed no interest in finding out what happened on the date—she could not care less.

"Aren't you going to ask me about my date?" I inquired.

"You will tell me about it when you are ready. There are lots of girls in the college who are interested in sleeping with you, and in the dormitory, they discuss you regularly. You are quiet, intelligent, good-looking, patient, courteous, generous, and respectful. These are rare qualities that are hard to find in Cuba, never mind in one person. They envy me; it isn't fair I get the most attractive guy, in looks, in character and attitude," she told me.

"I decided to go on a date, not so much to prove anything, but rather to determine if anyone or a group of individuals was conspiring to destroy our relationship," I told her.

However, I could not let her know that she was a potential suspect, since I knew that she was worried about me abandoning her after I slept with her.

"So, who was the girl that you went out with?"

"Marisol, a student in fourth year."

"I know her; she is like that; I could have saved you the discomfort of looking like a wimp if you had told me her name when I asked you. You aren't the first, and you certainly won't be the last. She isn't looking for a relationship. She just wants to have sex. She is on what appears to be some sort of a crusade because of a previous disappointment with her ex-boyfriend."

"What do you mean? She seems like a nice person; who would want to hurt her?"

"She was in a committed relationship, and her partner decided that he didn't want to go steady anymore; he wanted to see other people. He said that he was too young and didn't want to be bogged down with any one person. However, she only goes after who

she wants; she usually does the searching; she is a hunter; if you try to pursue her, she may get cagey and even reproach you."

"I have no intention of spending another of my weekends like that again."

"That is good because from now on, you will spend all your weekends with me, starting this coming weekend."

After a pause, both of us were silent for a few seconds.

"I have told my father about you, and I would like you to meet him and my stepmother when you visit me this coming weekend."

The week went by quickly without fanfare, save for Marisol sticking a note in my pocket during lunchtime one day. However, I ignored the note and left it in my pocket for several days without reading it or thinking about it because I told myself she was up to no good. Even if she did not consciously intend to cause a rift between Belkis and me, it did seem that way to me.

Chapter 26

On Friday afternoon, I packed my little bag with dirty clothes, as has been customary for more than a year, for Belkis to wash over the weekend, but on my way down the stairs to deliver the bag to Belkis, I recalled that I did not turn out my pockets, as I normally did on previous occasions. I ran back up the stairs and into the dormitory, emptied the content of the bag on my bunk and went through my pockets and among other scrap of papers, pencils, eraser and cigarettes, I saw Marisol's note; I repacked the bag and ran back downstairs to hand it to Belkis, who was waiting, and see her off.

"What took you so long?" she inquired.

"I was almost at the bottom of the stairs when I remembered that I didn't empty my pockets, and so I returned to the dormitory to remove the items that were in them," I responded.

"Did you have anything inside them that you didn't want me to see?" she asked.

"Don't I always empty my pockets before giving you my clothes on weekends?" I asked.

"Lighten up, estoy bromeando contigo," she said, "Walk me to the bus stop."

Arriving at the bus stop, we had to wait a while for the bus, and she reminded me that I was meeting her father over the weekend.

"Which day would you prefer to meet him?" she asked.

"Sunday afternoon. That way, you and I can return to the college together," I responded.

She proposed that we meet at the park in the centre of town, Parque Céspedes, at 3 p.m. She hugged me, kissed me on the cheek and then on the lips, looked into my face and said softly, I love you, papi; I reciprocated, and a couple of minutes later, the bus arrived, and she boarded it and waved back at me, and I blew her a kiss and in a matter of seconds the bus was on its way and out of sight.

I returned to the campus and stayed in the college yard for a while until it was dinner time; with a thousand thoughts going through my mind, I had already met Belkis' mother, brothers, and sister, and now she wants me to meet her father. Am I getting any closer to having intercourse with Belkis? What will her father have to say about me, about the relationship between his daughter and me? Will he approve? Will he lecture me on a topic I did not care to entertain? Or will he greet me and leave his wife to make my acquaintance? These and many other questions flowed through my mind. As I sat there deep in thought, I heard passersby offering salutations, but I was not listening, and they did not try to ensure that I got their attention. When I consciously recollected my thoughts, I noticed dinner *was being served; I stood up, rushed upstairs, picked up my utensils and drinking glass, hurried back downstairs to join the line, and received my dinner.*

After dinner, I went upstairs immediately, showered, brushed my teeth, and climbed into my bunk, I felt as though I was lying in trash, and I suddenly remembered that the content of my dirty clothes pockets was still on the bed, not put away. I began putting them away and came across Marisol's note; I hesitated to pull it open and wondered if I should read it, considering I was just a whisker away from kissing her last Saturday night. In all honesty, and I thought to myself, if I had to repeat that night, I doubt I could resist the temptation; it might be best to throw out the note and forget about her; I do not believe I was strong enough to combat her sexy body and personality. However, I decided that not reading the note was a sign of weakness, that I was incapable of managing my feelings and emotions, and that I was lacking in self-control and averse to challenges. Hence, I opened the note, and it read as follows:

Hi Desmond, thank you for reading my note; I wanted to let you know that I enjoyed our time together last Saturday night; I thought about you a lot since that night and imagined what it would have been like had you submitted yourself to making love to me. I am going home this weekend, so you will not see me around campus, but I will be thinking of you because I have an unfulfilled desire. I am taking this opportunity to remind you that you did not close the door to have a fling with me: you said, "Maybe some other place and time." Since you are reading this note, it is an indication that you value me as a human being, and that says something important to me about you. Hesitant to encourage me, you may not answer my note, and that is fine, but I would like to stay in touch with you even after I graduated college. Please have a delightful weekend. La tuya, cariñosamente, Marisol.

After I finished reading Marisol's note, I folded it as it had been before, stretched from under my mosquito net and opened my suitcase, which was on top of the cupboard attached to my bunk. I did not think too much about Marisol's note then because Sunday afternoon was first and foremost on my mind. I was deeply in love with Belkis and desperately wanted to be intimate with her; I wanted to get the meeting with her father over and done with and hoped that it was the final barrier between Belkis and me making love.

On Sunday afternoon, I had lunch early, ahead of most students, hurried back upstairs after I had finished eating, and tried to make conversation with my colleagues in hopes that the time would pass with celerity. Nonetheless, I became anxious; the time was not moving fast enough for me. My underarm began perspiring profusely, my heart was palpitating with alacrity, and my nerves were starting to embarrass me. I convinced myself that a long cold shower might help me to relax, so I took one and then went to bed, but I was no better off than before I took the shower. Finally, I decided to get dressed and be on my way; I told myself that walking would be better than taking the bus—It would help me to relax.

The distance from the college to the Parque Céspedes was three miles, but I could walk at least part of the way and, after I recovered, used the bus for the remainder of the journey. I reached the park at approximately 2:30 p.m. and was greeted by some diversions, tourists conversing with one another in foreign languages, a band playing Cuban music, and people dancing unenthusiastically. Their movements were off rhythm with poor coordination, shaking themselves around aimlessly. I was fine with watching them, passing the time, and relaxing my mental and physical being.

Minutes to 3 p.m., Belkis was entering the park, wearing a pair of tight-fitted light blue pants, a light greyish blouse, dark push-toe sandals, and her hair rolled into a bun at the back of her head, revealing her beautiful countenance. She was walking briskly, smiling broadly and graciously as she approached me. We made eye contact, moved towards each other at much the same pace, raised our arms at shoulder level, greeted each other, embraced, and kissed each other on the cheek.

"Are you ready to meet my dad and stepmother?" Belkis inquired. "They are in the living room waiting on your arrival."

"Ready as I will ever be, but I'm shaking; my nerves are beginning to fail me," I said.

"Relax, they are part of the human race; they aren't going to harm you. I'm not nervous, but I'm excited for you to meet them, and I'm sure they are curious about you. And that is about all there is to this afternoon."

After approximately seven minutes of walking, we arrived at the door to Belkis' father's home. A structure from the colonial era with about three feet of sidewalk between the house door and the vehicular road. We took one step up to enter the house. The entire block was similar on both sides of the road, one-storey townhouses, appearance tall, dull, and worn-out colours, mostly painted in white, grey, and yellow. Belkis had the door key in her hand all the time. She inserted the key into the lock and opened the door. We entered the building through a passageway. On the left, the neighbours dividing wall; on the right, two self-contained units, the first one Belkis' aunts, Esmeralda, lived there with her husband and two daughters. To the right of Esmeralda's, Belkis' other aunt, Conchita, and her son occupied the second unit. Belkis' father's dwelling was located at the back of the building, forming a rectangular shape with Conchita's unit, and the neighbour's dividing wall, a two-storey structure, as opposed to the other units, which were one story only, Belkis occupied the second floor which had only sleeping quarters, and her father and stepmother occupied the ground floor, which had two bedrooms, an open concept living and dining area, kitchen, and a bathroom. One of the bedrooms was used as a meeting room for religious purposes—Belkis' father, Pedro, practised the Roman Catholic faith.

The passage providing access to the three dwelling areas was only partially roofed. At the end of the roofed portion, about fifteen feet, it was open air, only the sky above. To the left, we had to make an L-shaped turn to avoid walking into a raised bed containing a lime and pomegranate tree. Next to the raised bed were four brown metal pillars supporting a brown water tank hoisted about 10 feet in the air. Continuing to the right, a seven-foot wall completed the passageway on the right. It formed part of a rectangular enclosed patio, which contained a laundry area on the short side, and on the longer side, there was a doorway which provided access to Conchita's unit.

Belkis' grandfather, Jorge, a medical doctor still practising at the time, owned the property but was living in Palma, where he owned another house and resided with his second wife after the passing of his first wife. He was in his late seventies and travelled from Palma to Santiago twice weekly to consult at the Santiago de Cuba General Hospital. The children from the first marriage occupied the home in Santiago, and the only child from the second marriage lived in Palma in his own dwelling immediately across the street from his father. Esmeralda was the eldest of the four children, followed by Pedro, then Conchita, and Ernesto from the second marriage.

As we approached the entrance of the living and dining area of Belkis' home, I noticed the eldest of her two brothers, Felipe, on the inside leaning against the doorjamb, suddenly a feeling of comfort befell me, the nervousness subsided, the pounding of my heart slowed considerably, and I was no longer feeling intimidated. Felipe and I greeted each other. Upon entering the living room, Belkis' Father, Pedro, stood to greet me. He flaunted a physique of medium built with an early bulging tummy. He was approximately five feet eight inches tall, had black curly hair, and his skin was light brown. Belkis' stepmother, Josefina, also of medium built but with no noticeable bulging tummy, was approximately five feet four inches tall, with black, permed, short hair, and had a dark skin colour. Belkis introduced me to her father and stepmother: "Papá and Josefina, I present to you my boyfriend, Desmond, a student at my college, and we have been dating for more than a year now."

The two hosts shook my hand and said in chorus: "It is a pleasure to finally meet you, Desmond." "We have been hearing about you for a while and wondered if" we would ever get the opportunity to meet you," Josefina remarked.

"I was in the same position as you were, but in my view the decision was for Belkis and for her alone to make."

"So, I understand that you and Belkis are novios," Pedro said, "Offer Desmond some coffee," Pedro told his wife.

Coffee was already on the table, black without milk or sugar, cold and in a stainless-steel coffee pot.

I declined the coffee, "Thank you, but I don't drink coffee." Belkis did not drink coffee either and no one wanted to partake of the coffee after I refused to have any.

Once I answered a few questions about my immediate family, brothers, sisters, mother, father, and grandparents and where exactly in Jamaica I was from, Belkis asked that we be excused, for a few minutes, she wanted me to meet her aunts and cousins.

We visited Conchita, first. Before we entered her domain, Belkis started shouting, "Tía, Tía, Tía," there was no response, but when we entered the patio, Conchita's son, Vinent, was there stretched out in a cot with a radio at his ear listening to whatever was on.

Finally, Conchita, without answering Belkis' yelling, showed up in her doorway smiling, and almost immediately, Esmeralda and her husband, Camilo, and daughters: Lilian and Odalys showed up on the patio as well. Except for Odalys, who appeared like a blonde, they all had light skin colour—and by Cuban standards, they were pretty, handsome, and beautiful. Conchita was slim, about five feet eight inches tall, with black curly hair; her son Vinent, was short with black curly hair, somewhat bulky. Esmeralda was noticeably older, slim built, with a salt and pepper colour hair, Camilo was slim built with a protruding stomach. Lilian was about five feet four inches tall, with a flat tummy, she had curly black hair. Odalys had long blonde hair, way below her shoulders.

Belkis introduced me, "Everyone, this is Desmond, my boyfriend, that I mentioned to you sometime back. We are studying at the same college, and we have been dating for a while now."

They all approached me but individually and greeted me, "Pleased to meet you," and then shook my hand with a smile on their faces.

"Desmond and I have to get ready to go back to the college, but he will be visiting in the future on weekends."

"We have a lot to talk about, because Conchita and I attended West Indies College in Mandeville, Jamaica," Esmeralda declared.

"I look forward to seeing you again," I said.

When we returned to Belkis' area of the building, Josefina was in the process of putting dinner on the table in anticipation of our return; Pedro was sitting in an armchair watching television and smoking a cigarette; he stood up and offered me the seat.

"Sit down, please," he told me.

"I prefer to stand; I like standing," I said.

I remained standing, and Belkis walked by her father, patted his neck and shoulder affectionately, entered the kitchen, and began assisting Josefina with the setting of the table. Josefina protested, but Belkis insisted on helping, and she got her way. Not long after, we were called to the table; dinner was ready. The five of us made our way there and sat down, and I was invited to partake. There was a separate platter placed on the table for me, fish as the main dish, and sides included avocado dressed in olive oil, pieces of fried sweet potato, and rice with peas. The other main dish was pork, but they shared similar sides as me, which were on a large dish, and all four of them helped themselves individually as the dish moved around the table. In addition, there was a large aluminum jug with limeade, and the lime in it was noticeably strong.

"Bon appetit," Josefina remarked. Then, she began probing, "Desmond, do you like Cuba? What do you

think of Cubans? How have you been spending your time? Has Belkis taken you to any fiestas?"

I replied affirmatively to all her questions; Belkis has made it easy for me to pass the time. Without her support and sensitivity, I would be confined to a life of solitude.

"Would you live in Cuba?" Felipe asked.

"When I reach a conclusion on that, I will let you know."

Belkis intervened and requested that they let me eat without inquiries—there was silence from everyone.

"Cuba is a beautiful country; crime is under control, no reporting of gang violence; besides, people are disciplined, friendly, courteous, organized, peaceful and kind," I said.

Pedro remained completely silent for the duration of the dinner consumption, mainly with his head bowed towards his plate.

After we finished eating, Belkis began clearing the table; Josefina told her not to because she would do it and the dishes, but Belkis paid no heed to her. Pedro requested coffee, Belkis brought it to him, he nodded his head in appreciation; he then motioned to me a cigarette pack, I took one and returned the pack to him and expressed my gratitude, and he bowed his head in acknowledgment.

Once Belkis was finished in the kitchen, she announced, "We must leave; time is running out. It is 6:40 p.m., and I'm planning on stopping at my mom's." She went upstairs, then came back down with her bag, our uniforms on hanging racks, handed the bag to me, kept the uniforms hanging over her shoulder, approached Pedro, kissed him on both cheeks and announced to everyone, including Felipe, that we were going.

They all told us to caminan bien or walk good; Josefina invited me to come again soon.

"No se preocupa, he will be back next weekend," Belkis promised. "Wait for me at the front door, I'm going to say goodbye to mis tíos, and primos."

Once she did not ask me to accompany her, I knew she was going to inquire what they thought of me.

After taking almost 15 minutes to say goodbye to her relatives, she confirmed my suspicion. She came out smiling, leaned into me and kissed me on the lips.

"What do they think of me?" I asked.

"How do you know we were discussing you?" she fired back instantly, smiling.

"Isn't it logical?"

She shoved me to go forward and said, "You are too smart. They are fond of you and my aunts think you are sympático."

We wrapped our arms around each other's waist, headed out into the street, and ambled along to the bus stop. In five minutes, the bus was at the stop opening its doors to pick up and let off passengers. We mounted the bus, only one seat was available, I invited Belkis to sit, she protested and wanted me to sit, I refused and insisted that she sit down, she yielded, and in the process, we were off on our way.

Thirty minutes later we were at the bus stop in front of the general hospital. We crossed the street and went over to Lorena's. The door was unlocked; Belkis pushed it open, announced our arrival, we entered the house, greeted those who were present: Lorena, Gladys, and Lionel.

"Why did you ask me to stop by Mummy?" Belkis inquired.

Lorena took her by the hand and led her into the kitchen, and she came back with a brown paper bag. Belkis and I bade everyone goodbye, and we set off walking towards the college. When we reached the sports village, darkness began to fall, the lights were on in the park around the village, but there were patches of darkness all about. We stopped to make out under a piece of shadow. We kissed, caressed, and fondled each other's private parts; Belkis was becoming swollen, her lips enlarged, her breasts became firm and pointed, I was burning with desire, and I suspected the same with her because she was scorching hot. I began to massage her pleasure spot, she bit my lips, I started to lower her underwear, and she whispered in my ear, "Papi, not here, not now; and she pulled away. I tried to pursue her, but she repeated, "Not here, not now." with a look of soberness in her eyes, and I obeyed her command.

I was disappointed, but I kept quiet, we started walking, she drew near to me, swung the brown bag at my head and remarked, Tu eres un hombre fresco. I held her hand, smiling at her in silence.

"You aren't mad at me, papi?" she asked, "Because if you are, I understand, but I don't want my first time to be ugly, cheap and in public view."

"No, I'm not mad at you, besides, you are the owner of your body."

We continued walking until we reached the college, the section on which her dormitory was located. Arriving at the staircase to her dormitory, she opened the paper bag, pulled out a paper wrap, and handed it to me, "Mummy gave us pastries," she requested her travelling bag, and handed my uniform over to me. "You'll receive the rest of your clothes afterwards, after I remove my clothes, I will bring you the bag, I'll not take out our clothes in public." She came close to me and wrapped her arms around me and said, "Don't get too comfortable in your dormitory, I'm coming back down momentarily with your clothes and to talk with you before bedtime."

I waited as she disappeared up the stairs to her dormitory. Once she was out of sight, I headed over to my side of the building, ascended the stairs, and noticed several of my colleagues in the common area of the dormitory playing chess and dominoes; a couple of them remarked, "Can't see you these days boss," but I just smiled and went into the dormitory, put away my things and went back downstairs so that Belkis would not have to holler for me to come down.

Not long after I descended the stairs, Belkis came bouncing towards me, smiling and bubbly; she was glowing and beaming with beauty; on arrival, she handed me the bag with my clothes and said, "You can give me back the bag later."

We sat on the edge of the ramp leading into the theatre; I took one of her hands in both of mine, looked her in the eyes and explained, apologized, "It wasn't my intention to make you feel cheap; I wanted you desperately, I was excited, my body was yearning, and for a moment I got carried away, thank you for reminding me that I was among the living.

Women, it seems, are much better than men at exercising self-control.

"I'm crazy in love with you, I wanted badly to end this celibacy, it is consuming me like wildfire to a parched forest, it is over a year now that we have been dating, and I'm beginning to wonder when will this chastity end," I told her.

"Do you think I'm not suffering too? At night, I tossed and turned. I dream about you when I'm asleep and think about you when I'm awake. I perfectly understand your needs and desires, mine are no different, but I want my first experience to be special. I'm not blaming you for anything; neither am I trying to *scold you for your advances; as a matter of fact, I like it when you fondle me because I get arousal from it, and that is an indication that I want you, we connect, there is chemistry, just be patient, estoy madura, so the day is near at hand."*

After hearing her submissive words, I became daring and excited, and I asked her: "Do you want me to rent a hotel for a day next weekend? I will provide you with the information so you could enter the Hotel separately from me. Being seen together may raise suspicion, and we wouldn't want your dad to hear any gossip. You could tell your dad that we are going to the beach, but instead you slip into the Hotel and spend the afternoon with me, and return to your home before late night, while I remain in the Hotel until the next morning."

Belkis agreed but provided a better idea on how we would get together.

"I will tell my dad that I'm going to spend the weekend with my mom and tell my mom that I'm going to the beach on Saturday afternoon—that way I could be with you until later in the night because my mom is less strict than my dad. Do you have money to rent the hotel room and have supper? Because if you don't, I could get some from my mom," she said.

"Yes, the 30 pesos I receive monthly from the college, I haven't spent much of it, because you and Lorena have been filling in whenever I missed meals at the college."

Belkis looked at me, held my hands, squeezed it, and said, "You are a rogue."

"I know,"

Then we hugged each other, kissed on the cheeks, bade goodbye for the night, and went to our respective dormitory.

Chapter 27

Over the next two days, I inquired from a couple of my colleagues, in confidence, if they knew how to go about renting a hotel room in the city and they had no knowledge of how it was done. Wednesday, we had a short afternoon; I told Belkis that I was going downtown to inquire how to go about renting a hotel room. She had no objection, so after class, I had a shower, dressed, went out to the street, took a bus, and got off at the nearest hotel, Hotel Libertad; I entered the hotel lobby, approached the receptionist, and asked her, "can I reserve a room for Saturday night."

"Yes, but you can't rent a hotel room on-site," she said.

"Where is it done?" I asked.

"You have to go to the reservation centre at 315 La Serna Street early on Friday morning and join the line in order to make your reservation. You can choose *from the available hotel rooms; the cost is 15 pesos per night, 24 hours stay, noon the first day until noon the second day."*

"What documentation do I need to present to make the reservation," I asked.

"Solamente your identity card," she replied.

I thanked her for the information, exited the hotel, walked to the bus stop, a bit dejected. I thought the process was simpler. I sat on a metal bench and waited for the bus. The bus came 20 minutes later, I inquired from another commuter the time. It was 5 p.m. I mounted the bus and returned to the college. It did not dawn on me to ask the receptionist how early I needed to be at the reservation centre.

After arriving back at the college, I saw a student who was residing in the same dormitory as Belkis, I asked her to take a message to Belkis for me, which was to ask her to come down to the landing level of the staircase. I wanted to update her.

She came down within moments of getting the message; I explained to her the procedure for renting a hotel room, as it was explained to me by the receptionist at Hotel Libertad.

"Are you going to follow through on the reservation?" she inquired.

"I'm going down to the reservation centre Friday morning bright and early. I didn't ask the receptionist how early I should get there, but I'll try to make it as early as possible."

I bade her goodbye on the landing, telling her as well that, "I'm hungry and going to see if I can catch the canteen before it closes its doors."

I rushed up to my dormitory to pick up my utensils and hurried back down to the canteen which was still open and serving meals. I joined the line, collected my meal, and sat down to eat it when I noticed Marisol two rows across from me. She was smiling and looking in my direction, I blushed and hung my head over my food tray and resisted with difficulty peering back at her. However, I gazed coyly in her direction occasionally and discovered that her eyes were in those moments incessantly fixed on me with an intense stare and I started to feel uncomfortable—my stomach was overrun with "butterflies, pins and needles."

After a couple of mouthfuls, I abandoned eating, got out from around the table and chairs, picked-up my tray, returned it to the side of the serving hatch where the other dirty trays were being stored for washing, and I dashed to the canteen exit, without looking back, and scuttled up the stairs to my dormitory. Upon reaching my bunk, I changed into my pyjamas, climbed into bed, and started thinking, why did I run? Marisol was attractive, beautiful, tempting, and I was beginning to lose control of my self-confidence and that was not a good thing, especially when I was about to reach the promised land with Belkis. I must avoid seeing Marisol and keep my focus on the looming grand prize that seemingly was only days away.

Friday morning took forever to appear and made me nervous, excited, impatient, and expectant, like a child anticipating a gift from Santa Claus at Christmas. I woke up about 4:30 a.m., went to the bathroom and freshened-up. Afterward, I dressed and set about my journey. It was still dark outdoors; hardly anyone was moving about. I walked down to Central Avenue, where the buses began their route schedule at 4 a.m.—unlike the feeder route buses that began their schedule at 5 a.m. On arrival at the bus stop, I noticed a bus was waiting, and I could mount it immediately; it was almost empty, just a few factory workers conversing amongst themselves about their end-of-the-week chores and plans.

I got off the bus at the stop close to Parque Céspedes and walked down to 315 La Serna Street. The lineup was already formed with approximately 40 individuals in waiting; the centre was still unopen, though there was a light on in the sales office. I joined the line, confident that I was going to secure a reservation. The reservation centre schedule was posted on the door: 7:30 a.m. to 12:30 p.m. The office opens on time, a short lady with light brown skin, long black hair, and an attractive profile came into focus; she greeted us and sat down to begin taking the reservations. She took approximately 15 reservations and declared, "Se acabó por hoy," and she put away the reservation book in a drawer, I was in disbelief, numbed, and shocked. The other patrons were outraged and began uttering foul words in Spanish, I understood a few, but I refused to join the fray and turned away and walked slowly towards the bus stop in a state of gloom.

Arriving at the bus stop, I hopped onto the first bus that came by, to get back to the college. When I reached the college breakfast time was almost over, so I decided to skip it that morning, went upstairs to my dormitory, took a quick shower, quickly put on my uniform, ferreted through my college paraphernalia, selected the books, pen, and pencil that I needed for class that morning. Then I headed back downstairs in hopes that I would see Belkis, crossing the college yard, so I could give her the disappointing news.

As soon as I hit the bottom of the stairs and looked straight ahead, I could see Belkis and a group of students walking towards me, she began smiling the moment we made eye contact, I began to make negative gestures with my hands and head, letting her know that I was unsuccessful, she did not seem disappointed or happy, but she broke away from her friends and came up to me.

"I wasn't able to make the reservation, but I will tell you about it at lunch time," I told her.

We agreed and met at lunchtime at the usual spot by the ramp leading into the theatre. I filled her in on the fiasco at the reservation centre, she seemed indifferent to my explanation of what went on, but she asked, "What do we do now?"

"I will sleep down there next Thursday night if that is what it takes to get a reservation."

"Next weekend is no good, because, I anticipate having my monthlies in the coming week, we will have to wait until the following week, because it normally lasts about five days." She told me not to worry, "It is going to happen, I desperately want to give myself to you, sooner rather than later."

I looked at her and smiled and told her, "Be on your way to class, because I'm going to class as well." We embraced and kissed each other on the cheeks and agreed to talk later in the evening.

I recalled that I had no breakfast and would have to visit the snack shop later in the morning. The snack shop usually opens for business at about 10 a.m., I am not a regular at the snack shop, because sugar and pork are the two main staples in the snack shops, in Cuba, and I tried devotedly to limit their intake if it were at all possible. However, that morning I was open to delve into whatever pastries were available, and so I was there waiting as soon as the scheduled break took effect. I ordered a glass of hot milk, a slice of cake, and two small sweet fried dumplings, paid the charge and proceeded to sit on one of the nearby concrete benches where I ate the grub before it was time for class.

On my way to class, I was joined by James who inquired from me: "Where did you go so early in the morning."

"I didn't think anyone had noticed."

"A couple of us noticed and that you missed breakfast as well."

"I had an errand to run, and it required meeting someone early," I told James.

Chapter 28

*A*fter dinner that evening, Belkis and I met up, and she brought her homework assignment with her. It was raining, so we decided to take cover in one of the classrooms, there were several other students present, hence no hanky-panky was possible. We sat at a desk and Belkis took out her assignment and began discussing it with me, mathematics as usual. She was doing better now than last year, and in less than an hour she had completed the task, with my help. The rain subsided and we decided to return to our respective dormitories, but not before agreeing that I would visit her, at her father's home, on Saturday afternoon.

I walked her to the bottom of the staircase leading up to her dormitory, and we embraced, as has been the habit following our meetings, and said goodbye for the evening. On the way to my dormitory, I ran into José; he told me: "The college is planning a party for the

Jamaican students at fin de año. The administration feels that it is necessary since the college would be on a week's holiday and the Cuban students are going home to pass the occasion with their family, it would provide the Jamaicans with some entertainment given that they could not go home,"

I thanked him for telling me and I said, "I will inform the other students."

I was thrilled. It was the best news I had heard from the administration in a long time. I could barely contain the excitement running through my body and mind. Finally, the opportunity to take Belkis to the land of ecstasy. The college was going to be empty, save for 31 Jamaican students and the college's maintenance crew, with nine dormitories at our disposal and several hundred bunk beds to choose from, my anticipation was overwhelming, and I had no doubt that the time had finally arrived to consummate my relationship with Belkis.

Friday afternoon, I called a meeting and shared the news with my colleagues; they welcomed the news and inquired, "What kinds of music are going to support the party?"

"I didn't ask, but if it is okay with you since several of us have cassette players, I could inform the administration that we would like to provide our own music."

They all agreed that we should supply the music. And as promised, I communicated the music source and preference to the administration and secured agreement that our music would carry the night of the party. I did not pass on the information to Belkis, but I did confirm with her before she left that afternoon for home that: "I will be coming downtown to spend Saturday afternoon with you."

"That is good, I will also inform them that you would be coming, that way you may socialize and get to know one another a bit better. My aunts will want to hear about Jamaica, particularly Mandeville," she said.

Saturday, after lunch, I went down to Belkis' home, it was 2:30 p.m. when I arrived, I used the brass door knocker to announce my arrival, Odalys answered the door and greeted me, "Hola Desmond, how are you?"

"I'm fine, thank you and how are you?" I inquired.

"Adelante, adelante, por favor," she also beckoned with one of her hands without answering my question.

As I entered, I spotted Belkis running full speed towards me, and she sprung into my arms and planted a kiss on my lips. We had not made out in about a week, and she did not seem to mind that Odalys was right there observing our exhibition.

"Could I go by your aunties' homes to say hello before I go to yours."

"That is okay with me."

I did the rounds and greeted everyone, this was good for me, it gave me an opportunity to practise my Spanish: listening and speaking skills, which I believe was fluent but not enough. After a brief chat with her extended family, we went to Belkis' home. She told me that she was doing laundry, and I should sit and make myself comfortable. Pedro was in his prayer room, and Josefina was away visiting with her mother.

"Turn on the television but keep the volume low in order not to disturb my father, he is praying."

I obeyed and quietly welcomed the opportunity to see and listen to a Spanish program.

I asked Belkis if we could go for a walk when she was through doing the laundry, she agreed, but asked: "Where do you want to go?"

"Anywhere"

"Maybe Parque Céspedes? It is bustling with local and foreign tourists at this time of the afternoon. However, seats in the park become available, in quick successions, the sun would be setting, and the temperature would be falling.," she explained.

"I have exciting, and wonderful information I would like to share with you," I said.

"Why can't you tell me now?" she asked.

"It's private, and I don't want the information leaked," I responded.

She acquiesced that we would go for a walk, but she said, "I have to at least get dinner started, in case Josefina is not back in time, because my father is accustomed to eating at a certain time. If he did not, his stomach bothers him, and the discomfort can last all night and sometimes well into the next day."

"That is alright, do what you have to, there is no urgency, at least not now, and we could make it a romantic stroll," I told her.

Not long after Belkis went into the kitchen and started preparing the meal, Josefina returned, greeted me, went into her bedroom, and in about 10 minutes she was out again, entered the kitchen and told Belkis she would take over. Belkis whispered into my ear. "We should eat before we go, especially if it is going to be a romantic stroll."

I concurred with Belkis, shortly thereafter the washing machine stopped with a buzzing noise.

"Can you come with me to hang the clothes?" Belkis inquired.

"Of course, I would be happy to help you," I replied.

"When we are finished, I'm going to shower, get dressed, and comb my hair," she said.

Pedro was still in the prayer room; I was at a loss as to what he was doing in there and inquired from Belkis. She told me he was communicating with the spirits—*that was sufficient for me. I did not wish to hear anything more about Pedro's antics in the prayer room.*

We watched television until dinner was ready and announced. Finally, Pedro exited the prayer room and greeted me, walked close by his daughter, and pulled her braids affectionately, then went to the washroom to wash his hands, before he came to the dinner table. When we were all seated at the table and began eating, Belkis announced: "After dinner, Desmond and I are going to dar un paseo in the city."

Pedro nodded in approval, but Josefina inquired, "Where are you guys going?"

"I'm going to show Desmond some of the attractions in the city, and we will hangout a bit at the Parque Céspedes," Belkis responded.

No other comment was made concerning the matter and when the repast was over, Belkis inquired if Josefina was okay doing the dishes, and she received an affirmative answer.

We bade goodbye, exited the house, and connected with Atrocha Street. We walked down to El Museo Carnaval, circled back to the Parque Céspedes, and sat on a bench made from iron and cured wood. The park was buzzing with passersby, tourists speaking in various foreign languages: Russian, German, Portuguese, among others that I was unable to decipher; Cubans and non-Cubans: Latin Americans and Spaniards, speaking in Spanish.

I pulled Belkis close to me, put my arms around her shoulders and inquired from her: "Do you wished to hear the information I have in store for you?"

"What is it?" she demanded.

"We don't have to rent a hotel room, for our first time, the college will be closed for the end of the year and new year. The college's administration is planning

a party for the Jamaican students, and we are allowed to invite a friend, and you are invited as my date."

She looked at me in consternation and exclaimed, "really!" Then she leaned her warm cheek against mine, with eyes closed. Her lips hunted mine, and when they found one another, they stayed together for a long and passionate kiss. We were both at the same place: we were on fire, yearning to give ourselves to each other, she desperately wanted to become a woman, and I badly wanted to end my "drought."

"The college will be empty, we could use one of the available bunks, we would leave the party early, I would fetch the sheet and bedspread from my bunk, and we would meet in the dormitory of the second floor below the Jamaicans dormitory."

"I occupy the first bed on the bunk that I share with another girl from Granma. We will do it on my side of the building, in my bed, I want to savor the moment, and knowing that I became a woman in my own bed would mean a lot to me," she said.

"I will provide you with the details as they become available," I told Belkis.

In less than two weeks we will end the torment, inquietude, suspense, and sexual deprivation. It was agreed upon that we were going to use Belkis dormitory and bed for our celebration and hence we changed the conversation to talk about her extended family.

I learned from Belkis: "Mi tia Conchita's former boyfriend, a dentist by profession, left her embarazada with Vinent, 14 years before, and migrated to Mexico, he stayed connected with Vinent but not with Conchita. However, my aunt now has a new man in her life, a married man with wife and children, my aunt, and her partner both work for the municipal government, and they meet regularly at hotels in the city. My aunt Esmeralda and my uncle Camilo have been married for more than 30 years, my aunt is a homemaker, my uncle works in a canning factory, as a supervisor. My cousin Lilian, the eldest of the two daughters, works for the municipal government, she has a lover, a married man, who is a member of the Cuban arm forces, with wife and two children. My cousin Odalys, the younger, works at a nearby primary school, as a physical and health education teacher, she is married to Alfonso, her college sweetheart; he works at the sport centre in El Distrito Frank País as a swimming instructor."

Thank you "I heard all I wanted to hear, besides the music is too loud, and you have to keep repeating yourself, at my request," I told her.

The evening was still young, though the streetlights were on, the park was lit thoroughly, and full of life, music bellowing from speakers located around the park while buses stopped intermittently, unloading passengers who were coming into the city for a night out; and loading people leaving the city centre after hours of shopping and window shopping. The evening chill began to make its presence felt; the park was famous for its evening chills; its location favours the condition.

Parque Céspedes is situated on land that sloped down from the back of Hotel Venus to La Alameda Avenue which was close to a large stream of water that produced cool air across the slope.

"I'm feeling cold, maybe we should get going," Belkis said.

I agreed with her, and we got up off our seats and started walking back when we noticed the line up for tickets to get into the movie theatre.

"Do you want to see a movie?" I asked.

"Yes, but it is going to be late when we get back home," Belkis replied. However, while you are in the line, I could run home and let my dad and Josefina know that we are going to the movie, and we will be late returning home.

She squeezed my hand and set off walking briskly towards Jiménez Street with her glutei maximi jolting with every step she took. I joined the line, which was not long, after about seven minutes, I purchased the tickets before Belkis returned, I waited for her return which lasted approximately 20 minutes. When she arrived, she was wearing a maroon sweater; she said, "Everything is fine, my parents are okay with our decision."

We held hands and entered the movie theatre, while the lights were still on. We shuffled across the backrow to find two vacant seats in the middle of the row and sat down. We avoided going down to the front of the theatre in case we had felt the need to make out, and the backrow was the ideal location, no one would be behind us to pry, and those beside us would be too focused on the film to notice what we were up to beside them.

The movie theatre was convenient for us since Belkis was not inclined to show her affection for me at her father's house. She was unnerved by her father and did not want to raise any suspicions as she was not sure how he would have reacted. Surprisingly, we conducted ourselves respectfully in the theatre, the movie "Spellbound," was riveting and interesting, it captured our attention, and we were hooked until the end of it. After the movie, I went with Belkis to her house, she insisted that I go inside and stay a while, she wanted to be near me. She wanted to spend time with me, she did not think she could sleep easily given what she had heard earlier.

I conciliated her, I went in and sat down in a balancing chair, Pedro and Josefina had already turned in for the night, though not yet asleep, Josefina inquired if it were we who had arrived, and Belkis answered in the affirmative. Belkis, aware that her parents were in bed, with their bedroom door closed, removed her sweater, threw it on the back of one of the chairs around the dining table. She came over to where I was, sat on my thighs, put her arms around my neck and began kissing me, then pulled her blouse open, put her breast in my mouth and whispered in my ear.

"I can't wait to get you inside me; I have been thinking about it all evening, I came a couple of times just thinking about you poking around inside me."

It was now up to me to be reticent. "Your parents are in the room close to us, and they may hear our frantic breathing," I reminded her.

"Look at who is talking, you are responsible for my current state, my behaviour is a result of your training," she whispered.

"That is true, but we have never made out in your dad's house before."

She then looked at me with her adoring eyes, put her enlarged lips to mine and kissed me and murmured: "I love you more than words can express."

"I need to catch the last bus or else I will have to walk to the college," I whispered.

"You better go now," she said.

We both stood up and she walked me to the exit door, then we embraced and kissed each other one last time for the night.

Belkis stood in the doorway until I reached the corner of Flamenco and San Miguel streets, we waved to each other, and she closed the door, and I proceeded to the bus stop. I reached the bus stop 25 minutes after midnight, the last bus was scheduled to run at 12:30 a.m., I waited until 1 a.m., and the 12:30 a.m. bus did not show up. I decided to walk approximately three miles, the streets were "naked," no vehicles, not a single person in sight. I walked all the way to the college, ground keepers were not in sight, the lights in the dormitories were off. I lazily climbed the stairs to my dormitory, removed my clothes, put on my pyjamas, and went to bed without going to the bathroom. I tried thinking about Belkis and what we were in for with a little over a week to go, but sleep overpowered me, and I woke up to the call for breakfast the next morning.

Chapter 29

L eading up to the big day, Belkis and I saw each other, every day, two or three times per day, morning, noon, and evening. We engaged in our usual conversation but existed in a world of trance. We were patient but anxious and wishing nothing would pop up to ruin the occasion for us. The party was planned for Friday, January 2, 1981, two days after New Year's Eve, 1980. Belkis and I made plans to meet at her mother's place at 7 p.m. on the evening of the party. I showed up on time and knocked on the door. Gladys appeared in front of me and invited me inside. The radio was on, and the time was announced. Almost instantly, Belkis and Lorena came out of the bedroom to join us in the living room.

Belkis was gorgeous. She was a natural beauty. She was wearing no make-up but sporting light-smelling lavender mint perfume. Her long black hair, the artificial brown colour removed, hung loose, and *swept to one side of her head, with a pink carnation fixed to the side where her face was left bare. She was wearing a dark polka dot dress with a V-neck cut above her cleavage, black loafer shoes, sterling silver earrings and necklace with a heart pendant and a dark shoulder bag. Her mother remarked, looking at me smiling.*

"Desmond, she is pretty, um?" hmm.

"Extremely pretty and glowing," I replied.

Belkis and her sister giggled for a moment. At about 7:45 p.m., we said our goodbyes and were told to have an enjoyable time—little did they know that we were going to have the time of our lives.

Belkis and I walked arm in arm to the college campus on our best behaviour; the silence around us was pervasive, our conversation was mainly about who would be at the party, apart from Jamaicans, and what could be expected. Upon reaching the steps of the building that led up to the corridor of the first floor, I held Belkis in my arms, looked her in the eyes and told her: "Sweetheart, you are very beautiful; an angel would have a hard time competing with you."

"You aren't looking too bad yourself," she said.

I pulled her in closer to me, put my hands around her rump, squeezed her against me and kissed her wildly. After that little display of affection, we went up the stairs to where the music was playing on the second floor of the academic wing of the building; we were greeted with words in English, like, "Way to go, Desmond. Don't let her out of your sight; she is wonderful!"

I ignored the comments, and Belkis did not speak or understand English. But she knew the partiers were referring to her.

"What are they saying?"

"They are paying you compliments but don't worry about what they are saying," I reassured her.

At that moment, Jimmy Cliff's song began playing: "Wonderful World, Beautiful People," and I asked Belkis if she wanted to dance, and she started moving her body even before answering me. The evening was hot because of how many people were in the room; after the playing of about four songs, I felt thirsty and wanted something cool to drink; I asked Belkis if she would like something as well, she responded positively, so I went and requested a cold beer for myself and a highball for her. The beer became hot before I had a chance to finish it, and about halfway through drinking it, I threw it away and asked for some water. We continued dancing and talking with other party attendees until about 11 p.m. I invited Belkis onto the balcony, and we discussed the revellers.

Burning with desire, after about 10 minutes, I wrapped my arms around her, kissed her, and told her: "It is time."

She said, "Let's go."

Chapter 30

We drifted away discreetly, descended the stairs to the corridor and walked across to the dormitories' wing of the building, and ascended the stairs to Belkis dormitory on the second floor. The dormitory was in darkness, the door was open, and she closed it, led me over to where her bed was and began kissing and rubbing against me. I lifted her dress and caressed her bottom, pushed my finger through her panties waist and lowered it to her knees; I opened the zipper in the back of her dress, pulled down the sleeves of her dress below her shoulders, and the dress fell to the ground. I removed her panties, bra, and shoes completely. She helped me to undress, I lifted her trembling body, light and delicate, and I laid her down on the bed; our bodies were burning hot, she drew me on top of her, but I shuffled off her body to the side and began kissing her all over, I caressed her soft but firmed breast and put her nipples into my mouth alternately and suck them tenderly.

She begged me, "Come inside me, please; I want to feel you in me."

I whispered pretty words in her ears, "I'm going to make you cum, I'm going to drain your swamp, you are here with me, then heaven must be missing an angel…" I caressed her vulva and labia; she shivered and moaned for a few seconds; I kissed her passionately and ran my fingers across, up and down her mound. She was moist; I made love to her; we exploded in ecstasy and rolled onto our sides. We lay kissing and caressing each other for a while.

"Thank you for liberating me; that was wonderful," she said.

"You are welcome; the experience was pleasurable for me," I assured her.

The continued kissing and caressing made us excited in short order, she climbed on top of me, spread her legs across my hips, made herself comfortable, ride herself to pleasure and screamed in joy, then fell on top of me and whispered above my face: "You make me really happy."

Belkis got out of bed, and told me she would be back shortly, in the dark, she ambled away, shortly thereafter, I heard water running; she was in the bathroom, tidying herself and when she came back, she said. "We should be going now," we got dressed and were on our way to Lorena's house where she would spend the night. Along the way, across the sports village and park, we stopped to kiss and embrace each other approximately every five minutes, wherever there were shades of darkness, behind the kiosks in the park; on one of our stops behind the pastry kiosk, we kissed and embraced with unbelievable force and energy, I was on fire with *desire; she was no different from me. I fumbled around in her bosom, found her nipples, and sucked on them alternately; she moaned and breathed heavily, I lifted her dress, I found no underwear; I moved my fingers up to her mound and probed her swamp; she opened my fly, took out my stiffness, helped me inside her, and began panting, breathing heavily, groaning, gasping, suddenly she clutched onto me and climaxed, then whispered to me, Desmond, "You bastard, what are you doing to me?"*

I whispered in her ears, "You are as guilty as I'm."

She held and squeezed my body and said, "Behave yourself now, that is it for tonight."

I walked her to Lorena's, the door was close but unlocked, we entered, no one came out to see us in, we kissed and embraced, I began fondling Belkis, she pulled away and whispered, "aqui no papi."

"You're right, cosita linda. The state I'm in; I better get going."

"You are correct; I'm in an awful way as well," she said.

I kissed her on the cheek and turned to leave, and she cautioned me, "Be careful, and don't forget to come and get me on Sunday afternoon,"

I returned to the college campus, walking leisurely, thinking about what we had just done, Belkis and me. I was pleased with myself and thought the wait was worth it. Belkis, with all her inexperience, turned me on amazingly.

I began to feel a profound attraction for her; she was in love with me; I knew it and could see it in her demeanour, her manner towards me, her kindness, tenderness, affection, and her willingness to give all herself to me and asked for nothing in return. She was unlike any other girl I had known and been with; it was a shame we were of two different worlds, and eventually, that was a subject we would have to discuss.

I went to get Belkis at Lorena's Sunday afternoon, but we did not hang around too long. We wanted to chat about Friday night and how we managed our emotions, needs and desires. We both agreed that we had a beautiful experience, missed each other terribly, thought about each other incessantly, overly anxious for another round. But we must exercise self-control, self-respect, patience, and good behaviour in the presence of others. There was already talk on campus about us: we were inseparable, the perfect couple, always together, and making others feel awkward. Furthermore, we had no intention of comporting ourselves like the maniacs on campus who took every opportunity to play out their sexual fantasies.

Chapter 31

We began the new calendar year and second semester and still have not received official communication from the newly sworn-in Jamaican Government or the Cuban authority. However, we tried as best we could to wear a brave face and not be fazed by the prospect of being recalled to Jamaica, though in our internal group discussions, we wished that possibility did not befall us. Furthermore, our anxiety intensified when less than half of the first-year group, who did the first of their two practicums in Jamaica, did not return to Cuba, and those who came back had to absorb the cost of returning themselves.

The arrangement was for them to do two six-month sessions of practice teaching in Jamaica, the first in their third year and the second in their fourth year. Fortunately, they received their placement before the elections were held. They received no support or instructions from the Government, and the opposition PNP was no longer "calling the shots." Hence, they were in limbo, and kept in the dark. The stipend from the Jamaican Government was discontinued, and the prospect of continuing and completing their studies became uncertain. We learned from them that they contacted the PNP about their predicament and were told that if they could find their way back to Cuba on their own, they would be allowed to continue and complete their studies. On that note, several chose not to return and remain in Jamaica.

Their practice teaching arrangement was modified, and instead of doing two stints of practice teaching, they only did one. That same year the college changed its requirement of two stints of practice teaching to one only. And our group was allowed to do our practice teaching in Cuban schools and sports centres. This development provided a glimmer of hope for us.

The weekend before classes resumed, I held a meeting to discuss our situation, tried to allay fears, and instill calm, which was important considering that we were kept outside of the loop of what was to be our fate. I reminded the group that if we were in Cuba, we would have the support of the PNP, and our chances of completing our program were promising. Further, I explained that I have no information from either the Jamaican Government or the Cuban authority regarding our fate; we have no control over the decision that may come down to us: politics trump everything, though our objectives are unchanged, our mission is to acquire the skills and education we came for, even if we are denied the opportunity to complete our studies; until then we owe it to ourselves to be resilient, resolute, disciplined, and confident in all our endeavours.

I cautioned the group against engaging in illegal activities, as those would be grounds for the Cuban authority to discontinue their support to us, which would make it easy for the Jamaican Government to demand that we return home before completing our studies. I opened the floor for others to speak or ask questions, and saved for one person, silence gripped the room.

"Will we be going home for the summer vacation? If we do on our own, would we be allowed to return to Cuba?" Andrea asked.

"You've as much information as I've on that matter," I told her.

However, we all left the meeting agreeing to continue our studies and attend classes on Monday after the weekend.

Once Monday arrived, the attitude was fairly positive among us. Most of us approached our studies with the fervour we had when we began the program in September 1979. The new semester schedule included the following subjects: mathematics, psychology, physiological anatomy, physics, chemistry, Spanish, Marxist thought, pedagogy, gymnastics, swimming, and basketball.

The second-semester schedule, unlike the first semester, carried only three physical activity classes. With one fewer class, the physical activity classes became longer. The introduction of new physical activities always stirred up mixed emotions, considering that several among us were not confident in practising certain sports either because they were not exposed to them or because they chose to avoid them deliberately because of relevancy concerns.

It should be noted that the sports that were practised widely in Jamaica were soccer and cricket by men and netball by women; the other sports were hit and miss, depending on whether one was from the city or the rural area. However, many of us attempted to practise all sports with determination because we were being prepared as physical and health education teachers to go back to Jamaica to work with children all over the island, and it was an opportunity to learn new things so we would be able to introduce them to the various schools and communities.

There were a few among us who resented the fact that we had a lot of new activities; these students were interested only in their specialization and often complained about having to do things that they may never use throughout their careers. But as the teachers often explained, our career development was multifaceted, so we needed the right tools and essential skills necessary to shape lives in a modern world. Diverse physical activities were and are important to our ability to multi-task and manage an array of assignments in a world where technology was leaving many people behind who were trained in unidimensional tasking and do not have the dexterity to adapt and change quickly to the new demands of society.

It is worth noting that even on the verge of us spending two years in Cuba and immersed in the Spanish language, academic requirements, and the support of street lingo, several students among us were unable to communicate effectively in Spanish, creating a barrier to their pursuit of knowledge. Their language fluency was limited in scope: "What happening buddy? How are things going? See you later, partner," and hand gestures.

"Learning Spanish isn't in my DNA, and hence I struggle to string multiple sentences together," Heather declared.

"I think some of us are averse to reading anything that isn't mandated by our program requirements," I said.

"Desmond, you're fortunate to have the aptitude to learn Spanish quickly," Heather said.

"Don't go believing that it's only like that. I've committed myself and invested a lot of time in learning Spanish," I told her.

"Then maybe I don't have your dedication," Heather expressed.

"It's more than dedication; it's also strategic; Spanish is an essential skill to acquire the education that I came to Cuba for," I reminded her.

"All I know is that it's difficult for me," she said.

"Then you should consider asking yourself if you're motivated enough," I told her.

"Believe me, it isn't for a lack of trying; I really do try. Andrea, a couple of the other girls, and I have even begun attending French classes to see if it would help us to improve our Spanish," Heather claimed.

"Then my advice to you is that you persevere and try to make friends with Cubans; it'll force you to learn Spanish in order to communicate with them," I assured her.

For some of us who were aptitude endowed, we were unable to fathom the inability of the others and judged that they were uninterested, maybe even lazy, without recognizing that each of us is wired differently, and our capability varied according to our genetic make-up. I did my best to be empathetic and encourage and support those that were always behind in their endeavours. Language was not the only adversity our group had to overcome or live with; several of the physical activities also posed challenges for several of my colleagues.

Our first swimming class was held in the small pool, fifty feet in width, seventy-five feet in length, and five feet six inches in depth at the deep end, which progressively reduced to about 18 inches at the shallow end. Our class was one of two held in the pool at the same time. For the lesson, we had a female teacher, Clarissa. A white lady with long brown hair hanging mid-way down her back, average built, wearing a one-piece swimsuit, she was a very competent and patient individual. Clarissa brought, apart from the attendance sheet and pencil, several kickboards, several large multi-coloured inflated rubber tubes, and a few floating rings, to class. She was a natural in the water, demonstrating the exercises; she displayed impeccable smoothness and grace, and she moved in the water like a swordfish. Clarissa was able to convince most of us to at least enter the water halfway through the length of the pool, hold on to the edge of the pool, and lift our bodies to line up with our outstretched arms. After several repetitions, she switched to doing water pumps; this activity was entertaining to most of us who were in the water.

Later, she instructed us: "Line up against the edge of the pool and take a kickboard. Once you have your kickboard in hand, follow my lead." She demonstrated the actions we should perform; she stretched out on top of the water with a kickboard in her hands, leveled on top of the water, and scissored her legs, with her face immersed in the water, holding her breath, across the width of the pool to the other end and back several times.

Once she was convinced that we had seen enough, she asked us to imitate her movements; no one was in danger of going underwater as we were all standing where our heads were above the surface of the water, we tried to follow her instructions to the tee, but it was not possible for several of us. There was frustration among the group as several students only made it to a few meters in the pool, while others stopped and stood up several times on the way.

Undoubtedly, swimming was the most daunting activity for the group; not a single girl in the group could swim, and several guys could not either; a few were only able to tread water, and maybe four or five of us could help ourselves appreciably. The teacher, realizing our weaknesses, was not hung up on perfection; she allowed us to leisurely do whatever was possible. No rush to move from one activity to the next. But she did encourage those who were slow in executing the movements to keep trying and reminded us that we were not there to become athletes but rather to acquire and manage the techniques in order to be able to properly impart them later to children and youth.

The Cuban students in the pool next door to us were attracted by our inability to manoeuvre the exercises. For every failed attempt on our part, they laughed and mocked us, but the teacher asked us not to be deterred and to stay focused. By the end of the fourth class, most of our students, except for about three or four, were able to perform the techniques of the activities as they were described and shown to us.

One of the things that was noticeable about the Cuban teachers was that they spent a lot of time explaining the activities they wanted us to perform, and Clarissa was no different. Her devotion to our learning to swim was admirable even though several of us never got beyond floating and treading water after three semesters of classes: learning freestyle, breaststroke, and backstroke. There was one guy, Marcus, who, after the first class, never again entered the pool. Furthermore, Marcus was frequently absent from most of the physical activity classes and showed no ability or disposition to practise any of the disciplines.

Separate and apart from the specialization subjects, basketball was a welcome discipline for almost everyone in our group; even the girls were enthusiastic about learning to play and fully participated in the classes without a murmur. This may be attributed to the fact that most of the interaction with the ball was done by hand, which provided better control over the dynamics of the sport. After all, how difficult could it be to run, jump, dribble, pass and shoot hoops? Of course, in addition to pivoting, defending, and rebounding, there were essential qualities that must be in place to undertake these elements effectively: flexibility, speed, and resistance.

However, the aim of our training was to acquire and develop techniques to train young people, not to prepare us to become athletes. With that said, I am reminded of Trevor who went back to Jamaica after just one month in Cuba on the grounds that he was not able to practise table tennis as a discipline, forgetting completely or did not care to remember our purpose for coming to Cuba in the first instance—to become a physical and health education teacher. We did one semester of basketball, which for all intents and purposes was an indication that it was not a complicated discipline.

Our basketball class was the first class we had after lunch, and it was a good event to wake us up from the drowsiness that usually sets in after eating. The teacher, Lázaro, was white, with blonde hair, tall, and medium built. On the first day, he had a mesh sack with eight balls in one hand and the attendance registry in the other. He lowered them onto the concrete surface of the basketball court. Then he retrieved the attendance registry and opened it to take the attendance but was unable to pronounce our names properly and so requested one of our students to mark the attendance.

As was customary from all the teachers, Lázaro lectured us about the rules and mechanics of the game, and he showed us systematically how to execute the various elements. For the first time, the mood and interest in an activity had changed, even though students were eager to play the game rather than learning how to effectively execute the fundamentals of the sport.

The teacher quickly recognized our enthusiasm and change in attitude and adopted new strategies and tactics to manage his game plan. Everything we did was done on the run, mostly in small groups. He capped off the class each day with scrimmage games at both ends of the basketball court with four teams and by rotating players daily. The students enjoyed the class immensely and sometimes continued playing beyond the allotted time, which often cut into the class time that followed it. The energy level among us was always elevated even though many of us were on a poor diet and were not eating properly.

Having been to Jamaica in the summer of 1980, several students brought back canned food, rice, and processed condiments. A few of them even brought back hotplates so they could do their cooking when the meal in the canteen was unsatisfactory. One girl cooked her own meals every day and often all three meals. To the college's administration, this was not known, we believed, and if they did know, they made no fuss about the situation.

Jamaican students purchased their food, leaf, and root vegetables, pastries, and ice cream from kiosks in

La Feria close to the sport's village; flour and bread were purchased at the nearby bakeries, and flour was also donated to them by friends they had and visited in the communities in and around Santiago. Their purchasing power was maintained and supported by their disposition to off-load their possessions, clothes, shoes, camera, cassettes, cassette players, or any items that were appealing to the Cubans.

The female students, as far as it was known, did not engage in these activities directly, but several of them relied upon their male colleagues to do the bidding for them. Several of our male students even went much further; they made deals with Cubans and used part of the proceeds from the sale of their belongings to purchase American dollars from tourists, then invested it in buying jeans, short sleeve shirts for men and women, or any items that could be disposed of quickly in the communities in and around Santiago. These activities netted a considerable amount of profit which was reinvested several times over to keep the money supply stable.

In addition to the in-dormitory cooking, my colleagues regularly ate at restaurants in hotels that were reserved mainly for tourists: locals, foreigners, and Cuban government officials who were travelling the country on business.

Often when dinner was being served, it was difficult to find more than six or seven of the remaining 31 Jamaican students in the canteen. They were either out on the streets or confined to their dormitory, sorting out their meals independently of the college's canteen. There were also male students who had novias in the various communities throughout the municipality. These students spent a lot of evenings and weekends away from campus and ate in the home of their girlfriends.

These behaviours, buying and selling merchandise and absence from the college campus in the evening, were not acceptable to the college's administration. The previous year, when the PNP government was in power, one member of the 1978-79 group of Jamaican sports students was identified as engaging in these sorts of activities and was returned to Jamaica, no questions asked. But for some reasons, members of the 1979-80 group were not subjected to a similar fate, even though those who engaged in inappropriate behaviour were known to the Cuban authority and or the college's administration.

In Cuba, news traveled at the "speed of light" amongst the people. Hence, there was no doubt that the Cuban authority was up to date on the comings and goings of the Jamaican students and their activities. I can only infer that it had something to do with the fact that there was a change of Government in Jamaica, and the Cuban authority was not interested in further straining an already tenuous relationship with the newly elected pro-Washington administration.

Those of us who were not engaged in these illicit activities were nervous, embarrassed, stressed, and mortified because we were under no illusion if the Cuban authority was going to act, all of us in the physical and health education program would be sent home before completing our studies after having spent almost two years persevering in Cuba, maintaining discipline and at times going hungry due to limited food choices.

Tom, having noticed how things were unfolding, approached me, and let loose, "It seems some of us are having a good time while others are held in a vise grip."

"It certainly seems that way, doesn't it?

"I'm doing my best to stay in line, even though I must tell you, Jefe, it's difficult."

"I'm with you on that, Tom, but I'm not tempted or influenced to do something I don't believe is appropriate."

"Don't get me wrong, I'll not violate the rules. I don't wonna be sent back to Jamaica in disgrace."

"That's my thinking too. Anything like that would kill my mother, and I couldn't look my friends in the face again. I would probably have to move away from my district."

"Are you aware that sometimes I go without eating?"

"I imagine so because I, too, missed meals on several occasions, often consecutively. However, I try not to miss classes."

"You're encouraging. I won't lie, I missed a couple of classes here and there but try to limit the occurrences," Tom admitted.

The only good thing we had going for us was that class attendance was consistently at an acceptable level. Except for four or five "bad apples," most of us attended and participated in the classes. We studied, with challenges resulting from new vocabularies and different accents, but we were keen on supporting one another with homework and sometimes mock sessions to ensure comfort amongst those who were unsure of themselves and how well they could perform on the exams.

On a couple of occasions, we had surprise visits from INDER officials who conducted evaluations of our teachers. During these sessions, we were able to demonstrate to the officials that the teachers were imparting their material competently; when the teachers questioned us regarding aspects of the lessons and asked for an explanation of learned concepts, we raised our hands eagerly, and when called upon, we answered the questions with demonstrability and confidence. The teachers, following the evaluations, expressed their gratitude and praised us for coming through for them—they usually received high marks from the evaluators.

July was upon us; classes were over for the 1981 academic year, and we were still waiting for word from the Cuban or the Jamaican authority regarding our status. We were in limbo and not knowing what, if anything, was being planned for us. Members of the group began to inquire: were we going to be called home? Find our own way home? Remain in Cuba for the summer, or until the four-year program was completed? By all accounts, there was no indication that we were going to leave Cuba, over the summer months, for vacation or otherwise.

Therefore, I called a meeting of the group and advised my colleagues to keep an open mind. While hoping for the best, whatever is decided, we will hear about it and must reconcile ourselves to the new reality. The matter is not in our hands, and choices are luxuries we did not have.

Funny how in times of uncertainty and crisis, all that is needed is a voice of reason to bring calm to those who are worried but who will listen and heed advice, especially when there are no competing thoughts around. The college continued to cater to our needs and wants in the same manner as before the Jamaican general elections. However, we were isolated. Cuban students went home for the summer vacation, teachers were on holidays, kitchen, grounds, and maintenance staff were reduced significantly, leaving on campus only as many people as was needed to ensure our continued existence.

Chapter 32

There was one occasion, Cuban officials invited us on a visit to the Friendship House in Santiago, a place where foreign students meet on occasion to commemorate or celebrate events in their homeland, to meet other foreign students and hear about their nation's challenges back home. That afternoon the focus of attention and discussion was on the Palestinian students and their description of the Israeli occupation of their homeland.

We all agreed that the visit was a great idea and would do us good to get away together for a well-deserved break from the college campus. However, we were apprehensive about leaving the dormitories unguarded and expressed our concerns to the college's administration about the security of our belongings, but our concerns were not taken seriously; instead, we were assured that no one would attempt to enter the college grounds and besides, all the Cuban students were away for the summer vacation.

It turned out our concerns were legitimate. When we returned from the visit, we found the dormitory in a cluttered condition; a significant amount of our things missing: jeans, running shoes, dress shoes, pullovers, t-shirts, and hats were all gone. We were in disbelief and angry at the situation, especially given that we knew that the scenario could have been prevented had the college's administration taken our concerns seriously. The girls were fortunate, they were not robbed. A couple of the girls stayed behind owing to ill health. In any case, women's garments were not in great demand in Santiago compared to those of men.

We concluded that the perpetrators were men, and they raided our possessions in order to sell their loot in out-of-town communities where the plunder would not be recognized. Everyone asked and expected me to take up the matter with the college's administration because we all believed that we should be compensated for our loss. I promised my colleagues that I would speak to the administration about the situation and communicate our desire.

I approached José, that same evening, who remained at the college throughout the summer months, and informed him of our discovery.

"We've been robbed. I would like you to visit our dormitory to see for yourself what has occurred."

"I'll accompany you right away," he said.

"We have been relieved of most of our clothing and accessories, and my colleagues are livid."

"I'm sorry to hear that."

"This situation could have been prevented if you guys had listened to me when I expressed concerns about leaving the dormitories unguarded," I told him.

"It seems you're being watched because outsiders rarely come on campus," he said. "They know if they're caught, they could get into serious trouble."

"Well, they entered the college and our dormitory and stole most of our belongings, and they haven't been caught."

"Let's see how we may manage the situation going forward."

As soon as we were in the common area of the male dormitory, my colleagues gathered around José, and everyone began talking at the same time and demanding that they be compensated for the loss of their belongings. I interceded, "Please be calm and allow José to hear our complaints in an orderly fashion, one after the other." The noise dissipated, but there were sounds of low chattering. Nonetheless, I invited José into the dormitory, and he looked around for approximately 15 minutes and asked me, "Can you accompany me to the office?" Then he told me, "Sit, please," "So you all believe that you should be compensated?"

"Yes, because some of us lost almost everything, and we don't see how else to replace them, given that there is no indication that we will be going to Jamaica anytime soon."

"Please discuss the matter with your colleagues and make a list of the articles that were stolen and the corresponding value in pesos."

"I have no problem getting the list, but my colleagues aren't going to be happy receiving compensation in pesos since they wouldn't be able to replace their stolen items from shopping at regular Cuban stores."

"Then we have a problem because the college isn't in a position to make amends in any currency other than Cuban pesos."

"I will discuss the matter with my colleagues and get back to you with both the list and any decisions we arrived at about currency."

I was not very optimistic about how my colleagues would receive and react to the news that they could only be compensated in Cuban pesos. However, I approached the matter as delicately as possible. We came together in the common area of the dormitory for a brief meeting; I explained the position of the college's administration. A few of my colleagues were incensed to hear the news, but the vast majority were inclined to go along with the proposal, which I believed showed a high degree of understanding. Besides, it was common knowledge that Cuba was having difficulty acquiring foreign currency, especially American dollars.

The objectors, once they found out that they were in the minority, decided to go along with the decision of the majority to accept compensation in Cuban currency. I set about compiling the list, and everyone listed their stolen items and associated costs as best as they could. The list was finalized late into the evening, so I decided to submit it to José the following morning, which I did at about 10 a.m. He thanked me and promised that he would submit the list and pertinent information to INDER. From that day forward, I was never able to get a straight answer from José regarding our compensation. Each time I brought up the subject with him, he would tell me that he was still waiting for a reply from INDER; surprisingly, my colleagues never once asked me about their compensation. After a while, I stopped inquiring about the issue's status, and the Cuban authority never compensated us for the loss of our belongings.

Despite our losses, we were all looking forward to the festivities that Santiago is famous for: Carnival in

Santiago. Carnival attracted local and international tourists, providing good business for the hospitality industry and welcome exposure for the Cubans and their way of life. The hotels in Santiago were usually booked solid for the duration of the carnival.

The streets were bustling with revelers; music was blaring everywhere and alternating between live bands and recorded music within a five-mile radius of the city centre where people concentrated, eating macho asado and rice, pork sandwiches, baked chicken, ayaca or hallaca (various meat pieces, wrapped in cornmeal dough, all folded within banana leaves, tied with strings, and boiled), and drinking mostly rum and beer from barrel, bottles, and cans.

During the day, it was not unusual to see groups of people sitting in booths, on street corners, in small parks, or on balconies, discussing baseball or politics. Other common manifestations were people sleeping on the sidewalks, on benches, in the parks, and accompanied by the occasional brawl. At night, people danced exuberantly to live bands, walked from street to street to observe floats located on flatbed trailers with models dressed in costumes, and frequently paraded the streets. Also, this was a time of new beginnings for many Cubans, initiating new relationships and dissolving old ones.

Carnival in Santiago was a time for merrymaking and partying, and several of my colleagues wasted little time getting into the swing of things. The guys were in the streets, night, and day, head-to-head with tourists and the Cubans, making new friends, hooking up with Cuban girls and occasionally with tourists, and engaging in illicit business transactions—buying and selling American dollars and items that were not accessible in Cuban pesos.

During the two months of summer, some of my colleagues spent a lot of time away from the campus at Cuban families' and girlfriends' homes, but they also brought girls into our dormitory, though not for sleepovers, for the purpose of sexual rendezvous. Often, their behaviour was atrocious and unbecoming of postsecondary education students, but no amount of advising and cautioning would deter them from carrying out their repulsive acts. It was reported to me that often several of my colleagues brought females to the dormitory to have group sex with them—a single girl at a time—the audience were spectators as well as participants—which, in my view, was an embarrassment to students who valued decency.

Chapter 33

Belkis and I continued our sexual rendezvous unabated. On the Saturday following our taste of paradise, Belkis and I went to the beach, Caleton Blanco, in the late afternoon and spent the night. Belkis and several other Cuban students did not go home that weekend and remained in the college.

We arranged to meet at about 5 p.m. on Saturday at the rear steps of the ladies' dormitory wing of the college; we were both on time, and we checked to make sure we were equipped with our needs and wants, snacks, bathing suits, toiletry, and beach towels. In 20 minutes, we were on a city bus going down to La Alameda Avenue, and after about 15 minutes wait, the country bus that ran between Caleton Blanco and the city of Santiago appeared, it was an hour drive, seating capacity was not attained, so we were seated comfortably. After another 20 minutes, we were on our way.

When we reached Caleton Blanco, we got off the bus one stop before the loading and off-loading buses depot. The road ran approximately 10 metres away from the beach. We went through a barbed wire fence. The time was about 7 p.m. We were alone and decided to eat. Belkis had brought guava and cheese sandwiches and sodas. The temperature was warm, but there was a strong wind blowing off the ocean. Mosquitoes, which were usually prevalent everywhere in Cuba after dark were absent.

We spread our bath towels and sat down on the ground between the fence and the sand, leaving enough space between us to put the sandwiches and sodas. Belkis unraveled the package containing the sandwiches, and we each took a sandwich and a soda. We offered each other a bite of sandwich, but we both refused; we were content with our own. After we finished eating and drinking, we removed our outer garments and promenaded on the beach, up and down for about 25 minutes, talking about what had happened the previous weekend and how much we missed each other and longing to relive the experience.

Belkis asked me: "Did you enjoy me? Did I do it right? Was my performance what you had expected?"

"You were wonderful; for a newbie, you made me happy," I joked.

"Now that you have conquered me, will you be going after other girls? Because I know there are several of them who are interested in you," she quipped back.

"I'm not done conquering you, I don't only want your body, but I also want your heart, mind, and soul."

She jumped on me, tied me with her legs and thighs around my waist, arms around my neck, and remarked, "I gave you my body because you had already conquered my spirit, and there was nothing else for me to give."

"Thank you for letting me know; I wasn't aware that my success was so great,"

"Well, now you know."

I fell to my knees and unwrapped her from around me, leaned over her body, and began caressing her from head to toe.

"Do you love me, Belkis?"

"With all my heart,"

I kissed her on the lips and told her, "I'm going to make love to you right here on the sand."

She shuddered and pulled me down on top of her and squeezed me tightly. We undressed each other and caressed our bodies until we were swollen, she was moist, but she crossed her legs tightly, so I had to use all the force of my upper body to release them; when I finally succeeded, she laughed, and relaxed and invited me inside, I made love to her fervently; we had second and third servings.

At about 10:30 p.m., we put back on our swimwear, decided to change our location, went back through the fence to the road and walked to the buses' depot, entered it, and picked up the beach on the other side. About a hundred yards away from the buses' depot, next to some shrubs and under a small tree, about six to seven feet tall, we spread out our bathing towels, put down our things, and headed for the water; we were alone, no one in sight, the half-moon shined on the water's surface and glistened everywhere on the ocean as far as our view could reach.

After a short swim and frolicking around, we returned to the beach area where we had left our belongings, got our towels, dried ourselves off, and laid down cuddling up to each other. With warm bodies exhausted from earlier activities, we fell asleep and were later awakened by raindrops smacking our naked bodies; our belongings were left exposed and began to get wet; we quickly gathered them up and pushed them into the bag in which Belkis had brought the sandwiches and bathing towels.

We checked the buses' depot and learned that the last bus to Santiago had already pulled out of the depot, and our only option was to spend the night on the beach. We shuffled under the shrubs and made ourselves as comfortable as possible, given the circumstances. The rain kept on coming for almost three hours, but the temperature was warm, and despite the rain wetting us, we were comfortable. We hugged each other and wrapped our bodies in bathing towels. Once the rain tapered off, we fell asleep and never woke again until the daylighted.

The next morning, we were ready to leave for Santiago at about 6 a.m. We got our stuff together and headed for the buses' depot, but the first bus did not arrive until about 9 a.m. By the time the bus arrived, we were awfully hungry, but there was nothing to eat, the snack bar was not open, and the bus was in no hurry to leave. There were hardly any passengers on board. It was Sunday morning, lots of people were coming to the beach, but no one was leaving, and we had had enough and wanted to get back to Santiago.

The bus pulled out of the depot at approximately 10 a.m., making very few stops along the way compared to when we were arriving. Therefore, the journey back to Santiago was covered much faster, and within an hour we were at the bus stop on La Alameda Avenue. Anxious to get back to the college, I was stopped in my tracks, and my enthusiasm was dashed.

Belkis remarked, "It seems I have lost my necklace; I can't find it."

She rummaged through our things and pockets without any success.

I offered to retrace our steps at the beach, hoping to stumble upon it, assuming it did not break loose while we were in the water.

"Continue to the college," I told her, "I will return to Caleton Blanco in search of your neckless."

"I'm sorry, papi, I should have been more careful."

"Don't worry about it, with these things, you never get any warnings."

"You are so sweet."

"And you are even sweeter, don't forget, I have tasted you a few times now."

I boarded the same bus we came on and went back to the places where we spent the night. I went over the areas meticulously but saw no sign of the necklace, a silver chain she received when she was accepted into the sports college from one of her maternal aunts who lived in Holguín.

Once I was satisfied that I would not be able to recover the necklace, I decided to hop on to the next available bus to Santiago; like the trip earlier, I was soon in Santiago and at the college. Upon arrival at the college, I saw a female student who I knew and asked her: "Can you go to Belkis' dormitory and inform her that I would like her to come down to the corridor because I want to speak with her."

"Happy to do it," she responded and ran off.

In a matter of minutes, I heard footsteps pitter-pattering down the stairs; not surprisingly, it was Belkis; with a broad smile on her face, she inquired, "Have you found the necklace?"

"No, but I looked everywhere we had been except for in the water, but that would be futile since the waves would have disrupted the sand and buried it anyway."

"It is okay; despite its sentimental value, it is nothing to worry about; thank you for making the trip back to search for it; I really appreciate your effort."

Then she said something that blew me away.

"I have collected lunch for you and asked James, your colleague, to put it up and give it to you when you arrive; hurry on because you must be very hungry."

I embraced and kissed her on the lips and thanked her. I bade her goodbye and went to my dormitory. As soon as I reached the common area of the dormitory, I saw James observing others playing chess.

"Your girlfriend collected lunch for you and asked me to save it for you; it is in your cupboard."

"Thank you, I'm grateful."

While I was eating, I could not help but think about Belkis' kindness, sensitivity, thoughtfulness, and how much she has given me without ever asking me for anything in return. I had no remorse in accepting her offerings, love, tenderness, affection, warm embraces, sweet kisses, and, most of all, her devotion.

Belkis and I discussed and agreed that we should spend more time together, getting intimate somewhere private, not on the college campus, and certainly not at her parents' homes, especially not at her father's.

I was under the impression that Belkis respected her father in a way that was much different from her mother's, and I also believed that she was intimidated by him. But more than anything else, Belkis did not want to give any hint that she was sexually active to her family and much less to her father. It appeared then that she was more comfortable with her mother than anyone else.

I remembered that on several occasions while we were at Lorena's place, she would often leave us alone for extended periods—a couple of hours at times. It was as if she was encouraging us by providing opportunities for us to relish one another. However, we conducted ourselves with restraint and never went beyond caressing, fondling, and kissing each other at Lorena's.

We decided that the most appropriate place for us to get together was at hotels, so we rented hotels at least two nights per month: I would use my monthly stipend from the Cuban Government and monies Belkis obtained from Lorena who was generous to her. Now my routine was that on Thursdays, I would spend almost the entire night at the hotel reservation centre to be among the first in line on Friday morning to be able to reserve a room for the upcoming Saturday night.

Belkis and I met in almost all the hotels in Santiago: Versailles, Venus, Las Americas, Libertad, Imperial, Casa Grande, Rex, Enramada, Balcon del Caribe, in addition to the cabins we rented at Siboney and Caleton Blanco Beaches. We were on fire, we had an insatiable appetite for sex, and we never missed an opportunity to compensate for the drought we experienced before, to make up for lost time, to enjoy each other's warmth, and celebrate our love.

After a while, we became careless; we were not being cautious; we entered and exited the hotels without regard for anyone, we occasionally spotted family acquaintances of Belkis, and we were certain that they had seen us even though they pretended not to. It was hard not to be noticed by individuals who knew Belkis' family; she was from the city. Almost her entire paternal family lived in Santiago; her mother, brothers, and sister also lived in the city. Cubans are also very communal; everyone knew someone in and around the city or in the entire province for that matter. Therefore, we were sure that any of those who we saw and assumed that they had seen us as well would have been likely to pass on the information to Belkis' parents—no Cuban can keep a secret; there is an old saying, the fastest ways to communicate are by "telegram, telephone, and tell-a-Cuban."

We were certain that her father had gotten wind of our hotel meetups because one evening, while he was in his prayer room. His wife was away visiting her mother. Belkis had the temerity to sit in my lap with her arms around my neck. Unexpectedly we were surprised by her father's sudden exit from the prayer room, and with a stern and angry look on his face, he inquired if Belkis and I were sleeping together. But neither of us responded, and Belkis remained seated in my lap. He walked away and entered his room without saying another word. In a few minutes, Belkis entered his room, and I heard muttering, not loud enough for me to discern what was being said. Belkis' voice was almost sustained for the length of time she was in the room. Belkis never revealed to me the content of her conversation with her father, and I never tried to pry, but I knew she was embarrassed by her father's remarks, so I did not want to make it a subject of conversation.

Other than meeting up with Belkis, the opportunity to eat a decent meal added value to my experience staying in the hotels of Santiago, if only for two days per month. The meals in the hotels were prepared for tourists, so the quality was never in question; I could choose from several meat options: beef, pork, lamb, mutton, duck, and chicken. I did not have to wait in long lines with locals to be seated and then be told it was all finished: no more food and no more cervezas.

One of Cuba's young couples' favourite hobbies was to eat out at restaurants— stand-alone restaurants or hotel restaurants; however, if they were not guests in a hotel, they had to wait in line for hours until after the guests were served, eaten, and exited the dining room. This situation was germane to months-ends when they were paid. Working Cubans got paid once a month, and their wages were not high, so they were not able to eat out more frequently.

Often, I joined the line; even though the Cubans were disciplined and did not cut the line, though the occasional person went ahead and took place among apparent friends, also it was noticeable when someone got called from behind me and seated at a table ahead of me. Such behaviour was dispiriting, especially when I protested the practice and was told that they had an appointment, which I knew was not true because I had asked more than once to make appointments and was told that no appointment was allowed: one got to eat on a first-come, first-served basis.

My experiences at restaurants, hotels, and stand-alone eateries were largely positive. They offered prompt service, courteous and friendly staff, and a clean atmosphere. Besides, my hotel experience was elevated by the fact that I was treated like a tourist, with my foreign accent, occasional eruption into English, and my attire, although not the best given that I had lost most of my garments and accessories due to the robbery that I experienced earlier. Therefore, I was disappointed when Belkis and I had to take a hiatus from our meetups.

Chapter 34

One evening Belkis and I sat down to chat as usual, and I noticed her eyes were welled up with tears. I inquired. "What is wrong mi melocotoncita? Why are you crying?"

"I think I'm pregnant because I missed my monthly, I'm not feeling myself these past few days, I'm always feeling nauseous, I fainted a couple of times, and my appetite is crushed. What am I going to do? My father is going to be furious. I have just a little over a year before graduation, I will have to leave college because I can't be in college if I'm pregnant, but I must graduate, or else the past two years plus would have been for nothing."

"Calm down. Let's talk this over wisely. This isn't only your problem. We are both responsible for this situation, so you aren't alone."

I knew that the pregnancy had to be terminated privately and discreetly, but I was hesitant to approach *the matter given the sensitivity involved. Terminating a potential human life is not a decision to be taken lightly; it requires extreme delicacy, absolute soberness, complete understanding, impeccable judgment, and the awareness that for every action, there are intended and unintended consequences. Furthermore, the matter was complicated by the fact that her family was of the catholic faith. However, knowing that a decision needed to be made urgently, I asked her: "Do you want to go through with the pregnancy?"*

"Yes, but I can't; my future will be ruined, and I'll not be able to care for my baby adequately; life in Cuba is already difficult; can you imagine it without a profession? I failed to follow my mother's advice: 'Belkis, don't get pregnant before you complete your studies.'

"Well, we will have to terminate the pregnancy, but you have to tell your mother about it, just in case of unintended consequences."

"Dios mío papi, I'm scared. Do you think we would be doing the right thing? What if my father finds out?"

"Let us worry about that if it happens. Right now, the matter at hand requires swift action. Every passing day makes the situation more dangerous both for your health and the chance that your father might find out."

I asked a second time, "Do you agree that we should terminate the pregnancy because if you do, I can begin putting the "wheels in motion;" I have a friend, Dialo Khumalo, an African guy, who attends the medical school in Santiago and is now an intern at the General Hospital, I will talk to him about the procedure and the requirements for arranging it."

"Yes, because right now, I don't have a good alternative."

Diallo was tall and lanky, with coiled black hair and dark brown skin colour; he was soft-spoken and walked with extremely long strides. He was the partner of Eleanor, a girl from the first Jamaican group who attended the sports college.

I visited the medical school regularly to check up on a couple of acquaintances, and after multiple encounters and conversations with Diallo, we became friends and kept in contact even after his partner returned to Jamaica to do her practice teaching. I contacted Diallo and described the dilemma to him. "My girlfriend is pregnant. It is still early, and we wish to terminate the pregnancy, but we want to keep the information private. We want to avoid the official channel at the hospital because her father mustn't know about it, and neither the college's administration."

"Don't disclose the information to anyone; I work and have contacts in the area where the procedure must take place; I will make the necessary arrangements and let you know the first available date."

Subsequently, the date, time, and location of the procedure were told to me within a week; the pregnancy was not two months old yet, not that it made the ordeal any more tolerable; I had difficulty sleeping at night, food was tasteless, and worry permeated my consciousness. What if anything unfortunate should occur? We were not going through the normal channel; I was putting the life of my girlfriend in the hands of an intern medical student; Belkis trusted me completely in the matter, she went along with whatever I said or did, and that was a burden I was not happy shouldering. But in my view, I had limited choices available to me. The responsibility felt enormous; I was tired and overwhelmed with emotions, my heart was dictating my feelings, and I felt close to Belkis, more so than ever before; the attachment was undetachable; I loved her profoundly and did not want anything unpleasant to happen to her.

I discussed the date of the procedure with Belkis and other arrangements that were necessary: she would have to speak with her mother, and I would speak with the director of lodging, Orestes, about her staying at the college for the weekend following the procedure. Orestes was a rough "dude;" all the Cuban students were intimidated by him; he was stern, mean, loud, and did not hesitate to suspend or expel students who stepped out of line.

In the evening, when it was bedtime, and Orestes made the announcement that everyone should proceed to their dormitory, no one disobeyed. Everyone would stop whatever they were doing and make their way up to their dormitory. If, by chance, anyone missed the directive, they would be dodging around corners and discreetly making their way to their dormitory without him noticing them.

I approached Orestes and asked him. "Would it be possible for my girlfriend, Belkis, to stay at the college this weekend?"

"Yes."

Without hesitation or questions, just like that, Orestes agreed to my request.

I had always thought that Orestes knew the reason for my request but preferred not to interfere. And as I have said earlier, in Cuba, there are no secrets from the authority. Nevertheless, I was grateful that he granted my request—sometimes, those that appear the meanest can be kind and understanding if they are given the opportunity.

I made the decision to be with Belkis when she told her mother the news and the unpleasant decision we were making. One evening after classes, we went to visit her mother, and as luck would have it, Lorena was alone in the house; Felipe, Lionel, and Gladys were not home yet, which made delivering the news a little more comfortable because we did not have to worry about anyone eavesdropping. We exchanged greetings, and Belkis holding one of my hands, told her mother, Mummy, "I have something to tell you."

"Tu eres embarazada?"

"Yes, but we aren't going to keep our bebé; we have already made arrangements to terminate our pregnancy."

"Have you told your father?"

"No, and we aren't going to tell him; you're the only one in the family we are telling, and you mustn't tell anyone."

"You are an adult and responsible for making your own decisions; I only hope you are aware of what it is you are doing and the long-term impact it will have on you."

I remained silent throughout the conversation; this was a matter for mother and daughter to iron out, the perception must be that it was Belkis' decision, and I was not an influencer; I was there only for moral support and, if necessary, to reassure that all would be managed professionally in a conducive environment.

Lorena concurred that it was best that no one else but the three of us knew about the pregnancy and inquired if we needed any help.

"The plan is for Belkis to stay in the college after the procedure for a few days so that she can recuperate, but she would like to come to your place for meals since no Cuban students are allowed to be in the college that weekend, and no accommodation was being made for them," I explained to Lorena.

"I will do whatever you guys need me to do; I'm here to help."

"Thank you very much," I said, "I will support Belkis for better or for worse."

I accompanied Belkis to the hospital; I engaged her in conversation to get her to think of something other than the imminent procedure, which I knew was impossible. But what else could I do?

"Do you think you are strong enough to deal with what is coming to you?"

"I'm nervous, but I believe so, and I hope everything goes well."

"You will be fine, and if you think that way, half the battle is already won."

"I'm really happy that you are here with me, papito."

"There is no place else that I would rather be, my love."

"I wish you could come into the procedure room with me."

"Don't worry about that now; I will be out here waiting for you to come back to me in the best condition possible."

"Can you hug me, please? I'm feeling cold."

"Yes, and anything else you want me to do," I said jokingly.

"Thank you, but there is just one thing on my mind right now."

"I hope you aren't thinking dirty because I'm not."

"Good, because I'm too sad and torn up right now."

"Belkis Sanchez," a young lady standing in one of the doorways of the hospital passageway called.

"Aquí señorita."

"Venga conmigo mi amor." Or come with me my love.

Belkis stood and went through the open passageway double doors.

In about an hour-and-a-half, she returned to me, looking pale, weak, exhausted, and with teary eyes, and I thought to myself, without saying it out loud, it must have been difficult for her—having to part with part of herself.

However, I picked her up in my arms, took her to the steps which ended almost in the street, Carretera Central, put her down to sit on a tread of the steps, turned to the street, and flagged down an unlicensed taxi, the driver was eager to stop and make a few bobs. He exited the car in a rush and opened the backdoor for Belkis, and I, too, got into the back seat. I told him our destination, and in less than 10 minutes, we were at the back entrance of the college, I asked the driver the cost, and he said 50 centavos, but I gave him a dollar and told him to keep the change. Cuban students were still on campus, so we pretended that everything was well, and Belkis walked as normally as she could; I asked her how she felt, "Are you in pain?"

"No"

"Can you make it up the stairs by yourself?"

"I'm okay; you just relax. I'm stronger than I seem."

"Try and get some rest, sleep even. I hope it'll not be difficult to do that."

"If you need me for anything, don't hesitate to send me a message."

"No te preocupes, or don't worry, I will be okay."

"We will talk later, if you are up to it."

"Absolutely, cariño."

We hugged, and after, I watched her climb the stairs and disappear out of view. Once she was out of sight, I went to my dormitory. Except for the dormitory cuatelero, students were out at class, and I prepared myself for the next scheduled class and waited until it was time. When classes resumed after the change-over break, I met a couple of students who inquired where I was and how it was that I was not in the previous class; I told them that I had an errand to run, and to my relief, they did not pursue with further questions. By that time, everyone in the group knew that I was not the kind of person who gave personal information at will.

Furthermore, I did not believe I was thinking clearly. Many things were on my mind, Belkis' health and state of mind, my role in destroying a fetus, and my first child being deprived of entering and seeing the world. What if this was my only opportunity to have a child? What are the mental consequences of having participated in such a cold-hearted escapade? I am not religious, but I have always believed in the pricelessness of life because I have little to no control over its conception or development. Except for providing part of the chemical components that produces life, which makes me only an active bystander or, let's say, a volunteer participant who is governed by the desires of pleasure and carnal gratification, I am powerless in the creation of life.

However, by lunchtime, I was beginning to think a bit more clearly in terms of past, present, and future; what was done was already done; the present was about ensuring that Belkis recovers intact from the ordeal, and the future was living and coping with the experience and knowing that the memory will never be erased from our minds, no matter how hard we try. We were to live with guilt and annoyance for the rest of our lives.

At lunchtime, I decided that I would collect my lunch and find someone to take it to Belkis for me since she might not have wanted to get out of bed for some time. In addition to finding a container, I needed someone to make the delivery for me; I recalled that I had a plastic container that I had brought back from Jamaica on our return to Cuba after the 1980 summer vacation. I had used the container to carry sandwiches *in transit with me for my snacks. I wanted to be prepared just in case what they served on the plane was not appealing to me.*

After class, I went up to the dormitory and fetched the plastic container, took it to the canteen, and asked one of the kitchen staff with whom I had a good rapport: "Can you put my lunch in this container and give me an extra piece of bread, and a glass of milk?" She did as I asked and gave me the items, and I was soon on my way to the bottom of the staircase that led up to Belkis dormitory. I waited, hoping to see someone that I recognized and who could take the meal up to Belkis for me.

In less than a minute, I saw Marisol coming down the stairs; apparently, she was going to fetch her own lunch. She had utensils in her hands. I inquired of her: "Can you take this container back up the stairs to Belkis for me? She isn't feeling up to coming down to the canteen today, and I don't want her to pass the day without eating anything."

Marisol looked at me and smiled with inquiring eyes, only to say, "I would be happy to do it for you."

"Please give this to Belkis and tell her she must eat it, even if it is tasteless."

"I will wait until you return—just to make sure you made a successful delivery; if Belkis is sleeping, please wake her up."

"Please keep my utensils until I return," Marisol said.

I nodded in affirmation and took her possessions.

Shortly after, Marisol returned empty handed, which meant the delivery was successful. She told me, "Belkis sent thanks and that she will speak with you later in the afternoon." I thanked her for the favour and returned her possessions to her.

I observed her looking at the bread in my hand, and so I told her this is what I will be having for lunch today; I am on a diet. I kept the extra piece of bread I requested from the canteen, which was going to be all I would have for lunch that day. I knew she did not believe me, but she remained silent as we walked towards the canteen and the stairs to my dormitory. I thanked Marisol for doing me the favour and told her: "I will see you around," then I ascended the stairs to my dormitory.

All the Cuban students went home that weekend, most left on Friday afternoon and the remainder on Saturday morning. Belkis came down to the corridor in the late afternoon, at about 5 p.m., and from her usual location, she shouted for me; I looked through the louver window, she saw me, and she beckoned with one of her hands for me to come down to the landing. I complied with her request, and upon reaching the landing, we greeted each other and decided to sit on the edge of the ramp to the auditorium.

"How are you feeling?"

"I'm feeling much better than earlier today. Papi, I'm torn inside, my physical state is fine, but mentally I am a mess; knowing what I know now, if I had it to do again, I wouldn't do it; it is as though I'm carrying the burden of the world on my shoulders, and I'm not sure how much longer I can persevere."

"Let us take it one day at a time; you aren't alone; I'm devastated too; my conscience is in turmoil, but I believe as time goes by, our transgression may become easier to live with."

We spent about an hour talking about our circumstances, the baby that will never be, her parents, my non-status in Cuba, our relationship, and the precautions we must take as we go forward. We decided from then on, we were going to use protection.

Our choice was the contraceptive patch since condoms were not frequently available in Santiago. Again, she was willing to put herself at a disadvantage—I had no opportunity to front up any responsibility. Our conversation ended abruptly when dinner was announced.

That Friday evening, we wanted to have our meal together before the Cuban students headed home for the weekend, so we decided to go and get our utensils and meet up again so we could collect our meals and eat together. When she returned, she brought with her my plastic container and thanked me for sending lunch to her and being considerate. I told her: "No need to thank me, I considered it my obligation; it was the least I could do. For you, I would go to the end of the earth and back."

In the canteen, at the table, we discussed plans for the weekend: she would remain in the dormitory, and I would go to Lorena's and ask her to prepare meals for her, and I agreed to pick up three meals per day for the two days. I wanted her to get as much rest as possible, after all, it was the doctor's order, no agitation, no heavy lifting, no brisk movement, and eat and drink normally as before the procedure. In order to divert attention and avoid the curiosity of her other children, Lorena decided to meet me in the park, La Feria, with the meals for Belkis. When she came to deliver the meals, she inquired, "Cómo está mi hija" Is she resting and eating properly? "I know she is stubborn, so please keep a watch on her."

"Don't worry, I'm looking out for Belkis, and she listens to me," I told her.

Chapter 35

Lorena was originally from Holguín, about two hours' drive from the city of Santiago, and her extended family was still living there; Lorena's mother, Consuela, and two sisters, Elvira and Christina, and Belkis wanted me to make their acquaintance. Therefore, during the summer of 1981, she invited me to make the trip with her and Lorena to Holguín. I was hesitant to make the trip because of college rules, but I decided to risk it given that the college was almost empty. We arranged to leave Santiago one Monday morning at about 8 a.m. via a coach bus to Holguín. We arrived at the Holguín bus terminal at approximately 10:30 a.m., we descended the bus and exited the terminal, and Christina was there patiently waiting to receive us. Individually, we greeted her by exchanging kisses on both cheeks and embracing. Of course, she was excited to see me *because she had heard about me from Lorena and Belkis' uncle, Estéban.*

Christina quickly led the way to the local bus stop, where we boarded a country bus to her little community of Valencia. It took us about 40 minutes to reach her home. The door was open because her teenage children were at home. Christina was a divorcée with three children: two girls and a boy. We entered the house through the front door that opens into the living room, behind which there was a kitchen wedged between the living room and the bathroom, all on the left-hand side of the house. The three bedrooms were on the right-hand side of the structure. In the beginning, the children seemed shy, but they quickly adjusted to me and began telling me about Jamaicans that were living in the community close to their house: one was an older single Jamaican man, and the others were descendants of Jamaican immigrants. I asked them if it were possible for me to visit these people, and they all shouted, "Of course, we will take you to see them." We made plans to see the old Jamaican guy after we had lunch.

In about 20 minutes, we were all seated at the table. Suddenly, Christina sprang me a question that no one had asked me before: "So Desmond, are you going to stay in Cuba?"

For a moment, I was speechless, and Belkis responded, "We haven't discussed that possibility yet, tía. Besides, what if I want to live in Jamaica? We have more than enough time to decide on where our future will be spent."

The children began questioning me about my family and myself: "How many siblings do you have? Where in Jamaica are you from? Are your parents and siblings living in Jamaica? What made you decide to come to Cuba? Do you like Cuba? Would you live in

Cuba? How come you look so different from the other Jamaicans we know? Are you mixed?"

"I'm mixed up; I represent all of the races in Jamaica; Jamaica is made up of people from the Caribbean, America, Europe, Asia, and Africa."

"You are already a Cuban, and you look so much like one."

Finally, Belkis intervened and declared, "That is enough questions for the day; give Desmond a chance to settle in and enjoy his meal."

Even though I was not too happy about being bombarded with questions, I nonetheless welcomed the opportunity to practise my Spanish, which was improving appreciably. I was by then not only speaking in Spanish, but I was also thinking in Spanish—no more mental translation from one language to the other before speaking. My Spanish fluency was almost like that of the Cubans, and everyone was telling me how well I spoke Spanish. I was often mistaken for a Cuban—my physical appearance and language skills gave me a new identity.

My native tongues, English and Patois, were fast becoming second languages because of my engaging approximately 85 per cent of my time speaking Spanish with students, teachers, Belkis and her family, the ancillary staff at the college, and, in general, members of the community.

While I was becoming fluent in Spanish, several of my colleagues were floundering even though we were all exposed to the same environment, and a few may have even been immersed in the community much better than I was. Therefore, the ability to speak a second language is largely conditional on one's mental capacity rather than the community or the ecosystem to which they belong. One can spend a significant portion of their lifetime in a country and never develop or acquire the skills required to communicate effectively in that country's language. This became apparent to me when I visited the old Jamaican man living in Valencia.

Christina's daughters and I went to visit the old Jamaican man. On approaching his house, we noticed the front door was ajar, and someone was lying across a bed in the front room. One of the girls yelled for the old man, "Hola padrino;" the first time, there was no response; however, on the second shout, a raucous voice came sounding from the back of the house, "Estoy en el patio?"

"We brought one of your countrymen to see you."

"Give me a few minutes, I will be with you shortly."

Upon closer look, the person we noticed lying on the bed was a lady; she could not have been more than 22 years old. She came and stood in the doorway and greeted us, and then pulled back inside and closed the door.

While we were waiting, Christina's girls decided to leave me since their home was not far away, and it was not complicated to find my way back to their house, but they waited until the old man appeared and greeted us. It took him about five minutes to make his appearance featuring a height of about five feet eight inches, dark-brown complexion, greyed hair, muscular but stocky, and wore a broad smile.

The girls introduced us and bid us farewell shortly thereafter. The old man and I struck up a conversation. I asked him: "What is your name?"

"Fredrich."

"Fredrich, would you prefer if we speak in Spanish?"

I was trying to be accommodating since it seemed he had been living in Cuba for a long time and may have forgotten his native tongue.

"Mi caan talk Spanish so good, mi talk Jumaican betta."

"How long have you been living in Cuba,"

"Mi coom yah in the 1920s, more dan 60 years ago, I was almost 25 years ole when mi coom a Cuba, now mi a 86-year-old and mi neva sick yet. Mi coom a Cuba pon di faam wok program to wok pon di sugarcane plantation."

During his 60-plus years in Cuba, he acquired more than one hundred acres of farmland for planting his own sugarcane but gradually disposed of the land after the revolution—most of it during the last 15 years because he could no longer manage on his own and hired help was difficult to find.

The Cuban Government was the sole purchaser of his land; other local farmers had enough of their own land and were not interested in acquiring more since they, too, were getting old and could no longer manage large farms.

I asked him: "Where in Jamaica are you from."

"Mi coom frahm Hayes in Clarendon, mi grow up in a di sugar belt in Hayes, mi fahda was a cane fama."
"Yu whuda like to drink a jelly cocanat?" he asked.

"Yes, please. I haven't had a jelly coconut since my arrival in Cuba."

Immediately, he kicked off his shoes and ascended the coconut tree. I could not believe what I was witnessing.

The old man picked four jelly coconuts for me, and when he came down, he said, "Mi no tink yuh caan drink all four a dem, but yuh caan tek weh yuh no drink back wid yuh."

He went on to tell me that he was still strong and in good condition, "The young lady in a di house is mi girlfriend," with a wry smile on his face, "I do everything fi miself: cook, wash, clean and mantain what property mi hah lef."

"Weh yuh ah do in a Cuba and weh in a Jamaica yuh coom frahm?

"I'm studying physical and health education to become a physical and health education teacher. I'm visiting Holguín with my girlfriend, Christina's niece, and I'm from St. Elizabeth in Jamaica." "Do you miss Jamaica and your family? Do you ever think of going back?"

"In a di beginning, I was hoom sick a lot, but di taout of gooing back a Jamaica frightened mi because jobs were neva easy fi find when mi did out deh."

"Do you have family in Cuba?"

"Mi neva get married, aan mi no ha no children and mi always lib by miself."

We chit-chatted about life in Cuba for a while, and he told me that no one bothered him, and he stayed out of trouble and politics—kept his opinion to himself most of the times. After about two hours with him, I told him, "I'm ready to leave."

"Tek this bag fi carry the cocanat wid yuh. "Tell Christina fi send back di bag wen she can."

We said goodbye with a handshake, "Coom again if yuh coom back a Holguín."

"I will certainly do that, Fredrich," I responded.

I spent my time in Holguín at Christina's home, with Belkis and Lorena, visiting close and extended relatives of theirs. We visited Elvira's home; she was married to a military officer, who was away on a combat mission overseas, and they had one daughter. Elvira's house was the most modern of all the family homes I visited: a three-bedroom structure located near the shoreline about a mile and a half from Christina's.

Belkis grandmother lived equidistant between Christina and Elvira. We visited her the Thursday afternoon of the week in question. Her house was the most modest of all that I saw. It was a circular shabby looking structure from the outside with lime and clay plastered walls held together by wooden posts placed approximately four feet apart with worn out, whitewashed finished wall, a rusted zinc roof, wood windows in dull grey, and the front door in faded oak. Inside the house, the floor was naked hard dirt, clean swept. The furniture in the living room where we stayed for the visit was old but beautifully finished in bronze-stained, and dust was not visible anywhere. It smelled of wood smoke even though the windows and doors were open, and there was a warm, dry air circulating inside as opposed to the outdoors, which was extremely hot and humid: typical tropical weather. I was not able to discern how many rooms were within the house, but the structure was large and possibly contained three to four bedrooms. Consuela was tall, between five feet 10 inches and six feet, with long white hair, slenderly built, hospitable, and humorous.

"My husband was a black man," she remarked, directing her gaze at me, "He died ten years ago." Pictures of him adorned the walls in the living room.

Consuela invited me to sit; I remained standing while the others sat, "Don't be shy; my home is yours." She offered us a snack: homemade cake and herbal drink—pru. Consuela, Lorena, and Belkis chatted for a while, and then unexpectedly, with her eyes focused on me, Consuela inquired, "So you like Cuban girls?" I smiled without commenting, and again she remarked, "Cuban women son calientes."

Belkis intervened, laughing, "Abuela no digas semejantes cosas."

Everyone burst out laughing.

Lorena added, "Es cierto Desmond."

"I'm well aware of that, Lorena; Belkis is candela."

In a little while, the conversation was over, and we were off back to Christina's house. I enjoyed my trip to Holguín; the people were warm, more welcoming, and friendlier than those in the city of Santiago. Belkis family showed me respect, politeness, courtesy, and kindness, which made me admire them unreservedly.

Chapter 36

The Jamaican authority largely ignored us, and the Cuban authority was mute regarding our circumstances even though they continued to treat us as before the elections were held. On my part, I had just one complaint: our personal belongings which were stolen were never replaced, and we were left with a shortage of casual wear, and most of us had no money to purchase any of the needed items neither in las tiendas de los extranjeros nor local Cuban stores. Notwithstanding, a few members of our group had items brought back from Jamaica for them by members of the first Jamaican group who had returned to Jamaica for the summer vacation at their own expense. They had contacted a few family members of students in our group and relayed messages about needs and wants and hence were given packages to bring back for the students whose families were supportive and had the means.

Those of us who were less fortunate had to make do with what was at our disposal; some of us practised sports in shorts and, at times, in our uniform since our sports clothes were stolen. However, there was hardly any protest from anyone except for the usual recalcitrant; most of us attended classes with the commitment and motivation with which we started the program.

The first semester of the 1981-82 academic year included subjects such as mathematics, Spanish, Marxist thought, pedagogy, the methodology of physical education, history of physical education, rhythmic gymnastics, handball, massage, corrective gymnastics, swimming, optional course, and a specialization. To date, this was the heaviest course load we had carried: thirteen subjects in total. However, the second semester was a bit lighter, even though the subjects were denser and mentally demanding. We carried eight subjects: mathematics, Spanish, Marxist thought, pedagogy, volleyball, swimming, optional courses, and a specialization. Those of us who attended classes consistently did not shirk from the challenges; we worked together, consulted the teachers, sought help when we needed to, and the results were encouraging.

For the year, we averaged above eighty; at the low extreme, the average was seventy, and at the higher end, the average was 95. Of course, the few who were not inclined to attend classes regularly, wasted their time complaining about the relevance of the subjects, and showed very little interest in managing their studies and were averaging marks between 50 and 60 per cent, and there were even a couple of failures, and they had to re-sit their exams.

This was our third academic year in Cuba, and we were now determined to complete our program despite the uncertainty hanging over our heads. Most of us were approaching our responsibility decisively and had stopped thinking about the gloom that was lurking all around us. We concluded that if the Jamaican government were going to demand our return, they would have done so by then. And it would have been stupid and irresponsible to recall 31 students who were on the verge of completing their teacher education program at no cost to the Jamaican government when Jamaica needed teachers given the initiatives that the previous government undertook to educate the Jamaican populace.

The previous government had built several new primary and secondary schools and implemented several training programs and centres, but there was still the same number of colleges, and one university on the island, which predates the island's independence in 1962. Our biggest concern, several of us, was that the wayward behavior of some of our colleagues might have been pushing Cuban authority beyond what was tolerable.

The illicit activities of several among us were spiraling out of control, and no signs of abating were apparent. Buying and selling on the "black market" was lucrative and attractive. Some of our students purchased goods at rock-bottom prices in the foreign-reserved stores and resold them to the Cubans on the streets at exorbitant prices. For example, they purchased a pair of jean pants for 30 American dollars and resold it in the Cuban communities for 150 pesos, five times the original price, with four hundred per cent profit. Officially, one American dollar was the equivalent of one Cuban peso. These transactions allowed a few of our students to "live large" in Cuba, given that the things that we desired most were food, drinks, hotel rooms, and travel. These items were priced cheaply in Cuba because they were intended, except hotel rooms, for local consumption and according to the purchasing power of working Cubans. Cubans at the time were earning an average 150 pesos per month.

"This business thing is getting out of hand," Tom echoed one afternoon in the presence of Andrea, Gregory, James, and myself.

"It's as if these guys haven't a care in the world about their future," Andrea remarked.

"Clearly, they've put the business above all else without even thinking of the consequences if they're caught," Gregory said.

"Maybe they've made enough profit which would compensate for losing their scholarship," James said.

"I doubt that. It's become an addiction for them. They can't help themselves," I intervened.

"Eating well and running wild with Cuban girls trump everything else for them," James said.

"Can't you talk to them, Desmond?" Andrea asked.

"I think it's beyond talking. As Desmond said, it's become a habit, and habits don't go away easily," Gregory said.

"Yes, I can, but I doubt it would do any good. Besides, I don't know all of whom are involved and would hate to single out individuals. You're aware of how many times I brought up this issue in meetings, and the practice continues."

"So, there's nothing that can be done?" James asked.

"I'm afraid not, and besides, I wouldn't want to be the cause of anybody getting sent home," I told the little group.

When it had been assessed that things could not have gotten any worse, there came another twist. It was no longer just buying and selling merchandise on the illegal market, which by all indications from the Cuban standpoint was unacceptable, but there was also wanton and blatant robbing of Cubans who requested favours from some of the businessmen.

It was not unusual for Cubans to approach Jamaican students and ask them to purchase items for them in stores that operated solely in foreign currency. But what transpired from these arrangements was horrifying; though they would have been considered misdemeanors in Jamaica, in Cuba, they were punishable by long prison sentences, if caught.

A few Jamaican sports students would often agree to make purchases for their Cuban associates, who accompanied them to the foreign currency store but could not enter the store. Therefore, they had to hand over their money to the Jamaican students to make the purchase for them—it was now a matter of trust. Inside, the store was not visible to the Cuban accomplices outside, so they had no way of knowing what may have occurred while they were out of sight. Prepare yourself: after a few minutes inside the store, the Jamaican students would suddenly run out yelling "Polícia, Polícia, Polícia" or for how many times were necessary.

The Cubans were fully aware of the risk and penalties if they were caught mixed up in "black market" activities and would follow the Jamaicans running away from the store. When calm was restored, the Jamaicans lied to the Cubans by telling them that the police confiscated the money or the store's salesclerk took it. The police intervened and they did not want to be arrested, so they bolted as quickly as possible. They could not wait to complete the transaction because the police were on to them. In these scenarios, the Cuban associates were always the losers because they had no way of verifying what occurred, nowhere to lodge their complaints, and no possibility of recovering their money.

"Can you inform your colleagues that they are playing with fire?" José told me one afternoon.

"What do you mean, and can you be specific?"

"Your colleagues are dealing in contraband, which isn't taken lightly in Cuba."

"Just so you know, I'm aware of the activities, and it is embarrassing for most members of the group, not that I think it matters."

"The punishment for engaging in these activities is harsh. They could go to prison for a long time before they are returned to Jamaica."

"I have addressed the group on this matter several times, but my pleas have been ignored and the situation has gotten worse."

"I would hate to see any of you get sent to prison or deported back to Jamaica for breaking the law."

"That would be unfortunate, wouldn't it?"

I listened intently to the concerns José was sharing with me on behalf of the college's administration without revealing my resolve to him. The situation became intolerable for me, and I considered renouncing the position of leader of the group. I did not want to be confronted with the matter again; I could only be responsible for my actions and not those of 30 other adult individuals; there were no babies in the group, and by this time, everyone was over 20 years old.

I let my little sounding board group in on my intention at our next study session. "I'm going to resign from the position of group leader," I told them.

"What do you mean you're going to resign?" Heather asked.

"What happened? Tom asked.

"You're not serious, I hope," Gregory said.

"Yes, I'm serious; I have been asked by José on behalf of the college's administration to speak with you guys about engaging in illegal activities."

"That's no reason to resign," Andrea said.

"For more than a year now, at our monthly meetings, I've been pleading with the culprits in general terms to desist from the practice of engaging in business transactions with Cubans. My pleas have fallen on deaf ears, and individuals continue their errant behaviour."

"I'm one of those who are involved in the practice of buying and selling merchandise. I do it because I can't eat in the canteen," John said.

"I don't know all those who're involved; I've no interest in knowing at this point, and to what degree you're all trading, but it's more than just for eating purposes. As far as I know, profit-making and robbery is going on. Thank you for coming clean, but I must say, I'm disappointed in you. I always thought this little group would keep its head above the fray."

"The other members of the group aren't going to be happy when they learn about your decision to quit. We all voted for you because we believe in your commitment and high standard," James joined in.

"I appreciate the loyalty and wish things were different, but I simply can't accept another complaint from the college's administration. They're looking to me to resolve the matter, which obviously I'm unable to do."

Fortunately, we had our monthly group meeting coming up on the Friday afternoon of that same week, and I decided that I would use the opportunity to announce my resignation. However, before I made my announcement, I outlined my grievances to the group.

"Your behaviour is tarnishing our good name; your actions are tantamount to criminal, and you are letting down our country and leader who negotiated the opportunity for us to study in Cuba. You are putting in jeopardy the scholarship of everyone, not just those of the guilty parties, and you are literally turning your backs on the children in Jamaica that we are being trained to go back to and prepare for the future."

I told them that I was disgusted by their behavior and attitude, among other things. They listened intently without interrupting me, and when I was through lambasting them, I heard and saw them muttering to one another. At that moment, I said, "I am relinquishing my position as leader of the group, and my decision is irrevocable; you should use this opportunity to select a new leader to interface with the college's administration going forward." One of the girls shouted, "No! no, you can't do this to us; please reconsider," but I did not respond. Furthermore, I did not tell them that José had spoken to me about the activities of the businessmen, nor did I give the reason for my decision in plain words.

I told them I would hold the floor until they chose a new leader if they were inclined to do so that evening. Someone in the audience shouted out, "Let's have a vote; we mustn't leave this meeting without a group leader," which I supported and asked that they put names forward or, better yet, those who were interested in the position could volunteer themselves to run for the position.

Keith put forward the name "Carleton Hanson" and the only name, and just like that, he was chosen without any challenges. Keith was the guy who chaired the meeting in Havana for my nomination and election to be the group leader.

After the confirmation of Carleton as group leader, I thanked everyone for their support over the past two years plus, and I vacated the limelight, took a seat in the audience, and listened while the new leader thanked the group for the vote of confidence and pledged to carry on from where I left off.

The following Monday, at noon, after the meeting, I went to the college's administration wing of the building and asked Juanita: "May I speak with Luis if he is available to have visitors? I only need about five minutes of his time," I told Juanita.

"Wait a moment. Let me check Luis' availability."

Luis was in his office. She called him on the interoffice phone and asked him, "Desmond is here to see you, are you disposed?" She hung up the phone and told me, "Luis will see you in his office now."

"Come in, come in; how can I help you?" Luis asked.

"I am no longer the leader of the Jamaican student group. I relinquished the position on Friday afternoon. Carleton Hanson is the new leader," I told him.

"What happened,"

"I resigned from the position."

"Why?"

"I can no longer lead individuals whose actions I can't manage or control," I told Luis without revealing the true cause of my decision.

However, I believed he knew my reasons, but he did not dwell on the matter. Instead, he proceeded to tell me: "A good leader doesn't walk away in the middle of a battle or a crisis."

"I wasn't aware of any of those things going on."

He wanted to explain what he meant, but I told him: "There is no need; I understand you perfectly."

"Then there is nothing else to talk about," he said.

I got out of the seat and told him, "I hope Carleton will be in touch soon," then I said goodbye and exited his office.

I must say that after exiting the director's office, I was feeling remorseful—not because I regretted my decision, but because I thought about the college's administration that had treated me respectfully over the past two years plus.

Except for the incident with the female students and their resistance to manual work experience in the country, most students were honest, upstanding, and followed the rules as they were laid down by the college's administration. Most of all, I was reconciling with myself the fact that they had elected me to be their leader in Havana in the summer of 1979 without knowing anything about me. They took a chance on me, and I let them down! But in my mind, my decision was based on moral principles, and they were not negotiable, so in the end I was more comfortable than uncomfortable.

For several days, I kept my distance from everyone, Cubans, and Jamaicans alike; I did not wish to discuss the matter with anyone; rather, I wanted to concentrate on myself and my studies to ensure I graduated. However, I did approach Carleton and suggested that he introduce himself to the college's administration as the new leader of the group, and I was available and prepared to accompany him if he wanted to meet with Luis and or José to talk about my handing over the reins to him so to speak. He promised to let me know his decision, but I never heard back from him on the matter. The meeting of his election was the last one our group had for the remainder of our time in Cuba.

Chapter 37

In the summer of 1982, most of us were spending the second consecutive summer in Cuba; I say most of us because several of our students went to Jamaica for the holidays. The first Jamaican group of sports students led the way and proved that travel was not prohibited; therefore, those students who had the means or those whose family had the means to give them a trip took advantage of the opportunity and went home for the summer. Nevertheless, several of us chose to remain in Cuba either because we did not have the means to go home or because we simply preferred to stay in Cuba until we had completed our studies. We pondered, why take the risk when we had just one more year to complete our program and graduate? By the way, two of those, a guy and girl, who went home for vacation that summer never came back and thus reduced our numbers to 29.

Those of us who remained in Cuba for the summer holidays were fully entertained with sports activities and exposure to a coffee plantation. We even had our living arrangements interrupted for a few weeks.

The INDER authority informed us that we were going to change residence for approximately one month. There were a few national sporting events that were going to be celebrated in Santiago; therefore, we had to vacate the college building to free up space to host the national athletes. We were moved to the sports village, where competitive athletes resided during training, accompanied by our regular living conditions: dormitory and meal arrangements remained status quo.

Furthermore, we had the opportunity to see the events, boxing, fencing, judo, volleyball, and basketball, during the night, and day, which were a welcome distraction from what would have been an otherwise boring and uneventful summer—save for the 1982 World Cup of soccer: Italy defeated Germany to claim the top prize that year.

As it turned out, we were okay with our time spent in the sports village, with fewer than half of our students there. We stuck together and enjoyed the time as much as possible. The Cuban authority continued to support us as best as they could, and we did not complain about anything. In fact, we were grateful for the hospitality and attention given to us. They helped us to pass the time calmly.

Mid-way through the second week of our stay at the sports village, Linda informed us: "A day of productive work is being planned for the Jamaican sports students on Sunday. You are all invited to go to the country to reap coffee."

"This is a good opportunity to see and enjoy some of Santiago de Cuba's natural beauty. One day is much more acceptable than a whole month like when we were in the first year," Heather told her.

Sunday morning, at approximately 8 a.m., one of the college buses was in the driveway of the sports village to collect and drive us to the coffee plantation. We started out at about 8:30 a.m., drove for about 40 minutes on the highway, and then exited onto a bumpy dirt road and continued for about another 35 minutes. When we arrived at the plantation, it was about 9:45 a.m., and Cuban workers were already in the field. There were several bins lying around, and Linda encouraged us: "Take a bin, work in pairs, and begin picking coffee. Pick only the red beans. Once the bins are full, empty them into one of the large drums at the entrance to the plantation."

We fell in line and followed the instructions given to us. The working Cubans said nothing to us, they were enthusiastically working away at filling their bins, but they were communicating with one another in what seemed like vernacular Spanish at a speed that was difficult for us to understand.

We worked and also spoke among ourselves in Patois; not because we did not want the Cuban workers to understand us, but because we were most comfortable speaking in our everyday Jamaican tongue.

Unexpectedly, at about 11:30 a.m., we were invited to have bocaditos: dairy-cheese sandwiches, and guava juice, and we were also treated to a 15-minute break. During the break, the Cuban workers came over to where we were and started enquiring about our nationality; they did not know who we were. No one had told them that they were going to have company, and they wanted to know what we were doing in Cuba. When the 15 minutes ended, we went back to picking coffee in our original pairs. One hour later, we were informed by Linda that we were to get ready to leave, and we would be returning to the sports village to catch lunch.

None among us were eager to return to the village because the experience was exhilarating with fresh air, cool temperature, quiet atmosphere, damp ground, no dust, and continuous shade, even though the sun was out, and it could have been seen through the gaping spaces between the towering trees. However, we did not protest the decision to return; we calmly followed the instructions we received.

Chapter 38

I was destined to visit Holguín a couple more times but not to visit Belkis relatives—in that vein, I made only one trip. Belkis specialization training was arranged to take place at the sports college in that province. She decided to specialize in synchronized swimming, and the discipline, at an advanced level, was not officially offered at the sports college in Santiago. Furthermore, not many Santiagueras practised the sport, which means there were not enough students to warrant incorporating the program into the curriculum of the sports college in Santiago. The closest sports college to Santiago that offered the program was in the city of Holguín, the province's capital.

Belkis loved to be in the water; she was an exceptional swimmer. At every opportunity, she took advantage of going into the pool or going to the beach. She liked to pretend that she was a mermaid. She scared me on many occasions at the beach: she would disappear out into the sea, and I would be at a loss as to where she was, but then as I began to get anxious, she would pop up out of the water laughing and would ask me, "Were you worried?"

"No."

I always lied to her because I did not want her to hold back from developing her skills. I believed if I said I was worried, she might have interpreted it to mean that I was concerned that she was not competent at what she was doing.

Synchronized swimming was not just her passion. It was her purpose. It would have given her an edge in obtaining employment, and I wanted to support her as much as possible. Therefore, when she suggested to me that she was going to change her specialization to pure swimming, I protested, "Are you crazy? This is your chance to remain a cut above the rest. You don't know what tomorrow will bring; you must be prepared for today and tomorrow if you are going to make it in this world. Cuba may not always be what it is today, and or you may not wish to remain in Cuba for the rest of your life either—remember tomorrow is filled with unknown."

She was not happy about going to Holguín and leaving me behind; she told me, "Separation isn't good; we might get distracted, begin to lose interest in each other, our love may begin to fade, and long-distance romance is tenuous at best."

"You aren't leaving the country, we will be able to visit each other, and if you love me as much as I love you, nothing can pull us asunder."

"Tienes razón, papi."

On the first Saturday in September, before classes began, she commanded me to come to the front of the college where she was to board the INDER bus that was to take her to Holguín. The bus was practically empty; maybe six or seven students were on board, but before she got onto the bus, we embraced, and with tears in her eyes, she said, "This is your fault. I'm sad; I'm going to miss you terribly; I don't know when I'm going to be able to see you again or when I will get a pass to come back to Santiago."

"Don't worry. At the end of the month, when I get paid, I will come to see you in Holguín, call Josefina and give her the address of the college and I will get it from her and be on my way to see you."

We kissed passionately, and we were reminded that we were not alone; someone spoke; it was an administration staff person, "Muchachos, you are still on campus," smiling, he told us it was time to go.

I initially followed the bus, walking, as it slowly exited the college campus, to the campus gate and waving and exchanging blown kisses with Belkis. Out of the campus gate, the bus picked up speed, and in less than a minute, it was out of sight, and so was my Belkis. I stood there for a while contemplating how I was going to manage without Belkis close by. It did not take long for me to start feeling lonely and missing her. Over the past two years, we became close, good friends, lovers, study companions, mutual supporters of each other, and comfort to each other when things were challenging.

The Thursday before she left, Belkis told me: "Go to my mother's every weekend, Saturdays, and Sundays, to eat lunch. I spoke to my mother, and she is expecting you, don't starve yourself to death; I know you are particular in eating, but you must maintain your strength and keep good health."

"I promise, I'll visit Lorena's whenever it is possible, but I'll not make it a habit of going every weekend."

She understood but reminded me it was not a problem, "I told my mother to take care of you."

However, before I got the chance to visit Belkis' mom, unexpectedly, Belkis would be back in Santiago. The first Friday evening after she left Santiago, I was scheduled for autoservicio. After dinner, my group of us Jamaicans was cleaning the dinner trays when James announced, "Desmond, your girlfriend is coming." I was astounded when I looked around; Belkis was already in the air as she sprung onto my upper body, I grabbed her, prevented her and me from falling, and we began kissing in front of everyone, including the kitchen staff.

When I was able to catch my breath, I asked her, "What are you doing here? How did you manage to get away from the college so soon?"

"I convinced the assistant director to allow me to return to Santiago for the weekend. But I must be back at the college before 6 p.m. Sunday evening."

Seeing Belkis resurrected the life in my body, which was lying dormant for a week, I was rejuvenated, exhilaratingly joyful, and it did not matter the length of time we would have together because what mattered most was that I was able to see and hold the girl I was devoted to and fervently in love with.

Belkis joined our working group and assisted us with washing the trays; she wanted me to get away early because she needed me to walk her home; she was staying at Lorena's for the weekend. My colleagues, having caught on to what was happening, suggested that I leave, and they would complete the task without me. "You won't be bothered by my leaving," I asked them.

"No, we are almost finished anyway. We can manage fine with the remainder of the chores to be completed."

"I will see you later then."

Belkis and I walked slowly, stopped occasionally in the park, and talked about the loneliness that overcame us in the past week, how we missed each other, could not wait to see each other, and all we could think about was each other. When we finally reached Lorena's home, it was more than two hours after leaving the college campus; normally, this would have been a twenty-minute walk. It was dark, but Belkis insisted that we linger. She told me, "I can't get enough of you, and I want to savour the moments since I will be leaving Sunday midday to return to Holguín."

"Anything you want, my darling; I'm here to please you."

I sat in the rocking chair in the living room at Lorena's house, and Belkis sat on my thighs with her arms around my neck; she leaned against my shoulder and kissed me incessantly for about 15 minutes. After kissing and whispering about how we were going to spend the weekend, we both fell asleep.

When we woke up, it was after midnight; I stood and picked her up in my arms and whispered, "I have to go now, and you need to get some good rest." I kissed her, put her down, and embraced her with all my strength, released her, and glanced towards the door. She followed me to stand between the ajar door and the jamb and asked me to come and see her early next day, at noon, because we were going to the Zoo and the adjacent Coney Island.

She stood in the doorway for as long as I was able to see her, from glancing back, and with that, I disappeared into the darkness. The next day I was punctual as usual; I was at Lorena's at noon, lunch was already underway, and not long after it was served, we ate and chatted. Lorena remarked, "My daughter is in love, Desmond. You have won her heart, and now she can't bear to be apart from you."

"I'm in love with her too; when she isn't here, I'm miserable—I miss her so much."

After lunch, at about 1:30 p.m., Belkis and I set off for the zoo. We took the bus, which came within five minutes, and in another 20 minutes, we reached our destination. We entered and promenaded the zoo for about 35 minutes and then decided to sit under a shade tree. First, Belkis leaned against me and rested her head on my shoulder where she was touching my neck, then suddenly she raised her head and pulled away from me, and with her eyes welled up and leaking, she said, "Papito, yo no quiero regresar a Holguín, or I don't want to go back to Holguin, don't make me go back, it is too painful being apart from you, I can't eat, I can't sleep, and I'm having difficulty staying focused in class."

"This isn't easy for either of us, but you can't back out now; you have worked too hard for this. This is your final year, and we are talking about your specialization, without which you'll not be able to graduate from college. If you are going to give up your career on account of me, then we should end our relationship here and now. Just think about what we have done and been through over the past year, which would have been all for naught. I can't let you do it; please don't let me get angry with you."

She began sobbing and attracting attention, and I said to her, "People are looking; please control your emotions, I can't let you do it, and that is final; I don't want to hear another word on the matter."

She pulled further away from me and stared at me with a piercing look, almost "sharp enough" to cut me into pieces. I looked back at her crossly and asked her, "Do you think this is easy for me? As a matter of fact, this relationship has never been easy for me; often, it is as though I'm going out of my mind thinking about the future, our future."

Eventually, she calmed down and asked: "Can you take me home, please?"

"You aren't interested in going over to the Coney Island?"

"No, I'm no longer in the mood."

"Fine, let's go."

We were back at Lorena's home before 4 p.m. Up on entering the house, Lorena inquired, "You are back already, what happened?"

"Belkis didn't want to continue the stay," I replied.

Belkis kept quiet.

Lorena continued, "Desmond, don't pay attention to her, she is spoiled."

Belkis went into a room and left me in the living room with Lorena, but I stopped talking and sat down in the rocking chair. Belkis did not reappear, and after about 40 minutes, I decided to leave.

"Goodbye," I told Lorena.

"Aren't you going to stay for dinner?

"No, I will take a pass this time."

On my way back to the college, I was furious and sad, but I kept going. The thought did enter my mind several times to go back and try talking to her, but I decided it was best to hold my ground. I did not see her again for the rest of the weekend, and neither did I before she went back to Holguín. I was left tormented and disparate, "My Belkis has abandoned me," and I wondered if she would ever speak to me again.

The following three weekends went by, and I did not hear from Belkis. I asked myself why I was torturing myself, but I could not help the way I was feeling; I loved her profoundly and wanted the best for her. She has been the only girl for me since I arrived in Cuba; I was lost without her kindness, gentleness, and tenderness, and the thought of her warmth could not be easily dislodged from my mind—I was in a confused state, a terrible state, and for the first time, I concluded that I had never been in love with anyone before Belkis.

Despite everything, I decided to go by Belkis' home to find out from Josefina if Belkis had called. And sure enough, she did call, but that was from the first week she spent in Holguín and left the address of the college. I took the address, wrote it down on a piece of paper, and decided to go to Holguín. So, Saturday morning of her fourth week in Holguín, I boarded the inter-provincial bus and headed to Holguín. I arrived at the Holguín bus terminal at about 10 a.m., but not knowing where the college was situated and unsure of geographical locations in terms of east, west, north, or south and which direction I should pursue.

However, as good luck would have it, I saw a few students I thought were from the college; their uniform was like ours in Santiago. I approached them to confirm that they were from Holguín Sports' College and if they could tell me how to get there. They were courteous, kind, and helpful to me and gave me the precise information I needed.

Upon arrival at the college, I spotted the swimming pools immediately and noticed that there were students frolicking around in the water. I approached the pools and students and inquired about Belkis, and I was told that she was not on campus but would be coming back soon. However, I waited more than two hours for her return; when she finally returned, she was with two other female students but ignored me, pretended not to see me, but I called out to her, and she came over to where I was and asked, "What are you doing here? I don't want to see you ever again."

"We did say mean things to each other in our last encounter, but don't you think we should talk about our situation."

"There is nothing to talk about, and I wish you would leave."

I felt dejected, flabbergasted, and hurt, and so I said, "If that is how you want it, I'll not bother you again." I abruptly turned around and started walking away from her and the college. I tried not to look back, so I did not notice that she was following me; when I turned the corner out of the college campus, out of the corner of one of my eyes, I observed her behind me, and I stopped to inquire, "Why are you following me?"

Acting in a rage, she ran towards me, and with folded fists, tears in her eyes, screaming in a loud voice, she began pounding me in the chest for about 5 seconds; I did not react; I just stood there and absorbed the blows. However, when I thought it was enough, I had enough, I took her two small arms in my hands and shook her a little, and said, "Please calm down; stop making a scene!"

"Were you going to go for real?"

"Yes, when you told me you never wanted to see me again, I was wounded, my heart, soul, and mind went dark, and I was broken, distraught, and in disarray, in that order."

"I don't know why I said that because I was overjoyed to see you; I know you would come to see me, and I wanted you to come, but our last conversation wasn't very civilized, and I guess it was still weighing on my mind. However, I know you are right, but I love you so much; from the bottom of my heart, you are my everything, and I want to be near you all the time."

"I'm so in love with you; when you aren't around me, I'm exhausted, feeble, lazy, and of low energy."

She took me by the hand and led the way back onto the campus proper and asked me to stay over Saturday night at the college, "We can't sleep together, but you can stay in the men's dormitory; most of them are away for the weekend. One of the girls you saw me with earlier, her boyfriend is staying over; I'm going to speak with the director of scholarship and request permission for you to stay over as well—he is an agreeable person."

Belkis obtained permission for me to stay at the college the Saturday night and to eat in the canteen as well! The other couple, Belkis, and I, agreed to go to the movies, later in the evening, in the city centre. The movie theatre was just about 25 minutes' walk from the college by paved road. We saw a two-hour movie, Roman Holiday, from 8 p.m. to 10 p.m. Afterwards we chose to bushwalk back to the college. On our way through the bushes, arms around each other, Belkis and I suddenly found ourselves alone; the other couple was nowhere in sight; we both smiled at each other knowingly. The other couple was apparently celebrating in the bushes.

Belkis pulled my head down to where my ear was close to her mouth and whispered, "I think they stopped to do it."

"Do what?" I said facetiously.

"No seas tonto." "They are having sex, and I'm feeling hot myself. Would you take me?"

"Where?"

"Right here."

I hesitated a bit because I had never done it in the wild before—discounting our stints after our first coitus: in La Feria and on the beach at Caleton Blanco—and neither did she. But we were both aware that it was commonplace in Santiago, given the lack of available facilities. Suddenly, I was burning up with desire, so I took her standing for the second time in our relationship. Doing it standing lasted much longer than lying down. We were in action for over 15 minutes and were still going at it, ravishing each other, when the other couple came passing by us. But we did not stop, and they just walked on by as if they had not seen anything interesting.

When it was over, we had to find our way back to the college on our own. The other couple did not stop to wait for us, but luckily there was a hotel near the college, and due to its shining lights, we were accurately guided back to the college.

Upon reaching the college, we embraced and kissed, occasionally laughing at our not-so-long-ago experience in the bushes, and said good night; it was about 11:10 p.m. I ascended the stairs to the second floor, where sleeping facilities were assigned to Belkis' friend's boyfriend and me. That night I slept comfortably and soundly and was relieved of the anxiety that I had endured for three weeks from not knowing if Belkis and I would continue our relationship. I slept through the night without even taking bathroom breaks and woke up the next morning at about 6:30 a.m. Once awoke, I freshened up and went downstairs to look around and waited for Belkis to appear, but she did not come out until about 7:30 a.m., just in time to catch breakfast before the closing of the canteen at 8 a.m.

After breakfast and a bit of digestion, Belkis wanted me to see what she was up to for the past month. She went and changed into her swimwear and told me to meet her at the pool. When she came back, she affectionately slapped me on the shoulder and ran and jumped into the water; she was like a fish, posing upside-down most of the time, moving her legs about, up, and down and around. She was a beauty to behold in the water, just like a mermaid; sometimes, I wondered if she were breathing under the water because she came up for breath so infrequently, and when she did, it was just for a few seconds. I was thrilled with her performance, and when she was out of the water, I told her, "You were graceful, exquisitely wonderful, and your future protégées are going to be lucky because they will have the best instructor ever."

"Thank you for the vote of confidence, papi. It means a lot to me coming from you. Can you wait here awhile?" she asked, "I'm going to change back into my casual wear."

I waited, and when she returned, she invited me to go by the nearby ice cream parlour, where they also served coffee and tea. Neither of us drank coffee, so we ordered herbal tea of a sort and settled at a table and talked about the past month and a little about the five more that she would be in Holguín.

When we went back to the college, lunch was being served, and we collected ours and ate. After lunch, we hooked up with the couple we went to the movies with and talked about the night and what we had done—no surprise to any of us—we knew what was unfolding all the time. After our foursome conversation, Belkis and I separated ourselves from the others and went promenading Holguín city centre, it was in many respects like that of Santiago, with old colonial buildings, narrow streets, well-kept parks, no outlandish skyscrapers, and hardly any cars, and everyone lined up patiently and highly disciplined to take the buses to wherever they were headed.

Before we knew it, time had elapsed rapidly, and it was time for me to return to Santiago. We were both sad to separate from each other but were painfully aware that the visit would end sooner rather than later. I did not have anything left back at the college, so we headed for the terminal. Belkis lingered around until I boarded the bus that would take me away from her. But before I boarded the bus, we embraced and kissed, and I wiped away the tears that was welled up in her eyes and running out slowly; I told her: "Never mind, I will be back to see you soon." The bus pulled out of the terminal, and we waved goodbye until we were both out of sight—as I have said sometime earlier, I was "tied" to her love and must add, I did not want to be separated from her!

Chapter 39

I began visiting Lorena's home regularly on weekends, and on the second Saturday in the second month since Belkis went to Holguín, she inquired, "Have you heard from Belkis?"

"No."

"Why don't you visit her?"

"I'm planning to go and see her at the end of the month."

She went into her room and returned with money in her hand and gave me 40 pesos.

"Belkis told me that you only receive 30 pesos per month, so I know you don't have much money to spend." I hesitated to take it, but she asked me, "You want to see Belkis, don't you?"

"Yes."

I took the money—this was a lot of money in Cuba at the time for Lorena to give me.

However, on the third weekend of the month, I went back to Holguín to visit my querida. When she saw me, she ran into my arms and started crying, "You have been on my mind all the time; where did you get the money? I hope you aren't starving yourself, because I know you do not get much money from INDER."

"Your mother gave me 40 pesos and suggested that I visit you."

"Oh, mi mama esta loca, but I'm happy you are here."

We discussed what we would do for the weekend and decided that we wanted time alone together. We had enough money to eat at restaurants, and go to the movies, knowing that everything else we could do needed no money. There were no costs to incur: the museum, beach, zoo, and window shopping were all free.

We wanted to sleep together Saturday night, so we inquired how to go about reserving a hotel room. It turned out the procedure was different in Holguín from Santiago. There was no lining up to make the reservation because the demand in the less developed cities was not as high. Therefore, one went straight to the villas or the hotels, even on the day of want, made their reservation, and moved in for occupancy any time after noon. And be prepared to check out the following day at 11 a.m.

We got help with finding a villa with inclusive services, meals, alcohol and gift items, sauna access, exercise room access, and swimming pool access. The villa was a hideaway in the interior of a well-kept forest-like setting—we did not have to share facilities.

We arrived at the villa, on foot, at about 6 p.m., after vagabonding most of the day. We approached the welcome area of the villa, which carried a sign that read

"Bienvenidos," and Belkis suggested that I made the reservation, which I did, presenting my identification card. I received our key and receipt without any interrogation from the attendant. We inquired about the dining room and received directions to find it, but we did not go there right away. Instead, we went to the room to leave our few pieces of belongings and freshen up before going to the dining room.

At about 6:30 p.m., we entered the dining room and were assisted in finding suitable seats; we were served ice-cold water and showed the menu. We ordered our meals, Belkis ordered pork stew and white rice, which came with tostones or fried mashed bananas and mixed garden salad: cucumber, lettuce, tomato, and mini carottes, and I ordered stewed chicken with rice and peas, which was accompanied by the same sides as what Belkis received. The camarero asked if we wanted to have anything to drink before the meals arrived, Belkis asked for a glass of white wine, and I asked for a cold beer. We both enjoyed our meal—it was delicious.

We ordered a second round of alcohol after dinner—"no dessert, please." We drank slowly and chatted, no one hurrying us on to make room for others, though the dining room was almost at capacity. But there was no one waiting in line. It seemed that dinner was prepared according to the number of guests in the villa.

Once we were finished drinking our second round of alcohol, I requested, "La nota por favor," paid it, and went back to our room. We gave and took from each other intermittently throughout the night; we enjoyed our time together, and the noises, screams of passion and pleasure, moaning, groaning, coming from the adjacent rooms. These sounds, though not very loud, were constant throughout the night, kept us awake, and contributed to our repeated arousal—it was entertaining, and we did not mind it.

The following morning, we got up at 6 a.m., took showers, dressed, and went to have breakfast. After breakfast, we went back to the room, got naked and went under the bed covers, and enjoyed the warmth of each other's body. We talked about Belkis' career and her imminent graduation and where she would like to work—but we did not talk about our future even though it should have been the most concerning for us.

At approximately 11:45 a.m., we vacated the villa's room, returned the keys, and waited for lunch to be served. When it was time, we ordered and ate lunch. After lunch we walked towards the bus terminal in the city centre. Arm-in-arm, we promenaded the streets and admired and talked about the beauty of nature's splendour, the frailty and dispensability of every living creature and thing. We discussed and agreed not to worry about the things we have no control over and things we have control over, we committed to never abuse them nor manage them perniciously but instead to appreciate, enjoy, and help to nurture them as wonders of the universe.

"We can't conceive anything outside the realms of possibilities," I said, "It doesn't matter how creative we are."

"Living things provided inspiration for all things created and or shall be created," Belkis completed my thought.

Soon we were in the bus terminal, ready to disentangle ourselves yet again from each other's presence, and without any presentiment to either of us, this was to be my last time driving away from the city of Holguín bus terminal during my four-year stint in Cuba.

Chapter 40

After a mere three months, not six, in Holguín, Belkis had to return to Santiago. Therefore, Saturday at the end of the third month when I called at Lorena's to receive my now routine lunch, as luck would have it, lo and behold, Belkis was there to greet me; I was stunned, because I had no prior warning, and I was not expecting her to be there. Immediately, I inquired from her: "What are you doing here?"

"I'm home for good; I'm not going back to Holguín," she told me.

"What do you mean you aren't going back?"

"I can't stand being away from you."

"Don't talk crazy; you must be out of your mind; you can't do that."

"Don't get mad papi, my trainer is sick, and they can't find a replacement in time for me to complete the specialization. I'm being sent back to Santiago, and it is now up to our college in Santiago to find a solution to my situation. I have already made an appointment to meet with the swimming department at the college this coming Monday."

"I'm happy to see you, but I don't like the situation you find yourself in one bit."

"The college is responsible for sorting out the matter so that I can be prepared for my graduation on time. I will let you know the outcome of the meeting on Monday, and don't worry," she told me.

Belkis' meeting with the college's swimming department was scheduled for 10 a.m. Monday morning, and I was anxious to know the outcome. But I had to wait until lunchtime to hear the result because I had classes all morning.

After my morning classes, I waited in the college yard, sitting on a concrete bench near where students lined up or assembled for lunch, to see Belkis before she went into the canteen for her lunch. She saw me before I saw her, and she came up behind me and slapped me affectionately on the back of my head to get my attention. As soon as I felt and saw her presence, I inquired from her, "What did your meeting with the swimming department resolve?"

"I was given two options: I could switch my specialization to swimming because I'm an advanced swimmer, or I could continue and finish my specialization under the supervision of a former national synchronized swimmer who is currently working in La Escuela de Iniciación Deportiva Escolar (La EIDE) or the Initiation School of Sports, in Santiago."

"So, what is your choice?"

"I told them that the latter was more appealing to me, and they gave me a form to fill out and sign, which also bore the signature of the director of the swimming *department of the college, and they instructed me to take it to La EIDE tomorrow."*

"Great, so you will be able to continue training in your specialization and be near me."

"We can only see each other on weekends because only students and employees are allowed on the premises of La EIDE. This is a school for children under 12 years old, and security is always on high alert, but never mind, if we need to see each other, I can come down to the college after my sessions in the evening and return before lights out in the night."

The following day, Tuesday, Belkis went to La EIDE with her particulars and was approved to start her sessions the following day—Wednesday. I was not able to accompany her. However, I was amazed at how quickly everything unfolds, the latest communication technology was still not available; in Cuba transportation was antiquated, and the telephone was the most efficient form of communication but was not widely available. Most businesses relied on face-to-face contact, and yet things moved along with considerable speed.

As it turned out, for the remainder of her specialization training, we saw each other mostly on weekends; we had to conserve our pennies for renting hotel rooms to celebrate our love and give undivided attention to each other. Therefore, buses and taxis were luxuries we could not afford.

Belkis specialization in La EIDE also included her teaching practice. Belkis became friends with her mentor and supervisor, Vivian, and so she wanted to show me off to her; they arranged for me to get a pass and asked me to visit the school. I arrived one Thursday, early evening, while classes were still in progress in the swimming pool. Upon my arrival at the school, Belkis spotted me first since she knew me and was not in the pool. She ran towards me and took my hand, and led me towards the pool, and I inquired from her, "Don't I have to report to the office of the school to let them know that I'm on the premises?"

"No, Vivian took care of everything."

When I arrived at the pool, everyone came out of the water to greet me. Belkis introduced me to Vivian and the kids as her boyfriend, and we politely exchanged greetings.

Vivian was white, with long blonde hair, approximately five feet two inches tall, muscularly built, and very beautiful. Several of the kids asked me to speak in English, having heard that I am from Jamaica. But I responded: "You'll not be able to understand me because you don't speak or understand English," but they would have none of that, so I obliged them and asked a few questions.

"What're your names? How old are you? Where do you live? Do you live with your parents? Can I meet them?"

They did not understand a word I was saying. Nonetheless, they were excited to hear someone speak whose native language was English, all the kids busted out in laughter and requested more, but Belkis and Vivian came to my rescue.

That, it seemed, was the last session for the day; Belkis and Vivian dismissed the kids, and Belkis signalled to Vivian that I was leaving. Vivian and I said goodbye to each other, and Belkis led me away from the pool to the bus shelter. She did not want me to be in that area after dark, and she also wanted to make out with me before I left. However, we got carried away by making out and talking about her assignment: her thesis.

Unfortunately, I missed the last bus and had to contend with the darkness and a six-mile walk back to the college. Belkis was apologetic and annoyed with herself because of the situation, but I told her not to worry. I will be fine, and I can find my way by keeping on the main road. I found my way back to the college without any difficulty, and the next day, Friday, I asked to use the telephone in the college's administration office and called Belkis to let her know that I had found my way back to the college okay, and I was fine. However, she informed me that she will be at the college for an appointment with her thesis supervisor at 11 a.m. on Saturday.

Chapter 41

After the meeting on Saturday with her thesis supervisor, Belkis and I walked to Lorena's but decided to sit in the park and chat for a while before arriving at Lorena's. We wanted lunch to be ready when we got there and not have to wait in the house for it to be prepared. We sat on a wooden bench in the park and talked about her thesis. She hated the quantitative aspect of the work; she was intimidated by numbers, especially large sets of data, I promised to help her, but she was still apprehensive about managing and manipulating the numbers. Notwithstanding, I told her not to worry, "You will be fine; just be patient; the worst thing to do is to get anxious and nervous because you will develop a mental block, and nothing will be accomplished under such a condition."

For a moment, we stopped talking and began gazing at the manicured grounds in front of us. I was thinking of how wonderful it would have been to have a child playing, running around, laughing, and screaming as we ran after him or her in a playful manner. Unexpectedly, Belkis declared, "I know what you are thinking."

"Now! How could you possibly know what I'm thinking? Are you a mind reader? Do you have psychic powers?"

"No, but I'm thinking the same thing you are," she said,

I asked her, "What would that be?"

"We are both thinking about a child playing in front of us on the grass," she told me.

I was flabbergasted, how was that possible? Even if she did not know what I was thinking, the fact that she was thinking about a child at the very moment that I was thinking about one was baffling to me. I had no choice but to admit to her, "Yes, we're both on the same subject."

Left in bewilderment, Belkis gave me another surprise. She told me that she wanted to have a baby, my baby, and it did not matter what happened. She would care for the child. This announcement was staggering, I shuddered in shock and quivered in awe, but I was destined to please her, and so I said yes, we would do it—without a doubt, the combination of love and madness is a recipe for stupidity.

Things did not end there. She further articulated that she wanted to be married to me because she did not want the child to be born out of wedlock. Aiming to please her, I agreed to marry her over the summer—in the absence of rational thinking, the mind is like an empty barrel. I was struggling to find the right words to at least provide enlightened reasoning to dissuade her from complicating matters, but dumbfoundedness overpowered my ability to think clearly, and all I could do was acquiesced to her demands.

We got up from the bench and slowly walked to Lorena's, and very few words were said between us. But I could tell that she was excited while I was perplexed, weak in spirit and unable to counter her position or convince her not to tread the path she seemed so enthusiastic about taking. When we reached Lorena's, lunch was almost ready, so we sat at the table and waited; in the meantime, she told her mother: "Mummy, Desmond and I are going to be married."

"I hope you guys know what you are doing," Lorena said.

"Desmond, don't be led by Belkis, she is crazy."

Neither Belkis nor I responded. We both smiled and looked at each other.

Lorena inquired further, "Belkis, have you told your father about this decision yet?"

Belkis replied, "No, but I'm going to tell him this evening, Desmond and I will be going home later, and we will break the news to him when we get there." "Chica loca," or crazy girl, Lorena murmured and said nothing further on the subject.

At approximately 3 p.m., Belkis and I hit the road to her/father's home. On the way, I asked her, "Do you think your mother approved of us getting married? Because to me, it seems she has reservations."

"I'm not asking my mom and dad for permission to marry you. I am telling them that I'm going to marry you, I'm now of age, and it is time I start making my own decisions. I will be graduating from college in a little while, and I will be expected to be responsible by the government as well as my parents," Belkis told me.

"You don't think that they might be concerned that in a year or so, I will be going back to Jamaica and

leaving you behind entangled in a marriage that may not be easily dissolved?"

"Let me worry about that," she said.

"What if your father disapproves and throws me out of his house?" I jokingly asked her.

"Well, indirectly, he is throwing me out, too," she said.

Subtly, I was also trying to make her take a reality check, a pause, but I quickly realized my efforts were fruitless, and I did not want to disappoint her. I was too much in love with her.

When we arrived at her home, it was about 4 p.m.; Pedro was in the living room watching television, and Josefina was in the kitchen preparing dinner. We greeted them and took seats in the living room. Without wasting any time, Belkis called: "Josefina, can you come in here a minute, please? I have something to tell you and Papa." When Josefina entered the living room, Belkis went to the television and asked permission from Pedro to turn it down, and he nodded in the affirmative.

"I would like both of you to know that I'm going to marry Desmond," Belkis announced.

Pedro remained silent.

"Are you pregnant?" Josefina inquired.

"No, but I'm planning to be."

"Chica loca," Josefina uttered, smiled, and went back into the kitchen.

To this point, no one took the announcement enthusiastically. I interpreted their reaction to mean that it was up to her because she was going to do whatever pleases her anyway.

I decided shortly thereafter that I was going to leave because I felt they might not feel comfortable discussing it in my presence. I knew I was leaving her to "face the music" all by herself, but I also knew if they could dissuade her, it would be difficult with me being there. I bade my goodbye, and she accompanied me to the door exiting the house onto the street. We embraced and kissed as usual, and she expressed, "Things might get heated with my father without you around, but I'm prepared for any opposition to my decision. We will have to contact the municipal administration office to set the wedding date and then plan the wedding, but I will do that Monday or Tuesday before I go to La EIDE. It is close to here and near the bus stop."

"I'm sure you will, my love," I responded.

Belkis went to the Municipal Administration Office the following Monday morning and got a date for our marriage, July 5, 1982, and the documentation for the necessary planning of the wedding and ceremony. The following Wednesday evening, she came down from La EIDE to give me the news and showed me the documentation: a card to rent the wedding dress and trappings, purchase a bedroom suite, television, stove, and fridge, contact information for the photographer and a hotel reservation number. In addition, we were required to have one witness present, and the person could be a family member other than a parent or sibling.

I did not ask her what had transpired that fateful Saturday evening between Pedro, Josefina, and herself, and she did not volunteer any information.

We were having a civil marriage, no celebration, so we skipped the wedding dress and trappings. We did not expect any support from her family, and my family was not in Cuba. There was not even enough time to alert them to the marriage or for them to participate in the wedding, even if they wanted to come to Cuba, and I doubted that very much. Money and time were not good bedfellows to us, and we had to take a pass on the things that ordinarily would have been welcomed to get a young family started in Cuba. We decided between us what was possible given our financial limitation.

The bedroom suite, television, stove, and fridge were out of our reach, because we had no money to make the purchases, which we knew going into the nuptial, and it did not bother us in the least. We offered the opportunity to her family members in Santiago, on both sides of her family, but no one showed any interest. I concluded that the announcement of our marriage was so sudden that no one had any time to prepare and save up for it, considering that Cuban workers did not get paid lavishly, and it would require a year or more to amass the necessary funds. According to Belkis, anything that we could do after the wedding would be put on hold, such as taking pictures.

"I'm not going to use the government-recommended photographer for our wedding pictures. I know of a skilled professional photographer in Palma, and I'm going to reserve a sitting with him for us to get our pictures taken once I start working in September. This photographer has everything we need for the sitting: suits, dresses, and paraphernalia at no extra cost."

Belkis did not consider material things important and did not give any serious thought to acquiring them. Her focus was on getting married and having a baby—hers and mine. The little money we had was supposed to go towards renting the hotel room and honeymoon expenses.

On this occasion, I did not have to line up to make a hotel reservation in Santiago; I only had to take the proof of marriage arrangements: a card containing the date, location, and certificate of permission number. Belkis asked me to make the hotel reservation, and she would ask her aunt Conchita to witness our marriage. I was able to reserve two nights at one of the most admired hotels on the outskirts of the city of Santiago, Hotel Versailles, and apart from being a world class hotel, it was situated on a hill overlooking a vast area of level land compact with lush vegetation—a beauty to behold.

Chapter 42

*T*he morning of the wedding, we were on time; Conchita, Belkis, and I were in the municipal administration building that executes civil nuptials at 8:30 a.m., and the citation was read to us in less than 20 seconds; we confirmed our coordinates were accurate, signed the register, and were congratulated and given a declaration slip to apply for our marriage certificate two weeks later.

Belkis' aunt worked at the City Hall, so she proceeded to work but embraced Belkis, told us to enjoy the honeymoon and bade us goodbye. Belkis and I went back to her home to "kill time" before heading off to the hotel. Pedro had already left for work, leaving Josefina alone at home. Josefina was a homemaker; she did not have employment outside the home.

"Josefina, please, can you get a key for Desmond? Belkis asked, and said, so that he doesn't have to *knock and wait for someone to open the door for him to enter the house."*

"I will get the key cut the next time I go out," Josefina agreed.

Our check-in time at the hotel was noon; at 11:30 a.m. Belkis telephoned for a taxi to take us to the hotel. The taxi, a Lada model, was at the door in 10 minutes. Belkis told Josefina that we were going to be away for a couple of days and to let her father know. We bade Josefina goodbye, and she wished us an enjoyable time.

We spent two wonderful days at the hotel going from our room to the pool, out into the hotel grounds, and window shopping in the tourists' boutique, but we did not go inside because we had no foreign currency to make purchases. On the first day, at about 4 p.m., Conchita called to make jokes and tease us. We had a bit of fun with her. At dinner time, we ordered room service; for the main dish, I ordered shredded beef with white rice, and Belkis ordered piernas de rana or frog legs with congri, or rice and peas. We also ordered dessert and alcoholic beverages.

For the first time in my life, I realized that frog legs could be eaten by humans. So, when Belkis ordered it, I frowned. She noticed and immediately told me, "It tastes like chicken."

"I never knew that it was edible and least of all by humans," I told her.

"It is a delicacy that is popular in Cuba," she said laughing.

When the meal arrived, she offered me a piece to try, and I refused: No, thank you, and she wasn't happy, but I told her, "I would never eat that thing."

"You are too particular."

"I know, very much so when it comes to food. I'm not going to kiss you until after you wash your mouth because I don't want to taste that meat in my mouth."

For the rest of that first evening, we spoke extraordinarily little, I knew she was mad at me, but I stood my ground.

After dinner, we sat in the sun loungers on the terrace that separated the swimming pool from the hotel building. I noticed her from time to time, but she never looked my way, not that I saw. She was paging through a magazine the last time I saw her before I fell asleep. When I woke up, she was sitting on my thighs and leaning over my face and kissing my lips. I opened my eyes and looked at her curiously, and she spoke immediately: "I washed my mouth and brushed my teeth;"

I smiled at her and pulled her down onto my body and squeezed her tightly. Then she took me by the hand and said, "Let's go inside, it is getting late."

Suddenly, events began to sink in, and I started thinking, I was now married to a Cuban beauty who wanted to have my child. I had about one year left before I finished my studies and had to return to Jamaica. I was in love with a beautiful girl who gave me everything and never once asked me for anything, but myself, in return. She was kind, considerate and sensitive; I hit the jackpot but could not collect the prize—it did not seem right or fair. Life is a complicated phenomenon; you sometimes get what you want, but you are unable to hold on to it

Chapter 43

We were now starting the final leg of our academic journey, and new responsibilities were coming our way, which required assiduousness. We were assigned our teaching practice locations in the first semester of the academic year, which meant that we had to spend a lot of time off-campus in areas where we were to complete our practicum: sports centres, primary and secondary schools. To fulfil the requirements of our program we were required to prepare lesson plans, and develop training plans for the children and adolescents, consistent with our specialization. Moreover, we were required to assemble data and develop our theses simultaneously.

I was placed in the "Ciudad Escolar 26 de Julio" to teach physical and health education. I worked with children between the ages of eight and 12 years old. My duties were confined to the afternoon from 1 p.m.

to 2:50 p.m., Monday to Friday, and I had to give two sessions of 45 minutes each day to multiple groups of students per week. Furthermore, I had grade five and six children as subjects of investigation for my thesis, using quantitative measurements.

My first order of business was to establish the objectives of the assignment, followed by the measuring activities, which included speed, resistance, agility, push-ups, abdominals, high jump, and long jump. I had to develop a compendium of results emanating from the activities completed by the children according to their age and gender. Then, I analyzed the data and constructed tables to group the results: 5th and 6th grades together and independently. And finally, I had to graph the results by gender in each grade: two graphs per grade. The students were cooperative most of the time and interested in learning and practising the activities.

However, they often got into tussles with one another, as is normal for children at that age. And this was one part of the assignment that I was reluctant to manage because parents came for their children every day, and I was leery of parting fights just in case there were to be any perceptions that I was partial to one student or another. One afternoon, I recalled, when two students got into a physical struggle, and I stood by and made no attempt to intervene. Unfortunately for me, my practicum monitor, Guillermo, was on hand to see the unfolding of the entire episode.

"You're responsible for managing the children's behaviour," Guillermo reprimanded me.

"I'm aware, but I was being cautious and not wanting to be the cause of anyone getting an advantage in the melee."

"This is your domain. You are the authority; your intervention is almost always required. Furthermore, your decision is the one that counts in these matters."

"You're correct, and I'm to be blamed for not managing these little brawlers appropriately."

"You're aware that I'll have to note this in your file, which will affect your marks."

"I suppose you'll have to do what you must," I told Guillermo.

From that day, I kept my eyes on all the kids as best I could, given that there were about 20 of them in each class at any given time. I tried to pre-empt any potential scuffles before they got underway. Incidentally, I received a final score of 91 for my practicum and thesis together. The penalty prevented me from achieving the maximum score, but I understood the reason and did not protest the decision.

During our practice teaching, my colleagues and I had to demonstrate respect, discipline, courtesy, expertise, impeccable behaviour, neatness, and levelheadedness because we were teaching, training, and shaping young children and adolescents for the future.

The wayward behaviour of some of my colleagues had to remain in the dormitory at the college until they returned in the afternoon, evening, or night. Our practice teaching was supervised, and we were rarely ever alone. An assigned Cuban teacher was always observing, and assisting us, mainly because several of us did not speak Spanish fluently, and all the children were not always on their best behaviour, so the Cuban teachers were there to ensure things did not get out of control. Besides, our assigned thesis supervisor, an activity monitor from the college visited us once per week while we were in action to monitor our performance and to ensure that we were following rules and protocols.

For the first time, most of us were getting an opportunity to work with children or adolescents in formal settings, and it required a lot of patience and social skills, which sometimes needed to be developed since they were not always innate. We were placed across the city of Santiago and saw very little of one another except at dinner time, and even then, it was sporadic because several among us stayed to eat at restaurants because the food in the college's canteen was not pleasing to them. Also, further contributing to the infrequency of connecting with one another was the fact that we had different schedules; we did not all leave the campus at the same time in the morning or afternoon, so we were not able to consult and compare notes until weekends.

Notwithstanding, the haphazardness of our comings and goings, we were all able to connect at some point during the week or weekend and validate our approaches and experiences. At the end of the semester, we all received high marks for our performance in practice teaching and thesis proposal and presentation. The scores were above eighty but mostly in the nineties.

The final semester of our stay at the college was now underway, and we had several subjects to complete before graduation, including mathematics, Spanish, methodology of physical education, optional course, specialization, medical check-up, and baseball. During this time, class attendance was more inconsistent with several of my colleagues. They did not believe it was important for them to attend classes, so they showed up whenever it pleased them, most times only to sit the exams; they got the class notes from others who attended the classes and were willing to share. Notwithstanding, there was a committed and dedicated group of students, who from the very first day of class through to the last day, did not waver or shirk from our purpose, and we were relentless in our pursuit of knowledge, good grades and mastering the Spanish language. We demonstrated that many of us appreciated the opportunity offered to us so that we could acquire knowledge and skills that would be invaluable to our respective communities back in Jamaica.

Our specialization was the discipline that we chose as the foundation on which to build our career as teachers, coaches, and trainers of children and youth. I chose soccer as my area to build expertise and exercise authority. The specialization included activities to demonstrate possessed playing skills, conducting training, and the development of a training plan. The areas of focus were speed, resistance, strength, and techniques. I was tasked to develop a soccer training plan for youth that encompassed training in stages for an entire year. The plan included general preparation: speed and techniques; specific preparation: resistance, strength, and techniques; pre-competitive and competitive: games, auxiliary sports, practice matches, tactics, strategies, and competition; and transition: cross sports, training, massages, meditation, stretches, juggling, heading and long passing.

I had three semesters to work on my specialization with the same teacher, so when the time came to develop my training plan in the final semester of the program, I had built a good rapport, so I was never lacking in guidance, support, and encouragement. My marks were excellent over the three semesters of specialization not just because I spoke Spanish fluently and understood it well, but I also had confidence in my ability to overcome every obstacle or challenge that confronted me even when I had no prior knowledge of the task that I had to undertake; one example that comes to mind is baseball.

I was excited about receiving instructions and playing baseball mainly because it contained similar characteristics to those in the game of cricket, which is widely played in most of the British commonwealth countries, and which consists of batting, throwing, fielding, and catching a ball. Also, it requires running at great speed in between bases, and it uses umpires to arbitrate the game. However, I noticed that there were marked differences, the pitching of the ball to the batter, there was a wind-up before releasing the ball to the batter, all the fielders wore gloves on their non-dominant hand, the bat was cylindrical in shape, to score a run the batter must cover approximately four times the length of the cricket pitch, and the playing area is approximately one-third of the size of the cricket ground.

During the first week of class, I found it challenging to pitch the ball because of my inability to successfully execute the wind-up and deliver the ball in a single motion, fielding or catching the ball using a glove, hitting the ball with such a narrow bat. I was always tempted to handle the ball with my bare hand. I was not alone, several of my male colleagues shared my experience, and the girls fared even worse at the game's techniques. Most of the time, the teacher divided the class into baseball for the guys and softball for the girls, and that approach was successful. However, the theoretical portion of the class was confined to baseball. In the end, no one failed the subject, and we all learned a new game—baseball—

which was not being played in Jamaica, though softball was widely played in Jamaican high schools.

361

Chapter 44

Belkis was selected to work in La EIDE, after completing her specialization and teaching practice and graduating from our sports college in the summer of 1982 because of having mastered the discipline and showed excellent work ethics. Her schedule was in the afternoon, from 11 a.m. to 6 p.m., and most evenings, I would go over to La EIDE to meet her at the bus stop, which was about a 10-minute walk to and from the school, and ride with her on the bus to her home. She wanted me to sleepover at her house, but I never attempted it. I was fearful it could become a habit and I was unsure of how the college's administration would react if they were to become aware.

On weekends, I stayed at Belkis' home until late in the night, but I would not be persuaded to sleepover, so often I had to walk from her house to the college because the time of night that I went out to the street, *no bus was available. I did not mind it because I wanted to spend time with her. She was adorable, she was my soulmate, and she brought out the best in me. I wanted to be with her always, but I was hesitant to go down a path that would invite reprimand from the college's administration. She understood my situation and never insisted that I stayed over at her house for an entire night.*

Notwithstanding, I spent a lot of time with her and at her mother's and father's home. Outside of my college schedule, she commandeered my time. Except for the occasional travel when she had to take her students to competition or undertook her professional development, I was hers completely, and I was never in need of anything; if she could afford any items I wanted, I would not be denied. Furthermore, each paycheque she received, she brought it to me, and we discussed how to portion it according to her obligations and my needs—her generosity had no limits as far as I was concerned.

Even though Belkis wanted to get pregnant, she decided to exercise some control over the matter. She wanted to settle in her job for at least three months. She knew that getting pregnant could have been disruptive for her work, and she wanted to lay down a foundation, get to know her students, build relationships with school staff and working colleagues, and make sure her work was valued. Therefore, she continued to take contraceptives.

"Papi, I'm definitely going to have your baby, but I want to get it right so that I can support the pregnancy and child on my own."

As I had done many times before, I asked her, "Are you sure you want to go through this all by yourself? I may not be here for you; to support you and the baby long distance may be problematic, especially given that the lines of communication between Cuba and the outside world are unreliable."

"Let me worry about that; you just concentrate on preparing yourself to play your part in the making of our child," she told me, "Besides, I want us to take our make-believe wedding pictures as soon as possible."

What else could I say? She had her mind made up, and I was too much in love with her to put up any resistance to her overtures. I wanted to inquire if her decision had anything to do with our first pregnancy, but I imagined that would hurt her, and I was too timid to go there, so I decided to leave well alone. Suddenly, the time to take the wedding pictures was at hand.

Three months after Belkis started her job in La EIDE, in early December 1982, she asked me. "How much money do we have stashed away for the wedding pictures; I want us to take the pictures before year-end. The new year must be about us getting pregnant, and I don't want to be pregnant in our wedding pictures. It will give the wrong impression."

"I have 30 pesos from our savings and another 30 pesos from my college stipend, which I received in November."

I kept all our monies at her father's house, in her room, in a bureau drawer, in a little brown pouch.

"We have enough money to go ahead with taking the pictures; everything will cost approximately 50 pesos; therefore, I'm going to call the photographer in Palma and reserve a date for the event," she told me.

The following evening when I went to get her in La EIDE, she greeted me with the news: "Our photo sitting has been arranged with the photographer for December 25 at 10:30 a.m."

"You're on top of things."

"Aren't I always? The photographer's residence is not far from where mi abuelo lives."

"Very convenient," I remarked.

In order not to be late for our sitting, we started out early. At about 8 a.m., we were on our way. The bus ride was about 35 minutes, so we reached Palma ahead of time, but we stayed at Jorge's until it was close to our appointment time. Jorge wanted to know what brought us to Palma, and Belkis explained our purpose to him. Also, we took the opportunity to visit Belkis' paternal uncle and his family, whom I had never met before. This paternal uncle was from Jorge's second marriage, and Belkis was not close to him; therefore, our conversation was brief. We greeted one another, asked a few routine questions, bade goodbye and returned to Jorge's.

At 10 a.m., Belkis asked Jorge, "Abuelo, can you collect the pictures from the photographer when they're ready and bring them to us in Santiago on one of your visits?"

"Certainly," he said.

Shortly after, we walked over to the photographer's residence, and he was expecting us, so he was prepared—everything was arranged. Belkis reserved a wedding gown, a crown, and a pair of dark brown heels. I did not need to reserve any attire because I had a grey dress pants and a long-sleeved light blue dress shirt, with black thread accented around the cuff, buttonholes, and collar, that I brought from Jamaica—I was not a fan of suits. The photographer saw me dressed and told me that I looked elegant, and that was good enough for me.

We posed for several shots, but my favourite was the one in which I was placing the crown on my queen's head. She was so beautiful I wondered if there was another person as lucky as I was in those moments.

We left instructions with the photographer to give the pictures to Jorge, who would bring them to us in Santiago on one of his morning visits. In little over a week later, Jorge brought the pictures and told us we were photogenic. The pictures were beautiful, and Belkis and her family loved them, so we gave family members copies.

Chapter 45

Saying goodbye to a zealous admirer, I was destined to see Marisol one more time before I left Cuba. After her graduation from the college, she sent me several notes with a student, Sonia, who was from Guama like herself. On the delivery of what would turn out to be Marisol's final note, I asked Sonia, "How is Marisol?"

"You haven't heard? She didn't mention it in any of her notes?" she inquired.

"Mention what?"

Sonia sighed and yelled, "Dios mío," and began to explain, "Marisol had an accident; she was thrown from her bicycle by a trailer, one of her legs is broken, and she sustained other injuries all over her body. I thought you knew from her notes."

"I had no idea. She never mentioned it. If you did not mention it just now, I would never have known."

"Thank you for bringing me the note and this bit of information. Can you give me directions how to get to Marisol's house?"

"Of course."

Sonia did not question my motive; she wrote down the directions and how to get there on a sheet of paper and handed it to me.

I made the decision that I was going to see Marisol, not because I have any feelings for her romantically, but I wanted to see her before I returned to Jamaica. I also decided that I was not going to tell Belkis. She may get ideas that were non-credible. I did not want her to worry in case she believed Marisol and I were an item. It turned out I made the correct decision because, unbeknownst to either of us, Belkis was already pregnant.

The opportunity to visit Marisol became available when Belkis was required, with other trainers, to take students practising synchronized swimming to western Cuba, Matanzas, as part of their training for an entire week, beginning on a Friday afternoon. The Saturday following their departure, I took the city bus down to La Alameda Avenue and transferred onto the country bus to Guama. I followed the directions that Sonia had provided me with, and they were spot on. When I arrived at Marisol's home, it was minutes after 10 a.m., and she was out on the patio sitting in a wooden chair with her fractured leg stretched out on a bench in front of her. She saw me approaching her house and blurted out, "Desmond, what are you doing here? I didn't want you to see me in this condition; I'm so embarrassed,"

"Sonia told me everything, including how to get here; I understand you had no wish for anyone to feel sorry for you, especially me."

"I'm happy to see you, and you haven't changed at all."

"Thank you for the compliment."

When I was close enough to her, I leaned in to embrace her and kiss her on both cheeks as was customary in Cuba. She smiled and shouted out, "Mama, Rosa ven acá, I have someone I want you to meet."

As soon as her mother and Rosa were on the patio, Marisol made the introduction, "Desmond, these are my mother Clara and my sister Rosa." Then she looked at me and said to them, "This is Desmond, one of the Jamaicans who are studying at the college I attended. I'm in love with him. However, he wants nothing to do with me, but here he is. He has come to see me because he has heard of my accident."

I smiled and remained silent until when her mother and sister began asking me the routine questions that every Cuban asked of me when they first met me. I answered their questions, and they disappeared.

Though I knew the circumstances surrounding her accident, I asked her how it happened.

"I remember riding along the main road with my back to the traffic on my side of the road, and at some point, I lost consciousness. I woke up in the hospital with my entire body in pain, with one of my thighs and leg in an ilizarov frame, blue dressing on my face and elbows and bandages on my hands and shoulders. I'm feeling much better now; everything has been removed except for the cast on my thigh. I had wanted it removed the last time I saw the doctor, but he insisted that I wear it for another four weeks. Now, I have three weeks to go, and I hope at the end, the doctor will authorize its removal."

"I'm sorry to hear about the accident and hope you will recover the full use of your thigh," I told her.

We chatted for over an hour, mostly about the college and students, my going back to Jamaica and my relationship with Belkis.

"Belkis and I are married, but at this moment, she is in training in Matanzas with other teachers and students of La EIDE, where she is employed."

"Are you going to take her with you to Jamaica after you are graduated?"

"No decision has been made about that yet."

"I'm feeling uncomfortable and want to lie down. Can you help me to get into my room? Besides, I want to feel your arms around me, maybe for the last time?"

"Sure."

I lifted her out of the chair and moved to the room she pointed to. As I suspected, in my arms, she tried to kiss me on the lips, and I turned my face away and told her: "If you keep that up, te voy a dejar caer."

She surrendered, and I put her in her bed as she had requested. I gave her a lecture: "I came to see you because I like you as a person; you are a beautiful girl who has a lot going for you, despite your accident. You are young and working, but you must not be in a rush to throw yourself at men; one man has hurt you; you are not the first, and you will not be the last. You must first start loving yourself, and then others will love you; if you love yourself, at least, there is one person in the world that loves you, the most important person, and no one can destroy that love. If I were not in love with Belkis, maybe I would sleep with you and the many others in the college and in the community who are making advances at me, but I'm in love, married, and respect Belkis, and could never betray her."

"You are different, maybe one of a kind, but you opened my eyes, gave me something to think about, and I will never forget you. Also, I believe if there is one

person in the world I can trust, it is you," she started crying.

"Don't worry; you will be fine." I wiped the tears from her cheek and eyes.

She asked me for permission to write to me in Jamaica, and we exchanged addresses.

"If you ever come back to Cuba, you should look me up."

"I promise and look forward to keeping it."

Just as I was about to bid my goodbye, the door leading from the living room to her room opened, and Rosa entered with her meal on a tray and told me, "Mama wants you in the kitchen."

I asked to be excused and went to find out what was the reason for my invitation to the kitchen. I entered, and Clara asked me to sit down at the table because she had made lunch for me, but I hesitated a bit before answering, and she told me: "Don't be shy, we have enough to share, and I prepared it myself, so you don't have to be shy about anything." She continued with a beautiful smile on her face, "I heard you talking to my daughter earlier, and I was moved, thank you very much. I believe she needed that, especially coming from someone who is not even a Cuban."

After hearing Clara, I decided to delay my exit and agreed to eat what she had prepared for me. Once I was through eating, I asked to be excused from the table, went into Marisol's room, and informed her that I had to be going, and she shouted out, "Desmond is leaving; come and say goodbye, you may never see him again."

All four of us gathered in the room, Clara, Rosa, and I hugged and kissed one another on the cheek, and I leaned over and kissed Marisol on her forehead and patted her on one of her arms, then told her, "You are beautiful, and you are going to be fine," and I made my exit from the room. When I was a few meters away from the house, I heard Rosa calling me.

"Desmond, wait for me. Marisol asked me to walk you to the bus stop."

"There is no need; I can find my way to the bus stop okay." I tried to discourage her, but it was useless, so she came to the bus stop and waited with me until the bus came, and I bade her goodbye and boarded it and was taken back to Santiago. I was able to visit Lorena well before nightfall.

Chapter 46

elkis was returning in one week, Friday evening, after her departure for Matanzas. The bus would leave her and others on the sidewalk close to the sports village, where they were collected for the initial leg of their trip. I made sure I was there to receive her once she alighted from the bus; she was all smiles, a sign she was happy to see me; her colour was much darker, and she was radiant. A few of the students got off the bus, but several others remained on board to be taken back to La EIDE. However, those who dismounted the bus were received by their guardians or parents. Once the students on the ground were in the control of their guardians, Belkis ran over to me and hugged and kissed me profusely and told me, "I missed you so much, I was going out of my mind; you're all I could think about, night and day, what are you doing to me, Desmond?"

"I'm glad you missed me, but you alone can tell what I'm doing to you; you're the recipient of my arrow. If it makes you feel any better, you're not alone; I, too, was longing for your return, and now that we're together again, let us go home because I want to lay you down and give you all of me."

"Don't worry, I will be yours, and whatever it is that you want to do with me, I will submit and surrender; we'll be in it together," she said, looking into my eyes and smiling; "we're not stopping at my mother's house, we're going straight to my father's where you can spend most if not all of the night with me."

"Thank you for the offer, but I can't stay out all night. Although I would love to, I never have at your home before and don't intend to start now."

"Tú eres muy disciplinado."

"Maybe, but I don't want anyone thinking that all this time in Cuba, I was putting on a show."

The ensuing Monday evening I went straight from the college to Belkis' home. I now used my key to enter the house, which meant I did not have to disturb Esmeralda and her family, the occupants of the first flat of the building. However, that Monday evening, I saw Esmeralda leaning down on the windowsill, her head supported by her arms and elbows, in the window facing the street.

"I wanted to be the first to break the news to you, you are going to be a daddy; the lady fainted on her way home this afternoon; Lilian found her spread out in the passageway, but she is okay, nothing to be concerned about, except that she is pregnant," Esmeralda told me.

"Thank you for the information, Esmeralda."

To myself, "I wondered: What if this had occurred on the street while she was walking from the bus stop to her house?"

I opened the door and rushed around to her father's section of the building and found Belkis sitting in the rocking chair. I did not look to see if there were others around. I went straight to her, picked her up out of the chair and spun around with her a couple of times.

"I heard the news that you are pregnant from your aunt Esmeralda."

"My aunt is a newsmonger. She robbed me of the opportunity to be the first to tell you."

"It does not matter how I get the information, you are pregnant, and that is the important thing in the final analysis."

I must admit, I was elated but sad. Belkis' wish was going to be achieved, and I was destined to leave part of myself behind in Cuba. Notwithstanding, my number one priority was to ensure that she received all the support she needed, keeping doctors' appointments and being with her at every opportunity. I cautioned her about overexertion, encouraged her to avoid crowded buses, which was difficult, if you relied on them exclusively, and use taxis as often as possible. For the next four and a half months, I was worried out of my mind, thinking about the dangers that came with her job, she had to be in the pool with her students given their age, demonstrating exercises was integral to her job and their training, and I did not want to hear of any accidents. I was a slave in love with a queen, my queen, the only girl I ever truly loved.

In July 1983, I had to go back to Jamaica, leaving my beloved behind in Cuba; the devastation I felt had no descriptors. Belkis was no less torn up.

"Papi, I'm going to miss you a lot. I have grown very close to you and your ways."

"Nena, I wish I didn't have to leave you behind in Cuba."

"For the first time in my life, I wish I had the power to make time stand still, just so we would never have to separate," Belkis told me.

"We will be separated physically, but in our hearts, and minds, we will always be together; no power on earth can rob us of that bond. Besides, I may not be here with you when the baby is born, but I will do everything in my power to come back in December, and at that time, we can begin to talk about our future."

"I don't want you to go away preoccupied about our situation. I believe you as well as I knew all the time what I was doing but didn't care to consider the implications. I love you and want to remember you always despite what tomorrow has in store for me. Our destiny was preordained. Whatever brought us together is now ripping us asunder, and we're practically helpless to do anything about it."

"It breaks my heart to hear you speak like that, Nena; you are really brave, which is one of the things I most admire about you," I told Belkis.

"I don't want you to leave thinking that I'm unhappy. I enjoyed the time we had together. I appreciate the love you have given me, the physicality we shared, and I'm joyfully proud of what I'm carrying inside me."

"I want to thank you for helping to make my life bearable in Cuba. Your kindness, understanding and commitment over the past four years have been splendid, and I will treasure the relationship we have had for all times."

The day I boarded the bus that would yank me away from my most precious responsibility, Belkis was five-and-a-half-months pregnant; one of the things that bothered me included losing Belkis, was that I may never get the opportunity to see my child—love is truly a hurting thing.

Chapter 47

After four years of studying physical and health education in Cuba, it all came to an end on July 1, 1983, when we lined up in three rows of seven in the front and one of eight in the back on a concrete platform, just below a set of concrete steps which formed part of the outdoor portion of the entrance to the administrative wing of the college's building. There was no fanfare, no valedictory message, or colourful ceremonial speech, no family members, or friends of our families, just a few Cuban teachers, administrative staff and college maintenance workers standing aloof to one side of the assembly.

Twenty-nine of us received congratulatory words from José Ramos, the assistant director responsible for academics. I was named the most outstanding student, having participated in all college activities, indoors and outdoors, and consistently attended classes over the four years. I was always punctual and received the highest score among my peers. If the event were being held to graduate the entire 1983 graduating class of the college, I would still have been named the most outstanding student, according to José. The only things that were missing were our transcripts and diplomas; they had to be sent to the British High Commission in Havana to be officially validated and stamped on behalf of the Jamaican government—the British High Commission had responsibility for Jamaica's affairs in Cuba. However, our credentials would be released to us in Havana before we departed Cuba.

Ten days after our graduation, we were taken by a college bus to the national bus terminal in Santiago to board a coach bus that would then take us to Havana. No one came to see us off, but we had bid farewell to our teachers, friends, and college staff before the morning of our departure.

Two of my peers brought their Cuban wives with them on the trip to Havana, one with two children and the other with no children. These wives would travel with us to Jamaica to live with their husband permanently; at least, that was the goal. Personally, I had no idea how the arrangements were made, who made them, or if any were made at all!

At about 10 a.m., the coach bus pulled out of the provincial terminal, and we left Santiago de Cuba behind us, taking with us only the good and bad memories we had acquired over the past four years. The drive to Havana was almost 14 hours in duration. Upon arriving at the bus terminal in Havana, there was a local INDER bus waiting to take us to the location where we were going to stay until the date of our departure to Jamaica.

We were taken to what seemed like a village of the past. I understood later that the owners of the houses had fled Cuba during and after the Revolution, but the government never reallocated the houses; rather, they were used occasionally for government purposes such as conferences and sheltering foreigners like us when the need arose. There were several dwellings in the village, and we were assigned three: two for the men and one for the ladies.

We spent the next several days just sitting around, sleeping, talking, and walking about in the city, mostly in New Havana, where we were located. We visited INDER's head office and got to know some of the officials whom we had only heard about but had not gotten the opportunity to meet before. We also visited tourists' hangouts: parks, the Malecon, hotels, and landmarks. The hotels in new Havana were well kept with beautifully manicured landscapes.

One day, I was walking around with five of my peers in New Havana, three guys and two girls. We decided to explore the lobby area of a conspicuously beautiful hotel; in it, I noticed a boutique with foreign-made merchandise, and through the glass frame, I was admiring the things it contained. Unexpectedly, one of the guys, Lance, asked me to purchase a cassette player for him from the foreign boutique. I wondered why he asked me since he had the same privilege as I did, but I did not think anything more of it; I just agreed to do him the favour. However, later, I concluded that he asked me to do him the favour because he had purchased several items previously, maybe not from the same store but from others, and he did not want to draw unwanted attention to himself.

During my four years in Cuba, this was the first time I had ever entered a foreign store, and it did not take long for me to find out that this was not my calling. When I went to purchase the item of interest and was about to make the order, as my luck would have it, two police officers approached me.

"You are under arrest," one of them told me.

"Why am I under arrest," I asked.

"Cubans aren't allowed to make purchases in these stores," he told me.

"I'm not a Cuban; I'm a Jamaican who has just finished studying in Santiago de Cuba, and I'm in Havana waiting for the flight to take me home."

I was, of course, speaking in Spanish. Then he asked, "Where are you staying?"

"For the time being, I'm staying in the neighbourhood of San Pedro on the INDER premises."

"Show me the palm of your hands," and when I did, he said to me, "You speak like a Cuban, your hands... and you have the hands of a working Cuban."

"All this because I speak Spanish well, and I have calluses in the palm of my hands; I'm suddenly a Cuban?"

"Show me some identification," he demanded.

"I believe those should have been your first words to me."

Before things got out of hand, I took out my passport and showed it to him; he took it, looked inside and at me and then handed it back to me; the look on his face told me he was shocked, he began to apologize, and I told him there was no need, "I get that a lot." Then he and his partner walked away.

During all that time, my peers stood by and watched it all unfold. I decided to rescind my offer to make the purchase of the cassette player and returned the money to my colleague. Once he retrieved the money, I walked out of the store and the hotel lobby and headed back to the house where we were staying. That incident made it the second time in my entire life that I had ever spoken to a police officer on duty: the first time occurred in Jamaica; a cop rode his motorcycle alongside me and stopped to ask me if I knew where a certain lady was living in my district.

After the incident in the hotel boutique, I decided never to wander about the streets again until it was time to board the plane that would take me back to Jamaica. However, I had to go, along with my colleagues, over to the INDER head office to collect our postsecondary credentials, which left me no choice but to venture out again, only this time, I was going into a protected environment. No one would mistakenly identify me as a Cuban, and I was almost certain not to have an encounter with the police. All 29 of the remaining Jamaican sports students showed up on July 20, 1983, to collect our credentials. However, only 27 of us received our credentials. Two men were told that they would not receive their diplomas because their record of absenteeism at the college made them unqualified to receive their diplomas.

The other 27 of us were murmuring with one another that it was not fair for the Cuban authority to treat the other two students like that. Though the Cuban authority was justified in their decision, I could not help but ask myself: Why were all 29 of us allowed to graduate? Why were the two students not informed of such a decision earlier?

Even though I was not the leader of the group any longer, I discreetly approached one of INDER's female officials and asked her the same questions I asked myself, and quietly she told me, "They will get their diploma; we are just giving them something to think about."

"Thank you, because I was beginning to have concerns when I thought that they would have wasted four years of their lives in Cuba."

I did not discuss with my colleagues the conversation I had with the INDER official; I went back to the house where we were staying and remained silent for the rest of the day and night. The next day at about 7 p.m., an INDER official came by the house to deliver to the two students their postsecondary credentials.

July 22, 1983, came, and at approximately 9 a.m., an INDER official informed us that we should prepare ourselves to be taken to the airport at 11 a.m. Now we were convinced that we were going home, and we started gathering our stuff while chatting about how good it felt to be going home. It was especially welcome news for those of us who had not been back to Jamaica since August 1980. The bus was on time, and we were taken to the airport, where we met up with other students who had graduated from other postsecondary institutions. Not long after our arrival at the airport, we began checking through customs and at approximately 1:30 p.m., we were ascending the airstairs into the chartered Air Jamaica plane to be flown out of Cuba. Suddenly nostalgia and solemnity usurped my being, and the emotional experience was tantalizing and demoralizing all in the same breath. For the past four years, Cuba has been home to me, and now I am abandoning it unhappily.

Afterword

This novel is inspired by a true story which describes the experiences of a Jamaican national who spent four years in Cuba as a member of a group of 29, initially 34, students studying Physical and Health Education with the expectation that after completing the program, he would return to Jamaica to help promote sports, physical and health education amongst children and youth. His experiences are bound up with those of the 28 other students who were tasked with a similar mandate. The story explains the lead character's experiences while observing his peers' behaviour and those of his romantic involvement with a Cuban damsel as he navigated Cuban communities, culture and way of life and "profited" from the hospitality of the Cuban government. Hence, the story is twofold, alternating experiences between the individual and the collective, providing an account of both the lead character and his peers.

On the one hand, the story repeatedly described the behaviour of his peers in a way that seemed out of line with the values akin to decency, honesty, and integrity, which caused embarrassment and humiliation to those who conducted themselves in a manner that was acceptable and consistent with civilized comportment. On the other hand, the story explains how his romantic engagement with the Cuban damsel encouraged his commitment and loyalty to love and one person. The story recalled academic experiences, illegal activities, criminal behaviours, and a passionate love affair that lasted approximately four years and ended with the acknowledgement that some relationships are destined not to survive.

In addition to academics, the life lessons learned in Cuba were instructive and inspiring and offered a chance to acquire knowledge in all its forms. Analogous to a "university," Cuba facilitates learning and equips learners so that they may create, produce, reproduce, and disseminate knowledge; and therefore, reinforcing the concept that one should not discard information irrespective of its source. Because to reject information is to wallow in closedmindedness and shallow interpretation of the universe and its myriad forms of manifestations.

The human mind is a repository of ideas, some good and some not so good, and as luck would have it, sometimes one good idea escapes, hits a favourable receptacle, gets germinated, and nurtured to maturity and changes an existing way of life: all material things that we used and rely on for our survival and sustenance came from ideas—from ideas we got computers, airplanes, cars and all the tools that we rely on to prolong our existence. There is value in embracing all humans as individuals and collectives and the information they have to offer regardless of its origin and or source because we need one another, even if it is to help us understand that we may be better or worse off than others—knowledge comes from everyone and everything. It is necessary to preserve things and people who provide challenges because, in the absence of challenges, human existence would have been confined to its pre-historic forms.

Acknowledgment

I owe the production of this book largely to the support of individuals who encouraged me to write the story within and contributed their time and talent to its development. I want to extend my sincere appreciation and gratitude to all of them for sharing their unyielding support and insight.

A big thank you to my daughter Olivia for her assistance in reviewing, editing, and critiquing the first draft of the book, as well as for her suggestions on how to write and organize a novel. Her contribution was essential in completing the final product.

I also offer sincere appreciation to my brother-in-law Steven Stunell for his kind and motivating words reaffirming my confidence that I could undertake and complete the novel.

Finally, I would be remiss if I didn't acknowledge my colleague from work, Tim Colfe, for his assistance and contribution to editing the second draft of the manuscript.